The Redemption of Joseph Heinz

MICHELE E. GWYNN

An M.E. Gwynn Publication

Cover by JC Clarke and The Graphics Shed.

Editing: M.E. Gwynn

The Redemption of Joseph Heinz is an *M.E. Gwynn Publication*.

Contents

Prologue

Leningrad, USSR

July 8, 1970

The ice cream cone melted, running down his small hand, and dripping onto his best shoes. The leather was scuffed, and the brown laces were becoming tattered at the ends, but they were still considered new despite the wear. It was summertime in Leningrad, and the day was hot and humid. The breeze coming in off the Baltic did little to cool the stifling heat, and the clouds gathering overhead were a clear indication that rain was imminent. He looked up. *It's going to rain on my presents if they don't let me open them soon."*

"Vladi, come! It's time." The towheaded boy turned away from staring off at the clouds and ran back to his mother's arms. She stood by a table set up on the front lawn of the tenement building where they shared a flat with his Uncle Pavo's family. Kommunalkas were common in the distressed neighborhoods throughout this major port city of the USSR. The Soviets called it good economic policy. All low-income families had a free apartment, but the people knew what it was really all about, keeping the poor corralled so that the aristocratic and privileged military families that ran the government and the major businesses could snatch up prime real estate for luxury condominiums. The market for property was booming in the northern region while the urban ghettos were ripe with poverty, crime, and suffering. But at the tender age of six, young Vladimir Alexei Brezhnev knew only that he had a table full of brightly wrapped presents to open.

His friends were herded in from their playtime to come and watch. He was about to rip the paper off the first one when his father noticed his shoe.

He grabbed the boy's arm. "What's this?" His finger pointed down.

Vladimir looked, noticing for the first time the mess on his foot. He shrugged. "I don't know, papa."

"You don't know!" His father's anger, always lurking beneath the surface, exploded. "This is how you care for the nice things I buy you with the money I work so hard for?" He shook the boy.

"Kirill, please!" His mother, Olga, pleaded as she ran over, and bent down quickly wiping the sticky sweet cream from the shoe. "There, see? It's all fine. No harm." She remained on her knees trying to gently pry her husband's fingers from Vladimir's arm.

"Of course there is harm, woman!" He slapped her, his expression fierce. "Do not defy me in front of our friends and family! The boy must learn to respect me, and to respect the things I provide for him. You cannot baby him anymore. He's six years old. Unless he is retarded, he understands that he is to take care of his belongings." Kirill turned his attention back to his son leaving Olga red-faced and embarrassed, avoiding the shock of bystanders. "Are you retarded, Vladimir?"

The boy looked around at his cousins, his uncle who stood with his eyes averted, his Aunt Ava who gathered her youngest to her side, and his friends from the apartment building, some of whom were laughing at his predicament. He looked back at his father keeping his eyes lowered while staring at the whiskers on his scarred chin.

"No, sir."

"You like your shoes?" The tone in his father's voice was deceptively soft.

"Yes, papa. I like my shoes very much." Vladimir's lip began to quiver, knowing his father's outbursts never ended well.

"You want to keep your shoes?"

"Yes, papa."

"Kirill, please, it's his birthday—" Olga began.

"Shut up!" He looked back at the boy. "I think you need to learn a lesson, a man's lesson. You wish to be a man, yes, Vladimir?"

Tears ran down the boy's cheeks now. He sniffled. "Yes, papa."

"Good. This is good. I'm going to teach you to respect me, and to respect what you own. You know how I am going to do this?" His son shook his head in the negative. "You are six now. Six is an age where you must start becoming a man. No more clinging to your mother's apron. So, Vladimir," his father put his arm around his small shoulders and turned him toward the crowd of children watching. "You're going to give away all of your presents to these children."

"But papa—" Vladimir gasped.

"No 'but papa', Vladimir! You will stand here, and pass these gifts out to your friends, and then you will thank them for coming to your party. When you are finished, you will go to your room and clean it. I expect it to be spotless when I come up and inspect." The look in his dark, brown eyes said, *'or else'*.

Vladimir wiped the tears blinding his blue eyes. Sobs wracked his small body as one by one, he handed out all seven of his gifts to the children who lived in the building. His uncle would not let any of his own children step forward. The look of shame in Pavo's eyes, and the tears escaping from his aunt and mother were too much to bear. Finally, the last package left his hands.

"Tha-thank you for coming to my pa-party," he hiccupped. With that, he ran inside, and up the four flights of stairs to the small flat with three rooms. No one else was inside, and young Vladimir Alexei Brezhnev slammed the door of the tiny space he shared with his older brother, Nikolay, and cousin, Oleg. He wanted to throw himself down on the cot and cry, but if he did, he'd lose time. His father would be up shortly, and if the room did not pass inspection, Vladimir knew he'd be on the wrong side of his father's belt. And even if his efforts to clean to his father's standards were good enough, past experience told him he would still feel the sting of the leather and the bite of the buckle. He sucked in the sob threatening to burst forth, holding it in, and began picking clothes up off the floor. The clock was ticking.

Saint Petersburg, Russia (Modern day Leningrad)

July 8, 2016

"Happy birthday, my son." The tiny gray-haired woman placed a small pineapple cake on the table in front of the well-dressed gentleman sporting a short salt and pepper beard. With shaky hands, she lit the single red candle that stood up from the fruit ring in the center.

"Mama, you don't have to..." Vladimir began.

"Shush. I am but an old woman, yet I can still bake a cake for my baby boy." She set the lighter down and cupped his face, smiling as she peered at him through rheumy eyes. "Fifty-one today, and still my baby." She kissed his cheek.

Vladimir smiled as he patted her hands. Olga Brezhnev was seventy-six now, and her back hunched with osteoporosis.

"Bal'shoye spasiba, mama."

Inside the small but well-appointed flat decorated with the best furniture money could buy, his mother lived with his Aunt Ava. His Uncle Pavo passed on the year before, and his own father met with the wrong end of a butcher's knife thirty-three years earlier.

"Ya tibya l'ublyu, Vladi." Olga pinched his bearded cheeks.

"I love you, too, mama."

"Now, make a wish quickly before the wax drips onto the cake." She stood behind his chair with her hands on his shoulders.

Vladimir closed his eyes and pretended to make a wish to please his mother. He didn't believe in wishes, not since his sixth birthday. That was the day everything changed. No longer could his mother protect him from his father's wrath although she never stopped trying. The drinking Kirill indulged in sporadically became a daily occupation as lack of work drove Vladimir's father to the streets. It was there he started peddling drugs for a local boss. Kirill was at first disgusted with this turn in his life, and then began to embrace it. He worked hard, selling the poisonous product to the poor who could little afford such a habit. He helped contribute to the vicious cycle of poverty and suffering in the ghettos with no empathy whatsoever. If someone overdosed, it was an opportunity to sell to the deceased's friends so they could numb themselves to their grief.

Kirill trained his oldest son, Nicolay, in the art of the deal when he turned thirteen. At first, he succeeded with passing the cocaine to his friends in the neighborhood. Kirill was proud of his oldest son until Nicolay, becoming too cocky, and trying to impress a young lady, took his first hit of the drug. Before long, he was hooked, and getting high on the inventory he was expected to sell. When he couldn't pay for the powder he'd blown through, Kirill had to step in and pay the boss out of his own pocket. Angry at the loss, his father focused his rage like a laser by beating Nicolay within an inch of his life. The beating was so severe, it broke Nicolay's leg costing Kirill even more in medical treatment. Nicolay eased the pain with more drugs, and when he couldn't afford more, he began stealing from his papa's stash. Two weeks before his fifteenth birthday, Nicolay was found dead, a needle hanging from his arm.

Vladimir was devastated. As a boy, he had looked up to his big brother. He also knew that despite his coke habit, Nico had never once injected the stuff into his veins. He snorted or tasted, but he was acutely afraid of needles, a fear he never admitted to anyone except Vladimir. No one ever questioned his death, but Kirill's demeanor grew more violent and erratic. He would come home late, and if dinner wasn't waiting on the table or not to his liking, he would beat Olga with his belt, and more often with his fists. He didn't seem to care if Vladimir or his cousins saw him do it, and his Uncle Pavo was too afraid of his brother-in-law to stop him. Life went on like that for a time.

Kirill tried again bringing a son into the business. When Vladimir turned fourteen, he started running the street sales to the other kids. He kept his head down, and did what he was told, not wanting to anger his father. He also learned from Nicolay's death to never, ever use drugs. Some of the older kids made fun of him, taunting him about being a "big pussy" too afraid to take a hit, but Vladimir knew that he would always have the last laugh. He would never overdose, and his pockets would always be filled with cash. Meanwhile, they would remain poor, and eventually die young or worse, die slowly, aging horribly while addicted to riding the white pony.

"Blow it out already!" Olga shook him out of his reverie.

He leaned over and blew out the flame.

His Aunt Ava shuffled in leaning on her cane. "We're having cake?" She was half blind at seventy-nine, but her appetite had yet to wane.

"Da, Ava. It's Vladi's birthday. You remember. I told you just this morning, you loony old bat," Olga chuckled. "Come, sit. It's time to eat." She turned to her son. "And what did you wish for?"

Vladimir accepted the slice of cake on the porcelain plate with a grin. "You know I cannot say or else the wish won't come true."

"Silly boy." She cut another slice and placed it in front of Ava.

"So, what's the occasion? Is it my birthday?" Ava picked up her fork, smiling through her few remaining teeth. "I do so love cake."

Olga looked at Vladimir who shook his head. His aunt was several marbles shy of a full bag anymore. Soon, he would have to hire a nurse to come in and help take care of them. There was nothing he wouldn't do, no expense he would not spare for his mother. She was dearer to him than anyone in the world. The three of them sat eating cake and sipping strong coffee for the next hour. Finally, Vladimir pushed his chair back and stood.

"I have to go now, mama."

"So soon? But what about dinner later?" She got up slowly and shuffled around the table.

"I can't. I have a business meeting, but I'll come tomorrow and take you both to lunch, yes?" He leaned down and kissed her forehead. Then, he did the same for his aunt. "I'll call tonight to check on you both."

"Such a good boy. I always knew he would grow up to be so good," Ava muttered through her second piece of cake.

Vladimir headed out the front door to the lift. On the way down, he pulled out his cell phone hitting number two on the speed dial. It was answered immediately.

"Have the car ready." He exited the elevator and walked through the marble hallway. The concierge held the door open and waited as he walked through.

"Have a good evening, Mr. Brezhnev." The man kept his eyes ahead as he stood at attention. In his uniform for the condominium complex, he resembled a soldier.

"Thank you."

A black limousine waited. A large, dark-haired man bulging with muscles covered in an expensive Navy-blue suit jumped out and opened the back door. Once Vladimir was inside, the man closed the door and climbed back into the front passenger seat. The driver wore an equally expensive suit, but was shorter, huskier, and bald. He looked in the rearview mirror. "Where to, Gospodin?"

"The warehouse. We have business to tie up," he said.

The man in the passenger seat smirked. The driver nodded, and put the car in gear steering into, and merging with traffic.

A thumping sound interrupted the quiet of the interior. Loud knocks were heard. The two men in the front seat exchanged a worried glance hoping their boss would not notice. Vladimir looked up from his mobile.

"Is that what I think it is?"

The man in the passenger seat fidgeted. "Yes, I'm sorry."

"Well, take care of it! I don't want to listen to that all the way to the warehouse." Vladimir gave the order, anger seeping into his words.

The driver pulled over past the bridge onto a dirt road. There, hidden from passing cars by an old, rusted-out shack, the man in the passenger seat got out and walked to the back of the limo. He popped open the trunk. The *thwack* of a fist cracking bone filled the air. Silence followed. The trunk slammed shut, and he walked back to the car, climbing in. Vladimir leaned forward. The man in the front seat froze, apprehension prickling the fine hairs on the back of his neck.

Brezhnev spoke in a deceptively soft voice. "Make sure that doesn't happen again, Petrovich." He sat back slowly, focusing once again on the screen of his cellular.

"Yes, sir," Petrovich replied, eyes cast down. He looked at his knuckles as a bead of sweat dripped from his forehead, evidence of his anxiety. The knuckles were already swelling. Next to him, the driver let out the breath he'd been holding. Once again, the car weaved into traffic heading toward the docks and warehouse number 214.

The drive seemed longer than usual. The tension inside the car coupled with the silence kept the men in the front seat of the limousine on edge. In the back, the man infamously known internationally as 'The Butcher' sent out a text message.

Delivery is expected within one hour. He hit SEND, then casually slid his mobile back into his inner jacket pocket.

Chapter 1

Berlin

September 3rd, 2016

"The royal purple with silver and cream is the perfect color scheme, Birgitta. I'm beginning to think you picked out these colors especially for me." Elsa Kreiss wrapped a swath of the purple satin around her body and posed in front of the mirror.

"Don't be silly. The cream and silver are best for my wedding gown, and the purple makes Joseph look majestic. His vest will be royal purple. It sets off his eyes." A dreamy smile danced on her lips.

Elsa bit the inside of her cheek to keep from laughing. The idea of Kommissar Joseph Heinz as 'majestic' tickled her. She did love the cranky old bear. He'd become a pseudo-father figure to her and her little brother, Anno, since he came into their lives three years ago. He was her hero after rescuing Anno from the Dutch pedophile who'd kidnapped him. After that, Heinz took it upon himself to look out for the two orphans, going so far as to take Elsa under his wing and helping her get out of her former career as Berlin's premiere dominatrix by assisting her in gaining enrollment in the police academy. She'd become a Schutzpolizei, and now, with the mentorship of Direktor Herman Faust at the Landiskriminalamt, she was on the fast track to advancing beyond patrol officer, up the ranks to detective, and maybe one day, Inspekteur der Polizei, Chief of all policemen. *A girl could dream, couldn't she?*

"I see you trying not to giggle, Elsa. You just wait until you're as in love as we are. You will find yourself softening, trust me." Detective Birgitta

Mahler turned to the seamstress and handed over the patterns for the bridesmaids' dresses. "I'd like the royal satin with silver piping." She turned toward Elsa. "But her dress must be special, not exactly the same as the others." The old seamstress nodded. Her dark-rimmed glasses sat low on her narrow nose. "The others have the bow over one shoulder, but Elsa's should be completely strapless like the top of my gown. She's my maid of honor, after all."

The woman took notes while Elsa grinned. "I'm so excited for you!" She reached out and hugged Birgitta for the millionth time.

"Good lord, Elsa. Control yourself," Birgitta gently admonished with a wry twist of her lips.

"I can't help it. I'm a fool for love."

"Does this mean you and Lukas...?" Birgitta arched a brow.

Elsa sighed. "I don't know yet. Things are going well and all, and we're taking it one day at a time. It's difficult enough just learning to be with someone new let alone a man you now share a bathroom with."

"Well, that was cryptic."

The seamstress came up behind Elsa and lifted her arms indicating how she wanted the redhead to stand. She then began taking measurements around her bust, waist, and hips.

"I didn't mean for it to be, but I've never been one to be open about what I'm feeling. It wasn't a desirable trait in my former career."

Birgitta laughed. "I imagine not, but it has been three years now. There's no need to shut off your emotions to Lukas. Scheisse, you're always gushing around me."

The smile returned. "That's because you're going to be Joseph's wife, which maybe sort-of makes you almost my mother." Elsa kept her eyes cast downward, unsure how Mahler would take her statement. She did love Birgitta like a mother, and everyone already knew that Heinz had become her father figure. Still, she worried that it might all be too much for the detective who already had a son of her own.

Birgitta set the patterns down and walked over to Elsa, who still stood with her arms out.

"Elsa, I couldn't be happier to be marrying Joseph, and that includes having you and Anno as part of my family." She tucked a stray strand of red hair behind the younger woman's ear. "Your mother would be so proud of you," she smiled, "just as I am. I'd be more than proud to someday give you away to a man who will love you as Joseph loves me. I'd be ever so proud to call you daughter."

Elsa's green eyes misted over, and she couldn't stop the smile that burst forth on her full red lips. She threw her arms around Mahler and hugged her tight. "Thank you."

Birgitta dabbed at a single tear escaping her own brown eyes. The two women, who'd been through so much together, in so short a period of time, made it official—they were now family.

"Lift!" The seamstress tapped Birgitta on the shoulder and held her arms out indicating she must do the same. "I don't have all day. If you want your dress completed on time, stop all this tearful nonsense in my shop and assume the position."

Elsa giggled, and Mahler shushed her. "Don't piss off Frau Kluge or she'll deliberately ruin my dress out of spite." Birgitta looked over her shoulder at the sour-pussed seamstress. "Is that not so?"

"Humph!" she grunted.

"Old-school, is this one, Elsa. She survived the bombing of Berlin."

Elsa's eyebrows climbed with surprise, and more than a little skepticism.

Frau Kluge stopped and looked up at Elsa from where she knelt measuring the length of Birgitta's legs noting the younger woman's expression. "You think you know tough, Red? I knew tough. I survived war. I held my own when my family and I were interrogated by the Gestapo. Didn't even break a sweat, and they knew when you broke a sweat. Made us all sit on hard cane chairs with paper beneath us while they grilled us all hour after hour without food or water or even a piss break."

Elsa's eyes widened. "What was the paper for?"

Frau Kluge's expression hardened. "For absorbing the sweat of our palms and asses. The more wet the paper, the guiltier you became in their eyes. My own paper? Ha! I wouldn't give them the satisfaction. I stayed as cold as Siberia, and as dry as a virgin's cu—"

"Frau Kluge! Language!" Birgitta interrupted.

Elsa chuckled. "I see. My hat's off to you, Frau Kluge."

"For what?" she asked, irritation in her voice.

"For surviving those assholes." Elsa didn't mince words.

Birgitta looked down at the seamstress. "Elsa here helped take down Yuri Ivchencko and the psycho who kidnapped the Russian girls from Charlottenburg. She's a survivor too."

The Frau's gray eyebrow raised up in disbelief as she surveyed the slender young woman from head to toe. She pointed to the back of the room. "You'll need to change. Strip down to your underwear so I can begin with the lining of your dress."

Elsa walked behind the curtain in the corner of the small shop and removed her jeans, blouse, and belt. She looked down at her body still wearing her under things.

"Well, are you going to stand back there all day?" Frau Kluge called out.

Elsa walked out, and stood on the small, round dais set before the three-way mirror. Frau Kluge stepped forward and stopped. Her eyes caught sight of hundreds of small white scars crisscrossing the younger woman's torso and the front of her thighs. They were fading, but still visible. Several ran straight across her breasts disappearing beneath the fabric of her bra, but it was obvious they continued over the very sensitive areolas. Kluge looked at Elsa, and her expression softened. She nodded slowly, acknowledging the evidence of torture.

"My hat is off to you, too, Officer Kreiss," she said softly.

The rest of the afternoon was spent finishing the initial fitting, and then shopping for shoes, gifts for the bridesmaids, and finally, picking out flowers. All in all, the day was productive. The wedding of Detective Joseph Heinz to Birgitta Mahler was on track. It was going to be perfect.

Joseph paced the short length of the cluttered corner office. "Denied? How can this be denied? We have credible evidence, Herman!"

Direktor Herman Faust sat with his hands folded on top of his desk watching his long-time friend, KriminalKommissar Joseph Heinz, wearing a path through his already threadbare carpet.

"I am aware, and so are they, but the case is nearly nine years cold, and now that both Ivchencko and Koslov are dead, the state is not willing to poke the bear, not for this. I'm sorry, my friend."

Heinz stopped, his expression both tortured and exasperated. After all he'd been through since the day Marlessa Schubert went missing, all the countless missing girls' cases thereafter, the kidnapping of Johann Kreiss, the Ivchencko/Koslov affair, and being shot and almost losing Birgitta, he'd finally stumbled upon a real clue. A ledger entry was found, documenting the girl's kidnapping, and indicating where she'd been transported. Finally, there was a way forward. Hope. To have such, and to have permission to pursue it denied, was wrong in Heinz's eyes. The German State Police didn't want to rock the boat by opening the cold case, operating, he was sure, under direct orders from the chancellor herself. Germany sought to bring Russia, and its president, Mikhail Mishin, to heel, to reign in his attempts to take over Ukraine. A trade deal was tentatively offered at the start of the year, one that would bring Russia into the fold of the European Union, creating avenues for trade, but only if Mishin agreed to abide by the Minsk Agreement and commit to a cease fire in Ukraine. So far, he hadn't, but the negotiations would surely end altogether if the state authorized an international investigation into sex trafficking through Saint Petersburg. Heinz was no fan of Mishin or politics. He cared only about justice.

He took a deep breath and sat down facing Faust. "How long have we known one another, Herman?"

Faust leaned back, shrugging his shoulders. A lock of his rapidly graying blond hair fell onto his forehead. He reached up and pushed it back.

"Over twenty-five years, I'd say, why?"

"And when in the last twenty-five years have you known me to abandon a case?"

"I don't like where you're going with this, Joseph."

"Just answer me."

The men stared at each other, neither blinking. Faust's blue eyes held steady with Heinz's determined brown ones.

Finally, the Direktor sighed. "Never. Not once. You're a stubborn son of a bitch, that's for sure."

Heinz sat forward. "I will do this, Herman, with or without you." He paused. "But I'd rather it be with you."

Faust pushed his chair back and stood up. Slipping his hands in his pockets, he walked to the window and looked down upon the busy street below.

"You know, I'll be fifty-one in a month. Frau Faust is looking forward to my retirement in two years. I'll have put in thirty years of service." He turned his head, smiling, and added, "She wants to travel, would you believe?" He chuckled. "Can you imagine me as a tourist, Joseph? Tourists are the first to get ripped off wherever they go. Me? I'd be casing every place we checked into, reminding Helga to keep her valuables in the hotel safe instead of her toiletry bag like she seems intent on doing. The woman can't seem to help herself, you know. She pulls money out of her wallet and counts it at the register." He shook his head. "At the register, for Christ's sake! Nearly thirty years I've been telling her to never, ever count her money in the public eye, and she shushes me, Joseph! She says, 'if someone steals my money, it's only money, and maybe they just need it more than I do.' What am I supposed to say to that?" He sighed. "She's going to be the death of me, God bless her, that or sheer boredom. What's an old cop like me supposed to do in retirement?"

Heinz remained silent, giving his friend time to mull it over.

Finally, Herman faced him again, speaking in hushed tones. "No one can ever know, Joseph. And if you get too deep, I won't be able to help you. There will be no official acknowledgement whatsoever of your presence there. If asked, I will deny you like Judas to save my own ass, for Helga's sake, of course."

"Of course." Heinz subdued a smirk.

"I can help get you in, but once you're there, you're on your own."

"That's more than I could have asked." Heinz stood, extending his hand. Faust met him halfway and shook it. "Thank you, Herman."

"Don't thank me yet. Birgitta is going to be pissed at you if you fuck up her wedding day, so you better make sure you come back in time." He shuffled through his rolodex searching for a card.

"I wouldn't dream of missing it. It's my wedding day, too, you know."

"Yes, but she'll blame me." He sat down and reached for the phone.

"Why do you say that?" Heinz arched a brow in amusement.

"Because she's smarter than you. She'll know I helped you, and then it will be shit sandwiches for me from here until eternity. You think Helga won't help her plot her revenge? Ha!"

Heinz grinned. He knew it was true, but he had no intention of missing his own wedding. He would get into Saint Petersburg with Faust's help, find the warehouse, follow the clues, and somehow, bring Marlessa Schubert home, dead or alive. Then, maybe, he would find peace.

Chapter 2

"But why now?" Birgitta calmly sipped her coffee as she watched Joseph search his closet for the dark green suitcase.

"Because now is when this seminar is being offered. If I miss it this year, I will have to wait two more years before I can apply for my A16."

His voice sounded muffled from within the small space. Finally, he backed up carrying the worn travel case over his head successfully removed from the top shelf. Joseph set it down and kicked a few items back inside the closet before shutting the door.

He looked at his fiancé. "I know it's cutting it close, but it's only for two weeks, and the wedding is still four weeks away." He walked over and sat down next to her on the sofa. He wrapped his arm around her shoulders, pulling her close. His voice dropped lower. "We've already settled the details, Birgitta. The venue is booked, I have my suit, and Elsa assures me your dress is being hand-stitched by an angel."

Birgitta laughed outright at the description of old Frau Kluge as an angel. More like a foul-mouthed devil woman, but she was gifted with the dress making skill of Vera Wang and the vision of Versace.

"Yes, I know, but that doesn't mean you should be rushing off. It's in Stockholm, for goodness sakes!"

Joseph smiled. "Worried I might run off with some tall, blonde, Swedish model?"

She hit him in the arm nearly spilling her hot coffee. "No! Worried some freak Swedish snowstorm might trap you in the land of smoked mackerel and Absolut Vodka. I'd never see you again." She half-joked, but it was clear she was worried.

Joseph had never seen his love agitated. Even when she'd been kidnapped by a Russian sadist, and tied up aboard his ship, she'd kept her cool, had even managed to escape. Still, here she was on the verge of becoming Mrs. Joseph Heinz, and his unflappable woman was ...flapping? He found it adorable.

"It's two weeks. It will be sheer hell without you, but when I come back, I can put in my formal application for Direktor, and we will be set to begin our very happy life together. It's a desk job, and you know how I've looked forward to that. No more haunting cases at two in the morning. I will get to hand them out to subordinates and sit back growing fat." He grinned down at her, smiling into her large, brown eyes.

"You're not allowed to get fat, Joseph Heinz. That is not part of our deal." She poked his ribs with a manicured fingernail.

"Well, then, maybe you can help keep me fit. Let's see..." He began ticking off possibilities on his fingers. "You can walk me every day like a pet dog."

She giggled.

"No? Okay. Um, you can feed me only carrots and hay like a horse?" He raised his eyebrows at her.

"When did you get so silly? What happened to the cynical grump I first met and fell in love with?" Birgitta asked, laughing out loud.

"I know!" Heinz snapped his fingers, grabbed her coffee cup from her hands, and set it on the table in front of them. He quickly leaned her back into the couch cushions, his expression suddenly very serious. His voice dropped lower still, growing husky with desire. "You can let your hair down and make love to me every day," he whispered hotly before claiming her lips in a sizzling kiss.

Birgitta melted. Her heart fluttered as the kiss deepened. Her body grew hot and needy as Joseph buried his fingers into her thick, curly hair effectively loosening her carefully placed pins. He slid one leg between hers and pulled her closer. Hands roved over each other's bodies as they passionately made out on the sofa.

"Maybe we can—" he began between kisses.

"No! Not until after the wedding." Birgitta turned her face away trying to cool down. She, too, felt the desperation between them. It was naughty, and oh so wonderful all at the same time.

"Birgitta, you make me feel like a fifteen-year-old boy," Joseph moaned into her exposed neck. He proceeded to cover the sensitive skin there with hot kisses and nibbles that made her squirm all over again.

"Oh," she moaned. When his lips found her ear, tingles skipped down her spine. "We have to stop, Liebling." Her whispered words filled the air, but they sounded unconvincing.

"Must we?" He licked her ear.

Tingles shot lower to her core. "Yes, we must." She grabbed his ears and lifted his head to look into his eyes. "Just think how much better our wedding night will be."

"But it's not like either of us is still a virgin, my love. We've both been married before. There are children, mine and yours. The cat's out of the bag." He smiled, amused at her insistence on no sex until they were officially married.

"I know, but we can pretend. And we are virgins, Joseph, to each other." She dropped a quick kiss on his lips.

He couldn't argue with her logic. Even though he was in man-pain at the moment, it was exquisite man-pain, and he had to admit that all their make-out sessions had been like a shot of youth serum because he felt like a young man when he was with her. All he could think about anymore was getting her naked. It didn't help that he'd already accidentally seen her naked, or maybe it did? He didn't know or care. All he knew was that he was head over heels in love with her, and if she wanted to wait until their wedding night, then he would oblige. Anything Birgitta wanted, Birgitta would get. He just hoped she would never find out the real reason for his trip to Stockholm because if she did, she might never forgive him. Whether or not it was for putting himself into unnecessary danger or for lying would not make a difference. She would see it as one in the same, and then his new, glorious life with her would become a living hell. He and Faust would both be eating shit sandwiches in the doghouse together wondering where they went wrong. But for now, he needed to keep her happy while pursuing the only other thing in his life that held meaning; finding out what happened to Marlessa Schubert. He needed to know, needed to somehow bring the girl home even if it was only by way of news of her passing, if that was the case.

He kissed her tenderly, then pulled back. "You're right, of course. But it will be difficult to keep my hands off you. Maybe this seminar is a good thing after all. Absence makes the heart grow fonder, does it not?"

She sighed. "I suppose, but I will miss you. Promise you'll call me."

"I will." He entwined his fingers with hers, holding her hand up to place a tender kiss on her knuckles.

They stared into each other's eyes, smiling, and enjoying a quiet moment alone.

The shrill ringing of the phone killed the moment.

"Damn." Joseph groaned and then shot her a half-smile before reaching for his cellular. "It's Herman," he said, eyeing the number.

"I'll go make us some dinner." She stood, turning toward the kitchen. "That is, if you have anything in your cabinets." She tossed him a look that said she knew him well, and that the possibility of finding enough ingredients to create a meal might be stretching it. "Otherwise, we may be calling for takeout." She left him alone in the living room.

Heinz hit the answer button. "Tell me you've planned my itinerary." He spoke in cryptic terms while glancing toward the kitchen.

On the other end, Faust cleared his throat. "Hello to you, too, you ingrate. Of course I have. You're booked on AirBerlin tomorrow morning to Stockholm. Once you're there, you will be meeting with a rather brilliant young woman who is making your fake passport as we speak."

Joseph blinked. "Is that necessary?"

"You cannot rightly go into Russia as Detective Heinz. They would be suspicious of any law enforcement coming into their country, but a simple Austrian tourist is another matter. She will meet you at the airport, by the way."

"How will I know her? What's her name?" Joseph pulled a pen out of his pocket and grabbed the electric bill sitting on the coffee table to write on the envelope.

"She will know you. Don't worry. She doesn't ever give out her real name. All I know is a contact hashtag, HackTwice." Faust grunted.

"You don't know her name? What about what she looks like?" Joseph was astonished.

"I have no idea. We've never met in person, but she came to my attention a few years back--highly recommended, and she's never failed to come through. Her work is perfect, undetectable from the real deal no matter what type of document is required. I trust her. She'll find you. From there, you'll purchase your ticket with your new documents to board the Air Baltic red eye to Saint Petersburg. I have your ticket for the first leg. I'll give it to you when I pick you up tomorrow. I'm driving you to the airport, in case you hadn't figured that out. What lie have you concocted for your bride-to-be, so I won't screw it up?"

Joseph could hear Birgitta rummaging through the fridge. He got up and walked to the bedroom. "A seminar to advance to my A16, for two weeks." He cleared the bed and headed for the bathroom where he closed the door and turned on the sink faucet.

"Not bad. Does this mean I have to put in a good word now to get you promoted?"

Joseph chuckled. "It does, but I was already on the shortlist after the Ivchencko affair."

"Okay, at least it's not a complete lie. I'll stick to the truthy parts. Less problem remembering."

"Remember, you old goat, if you screw up, you'll have ruined what will be a happy marriage."

Faust snorted. "And if you screw up, you'll have ruined mine so we're both on the hook, Heinz. FYI, I don't like shit sandwiches."

"Got it, so let's not mess this thing up."

"Once you're in, I can't help you anymore, not until you make it back to Swedish soil. Keep that in mind above all else."

Joseph turned off the faucet. "I will. I'll see you tomorrow."

"Seven a.m. sharp." Faust hung up.

A knock sounded on the door.

"Yes?" Joseph poked his head out. Birgitta stood near his bed holding a handful of menus.

"So, what are you in the mood for tonight? Chinese, Turkish, or Italian?"

He eyed the lists, realizing this meant he was sorely lacking in groceries. "That bad, eh?"

She smiled. "Well, you have Muesli."

He bit his lip and leaned on the door jamb. "It's a very good thing I am marrying you, Mahler."

She sauntered closer, grinning. "I know this. It's a charity case, really. I couldn't stand to see you wasting away from starvation anymore."

He wrapped his arms around her waist. "Oh, I see. So, it wasn't my good looks and charm." He kissed her forehead.

"No, not at all, not the charm part, at least. Good looks?" She eyed his face, taking her time.

"Mahler?" Heinz prompted her.

She laughed. "Yes, it was your dark, brooding stares. So sexy!"

He leaned down and kissed her lips, taking his time. Slowly, he pulled away. "That's better. Italian."

She blinked. "What?"

He kissed her again, laughing softly. "Let's order Italian. I'm feeling particularly romantic tonight."

"Oh." She let him hold her while she pulled out the menu for Valentino's. "What did Herman want?"

"He's picking me up in the morning to take me to the airport."

"So soon?" Her eyes reflected deep disappointment.

"Yes. But you'll be so busy with fittings and shopping, you'll hardly miss me. And Elsa will help keep you occupied, I'm sure."

Birgitta sighed. "After we get married, I don't want either of us to travel anywhere without the other. This is your last trip alone, Joseph. Try not to enjoy it too much." She made light of it, but behind his eyes, Joseph winced.

The last thing he was going to do on this trip was enjoy himself. In fact, it was going to be brutal. Hunting down the few clues he had in so short a period without any official help was going to be hell. He'd be lucky to make any connection at all between the ledger from the Vledelets and discovering what happened to his daughter's friend once she was delivered to Warehouse 214. But he needed to try. His tattered soul demanded it.

"I'd rather enjoy being here with you right now. Let's go call in our order, and turn on some jazz, drink wine, eat, and maybe I will steal a few more kisses from my lovely bride-to-be," he said with a waggle of his eyebrows.

"Maybe I'll let you. Maybe." She pulled out of his arms and ran back into the living room with a laughing Heinz hot on her trail.

Chapter 3

Heinz sat in his seat with his head back. He closed his eyes as the Air Baltic flight sped down the runway heading for Saint Petersburg, Russia. He'd had a long and strange day. First, it was an emotional parting with Birgitta that morning.

"Don't forget to call me when you get there!" She'd sounded worried, her usual calm deserting her.

"I promise." The look in her eyes reminded him of an old Jewish woman his mother, Helen, once knew. Zara Lieberman had lived next door to the Heinz family and was a survivor of the Holocaust. She didn't speak often, but when she did, it was with strict purpose. When Joseph and his younger brother, David, played in the front yard, she would stare out her window at them. The look in her eyes was one that bespoke of remembered horror. She seemed like she lived in a perpetual nightmare, and the two boys would make up stories about the spooky old witch next door. It wasn't until Joseph was grown, and understood what the poor woman had gone through, that he was finally able to pinpoint what he saw in her eyes all those years ago. It was fear. Fear had found a home inside Frau Lieberman, and it refused to leave. It was fear he saw that morning growing in Mahler's eyes, and he didn't understand where hers sprang from.

"What is it, love?" Joseph tossed his heavy coat into Herman's waiting blue Volvo and stood on the curb with his fiancé.

She bit her lip. "I don't know. It's nothing, I guess. Just a bad dream I had." She shook it off, and wrapped her arms around his waist, laying her head upon his chest.

Joseph stroked her hair and kissed her forehead. "Is that all? It's just some boring accreditation seminars, nothing to worry about," he lied, feeling like an ass.

"I know. It's silly. Just forget it and call me when you're there."

"Okay." With a finger beneath her chin, he tilted her head back. "I love that you worry so much for me. I'm a lucky man." He kissed her then.

The kiss deepened before the loud sound of a throat clearing brought the two love birds back to reality.

"I hear you, Herman!" Birgitta laughed. "You may have him—for now."

Faust leaned over to peek out of the open driver's side door. He was wearing his usual earth-tones; Khaki pants, brown plaid shirt, brown wing-tip shoes, and beige blazer with dark brown leather patches on the elbows. "And I will happily give him back to you, Mahler."

Joseph climbed into the seat. "Tell Elsa I'll call and check on her and Anno later tonight." He closed the door and reached through the open window to tug Birgitta's hand.

"I can't believe you still do that. She's a grown woman, Joseph." She admonished him for his overbearing protectiveness.

"That doesn't mean she doesn't need looking out for. She might do something completely hair brained if I don't check in. Anno, too." His signature cynical gruffness colored his words.

Birgitta snorted. "If you say so. Be safe." She reluctantly pulled her hand from his grasp and backed up.

Herman waved before putting the car in gear and steering away from the curb. Joseph blew her a kiss, then hit the button on the door, rolling up the window.

"I have some papers for you," he said.

Faust glanced at him.

"Legal papers," he said, his tone serious.

"Are you planning on getting yourself killed?" Faust turned right onto the highway.

"No. It's just my will."

"Just your will?" Faust chuckled without humor.

"And a few letters. One for Birgitta, one for Elsa, and one for Anno." He pulled out a sealed yellow packet. "I'm placing this in your care in the event I don't return."

"Joseph, what did I say about my lack of preference for shit sandwiches?"

"I know, Herman, and I plan to be back in two weeks, but I will feel better knowing I have everything settled should it all go south. Oh, and there's another...," he pulled out a single envelope, placing it atop the yellow packet. "This is for the Schuberts. If anything goes wrong, I want Marlessa's mother and father to know I died trying."

Faust sighed. "And what about your own daughter? What am I to tell her if her father doesn't come home?"

Joseph paused. "I have letters for her and my brother with my lawyer." He didn't like thinking about Ingrid. It was painful. Their relationship had gone by the wayside ever since his divorce from her mother, Eva. Sure, he phoned her for her birthdays and holidays, but the conversations were always short and stilted. He loved her with all his heart, and he hoped she would accept the invitation to come to his wedding. More than that, he hoped his lawyer would never need to call on her.

"Then why do I get the dubious honor of delivering bad news to your fiancé and semi-adopted children?"

Joseph threw his arm up over the seat and glared at Faust. "Because they know you, and they trust you. And if anyone can keep them calm by imparting the terrible news that I'd gone off to Russia to pursue an old cold case, and then gotten myself killed, it's you. I wouldn't want any of them to hear that from a stranger."

"Hmph," Faust grunted. "Maybe I'll leave my own letters with a lawyer to deliver along with your letters because God knows Helga will kill me, and Birgitta will jump up and down on what's left of my gizzards if anything happens to you."

Joseph patted his friend on the shoulder. "Cheer up, Herman. I may just come home in one piece."

"You'd better."

The rest of the ride was spent with Faust going over Joseph's itinerary. He handed over the round-trip ticket along with a fat envelope of his own. "Give this to my contact. She's expecting it."

"Are you sure she will find me in such a large crowd?" Joseph was skeptical.

"I'm sure. You're not the first operative I've sent off, you know. I've been conducting this rodeo for a long time."

"And here I thought you were just the clown." Heinz got out when Faust pulled up curbside to Tegal International Airport.

"I suppose it goes without saying you should be careful. Don't tangle with their police. I'd never be able to get you out of Siberia. It's cold as fuck there. Too cold for me to mount a rescue mission at my advanced age."

"I'll stay below the radar." Heinz walked to the back to pull his suitcase out of the boot. He tapped the back of the car once he closed the trunk. Faust gave a two-fingered wave and pulled into the stream of traffic going out of the airport.

His flight to Stockholm had been routine. No problems, no delays. He'd deplaned, making his way into the main terminal of Stockholm Arlanda Airport. He knew he would need to pick up his checked luggage as if he were staying in the city, rip off the travel tag, and then check in later at the Air Baltic counter with his new identity. He'd been anxious about that part of the plan. If anything went wrong, he would have a tough time explaining to Mahler why he was in a Swedish jail for using a fake passport.

The wait was the worst part. Heinz sat near the Air Baltic counter glancing at every person who passed by. He tried to remain casual, to conceal that he was looking for anyone, but it was difficult since he had no idea what his contact looked like. He eyed a few women who walked by. They appeared professional, wearing suits. None of them looked his way or stopped. One woman looked every inch an agent. Her bearing was strong, military, but her eyes skipped over him moving on to another man walking toward her from the opposite direction. They met in the middle and continued together. This went on for an hour. Heinz grew antsy, thinking Faust may have put his trust in the wrong person. He still had ten hours before he needed to check in. A whole damn day wasted in an airport. He pulled his cellular from his pocket deciding it was as good a time as any to call Birgitta. If he were really staying in Stockholm for a seminar, he would've arrived at his hotel by now, so he dialed.

"I'm here," he said as soon as she answered. He injected a little cheer into his voice.

"How was your flight?"

"Not bad. No problems." Joseph looked around, keeping his voice low.

"It sounds loud in the background. Where are you?" she asked.

"The lobby. I'm waiting for my room to be ready. Apparently, housekeeping is slow today." The lie rolled off his tongue, and he silently begged God to forgive him.

"Oh, that's too bad, but I'm sure it will be fine. When is your first class?"

"Tomorrow morning. The schedule is pretty much packed. I'll try to call you when it's over tomorrow night."

"That sounds good. I miss you already."

Heinz smiled. "I miss you too."

"Don't go bar hopping with those Swedes. They drink like fish."

He laughed. "I'm German, remember? I cut my teeth on beer. I think I'll be okay."

"Well don't be calling me when you're hungover," his love admonished.

"What, no drunk dialing?"

"Absolutely not! But seriously, have some fun if you can, but not too much."

"Okay. Well, looks like my room's ready," he prevaricated, ready to end the call before he said something revealing.

"Sehr gut. Go and get settled. I love you."

Heinz lowered his voice. "I love you too." He smiled, then ended the call.

"Well, isn't that sweet?" A female voice intruded on his privacy.

Heinz looked to his right. A young woman sat next to him. She was wearing all black. Even her fingernails and lipstick were painted black. She had a silver nose ring and one eyebrow pierced. Her blonde hair was obviously bleached, and was cut short except for the top, which was long and straight, and hanging over one heavily lined eye. She appeared to be all of seventeen.

"It's rude to eavesdrop." He tucked his phone back into his pocket and turned away, ignoring her. He started watching the crowd once again.

"And it's rude to ignore someone who is talking to you, Herr Heinz."

Joseph whipped back around to stare at her. His eyebrow rose. "You?"

"Yes, me."

His incredulity increased. "HackTwice?"

She blew out a bored breath. "Yes. Please get over your shock. Follow me." She got up and began walking toward the restaurant at the far end of the terminal, tucking her hands inside the pockets of her hoodie as she went.

Heinz jumped up grabbing his coat and the handle of his suitcase following her. He noticed she was quite petite. *"How could she possibly be some genius hacker and police asset?"* he thought. She went through the open doorway and found a table in the corner. He came in behind her and slid into the seat on the opposite side of the booth.

"I have your papers." She pulled a packet out of her shoulder bag and shoved it across the table at him. "Don't open it here. Just put it on the seat next to you. Inside is your new passport. Your name is Martin Lintz, and you are an Austrian schoolteacher. You teach mathematics to ten-year olds. Your birthdate remains the same for ease in remembering should anyone ask, and your address is your old house where you grew up."

Heinz's eyebrows shot up. "And how do you know that address?"

She shrugged. "I know everything about you. Faust provided most of it, the rest I dug up on my own."

"Christ, there's just no privacy anymore." He shook his head.

She remained unfazed. "No, none. You will find a new cellular inside. It's clean and registered to Martin Lintz. You can call whoever you need to, and it will route through your other account. "There is also a baggage tag for your suitcase. You can pick up your ticket to Saint Petersburg at the Air Baltic counter." She held out her hand.

Heinz looked at it. "What?" he asked.

"Hand over your phone and passport. You can't take them with you. They will give you away should you be caught."

"I'm just supposed to leave my personal phone and passport with you? How will I get them back?"

"I will express mail them to Faust as soon as I leave here. They'll be waiting for you when you get back."

Joseph sighed. He wasn't happy about turning over his personal information to this young woman, but it was also obvious that she already had all that since she freely admitted to digging around in his business. He pulled the phone and passport out of his pocket and handed them over.

"Now, in addition to the new phone, there is also Russian currency, so you don't need to stop anywhere to exchange. The amount is five thousand Euros in rubles. You have something for me?"

"Oh, yes." Heinz reached into his jacket pocket and pulled out the thick envelope, handing it over.

She held it in both hands, weighing it. When she was satisfied, she got up. "Thank you." She turned to leave.

"Wait!" Joseph sat straight, watching her.

"What?"

"That's it?" He was shocked at their short exchange.

"What more did you expect?"

That got him. *What did I expect?* He shrugged. "I don't know. I guess it all just seemed rather abrupt."

"I got the distinct impression that you didn't care for bullshit." She stuffed her hands in her pockets, her face absent any emotion.

"I suppose not. Never mind. Thank you."

She didn't say another word, simply turned and left. When she was gone, he picked the packet up off the seat and stared at it. A waitress approached, and he put it down on the table laying his hands on top.

"What can I get for you?" she asked.

Joseph looked around the table and then back at her. "A menu?"

She nodded, walking off to obtain one. After she dropped it off, he glanced through it, selected a hot roast beef sandwich and coffee, and then returned his attention to the packet after she left to place his order. Inside was his new passport. He was amazed. Not only was it perfectly unde-tectable from a legitimate passport, but it even had a couple of stamps in it, so it didn't appear like a newly issued document. Apparently, Martin Lintz had visited France, Italy, Sweden, and now he would be visiting Russia. His face stared back at him from the photo, the very same photo that was in his other passport only this one said he lived in Salzburg, Austria. He noted that the street address was his parents' house on the outskirts of Berlin. Easy enough to remember. He would just need to say Salzburg instead of Berlin. He pulled the money out, counted it, and then put half in his wallet and the other half inside his suitcase. There was a travel tag like the one he'd ripped off the case earlier. This one said the luggage had traveled from Austria to Sweden. He tied it around the handle. After putting his passport and new cell phone inside his coat pocket, he balled up the now empty packet. He would toss it into the nearest waste bin on his way out.

After eating his lunch, he headed for the Air Baltic counter. He knew he would need to get over his anxiety about the identity subterfuge and just do it. He felt like a sinner in church the entire time, but he had no difficulty in obtaining his ticket. It was already paid for. By the time the after-midnight flight had loaded, Heinz was exhausted. All he wanted was Scotch and sleep. He would need the three-hour nap because he had no clue where he was going to stay once he arrived. The plane was scheduled to land in the wee hours of the morning. He'd probably have to hang out in the airport until afternoon and then go obtain a room in the nearest hotel. He hoped his Russian was good enough to manage the transaction.

The plane taxied down the runway accelerating until the front end lifted and the back wheels left the tarmac. Once they were airborne, the drink cart came around. Heinz ordered his Scotch on the rocks, sipped it slowly, relaxing, and then, using his jacket as a blanket, leaned against the window and closed his eyes. He was heading into the unknown without a safety net. He just hoped he would find an answer that he could live with.

Chapter 4

Elsa Kreiss no sooner clocked in for patrol duty when she was called into her Captain's office. Karl Keller sat behind his desk sipping coffee. The rich aroma filled the small space. He didn't look happy as evidenced by the constant tug he gave to his dark mustache. His balding head tilted at an angle as he glared at her. She wondered just what the hell she'd done to earn his ire so early in the morning.

"I see that your knee troubles you no more. You've been successfully completing patrol duty."

Elsa remained quiet since he hadn't asked a question yet. She gave a silent nod of assent.

He continued. "So here you are now on your second month back on duty, and I get a call to send you straight away to the LKA, to Direktor Herman Faust, no less. I'd heard a rumor or two flying around, but nothing confirmed, and you've been suspiciously quiet yourself."

Elsa's mouth opened.

"Save it, Kreiss," he said. Looking down at her file, he flipped through a few pages, stopping to read one before flipping to the next. Finally, he looked up.

"I don't know whose ass you kissed, but most Schutzpolizei wait years, working their tails off, moving up the ranks organically, and only after proving themselves time and again, completing courses, and sweating it out the hard way before being tagged for upper echelon positions."

"Sir?" Elsa couldn't hold her tongue any longer. She was confused and taken by surprise. The last time she'd seen Faust was when he and Heinz had dropped by together to check on her home therapy. Sure, Faust had made one passing mention concerning advancement during the Ivchencko affair while she was still in hospital, but he'd not brought it up since, so she didn't put any more thought into his words. They were just praise and encouragement in the heat of a very intense moment. At least, that's what she thought when more than a month passed, and no further word was received on the subject. She had to admit, she'd been a little disappointed.

"Nein!" He held up his hand, and for a moment, bore a comedic resemblance to Germany's greatest shame, Adolf Hitler. "I always knew you were Heinz's little protégé, but I had no idea you'd moonlighted even above his graces. At least he never interfered or tried to throw his weight around here. He left you to fend for yourself and earn your way, and up until this morning, I thought that was who you were. I respected that, but now I just don't know."

This pissed Elsa off. Heat bloomed around her ears as she forced herself to bite her tongue. She'd had nothing to do with anyone requesting her anywhere, and now her Captain sat before her all but accusing her of what, screwing her way up the ladder?

She glared at him, waiting for him to finish. He stared back, and the standoff continued until he realized she wasn't going to back down. Keller cleared his throat.

"Here." He handed up the file. "Take this, clock out, and go to the LKA office on Tempelhofer Damm."

Elsa stepped forward and grabbed the file. "When do I return?" she asked.

"You don't. You don't work here anymore, Kreiss. You're their problem now. Dismissed." He gave her a mocking salute.

She stared at Keller a moment longer. He ignored her, turning to his computer. She spun around and marched out of his office. As she passed his secretary's desk, she stumbled. Sigrid jumped up, reaching out a hand.

"Are you okay, Elsa?"

Kreiss looked at the woman. She appeared like she always did, sweet, kind, plump, and now wearing a gold and diamond engagement ring. Her partner--scratch that, *ex-partner*, Hugo Beimer, had proposed to the woman, and Sigrid had said yes. They were set to be married a month after Heinz and Mahler's own wedding.

"Yes. I'm okay. Just angry and confused." She straightened up and offered a half-smile to the woman.

Sigrid nodded. "I know. I transferred the call in to the captain." She glanced back at his door, then leaned closer to whisper, "He's not really angry with you, Elsa. He knows you didn't have a hand in the transfer. He's just mad at himself." She looked back once more to make sure Keller couldn't hear their conversation. "He's been passed over by the LKA for years, and now they've personally requested you, a rookie. It's just jealousy."

Elsa blew out her breath. "Well why the hell did he all but accuse me of screwing someone for the reassignment?"

Sigrid shrugged. "I don't know. Maybe because he's a bit of an asshole?"

Kreiss tried not to smile, but hearing sweet, sensible Sigrid say 'asshole' got her.

"He did try to fight for you, Elsa. I heard him tell Faust that you were a good officer, and that a few more years would only make you better. He wanted to keep you on, tried to look out for you, I think."

Elsa looked over her shoulder at Captain Keller's open door. Some of her anger melted away. "Well, he has a shitty way of showing his regard." She sighed. "I'm to leave immediately and report to Faust. I am happy about it, but I'm nervous, Sigrid. What if I fuck it all up?" Elsa turned her green eyes toward the woman.

Sigrid smiled. "You're going to be great, Elsa. This I know!" She reached out and gave her a hug.

"Thank you." Elsa returned the hug. "And how is Hugo doing with his training?"

Her partner was called to begin his own new career path only two weeks ago with the SEK. Beimer had made his own impression in their last case, and thanks to her boyfriend, Lukas, had received high praise, and a new commission.

"He's doing very well although he says he's bruised and tired all the time from the physical training. And he misses me, of course," she blushed.

"That complainer! Tell him I said to suck it up, and then tell him I finally got the call!" She held up the file folder. "I thought Faust had either forgotten or decided he didn't think I was LKA material. God, when Hugo got his new assignment, we threw him a going away party. I get this." She tossed another renewed look of anger at Keller's office.

Sigrid nodded. "It's the old boys club, Elsa. Some things never change."

"Well, maybe I'll change them."

Sigrid smiled. "Maybe you will."

The two women grinned, sharing a momentary celebration over Elsa's promotion.

"Sigrid!" Keller barked. "Bring me the Gunderman file."

"Duty calls. Good luck, Elsa." She hugged the shorter, redheaded woman one last time.

"Thank you, Sigrid. I'll see you soon. At a wedding, I believe?"

"At two! First Heinz and Mahler, and then me and Hugo." She waved as she set off for the file room.

Elsa chuckled and clocked out, then cleared out her locker. She left, making her way to the UBahn. She hopped the next car to Tempelhofer Damm. On the ride over, she called Lukas to share her news. At least he would be happy for her, and perhaps later, they could celebrate, just the two of them.

Heinz found a cheap hotel room in the Kseniya Guest House near the docks. He checked in, handing over his passport to show identification. Martin Lintz was now an official guest. He paid a week in advance in cash. After settling into the single bedroom, and taking a quick shower, he headed out again, shrugging into his coat as he walked out the front door. Across the street he spotted a café. Heinz stopped there first for brunch and a cup of strong, black coffee, and then grabbed a taxi to the warehouse district on the docks. He wanted to get a look at warehouse number 214 during a drive-by first. Once he saw exactly where it was situated, he directed the driver to take him to the nearest car rental service. He couldn't very well conduct a stakeout in a taxi. Once again, Martin Lintz made a transaction, this time, signing on the dotted line for a Volga Siber, similar to the American Chrysler Sebring. The black vehicle waited in the parking lot, gassed up and ready to go. From the rent-a-car service, he found a small grocery store where he stocked up on bottled sparkling water and a few snacks. Finding a hardware store was a little more difficult since his command of the Russian language was iffy, but he found a place where he picked up a set of screwdrivers in various sizes—great for picking locks—and even a small pair of hunting binoculars.

What he really needed was a gun. He couldn't bring his own police issued Glock. It would've given him away, but if push came to shove, Saint Petersburg would surely have its own black-market dealers, and criminals were never hard to find. For now, he'd stick to surveillance. With the minimum supplies needed acquired, Heinz threw his purchases on the passenger seat, and turned the wheel of the car, heading back to the docks. He made one wrong turn before correcting course and arriving at his destination. The only problem now became finding an inconspicuous spot to park.

As he watched, Heinz noticed two other cars pull in from further up the dock. They drove into a fenced area where they parked, and the drivers got out, walking down the ramp to a lower-level loading dock. The chain-link fence stood wide open with no one to monitor who came and went. It also sat across the road, and two buildings down from Warehouse 214. It wasn't as close as he'd like to be, but it would do. He steered the Volga Siber into the fenced-off parking lot and backed into a parking space. This allowed him to at least face the warehouse he planned to surveil. Heinz settled in, preparing for a long vigil. He wasn't sure what he was looking for. He only knew he'd know when he saw it. Then, he would have to figure out what to do with that information. Whatever he decided, it was going to be dangerous.

Chapter 5

Faust looked up from the file he was reading. He heard women's voices coming down the hallway. One was his secretary, Lora, a woman in her forties with short, black hair, and the other came from someone he'd grown quite fond of recently. He smiled to himself, got up, and walked casually to the door of his office where he stood, hands in his pockets, waiting.

"Well, it's about time you showed up. I hope this isn't going to be a regularly occurring problem, Kreiss. Tardiness will not be tolerated."

Elsa arched her brow. A laugh threatened to burst forth, but she contained herself. "Herr Direktor, I promise you it is not."

Faust glanced at Lora. "Thank you for bringing this delinquent in. I'll take it from here."

Lora smirked, knowing her boss's dry sense of humor after working for him for the past seven years. "Yes, sir." She turned to leave, patting Elsa on the shoulder. "Good luck," she whispered.

Faust waited as Elsa walked inside his office before following her in and closing the door. "Well, how did Captain Keller take the news? Is he green with envy?" He stood behind his desk, with a look of glee on his face.

Elsa continued to stand, unsure as to whether she should sit or not. On one hand, this wasn't the military, but on the other hand, Herman Faust was now her commander, which meant the casual rules regarding men and women in social situations did not apply. He was the direktor, and she, a subordinate.

Faust watched as she stood there, practically at attention. Finally, it hit him. "Oh, sit, sit." He waved at the chair behind her.

Elsa took a seat, and Faust followed suit, sinking down into his old, worn leather chair.

"Well?" He leaned onto his elbows, waiting.

Elsa leaned in as well. "He was not happy. In fact, he practically accused me of sleeping with you to get sent here." She refrained from stating "*to get this job*" because she wasn't yet sure exactly what position she would be gaining at the Landeskriminalamt, or LKA, as it was commonly called.

Faust hooted a loud guffaw.

"Ha! He just wishes he had the opportunity. I've no doubt Keller would drop to his knees if I asked, all for the chance to work here, the fool. I've dodged his verbal hand jobs for years now. Truly, Kreiss, he is a bit of an asshole, and I never took to him. Too self-aggrandizing, that one. I could hear the animosity bubbling inside of him when I gave the order to relinquish you. I thought his head might pop off from all the steam boiling his blood. Good times, yes." Faust sat back, grinning in a self-congratulatory way.

Elsa stifled a smile. It was plain to see that he enjoyed stealing her away. Why, however, was another question.

"What did Keller do to earn your dislike, Direktor?"

"Herman. You must remember to call me Herman, Elsa, but only when we're alone or in casual company, of course." He tapped the desk lightly. "Keller and I go way back. Heinz, too. We were all in the academy together, you see. Long story short, we'd gone out to celebrate the completion of our training. Somewhere around the third or fourth pub we visited we met some lovely ladies."

"Oh, really?" Elsa smiled, and sat back, legs crossed.

"Yes, yes. You know, I wasn't always an old, married fart. Anyhow, one of them was particularly beautiful. Like you, she had long, red hair, but her eyes were blue, the bluest I'd ever seen. Well, Keller began to brag he could get her. Heinz and I were never ones to back away from a challenge, and it became a competition, one that I won, mind you." He smirked to himself.

"And?" Elsa waited, knowing there was more to the story.

Faust's smirk spread into a full grin. "And I'm still married to her today. Keller has been jealous ever since, especially since my career also outpaced his own."

"Helga? Helga is the red-haired girl? Why, Herman, you sly dog!"

"I know. See? I told you. There was a time this old dog could hunt."

"Well, you're not an old dog, Herman," she winked, chuckling. "I can see why she chose you. But what about Heinz? Are you telling me he tried to date Helga too?"

"Heinz was the most excellent wingman as it turns out. I did ask him once, right before Helga and I said our I do's, why he backed off from the challenge that night. You know what he said?"

Elsa waited, enjoying learning more about her mentor.

"No, what?"

Faust's eyes grew distant as he looked out the window, happiness radiating from his face.

"He said, 'Herman, the minute you laid eyes on Helga, I knew it was all over.' He said, 'I've never seen anyone fall in love so hard, so quickly, and what kind of friend would I be if I tried to stand in the way?' That's a good friend to have, Elsa."

"I take it Captain Keller hadn't noticed Cupid's arrow sticking out of your hind end?" The tongue in cheek comment brought Faust back to the moment.

"Indeed. The fool kept trying to make Helga dance with him. She obviously wasn't interested, not after we were introduced. I tell you, if it wasn't already love at first sight, her next action would have clinched my heart. Keller made a clumsy attempt to kiss my girl, and she balled up her fist and walloped him. How could I not marry her after that?"

Elsa laughed. "I can see it was a match made in heaven."

"Most days, yes." He looked down, bashful.

"Did you two ever have children?" As soon as the question left her lips, she regretted it. An immediate look of pain crossed his face.

Faust noticed her regret and held up a hand. "No, it's okay. We did have one child, a little girl. Her name was Therese."

Elsa sat quietly. She mentally focused on one word; *was*.

"God took her from us when she was only three years old. A dark time, it was. She was beautiful too. Long, curly, red hair like her mother, and the tenacity of a bulldog like her old man." He sighed. "It was an accident, no one's fault, really. At least, that's what Helga keeps telling me. I still wonder..." His voice trailed off as he stared out the window. "She fell off her tricycle. A few scrapes, but we didn't realize at the time she'd hit her head harder than we knew. Over the next couple of days, her brain swelled. She lost consciousness. She was in the intensive care unit for a week. The doctors did all they could to reduce the swelling. They kept her in an induced comatose state, but nothing worked. She was already brain dead. It just took her body a little longer to catch up." He sniffed, surreptitiously wiping his eyes. "See? Tenacious. She wasn't going to give up without a fight."

Elsa leaned forward, reaching across the desk to pat his arm. "Just like her papa," she smiled.

"After that, we grieved. We did think about trying again, but it seems we waited a bit too long, and conceiving became more difficult. It just never happened. Now, we have pugs, two of them. Weasel and Monk."

"I like those names. Very unusual." Elsa sat back.

"Helga's idea, both of them. I don't know where she comes up with these things." He sat back, clearing his throat. "Well, officer Kreiss, it's time to learn about what it is you'll be doing here; don't you think?" Faust changed the subject.

"I'm ready." She sat up straight.

His face grew serious. "To begin, you're going to help me monitor a situation, one that is under the radar, unsanctioned, and only has two names approved for clearance on the matter, mine, and yours. You cannot speak of it to anyone no matter their occupation or personal relevance in your life. Understood?"

"Understood."

"Good, because if it gets out, it's both our asses."

Elsa sat quietly as Faust began briefing her about a new lead on a cold case, explaining how she, herself, helped bring about this new information with her involvement in the Ivchencko affair. Her eyes grew wider as her new superior shared that the case itself was the very one that nearly derailed the career of her mentor, and that Detective Heinz was now deep undercover, and deep into the former Soviet Union where diplomatic relations were only surface niceties. It was clear by the end of the telling that Elsa understood the very real danger Joseph Heinz was in, and worse, she couldn't tell Birgitta, couldn't express her concerns out loud to Lukas or even answer her own brother's queries as to Heinz's whereabouts, which she knew would eventually come. All she could do was utter the lie about a training getaway in Sweden.

Faust watched her face looking for any reaction beyond the large, green-eyed stare. "Well? You see now why this must be kept under wraps?"

Elsa drew a deep breath, letting it out slowly. "I do, and if I may speak plainly?"

"You may."

"This sucks!"

Faust raised an eyebrow. "It does. Welcome to the world of the LKA, Kreiss."

"So, you and I are the only two people who have Joseph's back, and we're too far back to be effective. If something goes wrong, we won't know until it's too late, if at all?"

"That about sums it up."

Anger flashed in her eyes. She tried to tamp it down. "What in the world made him think he could just go off like this, without one of us with him?"

The direktor sighed. "It is not unusual for an agent to undertake a solo mission, Kreiss. It happens every day." He pointed to a stack of files on his desk. "There are seven in front of me." He lifted the first file and opened it, scanning it briefly. "One in Syria undercover with the resistance." He pulled another. "Two in Saudi Arabia not even aware of each other, set in motion to infiltrate the Kingdom's highest echelon." Faust flipped open yet another. "And several inside the United States awaiting orders." He stacked them again, pushing them off to the side. "These are the risks these agents take, the very risks you, yourself, will one day take upon completion of your training to my satisfaction." He folded his arms on the desk, leaning forward.

Elsa sat forward at the same time locking eyes with his. "Yes, but Joseph is not one of your agents. He's a police detective," she pointed out.

"Heinz is better than any agent under me, and I trust his instincts even if I don't agree with his methods. He's also a friend, and I owe him the opportunity to find peace within himself. He's been haunted by this case for too long."

Elsa read the lines on Faust's face. Something in her softened. "And you know what it's like to lose a child."

They stared at each other in silence.

Finally, Faust grunted, "Exactly."

Accepting her new role as co-conspirator, Elsa sat back. "What now?"

"Now, we wait for him to contact us, and..." he turned to his computer. "...we see if my inside contact has any news to share." He leaned around and looked over the top of the screen. "What? Did you think I wouldn't provide him some kind of backup?" He typed in his password.

"Herman, you softie. You do care." Elsa smiled and waited to hear if there was yet any news of Detective Joseph Heinz inside Russia. "Does he know?"

He scanned his inbox. "No, and that's the way we shall keep it. Heinz would be pissed to know he is being followed. The agreement with my insider is for surveillance only, just so we have some way of knowing if he's safe, and a pathway in case we need to get him out sooner than planned. It was the best I could under the circumstances."

Chapter 6

Birgitta Mahler reported to her superior, Erster Hauptkommissar Karl Levitz. The tall, blond man sat at his desk aggressively banging on his computer keyboard. He didn't even bother to look up when Mahler walked in, but simply lifted one hand to wave her to a chair on the opposite side of his desk.

"Mahler, have a seat."

Birgitta sat down and waited for him to continue.

"I know your leave begins in two weeks, but I have an urgent request out of the Federal Ministry of the Interior, and since Heinz is in Sweden for a seminar," he rolled his eyes, "you're next on my list."

Mahler remained silent knowing Levitz didn't like being interrupted even when it seemed he'd stop talking. She knew better. Experience taught her that he was gathering his thoughts.

He finished whatever he was typing with a final bang of his fingers and then sat back, his blue eyes focused on her. His short, military-styled haircut framed a rectangular face with an unusually sharp chin. There was a small dimple in it, but it did nothing to soften his otherwise austere countenance. Two lines furrowed his brow showing the years of worry he'd shouldered in his life, and career. Levitz was a former Major in the German Army, and an artillery specialist. He was ranked as the number one sniper in his division, and he brought that experience with him into the police force.

He cleared his throat.

"There have been threats made on the life of the Minister. Several have been issued anonymously through email, voicemail, and post." He pulled out a packet from his drawer and tossed it onto the desktop. "These are the email copies with IT reports that show the ghost IP used to send them has been routed through so many servers, we have yet to be able to determine the original owner. The voicemails are being analyzed by our lab to see if we can match them to any registered convicts in our system, and there are three physical posts that are clean of fingerprints. I want you to go over everything, and in the morning, report to the Minister's home address. It's all inside the packet. You're being assigned to shadow Ritt Obermeyer throughout the day from the moment he wakes until he arrives back home. I have another officer assigned to guard him overnight with patrol units going by every hour until we neutralize the threat."

Birgitta bit her lower lip. She'd planned to finish tying up the loose ends for her wedding, but now she didn't know how she would accomplish that massive task while babysitting the Minister of the Interior. She would need to rely heavily upon Elsa which, while she trusted the younger woman to handle things, still didn't seem fair. She was a hands-on person, and relinquishing control to someone else irked her.

"Are there any suspects yet? Anyone he's recently angered, a co-worker, a lover?" Mahler knew all about Herr Obermeyer's penchant for young, beautiful women, and his politics were not popular, especially among the police state that he and his under-secretaries oversaw.

"That's what I expect you to determine. This is a shit assignment, I know. None of us are fond of Obermeyer, but it is still our sworn duty, despite his recent cuts to police funding, to protect him." Levitz's nostrils flared. It was plain he did not like having anyone in his department running to the rescue of the man who had cut the budget for new protective equipment and was hell-bent on privatizing law enforcement retirement pensions. "Do your best. If you manage to keep whoever wants him dead from killing him, you've done your job."

"What if I fail?" Birgitta asked, a delicate, dark eyebrow raised.

Levitz looked her in the eye. "I'll recommend you for a commendation." He turned back to his computer.

That was her superior's idea of humor. If one didn't know him, they would believe he was serious, and perhaps in this case, he was. She rose, picking up the packet from his desk, and quietly walked out of his office. At her cubicle, she pulled out her phone and fired off a quick text to Joseph. *New assignment protecting the MP of Budget Cuts. Yay, me! Someone wants to kill him. Can't imagine why. Miss you. B.*

She set her mobile down and opened the packet, dumping the contents out on her desk. Sifting through, Mahler placed the emails to one side with the small flash drive on top of that short stack and reached for the physical posts. Those interested her the most because while most people who sent death threats through email were often disgruntled, angry people typing out their frustrations in a moment that was usually gone by the time law enforcement showed up on their doorstep, delivering an actual, physical post showed more disturbing intent. Snail mail took far more time to hand-write, or in this case, cut out what appeared to be individual words that came from several newspapers. Each word was carefully cut into a square and glued down onto standard white typing paper creating an obviously well thought out message.

Herr Obermeyer, Money cannot buy silence. Money cannot protect you. Money cannot save you.

That was the first message. The second showed a picture of a Euro with a bullet flying through, ripping the paper. It was underscored with the words '*Money cannot stop a bullet.*' The last one simply said, '*How does it feel to be scared to walk out your front door?*'

Someone was definitely mad at the Minister, but Birgitta reread all three posts before going through the emails. There were more of those, and each was crazier than the last. The perpetrator was engaging in full-out psychological terrorism dating back a month but had yet to strike beyond the delivery of threats. It was as if the real purpose was to terrorize him, not physically harm him. Still, without investigation, she would not be able to make that determination with certainty. She picked up the flash drive. The voicemail recordings were contained within. She plugged it into her computer and pulled up the mp3 file. One mouse click on the play button revealed a low-pitched, mechanical voice with a sinister warning.

"You will know no peace and will suffer until the moment when your suffering ends!"

It was obvious that the pitch and tone of the voice had been altered, but what could not be determined was whether it was originally male or female. The message itself was vague. All that was certain was that whoever was threatening the Minister wanted him to be fearful. Mahler unplugged the flash drive and then put the contents back inside the packet. She would look over each email again later, and tomorrow, she would meet up with Herr Obermeyer at his home and escort him to work. On the way, she planned to grill him about any knowledge or suspicions he had as to who might be making these threats. For now, she needed to use the rest of her day to finish off a report, and then make a list, a very long one, of things she would need Elsa to do in order to cement plans for her and Joseph's wedding. Joseph. Thinking of him made her reach out and pick up her mobile, checking for messages. Nothing. He still hadn't responded to her text. Perhaps he was in one of the many seminars and had his phone off. She sighed. The next two weeks were going to be long and grueling, and she didn't look forward to providing protection to the Minister while investigating the threats to his life. She just hoped it was nothing more than a scorned lover, and she prayed the time would fly so she could walk down the aisle and marry the man she loved. She'd waited long enough, and now, the moment was drawing near. Birgitta pulled out a sheet of paper and began writing out her list. She was sure that with everything planned out to a T, the wedding would go off without a hitch.

It was late afternoon, and Heinz still hadn't seen anyone come into or leave the warehouse. He had, however, watched a few cars roll in, and out of the parking lot where he sat. Dock hands and sailors left for the day and others came to work. He'd also drunk two bottles of water and had eaten a package of nuts and dried fruit. At one point, he'd even climbed out after making sure no one was around, stretched his legs briefly, and took a piss behind the car. Now, the sun was beginning its descent, and temperatures began to drop. He desperately wanted a hot cup of coffee, and a hotter meal. He was about to call it a day when a dark limousine pulled around the corner and headed toward number 214.

Heinz pulled out his binoculars to get a closer look.

The limo rolled to a stop just outside of the massive double doors, doors that had been closed the entire time he'd surveilled the building. A large, muscular man in a dark suit got out on the passenger side, walking to the warehouse doors where he inserted a key into the lock, and then punched in a code on the black box above that lock. The doors began to slide open automatically. He stood aside, leaving room for the limousine to drive past and through the doorway.

Heinz aimed the binoculars down to get a look at the license plate. He reached blindly for the small notebook at his side and scribbled down the numbers. When the limo stopped, only a small portion of the trunk was visible. He cursed. "Damn!" He could not see any more from where he sat. He craned his neck around, straining to gain more visual access. The man standing outside walked in and approached the trunk. He popped it open and reached inside. Another man came around to join him. He was shorter, broader, and bald. The setting sun reflected off his head making it appear waxen. Together, they leaned into the trunk, and when they pulled back, Heinz could clearly see a large, dark green, duffel-style bag being lifted out. It moved, bucking them. He couldn't see the rest of it as the two brutes handling what seemed to be a body blocked the rest from view, but it was clear someone or something was struggling, putting up a fight. As they carried their squirming load around the car, a third person came into view, following them. He was a tall man, distinguished-looking with an expensive haircut. Even his salt and pepper beard was meticulously groomed. His attire was tailored; dark suit, probably Armani or an equally fashionable brand. He was speaking, although Joseph could not hear what he was saying, and gesturing. Probably giving orders. Something sparkled on his hand. Heinz zeroed in noting a gold pinky ring, but it was the tattoo on the back of his hand that held his attention. A five-pointed star, insignia of the Russian mafia commonly showing the number of years a man spent in prison. Below the faded blue star, tattooed around his index finger was a crown. Heinz was not familiar with that one, but the Cyrillic acronym spelling out SLON across his knuckles in between the other two symbols, that one he knew. It meant *'From my early years, only misery.'*

Given his appearance, issuing orders, and those tattoos, Heinz knew the man held high rank within the Bratva. How much was another matter. He made a mental note, and watched as the man glanced outside, casting a look around before retreating to the interior. The large doors began to close, running mechanically on their metallic tracks. The screeching of the gears echoed across the divide and reached Heinz's ears. He waited another hour. The light grew dimmer, but finally, the gears began to grind once again, the doors opening wide. The limousine pulled out, and the same large man from before stood outside waiting for the doors to close. He inserted his key, turned the lock, and punched a code in, presumably setting the alarm. When he was finished, he climbed into the passenger side, and the car drove off, back around the corner, and out of sight.

Heinz scribbled a few words into his notebook. He thought about the wiggling bag he saw the men take out of the trunk and haul into the warehouse. Possibly one of their own, or someone on their shit list. He wondered if he should try to get inside because the prognosis for someone in that position was not good. Still, he had no way of knowing if the person was still inside. He could even be dead already. Heinz knew he didn't have enough information, and he also had neither any official capacity to investigate what he saw, nor any backup to help him. It was hard to walk away, but it was what he needed to do now. He knew he needed more than what he'd just witnessed. He started the car, and pulled out of the parking lot, heading back toward his hotel. It had been a long day of sitting and waiting. He was tired from traveling, tired from his stakeout, ready for dinner, and a good night's sleep. He would return in the morning to see if the limo came back and, perhaps, might reveal more activity. With the grit of weariness in his eyes, and upon his soul, he didn't notice the small, dark sedan that pulled in behind him, merging with traffic.

Chapter 7

The hotel room was quiet. Usually, Heinz enjoyed this, but after spending the day alone on a stakeout, it was unnerving. He'd grown used to spending his nights with Birgitta, that is, until she would send him home. He smiled. Her no sex before marriage ban tickled him. It was fine for the moment, but as soon as she said "I do", he was going to make her pay dearly for every night spent nursing a tender pair of blue balls, and by 'pay', he meant to mercilessly make love to her until they both collapsed from exhaustion. But he also missed talking to her, something he'd been doing long before he fell in love with her. It was 6:30 in the evening in Saint Petersburg, but it was only 4:30 in the afternoon back home in Berlin. He would need to wait at least another hour and a half before he called. She was still at work, and then there was the text message he just noticed popping up on his burner phone.

New assignment protecting the MP of Budget Cuts. Yay, me! Someone wants to kill him. Can't imagine why. Miss you. B.

According to the time stamp on the message, and the current time on his bedside clock, the relay time HackTwice set up was more than five hours. Maybe that couldn't be helped. He didn't know, but that was going to prove problematic if Birgitta texted him again. He would need to find creative ways to explain why it took so long to answer. He noted the content of the message and frowned. He was no fan of Obermeyer, and he knew it was his own absence that put Mahler on the case. The Minister of Parliament was scum in his eyes, not only for his policies or lack thereof, but also his well-reported personal activities. He didn't like the idea of

Birgitta being assigned to the man. He planned on talking to Levitz about it when he got back, for surely there was someone else he could have put on a security detail for the MP who wasn't female, beautiful, and also his woman. He ran his hand over his face. *Christ, listen to me. When did I get to be such a Neanderthal?* Heinz didn't care. His protective instincts were now activated, and he felt frustration set in at being too far away to do anything about the situation.

He pulled up the list of phone numbers stored in the burner. Birgitta, Faust, and Elsa. He smiled. There was one more listed simply as Emergency. He had no idea who that was, and the number below was unfamiliar. He ignored it for the moment and hit number three on the speed-dial.

"Hallo?"

"Are you staying out of trouble?" Heinz asked in a stern voice.

"Of course not, Papa," the feminine voice answered. He could hear the barely contained laughter bubbling just under the surface of her statement.

Heinz laughed. "I figured as much. Who have you pissed off today, Elsa?"

She giggled, then grew serious. "Well, for starters, Captain Keller thinks I'm screwing Herman."

His eyebrows shot up. "What?"

"Yes, can you believe it?"

"Why would he think such a thing? That's ridiculous! Faust is an old dog with his own porch to lay on."

Elsa snorted. "What is it with you and Herman and your old dog references?" She paused, then continued. "Keller got his nose out of joint. It seems he's been vying for a position within the LKA for quite some time, and he was none too happy to lose me to Faust. That is what prompted the egotistical man to infer I was sleeping my way up the ladder."

Joseph slapped his knee. "You've been promoted?"

Elsa considered his question. "Well, I suppose so, or maybe it's a lateral move. Faust has me working for him right now..." She stopped, knowing she could not reveal too much.

"Elsa, if you're working directly for the Direktor of the LKA, you've been promoted. Maybe Herman didn't make that abundantly clear but let me do so now. Congratulations. I'm proud of you." The last sentence was stated with feeling.

Elsa felt it. His words touched her heart. She swallowed a tight lump in her throat and blinked back a happy tear. "Thank you," she said, softly. A smile she couldn't contain spread across her lips. "Well, needless to say, Keller was unhappy."

Heinz laughed out loud. "Well, Keller always was the jealous one. He and Faust have an old rivalry."

"I heard."

This surprised him. "You did?"

"Yes, Herman told me all about the competition for Helga all those years ago. It was rather cute, actually. He's really an old softie."

A loud snort echoed across the line. "Don't let him fool you. Faust is tough as nails." A small smile tugged his lips. "Just do what he tells you to do. He won't steer you wrong."

"Will do, Herr Kommissar."

"How's Anno?"

"He's well. His grades are good, and he's dating a girl named Jules from England. She's an exchange student."

"Did I ever have the talk with him?" Heinz began, worried.

Elsa cackled. "No, I did! Don't worry. I've already explained the birds and the bees to him, and he knows to slap a raincoat over his cock or else I'll beat him within an inch of his life."

Joseph winced. "Elsa, language!"

"Don't be so provincial. We're all grownups." He could hear the laughter in her voice.

"That may be, but I'm still your elder, and hearing you say words like "cock" just does not strike me right."

"Sorry, papa," she mocked.

"And stop calling me papa," he said with a grumpy inflection. He didn't really mean it. "Well, I just wanted to check in. Will you be celebrating tonight with Lukas?"

"Maybe a small celebration, dinner or something."

"Tell him hello for me."

"I will."

Heinz was quiet for a moment, staring at the faded, floral wallpaper where it peeled away from the corner by the door. "Keep an eye on Birgitta for me. I'll call you again this weekend to check on you."

Elsa felt love fill her heart. Heinz could never say it, but she knew he loved her, and loved Anno. It was in every phone call to 'check' on them, and every weekly dinner out, and every action he took to help them along their paths in this world.

"Okay, I will. Be careful," she said before she could censor her words.

He chuckled. "At a police seminar? I'm sure I'll be fine. Just bored."

Elsa replied, "You know what I mean."

"I do. Auf wiedersehen."

He ended the call. A growl erupted from his stomach reminding him he'd hardly eaten a thing all day. With time to kill, he got off the bed, and left his room to seek out the hotel dining room.

The restaurant within the Kseniya consisted of five tables set in a darkened room with only two windows facing out onto the front and side streets. Small candles lit the individual tables, and Heinz felt sure the low lighting was intentional to hide the down-trodden conditions of the furniture, carpet, and wallpaper, which looked suspiciously like the peeling paper on the walls of his bedroom. Still, the scents coming from the kitchen were appetizing, and he was hungry enough not to care how much of a hole-in-the-wall joint the hotel dining room was.

A plump, dark-haired, older woman led him to a table by the window facing the side street. She handed him a menu, which he took, and asked him for his drink order. Thankfully, Heinz knew enough words to recognize what she was asking. He ordered a cup of hot tea and a shot of Vodka. The woman raised a bushy, black eyebrow as she gave Heinz the once-over. He noticed the mole at the very corner of her thin lips. It was nearly as dark as her hair. He tried not to wince and nodded his head instead. With a final pointed stare, she left to fill his order.

Opening the frayed paper menu, he scanned the list. It was, thankfully, written in English in addition to Russian. His English was better than his Russian any day of the week. When she came back with his drinks, he ordered the Shchi, a soup made of beef stock, spices, vegetables, and pickled cucumber water, and two steaming Pirozhki stuffed with boiled meat and onions. Both were typical Russian fare, and both would fill the empty, growling space otherwise known as his stomach.

She wrote it all down and took her time returning to the kitchen. The older woman didn't seem to be in any hurry, and in his current state of hunger, that didn't sit well with him. Heinz sipped his Vodka. It was cool and smooth, and potent. He sucked in a breath and blew it back out. He was used to German beer, which was also fairly potent, but this was stronger. Slowly, a sensation of warmth spread through his body, and he felt himself relaxing. He began going over his notes in his head. There was no doubt he'd witnessed a crime being committed, but he was in no position to do anything about it. This weighed heavily on his conscience. A man or woman could have very well been killed while he sat outside observing.

Before he realized it, his shot of Vodka was gone. He reached for his tea and was interrupted.

"Looks like you need a refill." The words, spoken in Russian, did not register fully at first.

Heinz turned from the window, startled out of his thoughts. A tall woman stood next to his table staring down at him with a small smile on her lips. The first two things he noted were that she held two shots of Vodka in her hands, and she was uncommonly beautiful. Her dark, blonde hair fell over one shoulder onto her Hunter green blazer, which matched her slacks. She wore a silky white blouse beneath, and small gold hoops dangled from her ears. Her eyes were dark, somewhere between green and amber, but Heinz was not positive. The lighting was a bit too dim. He responded in his native tongue.

"I'm sorry. What did you say?"

She switched to German with ease. "I said it looks like you need a refill." She set one of the two shot glasses down in front of him, and then glanced at the seat opposite.

Heinz nodded, indicating she should sit. Once settled, she introduced herself. "I'm Lana Karakova."

"Martin Lintz," said Heinz.

She smiled. "It is nice to meet you, Martin Lintz. I hope you don't mind," she gestured toward the table, "but I hate to eat alone."

Heinz wondered just who she was and where she came from. Beautiful women didn't just walk up and join him for dinner every day. "Not at all. Are you a guest of the Kseniya?"

"Yes, just for a few days." She didn't offer any more.

"Business or pleasure?"

"Business, of course." She lifted her shot glass, clinking his before taking a sip. Heinz offered a benign smile and lifted the glass to his lips but did not drink. His brain was on full alert.

"And yourself? What brings you to Saint Petersburg, Herr Lintz?" She smiled through her eyes. They were lovely eyes, and the effect was not lost on him, but he remained guarded.

"Pleasure. I'm enjoying a small vacation."

"In Russia?" She chuckled. "And what do you do when not on vacation?"

"I teach." He sat back and away from the table as the older woman returned carrying a hot bowl of soup and a plate of steaming meat pies. She glanced at the woman now sitting across from Heinz.

"Are you ordering too?" she asked, irritated.

Lana Karakova switched tongues again and replied in rapid-fire succession with, "I'll have the Shchi with a slice of warm bread, and please bring two more of these." She held up her shot glass.

The older woman huffed and ambled away, grumbling under her breath.

Heinz watched her go before returning his attention to his unexpected dinner companion. Lana took another sip of her liquor, watching him. "So, what is your business, Frau Karakova?"

"Lana, please."

"Then you must call me Martin," he easily replied.

"Well, Martin, I work in the tech field." She leaned forward.

Heinz surreptitiously observed the woman. She wore a business suit with minimal jewelry; only her earrings and a gold-tone watch. No rings. Her nails were unpolished, filed short, yet shapely. On her feet she wore whiskey-colored leather boots with a pointed toe, and a mid-height heel; neither formal nor informal, but somewhere in between. She didn't seem to be carrying a handbag which told him she was probably telling the truth about being a hotel guest. She most likely left it in her room. Still, he was thrown by the forward way in which she invited herself to dine with him. *Am I being too cynical?* He asked himself the question knowing that in his line of work, second-guessing was never a smart move. He commanded himself to take a cautious approach. No one knew he was here except for Faust, so the woman's story was completely plausible. He was probably overreacting, but the habit was ingrained. If she was simply Lana Karakova, businesswoman from the tech industry, then he had to wonder why she decided to boldly join him. And, he had to admit he felt just a little guilty because he was a man engaged to be married in just a few weeks, and his beloved thought he was in Stockholm attending seminars to advance his career. In a flash, he realized his guilt had to do with only one thing – he found the woman attractive.

"And do you enjoy it?"

The old woman returned once again with a tray containing Lana's soup, bread, and two more shots. She placed the items on the table, saving the Vodka for last, which she put in the center between them.

When she left, Lana pushed one toward him. "Go on, drink it. I hate drinking alone. So boring." She set her own down and picked up her spoon.

Heinz took the shot. This one he lifted and sipped before delving into his own meal. Manners dictated that he wait until she was served. They ate in silence for a moment before she answered.

"I do enjoy it," she said in between bites. "Tech is always changing, so it's never dull."

"Exactly what type of tech?" He took a bite of his pirozhki.

She looked up, holding his gaze. "Weaponry."

Heinz stopped chewing, and then swallowed. "Military or civilian?"

A second passed before she answered, "civilian."

Heinz wondered why she hesitated, even if only for a split second, but she continued to eat her soup calmly. He began to wonder if he'd grown too jaded, being so highly suspicious of a lone female. Still, Mata Hari was a lone female, and look at the grief she caused both France and Germany during World War I.

"And what do you teach, Martin?"

"Mathematics," he answered.

She groaned. "That was my worst subject." She glanced up and smiled. "But if my instructor had been half as handsome as yourself, perhaps I would have paid more attention."

Heinz chuckled, surprised by her blatant flirtation. "I have a feeling you managed to pass the course."

She sat forward. "And how do you know this?"

He lifted his Vodka in a mock salute. "Because you are obviously a successful woman now."

Lana's smile spread revealing white teeth in a dazzling display. Her eyes twinkled as she picked up her own shot glass and clinked it to his. "Are all German men so charming?"

Heinz pursed his lips. "I don't know. I'm Austrian," he said, maintaining his pseudo-identity.

"Oh, I see. My mistake. And where from in Austria?"

He took a sip before answering. "Salzburg."

"Home of Mozart. Lovely. I visited only last year." Lana sat her drink down. "There was a wonderful café not far from my hotel that served delicious food. It was near Mozart's actual birthplace. It was on...," she sat back, trying to remember.

Heinz finished off his Vodka. "Getreidegasse. The whole area is a popular tourist attraction." Thankfully, he knew what she was talking about having visited Salzburg while still married to his ex-wife, Eva. But those were altogether different times.

"Yes, that's it exactly." Lana returned her attention to her soup while Heinz continued to work his way through his own meal. They grew quiet, both staring out the window at the foot traffic passing by.

He felt more relaxed. She'd ceased her questions which left him silently berating himself. He knew, as a career detective, that anyone seeking information, either police or the criminal element, would have continued chatting in hope of lulling the other person into revealing more about themselves. Lana seemed satisfied with his brief answers, and what he thought might have been a ploy to trip him up about his origins in Austria turned out not to be the case at all.

A cell phone buzzed. She reached into her jacket pocket and pulled out her mobile. Looking at the screen, she smiled. "Sorry. It's my son." She let the call go to voicemail but backed up her chair preparing to rise. Heinz shoved his own chair back and stood. "I'll need to call him back. He worries when I'm away."

"How old is he?" Heinz asked.

"Nearly fifteen but thinks he's thirty." She chuckled. "Thank you for the company. It has been quite lovely." She reached out, and Heinz took her hand. He gave her a gentlemanly handshake.

"Not at all. It is me who should thank you. You've made my dinner most enjoyable."

She held his hand a moment longer than seemly before turning to walk away. "Goodnight, Herr Lintz." She threw a smile over her shoulder, and then walked out of the dining room.

Heinz watched her go noting the sway of her long, blonde hair, and how it matched the sway of her hips. He shook himself suddenly. *Stop looking! You're engaged, you dog!* The silent reprimand brought him back to the present. He sat back down and finished his now cold tea. It was almost eight in the evening which meant back home in Berlin, Birgitta would be getting home soon. He flagged the old woman who'd served him all night and asked for the check. Too late, he realized that Lana had not paid for her meal, but rather, had left him with the bill. He laughed at himself. *Sucker.* He knew karma had just paid him back for lying to Birgitta about this trip, and for enjoying dinner with a woman who was not his fiancé. He left the restaurant and headed back to his room.

Chapter 8

Elsa moaned. Lukas kissed a trail down her back as he slowly removed the little black dress she'd worn to dinner. He'd made reservations at her favorite spot, Oma's Haus. He didn't know why she loved it so much. The food was good, but it was casual and designed for tourists. Far too 'cutesy' for his own well-traveled tastes. Still, it was her celebration for her promotion, and anything his woman wanted, she got. On the way home, she informed Lukas that she wanted him, and he was about to fulfil that request as well.

He tugged the small scrap of black, silky material down over her slender hips revealing the smooth skin of her perfectly shaped bottom to his greedy eyes. From his vantage point crouched down behind her, he was able to enjoy the full view including the red string thong she wore that hid nothing from his gaze. He pressed his lips to a cheek, rubbing them back and forth before slowly rising and licking a wet line up her spine.

"I love when you do that," she said with her head lolling back and to the side as he stood fully and buried his face into her fragrant neck.

"I know." He reached around and cupped her breasts, kneading them in his warm palms.

She could feel him growing hard pressed up against her backside. She smiled and reached one hand around to caress his hip through his slacks. "You have on too many clothes." She pushed away from him, breaking his hold and turned around. "Strip for me," she purred.

Lukas chuckled. "Here? Now?"

He watched as she stepped backwards and sat on the edge of their bed. She spread her knees, placing her hands on them while she kept her feet firmly planted on the floor. She still wore her black stilettos. The image she presented sitting there in nothing but the barest scrap of a thong and her high heels with her red hair tumbling down around her shoulders in loose curls was the sexiest thing he'd ever seen, and he'd seen a lot since his relationship with Elsa began. She never ceased to surprise him. Just when he thought he'd seen it all with her, she'd do or say something new that enchanted him all over again. He was addicted to her beauty, her scent, her sexy moans, her laugh, and her indomitable spirit. He was hopelessly ensnared by every single freckle that dotted her small, perky tits, and he'd become intimately acquainted with each and every one. He wanted to visit that land of milk and honey again, but she wanted a show first.

"Yes. Here and now." She leaned back onto her elbows displaying herself to the fullest advantage.

He grew harder, if that was at all possible. Already, he could hammer nails into a wall. He reached down and popped the button on his black slacks, and then slowly tugged the zipper down. He kept his eyes on her the entire time. It took a few more tugs to unzip the strained material, but finally, his fly was open. He ran his hand over his crotch and gyrated his hips. Elsa smiled.

"Turn around. Let me see that ass." She growled her words, and the vibrations of her voice made his gut clench. He obeyed her command. "Reach your hands around and grab your ass. Give it a good squeeze."

Lukas's lips tugged at the corners, but he controlled the smile that threatened to burst forth on his face. Instead, he glanced over his shoulder at her, sending her a smoldering look before reaching back and cupping his behind. He squeezed and released twice.

"Take off your shirt, darling."

He unbuttoned the cuffs, and then each button down the front of the dark green dress shirt. When all buttons were released, he slipped it off one shoulder, and then the other, before letting it fall to the floor. His bare back greeted her gaze showing off the muscles and the tribal tattoo he got on an art buying trip to Cairo that extended from his chest partially over his left shoulder.

"Nice. Now drop those trousers."

Lukas could tell she was enjoying herself back there. He could hear it in her voice. He slipped his thumbs under the seam of both the pants and his underwear, and shimmied them down, flexing the muscles in his arms, and tightening his buttocks as he went. She wanted a show; he'd give her one. He heard the hitch in her breathing and smiled to himself. He knew then his efforts were paying off and was mentally congratulating himself when he snuck a look back at her and froze. His own breathing stopped.

Elsa was now completely naked and lying on the bed with her legs spread wide. She was fingering herself while watching him. Her green eyes were barely open, appearing languorous, and the motion of her delicate hand working herself as slender fingers disappeared between her wet folds made his heart skip a beat. The exquisite pain searing through his cock told him if he grew any harder, he'd burst.

"Elsa!" His husky voice rasped out her name.

She lifted her free hand and beckoned him with the crook of her finger. He didn't need any more encouragement. Lukas kicked off his pants, and in one predatory motion, positioned himself between her splayed knees. He moved her hand out of the way, angled himself, and pushed deep inside. Elsa wrapped her slender legs around his waist as he pumped, sliding in and out in sure, powerful strokes.

"Yes!" She moaned, throwing back her head.

Lukas leaned in and licked her neck up to her delicate ear where he nipped the soft lobe.

"Bite my neck," she urged.

He did, applying just enough pressure to excite her further.

Elsa lifted her hips, meeting each thrust with vigor. She loved how he filled her up so completely. She delighted in the raw, animal sexuality they shared. He swiveled, sending hot, tight sensations throughout her body, and she could feel herself moving closer to climax.

"Fuck me hard, Lukas!" She turned her head to stare into his eyes. Strain showed on his handsome face as he kicked his cock into overdrive. The muscles in his shoulders and arms bulged, and his skin glistened with the effort he was putting in to please her. The intensity in his hazel eyes pinned her where she lay as he slammed into her driving her up, up, and over the edge towards a spectacular orgasm. He pumped two more times and joined her in the freefall.

They collapsed together sprawled along the edge of the bed, slowly sliding off.

"I'm falling," she laughed, patting the back of his head.

His face was still buried in her neck where he was working to catch his breath. His knees hit the floor. "Ow!" Lukas chuckled, and then slid his arms beneath her, lifting them both, and landing in a half-hazard manner somewhere in the middle of the bed. He rolled off and threw one arm over his eyes. "You're trying to kill me, woman."

The complaint was only semi-serious. Elsa curled into his side and rested her head on his chest. "And you would die a happy man."

He wrapped his arm around her and smiled. "That I would. God, you're the sexiest woman in the world, do you know that? Just when I think I know you..."

She drew a small heart on his chest with her finger. "I'm all about keeping you on your toes." She kissed the center of the imaginary heart.

"That's what I lo...," his words trailed off, incomplete.

Elsa looked up. He still had his arm over his eyes so she couldn't see his expression. "Yes?" she prompted softly, "that's what you ...?" She whispered the last line, hesitant.

He didn't respond. Finally, he emitted a soft snore.

She lay there watching him sleep trying to decide if she was heartbroken he hadn't said he loved her or relieved. She cared deeply for Lukas, but she still didn't know if what she felt was love or lust. Worse, although she knew she'd been keeping him sexually satisfied, she had no clue if what he felt for her went beyond the bedroom, even though they now shared his apartment. The word love had not come up. With two weddings on the horizon, Elsa had been thinking quite a bit on the subject. For Hugo and Sigrid, it all happened so quickly. She could plainly see they were meant for each other, but she wondered when and how they knew it. And then there was Heinz and Mahler. The two together seemed a perfect fit, but perhaps not to everyone who first met them. Joseph was a cranky police detective who never appeared cognizant of such things as finer feelings until the subject of abducted children came up. Then, a person could easily see his heart, see the passion of a father, a protector. Mahler, on the other hand, was quiet, contemplative, and observant. She had endless patience, and that patience worked well with Heinz's impatience when it came to pursuing cases. She was his opposite, and they attracted each other in a way that was not obvious until it was...obvious, that is. For Heinz, the realization that he loved Birgitta came when he almost lost her to a sadistic Russian billionaire. Indeed, the Ivchencko affair was a turning point on many levels for them all. It brought her and Lukas closer together. After the arrests of all involved, he asked her to move in with him. Since then, life had been good, but in moments like this one, she found herself questioning whether it was temporary or not. Would he ever commit? Did she really want him to?

Her phone buzzed. It was set to vibrate and nearly fell off the nightstand. She rolled away from Lukas in a smooth motion and picked it up. She read the text.

Message received. H arrived. Identity secure. Faust.

Her new supervisor was letting her know he'd heard from his contact, and Heinz had arrived in Saint Petersburg safely. She already knew since he'd called her earlier in the day. She texted back. *Thanks for the update. EK.*

She set the phone down. Explaining about the phone call would require too much texting, and she was tired. She would tell Faust in the morning.

Elsa stood and headed to the kitchen, still naked. Lukas snored on. It was dark throughout the flat save for the ambient night lights in the hallway and one in the kitchen. The tile floor was cold on her bare feet as she made her way to the refrigerator. She opened it and found the orange juice. Removing the jug, she set it on the counter and reached into the overhead cabinet for a glass. Pouring out a generous amount, she sipped it while leaning against the sink. A ping alerted her ears. She glanced at Lukas's laptop. He'd left it plugged in on the small dinette table.

A soft glow emitted between the crack of the casing. Curious, she went to the table, lifted the monitor open, and looked at the screen. An email alert flashed, and before it faded, she caught a name. Korvettankapitan Dieter Kelner. Kelner was one of two army buddies from Lukas' days as a soldier. Without offering very much information on his former occupation, she knew that he was somehow connected to a special operations team, but he was retired now, wasn't he? The subject of the email read, 'BIRD IN THE HAND'.

"What are you up to, my darling?" she whispered. Elsa pulled up the email server, but it was password protected, and she couldn't get past the login screen.

She closed the computer and stood staring out the window sipping her juice. It appeared that Lukas was keeping more from her than the extent of his feelings. This did not sit well with her. She finished off her drink and rinsed out the glass before setting it on the drying rack. The wheels in her brain were spinning. Until she knew what was going on, she vowed to keep her business to herself. Elsa went back to bed, curling up on her side and away from the man snoring softly, unaware that everything had just changed.

Chapter 9

Birgitta Mahler arrived promptly at 7:30 a.m. on the doorstep of Minister Obermeyer's residence. She rang the doorbell and waited. Standing in the chill of the early morning air waiting on a man she intensely disliked for a multitude of reasons was no way to start her day. She tugged her coat tighter around her shivering frame. The door swung open revealing a tall, ginger-haired man with blue eyes. He nodded his head in deference to her.

"Good morning, Detective Mahler." He stepped outside, pulling on his coat as he passed her.

"Officer Edelmann," she acknowledged.

The man faced her. "Nothing new to report. The night was quiet. Herr Obermeyer will be out shortly. He's on the phone." Officer Edelmann finished his briefing and tucked his hands inside his pockets to keep them warm.

Mahler nodded. "Sehr gut. You are officially relieved then. Have a good day. Get some sleep."

Edelmann offered a small smile and then cast a sideways look at the interior of the house he'd just exited, sighing. "I'll see you tonight."

Birgitta stifled a chuckle. She knew that look. No one wanted this detail. Obermeyer had made many enemies within the department with his budget cuts, and the irony of his needing their protection was not lost on any of them.

Edelmann walked to his car, leaving Mahler standing outside waiting for Obermeyer to finish his phone call. She could hear him inside, speaking in a hushed tone. She wiped her feet on the mat and stepped over the threshold. The inside of the Minister's home was opulently appointed with marble tiled floors covered in Aubusson carpets. Expensive artwork graced the elegantly painted walls, and in the center of the foyer sat a granite-topped round table with a massive crystal vase containing fresh flowers and greenery. It reminded her of a five-star hotel. It also reminded her that the man had cut millions from the police budget allocated for protective gear and new weapons as well as department upgrades such as vehicles and technology, yet here that same man lived like some kind of king in his palace. It sickened her, but she kept her expression blank, and her emotions in check as always.

Obermeyer appeared from a doorway off the left side of the foyer. He was about six feet in height with graying brown hair cut short on the sides. It looked like he moussed the lengthier top strands, as the waves had a shellacked appearance. His mustache was still dark, but to Mahler's eye, it was kept that way with chemical hair dye. Women can always spot a dye job. His dark eyes were deep set and dark brown beneath bushy brows in a narrow face. His expression was that of a bear with a sour belly. The man caught site of her and assessed her from head to toe. Birgitta felt immediately violated.

"Detective Mahler, I presume?"

"Yes," she answered, keeping her hands in her pockets.

"I was expecting Kommissar Heinz, but Levitz tells me he's at some seminar in Sweden. I suppose you'll do." He spoke down to her as if she were nothing.

Mahler's blood boiled, but she maintained her stoicism, turned halfway toward the door, and said, "Are you ready?"

He grumbled to himself as he grabbed his overcoat from the hall closet. "Are you going to nag? Women, always nagging."

Mahler counted to ten.

Finally, he shrugged into the coat and picked up his briefcase. Keys in hand, he walked to the front door. "I assume you're driving?" he said over his shoulder.

"I am." Mahler followed him out and then stepped around him as he closed and locked the front door. She looked left and right, scanning as she made her way to the black BMW sedan she'd checked out that morning. Levitz had insisted on upgrading her usual Audi since it was in service to a Minister of Parliament, even if it was one they all hated.

Obermeyer eyed the older model car with distaste. "Is this the best the Kripo can do?" He waited for Mahler to open the back door. She stood staring at him with one eyebrow raised, incredulous at being treated like some hired driver. She blew out an impatient breath, unusual for her as it bespoke of her losing her cool, and reached out to open the back door.

"Yes, under our depleted budget, this is the best the department can do...unless you prefer to walk?" She spoke calmly, letting her words sink in.

The Minister looked at her more closely, then chuckled without humor. "You will do just fine, I see," he said, sliding into the back seat. His faux humor was gone as quickly as it appeared.

Mahler closed the door, only barely refraining from slamming it, and went to the driver's side, climbing in. "Now," she said, "I have some questions for you on the way."

"Haven't you been briefed already?" Obermeyer shot the words at the back of her head.

Birgitta's eyes narrowed, but she kept them on the road ahead as she pulled out into traffic. "I have, which is why I have questions," came her arch reply.

She accelerated onto the Autobahn, moving in between a delivery truck and a Fiat. The flow moved along quickly, and she knew she wouldn't have a lot of time to gain new information before reaching their exit.

"First, I did not see in any of the reports if you had an idea as to who might be responsible for the death threats. I find it difficult to believe you weren't asked this by the officers who opened the investigation."

Obermeyer carefully set his briefcase on the seat next to him and caught her eye in the rearview mirror. "They asked. I had no answer. That's why my office reported the threats in the first place. You are detectives. Investigate. I've turned over all the relevant information. Clues, aren't they? Well, work them and figure this out so I can get back to working without this cadre of police escorts."

Birgitta listened carefully to his words. "You said *relevant* information. Is there some *irrelevant* information withheld?" She glanced back to the rearview in time to catch Obermeyer's eyes narrowing before he composed himself.

"I've turned over all that you need. Just find the malcontent, toss him in jail, and let's be done with this business. I do not enjoy being flanked day and night by police, and I'm well aware your kind are not fans of mine either." The sharp edge of his voice cut through the small space of the vehicle's interior."

Mahler realized her questions were needling him, and secretly, she was enjoying that fact, but his answers, or lack thereof, were also telling. Why was he so angry about being surrounded by protective officers unless it was keeping him from seeing someone?

"What makes you so sure the threats are being issued from a *him?* It could easily be a woman. The very nature of the threats reveals a desire to see you suffer, to not feel safe no matter what you do, and yet there has been no physical violence. Men are particularly physical in nature when making threats, whereas women will more often play head games." She let that sink in, watching his face closely.

He looked into the mirror. "Maybe you should keep your eyes on the road." He stared a moment longer before picking up his briefcase, opening it, and pulling out some papers, ignoring her.

Mahler looked ahead at the back end of the delivery truck. Their exit was coming up next. "I will need the names of any women you're currently seeing, and those you've recently cut ties with."

Obermeyer looked up then. "There are none such." He dismissed her, but a small hitch in his voice told her she'd hit a nerve.

"Let's not play games, Minister. Someone wants you dead, someone who is making a very concerted effort to forewarn you of the event. If it were simply online threats, it could be considered of minimal security risk, but this person has gone so far as to hand-compose physical correspondence directly threatening your life. That is serious. It means this person is thinking very carefully about your demise, and not just in a hot moment on the internet, but in the privacy of their home while slowly cutting out the precise words needed to formulate a death threat from newspaper clippings. That is not someone to dismiss out of hand. Make no mistake, this person wants you dead, and if I'm to discover their identity, I'll need your full cooperation. Otherwise, why bother asking for our help? Why am I here?"

Obermeyer stared ahead, thinking. With an annoyed sigh, he gave in. "What do you need to know?"

Mahler silently congratulated herself on getting through his thick, stubborn head. "There are generally three reasons someone seeks to murder another; sex, revenge or money. Each threat made to you has mentioned money specifically. We'll start with anyone you've angered over money – contracts, budget cuts, and the like."

"That would make the entire police state suspect, and you, Detective." He tossed a look at her in the rearview.

A dry chuckle passed her lips. "I'll let Levitz know his department is on the list. But money can be connected with sex, and that leads to women in your life, or a single woman. I will need names. In addition, anyone you've pissed off politically needs to be added. I need to start narrowing down the possibilities." She flipped on the blinker and took the off ramp. "Oh, and this person has delivered posts to your office and home by hand. There was no postage. I'll need the exact dates you received them, so I can check traffic camera footage. This person knows where you live."

The edges of Obermeyer's eyes tightened on her last words. He said nothing for a moment. Then, "I'll write up a list as soon as we get to my office. My assistant, Rudi, will help you with any other information."

Mahler turned right, and then right again into the parking lot of the Reichstag building where the Bundestag convenes. There was already a line of tourists at the visitor center. The Reichstag was one of the most popular attractions in Berlin for visitors. Maintaining a check on who was allowed in and around Obermeyer's office was not going to be easy. Mahler found a parking spot and turned off the engine. She got out first, scanning left and right before opening his door and letting the minister out. She stayed at his flank as they bypassed the visitor center heading for a side door for employees. She showed her badge to the guard at the interior checkpoint. He waved them past, and she followed Minister Ritt Obermeyer to the lifts. It was going to be a long day of compiling a list of suspects, and then beginning to rule them out one by one. She did not look forward to delving into this man's personal life. Knowing the tales and tidbits reported by the press, she knew it was going to be a shit-pile of a mess.

Chapter 10

Saint Petersburg
   The Kseniya

Dawn arrived gray and thick with the promise of snow. Heinz showered and dressed quickly, heading downstairs to the dining room for a quick breakfast of boiled egg, toast, and hot coffee. It was still mostly dark outside, but the kitchen staff was busy with cooking up the morning meal. The older woman with the mole who'd served him the night before was not in the dining room. Instead, a young man of around eighteen took Heinz's order, returning promptly.

Only two other people sat in the small room eating. They were a young couple with heads bent together whispering low and smiling often. Honeymooners or at the very least, lovers who still found adventures in foreign countries to be exciting, so long as they had each other. Heinz envied them. Not a care in the world. He looked forward to enjoying that very same feeling with Birgitta in a few short weeks.

He finished his meal, paid the bill, and left.

Outside, the temperature was far colder than the day before. The thick, dingy gray clouds overhead blocking out the sun hung heavy with unshed snow. Heinz pulled his overcoat tighter around his body as he retrieved his rental car from the parking garage across the street. The Kseniya did not boast its own. Once again, he found the corner convenience store where he purchased bottled water and snacks to hold him over during his vigil at the dock.

The drive to port was slow. Traffic was heavy, and one accident along the way pushed three lanes of cars into one inching along as everyone rubbernecked to see what had happened. At the turnoff to the docks, Heinz noticed a black limo ahead of him. It pulled through the entry and drove smoothly to Warehouse 214. The large, muscular man from the day before got out of the passenger side and pushed the buttons on the alarm unlocking the bay door. Heinz kept his eyes straight ahead, using his peripheral vision as he drove past and pulled into the parking lot surrounded by chain link fencing. He backed into a spot near where he'd parked the day before, but this one offered a slightly better view of the warehouse. Several more vehicles drove past, dock workers on their way to punch in, as the limo glided inside the warehouse. Today, however, the door did not close immediately. Instead, it remained open for a full thirty minutes.

A large truck turned onto the dock and drove straight to the warehouse where it pulled inside. It was the type of truck that would usually transport produce of some type. The side logo showed a bright yellow ear of corn with a smiling face. The Cyrillic writing meant nothing to Heinz, but he photographed it with his camera, zooming in on the driver, an older man with heavy jowls and graying brown hair, and then focused on the license plate. Noting the time, he wrote it down in his notebook. As he scribbled the information, the driver hopped out and went around to the back. He yanked the lock sideways and slid the metal door up. A girl ran out, screaming for all she was worth, onto the dock.

Joseph looked up, and saw the brawny muscled man chase her, catching her easily, and lifting her up into the air. He hauled her back inside, one hand clamped over her mouth. He glanced left and right, clearly angry, as he moved fast to get back inside the warehouse. Loud words were exchanged between muscle man and the truck driver, with the driver backing down, head bent in submission. He appeared afraid.

Heinz wrote down the details. *Young girl, approximately 15-17 years of age, long dark hair, blue dress, no shoes, hands tied. Distressed.* For Heinz, this changed everything.

The warehouse door closed and remained closed for two hours. When it once again began to open, the limousine came out first, heading for the main road. The produce truck with the bright yellow smiling corn cob drove out behind it, stopping as the muscled man who arrived in the limo hopped out to close the door and lock the warehouse. The driver sat in the truck waiting. Heinz knew beyond a doubt that the truck contained at least one kidnapped teenage girl, if not more. It was surely on its way to deliver its cargo to a brothel where the girl or girls would be drugged and prostituted. Turning the key in the ignition, Heinz prepared to follow them. This was the clue he'd been waiting for. This was, undoubtedly, what had happened to Marlessa Schubert. This, he told himself, was why he was here.

He pulled out as soon as the truck was in motion, careful to hang back just enough to remain undetected. Heinz flipped on the GPS in the rental as an afterthought checking to make sure he'd remembered to input the address to the hotel. Getting lost in Saint Petersburg was not something he wanted to experience. For the next half hour, he tailed them, all along thinking hard about what, if anything, he would be able to do once the produce truck arrived at its destination. He had no weapons, no backup, and as the vehicle in front of him slowed to turn into an upscale neighborhood, Heinz knew he was running out of time.

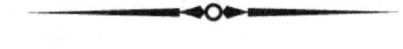

Mahler stood next to a man of medium height. He was petite, dark of hair, with blue eyes. He wore a tailored suit in charcoal gray with pin stripes. His tie was blue silk with an antique silver tie pin reminiscent of one that her Opa Walter used to wear to church on Sundays. Walter Mahler was very particular that a man should dress well and respectfully before going into the house of God even though the other six days of the week he wore work clothes that were frequently dirty from farming. Although not nearly as robust, Rudi Oppel's style did remind her of her Opa. That's where the similarity ended, however. Obermeyer's Undersecretary tried to project a quiet confidence, but it came across more as ingratiating in the manner of a woman trying to suck up. It didn't help that his eyes held a slyness that struck Mahler as deceptive. What he had to be deceptive about, she didn't know, as she'd only met him for the first time three hours prior. Since then, he'd been helpful in providing a list of people who might wish to snuff out the Prime Minister.

Oppel went through the appointment book reading off names of recent visitors to Obermeyer's office. When he reached the end, he closed the ledger carefully, running his hand over the black leather binding. It did not escape Mahler's scrutiny that in the age of computers, Oppel kept all of Herr Obermeyer's appointments written down in what could only be categorized as a fancy notebook. On the man's index finger was a gold signet ring with a raised star, possibly a Jewish insignia. His hand motion was graceful, effeminate. He glanced up, pinning Mahler with his stare.

"And now, I suppose, we can begin with the juicier list."

She waited patiently; pen poised over her own, far cheaper notebook. "I'm ready."

Oppel smirked before taking a seat behind his desk. "His paramours may surprise you, Detective, and public knowledge of them could end his career. I need to know that you will protect the information I give you, as it has been my job to help the Prime Minister to maintain absolute discretion."

Mahler swallowed down a laugh. The man was odious, and tabloids had already had a field day with his supposed discreet affairs, but here sat his assistant, more concerned about appearances than preventing murder. "You have my word," she said.

Oppel held her gaze a moment longer, and then sat back. "Most of the minister's *dates* come from an agency," he began. "They are paid escorts that he sees once or twice before moving on to the next. Most of those I would discard out of hand since no relationship ever develops beyond the night."

"I will need the name of this agency," Mahler interrupted.

"And I will provide it, but only after you promise not to cause a problem there. This particular agency doesn't advertise to the public. Their client list is top secret. Discretion is everything for both the employees and the clientele. I promise you they operate completely within the law." Oppel watched Mahler, pinning her where she sat with his blue stare.

She gave as good as she got, not blinking as she showed with minimal emotion that she was losing patience with his insistence on promises. It was her hardened detective look. "Herr Oppel, the name of the agency, bitte."

Silence stretched out for fifteen excruciating seconds.

"Alright. It's the Midnight Belle Agency. I trust we understand each other?" He raised a manicured eyebrow.

Mahler was struck again by his effeminate mannerisms which conflicted with the passive-aggressiveness he was displaying now. Of course, she could simply pinpoint his behavior as bitchy, but that might be too easy, and a gross underestimation. She didn't like to make those types of generalizations. Instead, she made a mental note, filing it away to revisit later.

"Clever. And an address, please." He rattled off the address, warning her at the same time that without a recommendation from a person in the inner circle, no one there would speak with her.

"I will, of course, be pleased to accompany you, and make an introduction." A self-congratulatory smile spread across his rather full lips.

Mahler counted to ten in the privacy of her own head, and then said, "Kind of you, Herr Oppel. Now, who else shall we add to this growing list?"

The man sat forward. "Well, there really is only one other I can think of."

"Yes?"

"Vera Wolf." He let the name hang upon the empty space between them.

Mahler knew the name. Wolf had been in the news often lately. Within the Socialist Democratic Party of Germany were many activist groups. The most vocal of these recently was the Women's Socialist Alliance headed by none other than Vera Wolf, an accomplished prosecutor and defender of women's rights, and very popular throughout Germany. Everything that she stood for was directly opposite that of the Minister of the Interior whose policies were conservative. This was very interesting.

"Are you telling me that Obermeyer and Vera Wolf are having an affair?"

Oppel grinned, wide. "Had. It has been over for the past three months, but yes. Politics do, indeed, make strange bedfellows."

There was something in his eyes. To Mahler, it almost seemed like glee, as if the fact that the minister bedding the head of an opposition party leader pleased him greatly. Why, she couldn't fathom, but she made yet another mental checkmark.

"And why did the affair end, do you know?"

"The same reason all affairs end, Detective. She wanted more."

This time, Mahler couldn't prevent the dry laugh from bursting forth. "You're saying she wanted to marry the minister and that he refused?" Somehow, the idea that Vera Wolf would even condescend to date the man was laughable, but people could often be surprising when the laws of attraction were at work.

"Why laugh? Isn't that what all women want? Always more? Always a legal contract to bind themselves to a man's fortune?" The slyness entered his eyes again. "You're marrying soon, aren't you, Detective? Your partner, I heard. You would know better than myself what it is women are after."

His snide insult did not go unnoticed, but Mahler was more interested in how he knew anything at all about her personal life.

"I'd hardly call marrying Joseph an opportunity to hitch my wagon to his star. We are both adults, both equal, but that is neither here nor there. We're discussing your boss."

"Interesting that you'd say you're equals. Everyone in Berlin knows the reputation of Kommissar Heinz, but until recently, I'd never heard of you." He stood.

Mahler closed her notebook and joined him. "And why would you hear about me, Herr Oppel? Unless, of course, you're up to no good?" She let her words hang between them, and then, "I have a list to begin working on. I trust you will set up that introduction expeditiously."

His eyes narrowed briefly before his face relaxed, and the *undersecretary* returned. "Of course. Give me an hour. I have to remind the minister of his afternoon appointments and tie up a few loose ends."

"Of course." Mahler watched him as he picked up the black leather appointment book, tucked it against his side, and sauntered off to the minister's office. She walked out into the hallway just outside the door and pulled out her mobile. Names needed to be run through the police database. She needed rundowns on everyone so she could begin ruling people out. She also wanted as much information on Vera Wolf as she could garner. It really did seem implausible that Wolf and Obermeyer would be a couple no matter how briefly, but Oppel seemed sure of his information, and he obviously wanted to direct her attention to the woman. All of this had her wheels spinning, and she spent the next hour doing what she did best, running background checks, collecting all the details, and sifting through each systematically.

Chapter 11

Heinz was impressed. He'd never imagined the upscale neighborhoods of Russia before. It wasn't a thought that entered his head, ever, but now, he was seeing firsthand how the upper echelon of Russian society lived. Every house he passed was a mansion made of hand-carved stone and gold. Compared to the region where his hotel was located, this was an entirely different world. Ahead, the produce truck turned into a long driveway. It came to a stop at a security gate that stretched around the property. Beside the gate was a gray, concrete guardhouse. A large man with a blond crew cut stepped out. He wore a tailored black suit and dark sunglasses. The man approached the driver. There was a brief exchange, and then he reached up to touch his ear. That's when Heinz noticed the earpiece the man wore. He nodded absently, and the gate began to roll back on its rail, allowing the truck to pass through. The driveway continued up, winding back to a large three-story house partially obscured by tall trees. The blond crew cut stood in the driveway until the gate closed once again, locking into place. He re-entered the gatehouse, and stood at attention, waiting. This was no ordinary guard.

Heinz noted all of this as he slowly drove by, continuing down the long, residential street until he came to a crossroad. It was there that he turned right, drove approximately three houses down, and pulled over. He wrote down the address gleaned from the front of the gate, inputting it into the car's GPS. He then pulled out his mobile and searched the address in Earth Maps on Yandex. It took a long time to pull up on screen. "I miss Google already," he said.

Finally, the site opened, showing him a street view of the house. From there, he was able to see the front and backside satellite images and determine the acreage it sat upon. There was approximately four acres of land, and all of it was surrounded by the wrought-iron fencing. It was possible the fence was electrified, but he hadn't seen any posted warning signs, and the only way to know for sure was to touch it, which wasn't smart, or throw something against it, which would alert security. There had to be a way in, but in broad daylight, he would not be able to recon the area. He'd need to wait until nightfall, and if he was truly going to do this, he'd need to procure a firearm. Heinz checked his watch. It was noon. He had five and a half hours to sniff out a criminal arms dealer, convince him to sell a gun to a complete stranger, who was not Russian, and could not, if need be, properly defend himself should it all go south. Great.

He took the next street over to go back out to the road on which he came in. From there, Heinz headed back towards the docks. Not far from the busy, industrial Baltic was a commercial road upon which there were at least three pubs. None of them looked particularly welcoming. He decided to begin with the least welcoming, hoping to hit a home run on his first try. He mentally prepared himself as he parked and got out. Shrugging into his overcoat, he worked out his angle; a lover's quarrel. He would play the part of the cuckold whose wife had run off with the Russian playboy that visited his faux hometown of Salzburg. Russian men were known for their machismo and would respect a man trying to bring his own wife home and reclaim his honor, if nothing else. There would be few questions...he hoped.

Inside, smoke filled the small room creating a blue haze that stung Heinz's eyes and filled his lungs. He'd kicked the habit a couple of years back and hadn't really noticed until now how badly it stunk. Still, there was something satisfying about it, and with each breath he drew, that region of his brain responsible for his addiction began to unfurl, expressing its pleasure. By the time he reached the bar, he desperately wanted a cigarette. It was like putting rows of white powder before a cocaine addict. As his craving increased, his irritability grew. It made him edgy, and there was only one thing to do now, use it to his advantage and get the hell out as quickly as possible.

A short, barrel-chested man with a shaggy beard stood behind the bar. He had the worn look of a person who'd had to work hard all his life with very little reward. His stained white shirt sleeves were rolled up to his elbows, and he sported a faded tattoo of a sleeping infant laying on a bed of white roses on his right forearm. The Russian equivalent of Rest in Peace was written in formal script above the child's head. It was telling. The man had lost a child. Heinz felt his pain, and instantly determined that if anyone would understand a gentleman's need to keep his family together, this bartender would. His cover story just acquired another layer, children waiting back home for their wayward mother swept off her feet by a smooth-talking Russian playboy. It had to work. He had no other alternatives at this point.

"What will it be," he asked.

Heinz picked out two of the words and understood the question. He answered with his own stilted Russian, "Vodka, neat," and then switched tongues, "und sprechen Sie Deutsch?"

"Da, ein bisschen." The man pulled out a small tumbler, poured two fingers of vodka, and passed the glass to Heinz. "That will be two-hundred twelve rubles," he answered.

Heinz placed the money on the bar, but kept his hand over it as he asked, "And how much for some information?"

The man held his gaze. "Are you police?" He kept his hands down below the bar, out of Heinz's line of sight.

"Nein. I am a man in need of finding his wife and taking her home. Our children are waiting, and I have very little time."

The man relaxed. "I see. And what kind of information are you looking for?"

"I need to purchase a handgun." He offered no prevarication. Simply straight to the point as a desperate, jealous man would be.

"Go to a gun manufacturer," the man stated, still taking Heinz's measure.

"I don't have time for that, friend, nor would I qualify. I'm an Austrian national, not a Russian Federation citizen. What I require is immediate, short term, and cash only."

"You don't think you could convince your wife to come home with you otherwise?"

"It's not for her that I need a gun. This man she has run off with, let's just say he's a bit younger and more athletic than me. A real smooth operator with honey dripping off his lying tongue, and no real intention of doing anything more than ruining her. He already convinced her to empty our bank account and leave our children. I'm not the least bit happy about it, but I'm willing to forgive and forget, for the sake of our daughters," he added. Making his fictitious children girls was a gamble, but he was more than sure the child tattooed on his arm was a daughter.

The gamble paid off.

The man nodded. "It's the children who suffer when women lose their minds and their virtue. I may know of someone." The man reached out his hand. "I'm Viktor."

Heinz took the man's hand, shaking it. "Martin. And thank you."

"How soon?" he asked.

"By day's end, if possible."

Viktor walked to the end of the bar. He leaned over and spoke to a man sitting there reading a newspaper. The man appeared menacing with dark hair and thick brows. A scar cut across his forehead down his left cheek to his jaw. He glanced over at Heinz, checking him from head to toe. Heinz sat down at the bar, and sipped his vodka, trying for all the world not to look like a cop. He ignored the man as Viktor spoke to him, relaying the story. Finally, the bartender returned.

"Nine hundred rubles, cash. Finish your drink, and then in thirty minutes, go out the side door. Take a left. The transaction will take place there."

"Thank you, Viktor." Heinz reached out to shake his hand once again. "I won't forget your kindness."

"Just bring your wife home to her children, and make sure she understands what she has put her family through, make sure she never leaves again." The look in Viktor's eyes conveyed exactly what he meant. The man clearly advocated a good beating. It was repulsive to Heinz's way of thinking, but he wasn't here to preach against domestic violence. He was here to find answers. At least part of his story was truthful. If God answered his prayers, he'd find a way to either bring Marlessa Schubert home, or at the very least, put her ghost to rest.

"I will." Heinz looked at his watch, and then slowly sipped his drink. When thirty minutes passed, he placed a few extra rubles on the bar, got up, and walked out the side door.

"This is the place." Rudi Oppel kept up a running one-sided dialogue as he drove them to an exclusive neighborhood in Reinickendorf on Berlin's northwest side.

Mahler let him talk. Now and again, she nodded or offered a short reply. She concluded that Oppel liked to hear himself speak, and that he held himself in very high esteem beneath the deferential demeanor he presented to his superior.

He turned to her after parking his Audi in the long driveway that curved around the front of a four-story mansion set at the end of a picturesque drive. It was opulent, to say the least. The grounds surrounding the estate were meticulously manicured with tall trees forming a boundary at the edges of the property. The house screamed money, but looking at it, the last thing anyone would guess was that it served as the site for a high-dollar escort service.

"Madame Denouve has granted you this interview, but not without reservations. I've assured her you're here only in the capacity of helping the minister, and not to interfere with her business." He said this while giving her a stern eye.

It was all she could do not to laugh at him. Only someone who knew her well would understand the slightly raised eyebrow in an otherwise blank expression.

"Understood, Herr Oppel. Shall we?" Mahler opened her door and stepped out, leaving the assistant to catch up as she walked purposefully toward the massive, dark oak double doors with intricate, stained glass, arched windows.

As she reached out to knock, Rudi Oppel caught her hand and stopped her. He pointed to the doorbell on the left wall of the porch enclosure, and then pressed the button.

Church bells chimed alerting the occupants inside of visitors. The irony was not lost on Mahler.

The door opened, and they were greeted by a tall brunette in a burgundy silk sheathe. Her makeup, hair, and nails were immaculate, and her legs beneath the mid-thigh-length dress seemed to go on for days ending in matching burgundy leather stilettos. Mahler looked up at the woman who topped her by a good six inches. Her bosom was impressive, she'd give her that. The amount of cleavage revealed by the low, scooped neckline bordered on pornographic yet stilled appeared elegant within the silken material.

"Herr Oppel, Madame Denouve is expecting you. This way, please." The woman's accent revealed a possible Georgian background, maybe Ukrainian, but Mahler wasn't completely sure.

"Wonderful. Thank you, Salome. Detective?" Oppel glanced at Mahler indicating she should follow.

Birgitta stepped inside the opulent manor behind him. Salome closed the door and caught up to them. She slid a sideways look at Mahler, a small smile on her full, red lips. The woman took her measure, raking her dark eyes over the detective from head to toe. Birgitta felt every inch of her perusal in a disturbingly familiar way. She pulled her shoulders back and straightened her spine, subconsciously showing her full height of five feet, four inches of no-nonsense policewoman.

As they neared an open doorway at the far side of the impressive foyer, Salome stepped in front of them, reaching out to offer a perfunctory knock. She stood just inside the doorway and addressed the room's occupant, leaving Oppel and Mahler standing outside.

"Madame, your guests have arrived."

"Send them in, Salome," a sultry, low voice answered.

Foregoing gentlemanly etiquette, Rudi Oppel walked inside first. Mahler trailed in behind him, but not before she felt a hand touch her shoulder and slide down to the small of her back as she walked through the doorway, directing her as a man would his lover. Birgitta threw a sharp look over her shoulder at Salome. The tall woman smiled down at her, cat-like, before finally removing her hand, and stepping out of the room.

Mahler didn't like this one bit. It was bad enough when men took liberties, but this was the first time she'd experienced the phenomenon at the hands of a woman. The fact that it happened inside what could only be legally termed a brothel made it that much seedier. Worse, she didn't quite know how to handle it. When a man took advantage, it was easy to rebuke him straight out with a look or a word. But what does one say when it's another woman? First, she'd have to admit she assumed the woman's intentions to be sexually motivated when perhaps the woman in question was merely the 'touchy-feely' sort. The second guessing is what allowed this type of thing to happen every day to women everywhere. No, overthinking was never the answer. Trusting one's natural instincts was usually the truer course of action, and her instincts told her she'd just been felt up. The bitch.

"Welcome, Rudi. I see you've brought your detective with you. Let's have a look, shall we?"

A petite woman with silver hair and clear blue eyes sat in a cream-colored, wing-back chair. She wore a dark gray Chanel suit over an ice-blue blouse. Her upswept hair enhanced her prominent cheekbones, and teardrop diamonds adorned her ears while a matching pendant graced her long, slender neck. Despite her advanced age, her skin was smooth, taut over what Mahler's mother would call a blessed face, one that aged well. Madame Denouve had obviously been quite beautiful in her younger days, and she was still a stunner today. There was something familiar about her face, but it was fleeting.

"Yes. Allow me to make the introduction. Madame," he nodded in deference to the lady, "this is Detective Mahler. She is here to ask you a few questions related to the minister's, eh, time spent here with your talented staff."

"I know why you say she's here, Rudi," Madame stated sharply. "What I want to know is how my establishment has anything to do with the minister's need for protection by the police?" She directed the last question at Mahler. "Come, detective, and sit." She indicated the royal blue wing-back opposite. "Rudi, you may go and amuse yourself. I'll have Salome find you when we're finished."

Oppel sputtered. "But should I not be here for this interview? It is, after all, concerning my employer."

"It concerns no one but my business, which, in this arena, is not *your* business. Thank you, Rudi. That will be all." Madame Denouve turned her attention to Mahler, effectively dismissing the man. After hesitating for a moment, he nodded, and made his way out of the drawing room, red faced.

"Now, let's discuss this without men around to fuck it all up."

Mahler had to smother a laugh. Hearing the elegant woman before her casually uttering the course expletive surprised her, and she was rarely surprised these days.

"Tell me, detective, are you truly here solely for the purpose of ferreting out whoever is making threats to Minister Obermeyer or is there an ulterior motive? Come, come, I have no time for prevarication."

Mahler held the woman's steely gaze. "I've been assigned to investigate the threats against the minister, Madame Denouve, and nothing more. As for your business, as long as you are operating within the letter of the law, I'm sure we have no issue."

"Indeed," the Madame replied. A moment passed before the woman let out a small sigh, and sat back, crossing her legs. "So, ask your questions, Detective."

"I need to know which of your staff are intimately acquainted with Herr Obermeyer, all of them, but especially, those of whom he spends the most time. I'll need to question each, and if there is any background information you can offer that will help me eliminate them as suspects, it would be appreciated."

"What makes you even consider that the individual threatening the Minister is a female?"

Mahler leaned forward. "A hunch." She offered the vague reply, refusing to share any details of an ongoing investigation.

Madame Denouve smiled slyly. "Women always know. We know because we recognize what we, ourselves, would do. Tell me, when did the threats begin?"

"Why do you need to know?" Mahler asked.

"Because, my dear, it will help me to pare down the list of the Minister's...how did you state it? Ah yes, his intimate acquaintances. If I know when this began, I can have Salome compile the list from that date on."

"Of course." Birgitta opened her notebook. "The threats began approximately four and a half weeks ago."

"So, around the first of August?" The older woman reached over to the small table next to her chair and lifted a ledger which she opened in her lap. She spent a quiet minute running her manicured fingertip down the pages. One eyebrow raised and lowered, and then she called out, "Salome?"

The tall woman entered, walking to Madame Denouve's side. "Yes, Madame?"

Denouve handed the ledger over. "Please pull the files on all the Minister's appointments from August 1st forward. Make a copy of their applications, and bring them to me, please. Also, call each and have them come in," she looked at Mahler, "tomorrow afternoon? Will that work, Detective?"

Mahler checked her schedule. She would still be on the clock protecting Obermeyer. "Actually, I'm on duty until around 6:00 p.m."

"Then make that 7:00 p.m., Salome, to give the Detective time to get here." She looked at Mahler. "You'll be here during business hours, Detective. I trust you will be discreet, but just in case, I shall be joining you—a silent observer, of course—but it's my duty to protect my employees, and to ensure my clients' appointments are not interrupted. We'll meet back here," she stood, "but please, dress appropriately for after five." She ran her blue eyes up and down Mahler's usual, dark utilitarian pantsuit. "No offense, dear, but you look every inch a police detective. I can't have that. Not here. You understand?" Her silver eyebrow rose as she stood, waiting.

Irritation nibbled at Birgitta's patience. "I understand." She did, but she didn't like it. It was already bad enough that she had to spend her days shadowing Ritt Obermeyer, but now, she was expected to dress up for a cocktail party to conduct serious, investigative interviews. Worse, she would have to maintain her professional dignity while questioning call girls inside a residential brothel as the powerful men of Berlin cavorted in rooms above her head. It reeked to high heaven. She felt a rising anger towards the Minister, his stalker, her captain, and even her fiancé for not being here.

"Good, then we're finished. We'll see you tomorrow night." Madame Denouve exited the drawing room, regal as a queen.

Salome turned to Mahler. "I'll have the files for you shortly. Can I offer you a drink while you wait?" She stepped closer.

Birgitta held up her hand. "No, thank you. I'll just wait with Herr Oppel."

"Herr Oppel is otherwise occupied at the moment, but you're welcome to stay here. I won't be long." Salome smiled.

"He's occupied? As in..." Mahler's words trailed off.

"Yes. He is upstairs fucking Ekaterine."

To Mahler, it seemed as if Salome chose her words with purpose. The glint in the woman's dark eyes confirmed this. A telling hint of amusement.

"I see." Birgitta's discomfort rose.

Salome stepped closer still, her long legs now directly in front of where Birgitta sat offering her a full view of their length. "Is there anything I can interest you in...while you wait?" She bent down, placing one hand on the armrest of Mahler's chair while locking eyes. The woman's breasts nearly fell out of their silken confines.

"Nein! I mean, no thank you. I'm good." *Good Lord, what is going on? If Joseph were here, he wouldn't believe this. Or maybe he would. Probably would blush bright red in embarrassment, just like he did the first time he saw me naked. For sure, Elsa would get a laugh out of it.*

Salome remained positioned provocatively a moment longer, and then slowly straightened. "You have only to ask. I'll be right back." She sauntered from the room, swaying her hips more than necessary.

When she was gone, Mahler let out a breath she didn't realize she'd been holding. It was followed by the laugh she'd smothered earlier. She stood and pulled her mobile out of her pocket. Walking toward the window, she began texting, '*You won't believe this, darling...*' As she finished typing the details of her encounter, she prepared to hit SEND, but stopped. Her eyes caught movement out front. Looking up, she saw a man in a suit exit the front door, and get into his Mercedes, which had been brought around by a valet. She knew that car, and she knew the man getting in. It was Lukas Trommler.

What the hell is he doing here? Mahler's jaw dropped. Her brain raced ninety miles a minute trying to come up with one good reason why her maid of honor's boyfriend would be leaving a brothel, and she couldn't come up with one. If she asked Salome about him, no doubt the woman would refuse to answer. Discretion was the key to the success of businesses such as this one, and with it already successfully serving some of the richest, most powerful men in Berlin, she knew she'd get no information. Now, she was faced with a dilemma. Tell Elsa she'd seen Lukas leaving the brothel or keep her mouth shut.

Chapter 12

Two hours after the sun went down, Heinz found himself back at the gilded home in the upscale neighborhood where he'd last seen the produce truck. The temperature dropped. He could see his own breath every time he exhaled, and if it kept dropping, the moisture in the air would turn once again to snow. This would not be good. He couldn't cover his tracks in the snow, and he planned to get as close to the house as he could without being caught. He hoped to find his way discreetly inside, but that might be asking the powers that be for too much. However it played out; he knew he wanted to find some concrete answers.

Heinz stood under a thick copse of trees in the alleyway at the back of the house, watching intently, seeking a way in. There were lights shining from the floor to ceiling windows of a large room on the right. He could see several people milling about with drinks in hand. It appeared for all the world to be a simple but glamorous cocktail party, but he knew better. On the second floor, softer lights glowed from smaller windows, at least eight single rooms. Now and again, he could see the shadows of people passing by, and in one, a couple embracing. He wondered how old the woman was, and then, he wondered if somewhere inside this home, he would find Marlessa Schubert. He shook himself. Heinz knew it was a longshot. The number of years that had already passed since she was abducted made that probability very small. But he still hoped.

Rubbing his hands together, he looked around noting that a guard had already walked around the inner perimeter of the house twice. He glanced at his watch. Eight minutes. Every eight minutes so far. He waited, clocking the time to make sure. Exactly eight minutes later, the guard, carrying a semi-automatic rifle slung over his shoulder by a strap, marched by again.

"Okay," he mumbled to himself. "Now to see if this fence will kill me quickly or slowly." He cast his eyes around the ground and found a stick not far from his feet. It would do. He picked it up and crouched low, approaching the wrought iron fence. Cautiously, he reached out, placing the stick next to one of the rods. Then he gave it a little kick with the rubber sole of his shoe, sending it right up against the metal. Nothing. No sparks. No alarm tripped. All was quiet. The fence was not electrified.

"So, you'll kill me slowly then." Heinz sighed, then stood. The fence was at least a foot taller than his own height of six feet two inches. He gripped the bars, took a deep breath, and began climbing. It was no small effort. At the top, he hauled one leg over, and then the next, trying to avoid emasculating himself. Finally, he dropped down on the other side. "I'm too old for this shit." He puffed, catching his breath.

He checked his watch. There were still four minutes left to get from the fence to a spot at the back of the house where he couldn't be seen. Dark eyes gauged the distance. He was pretty sure he could make it. Towards the left-hand side was a wing of the house in complete darkness. No lights illuminated the windows on the first or second floor. One faint glow showed through a third-floor window at the very end of the building, but that was all. It seemed his best chance to stay under the radar, and if it was as deserted as it appeared, his best chance for gaining entry.

Three minutes. "Dammit." Heinz sucked in a breath and took off running, keeping low. By the time he reached the darkened wing, the guard was coming around the corner. He didn't have time to locate a nook, so he threw himself to the ground, rolling against the wall amid the low shrubbery. A branch scratched his cheek, taking some skin with it. Heinz stopped breathing; eyes focused like a wild, cornered animal on the booted feet walking by. The sound of dead grass and ice crunching under the man's heels seemed as loud as thunder. Louder still, was the beating of the detective's heart when the crunching noise stopped. The guard turned, looking around. Heinz bit his lip, frozen into place. The guard reached into his hip pocket, and slowly pulled something out. The strike of a match lit up a square, rugged face with dark stubble along his jaw. He stood there, taking a long drag from his cigarette. On the ground behind him, hidden between the low shrubbery and the stone wall, Heinz waited, the cold seeping into his bones.

Five minutes passed as the armed thug enjoyed his nicotine fix. Five long minutes. Heinz considered just sneaking up behind him and snapping his neck, anything so he could get up off the frozen ground, but he waited. Finally, the guard dropped the butt, stepped on it, and resumed his rounds. As he cleared the wing, hooking around to the right-hand side of the manor, Heinz exhaled, and got up. His knee popped, and his left side reminded him painfully that he was not a spring chicken anymore. The search began for a way inside.

The first-floor windows were secure. The only doorway along this wing was inset, at the bottom of a slope going into the back of the house. Heinz realized it was a basement entry. The lock was old-fashioned with a large keyhole, the type that accommodated large keys that most people didn't use anymore. If he could manage to turn the tumbler just a bit, he could slide a credit card between the latch and the strike plate. He just needed a tool. Reaching into his pocket, he pulled out the small screwdriver set he purchased when he arrived. He surveyed the sizes, selecting one.

Heinz bent down, keeping to the shadows cast by the shrubbery at the top of the slope, and inserted the Phillip's head. The tool tried to catch on the grooves inside the lock. It turned a bit, then slipped back into place with a click. Heinz cringed, and then looked over his shoulder. He knew the guard would be coming back around in less than a minute, so he waited. Within seconds, his ears picked up on the crunching of booted feet on icy dead grass. Holding his breath, he shrunk lower still, fitting his frame into the corner of the door and the side wall. The guard passed, not slowing down and stopping this time. Eight more minutes left to pick the lock.

This time, he slipped his hotel room keycard out of his pocket, preparing for that small window of opportunity when the tool caught just enough. He turned it cautiously, just shy of the point where it stopped, hitting the locked tumblers. Slowly, he inserted the Kseniya's keycard into the miniscule space between the strike plate and the latch. Wiggling the card, he inched it in like a patient lover seeking to penetrate virgin skin for the very first time. "Come on, baby. Work with me," Heinz whispered. Finally, the card slid all the way home, and the latch clicked. This time, the sound was welcome. He pulled the doorknob, and the door cracked open. With three minutes remaining, the detective slipped inside, wiping a trickle of sweat from his brow.

The interior was dark. The only light by which to see filtered in through two small, grimy basement windows. Still, he was in. Now, he needed to find the stairs, and see exactly what, and who, was above. Ten steps across the concrete floor had him at the foot of an old, wooden staircase. Twenty steps up brought him to the door. He hoped it wasn't locked. Heinz pressed his cheek to the cold surface and listened. No sound greeted his ear. With a quick prayer, he turned the knob. As the door opened quietly, he breathed a sigh of relief. In another moment, he was through, into the hallway, and he prayed, on his way to finding answers.

A uniformed butler greeted the two men in the grand foyer. The servant took the overcoat of the first gentleman, showing great deference before turning to take the coat and hat of the second man, who stood, shoulders back, waiting. His graying brown hair was cut short above his large ears which seemed to protrude from beneath his head cover.

"Egor, this is Colonel-general Dmitry Vasiliev. You will make sure he enjoys himself tonight, yes?" The first gentleman addressed the butler.

"Of course, sir. Valentina," Egor snapped his fingers and a tall, blonde woman sauntered over. She wore a sheer, black gown that hugged her curves, and nothing underneath. Her heels clicked on the marble flooring as she came to a standstill next to the men. "Please take care of the Colonel-general. Show him the menu and take his order."

Valentina slipped her arm through the Colonel-general's, leaning in. The man smiled, clearly pleased. He tossed a look to the gentleman. "You do know how to treat your friends well, Brezhnev."

"Indeed, I do. I'm sure you'll find today's menu thoroughly satisfies your appetite." Brezhnev nodded, a tight smile on his lips.

"And what can I do for you, Colonel-general?" Valentina pouted her full, red lips as she led the man away.

"You can order me up two of your freshest dishes. And I like them quite young. Inexperienced is best." He patted her hand that rested on his arm. "No offense, my dear, but you're well past the expiration date for me."

Brezhnev waited until the Colonel-general and Valentina disappeared into the sitting room before turning to Egor. The small, tight smile on his face vanished. "Our new arrivals, are they being groomed?"

Egor stood at attention with the coats over one arm, and the Colonel-general's hat in hand. He kept his gaze averted just south of his employer's, never fully looking the man directly in the eye. Everyone employed in the manor knew to never make full eye contact with Vladimir Brezhnev. To do so was to put one's own life at risk. "They are, sir. Maya has seen them bathed and prepared, and has taken them to their training in the east wing."

Brezhnev offered a nod, and turned to go to his office, then stopped. "And who drew the lot this week?"

"Nestor, sir." Egor waited.

"Nestor?"

"Yes, sir."

Brezhnev chuckled, but it was without humor. "He will be no help at all. No control, that one. Send Arkady in as well but remind him he is not allowed to penetrate them, or I will cut off his balls personally."

"Very good, sir. Will that be all?"

"Da. I'll be in my office. Unless the Colonel-general requests my company, I do not wish to be disturbed." Brezhnev left, heading toward his office.

As he walked to the coat room, Egor's tense posture relaxed. Relief showed on his face as he left the foyer to put away the coats and deliver his boss's instructions.

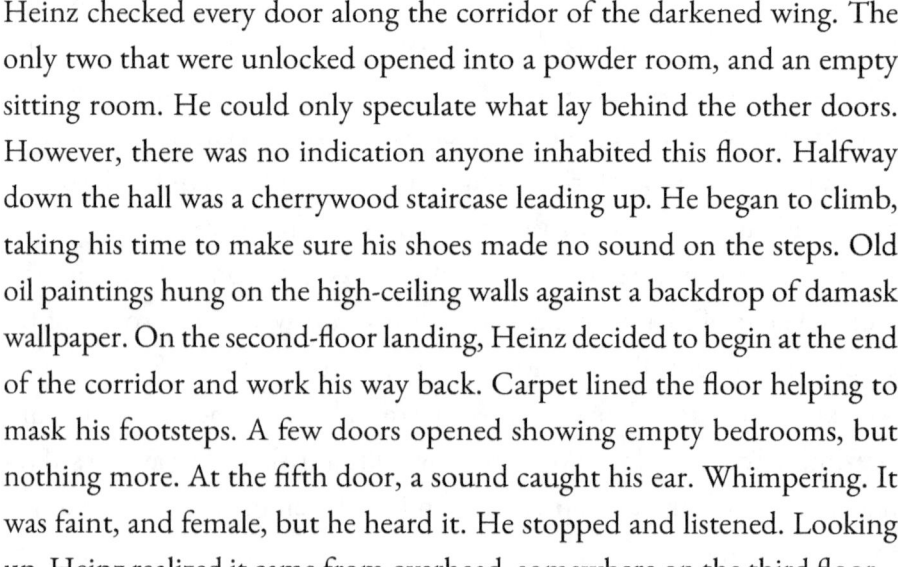

Heinz checked every door along the corridor of the darkened wing. The only two that were unlocked opened into a powder room, and an empty sitting room. He could only speculate what lay behind the other doors. However, there was no indication anyone inhabited this floor. Halfway down the hall was a cherrywood staircase leading up. He began to climb, taking his time to make sure his shoes made no sound on the steps. Old oil paintings hung on the high-ceiling walls against a backdrop of damask wallpaper. On the second-floor landing, Heinz decided to begin at the end of the corridor and work his way back. Carpet lined the floor helping to mask his footsteps. A few doors opened showing empty bedrooms, but nothing more. At the fifth door, a sound caught his ear. Whimpering. It was faint, and female, but he heard it. He stopped and listened. Looking up, Heinz realized it came from overhead, somewhere on the third floor.

Quickly, he returned to the stairs and went up. At the top of the landing, he paused, allowing his senses to reach out, seeking evidence of anyone else around the corner. He heard nothing. Peeking around, his eyes confirmed he was alone. Moving fast, he cleared the length of the hallway, arriving near the end. He remembered seeing a dim light shining through the last window on this level while he was still outside trying to get in. Someone was in that room, someone who was crying, and female.

Outside of the carved, cherrywood door, he stood, listening. What he heard made his blood boil.

"Stop crying, bitch, and stroke it!"

"Please, don't make me—" A soft voice replied, filled with fear.

A loud slap echoed. Heinz bit his lip, pulled out his ill-gotten gun, and without further thought, barged in, ready to shoot to kill.

A tall man in his twenties with short black hair and acne scars covering his thin face turned.

"Who the hell are you?"

Heinz's eyes took in the scene before him. Three young girls sat naked on the side of a four-poster bed. He recognized one as the girl he'd seen trying to make a run for it from the produce truck. The other two were huddled together, obviously terrified, and seeking to comfort each other. None of them appeared older than fifteen or sixteen. In fact, the smallest one looked to be all of ten years of age.

"You sick sonofabitch! Back away from them, now! Do it, or I will shoot you where you stand!" Heinz gave the order to the stunned man. To the girls, he said, "It's going to be okay. Cover yourselves and get over there by the wall."

The tall man stood with his pants down and cock out. He was clearly at a disadvantage. Yet he smiled.

Heinz didn't like this. "What the hell have you to smile about? Back away, I said!"

The man continued to grin. "I don't think so, you stupid bastard," his accent thick as he switched from Russian to German, recognizing Heinz's language. "You're just in time, Arkady." His eyes flitted to a point over Heinz's shoulder.

Heinz turned, seeing a large, bearded man behind him, and then a split second later, a meaty fist flying straight at him. Then, everything went black.

Chapter 13

Pain shot through Heinz's skull. He felt a tremendous amount of pressure and weight sitting on his face. He struggled to open his eyes and blinked several times. Reaching up, he felt the lump. It was his nose, and he was sure it was now broken. Memories came flooding back, and he jerked upright.

"So, you're awake now." A deep voice spoke.

Heinz turned and focused on the well-dressed man with salt and pepper hair, and short, well-manicured beard. It was the man from the warehouse, the one who appeared in charge that day. He stood flanked by the guard from outside, and the one who'd punched his lights out.

"That's quite a bruise you're developing." The man squatted down in front of Heinz, pointing at his nose. "Now, do you mind telling me just who the hell you are?"

Heinz held his tongue. He knew he was in a bad situation, and he needed a moment to think.

"I see. Not much of a talker, eh? Let me guess, a father? A brother? A jilted lover? Certainly not a dissatisfied customer, I would hope. Just why is it you're here? Who did you hope to find?"

He seized the opportunity. "My daughter."

The man chuckled. "And who is your daughter, and more importantly, why would she be here in my house?"

"Her name is Marlessa, and you know why."

The man cocked his head, quiet for a moment as he stared out the window. "Arkady, is there anyone here by that name?"

"No, sir."

He looked back at Heinz. "You see? No one here by that name. Is that what you broke into my house for? Or do you have more to share?"

The deceptively soft tone of his voice was not lost on Heinz. He knew the man was dangerous. "That is all," he replied.

The man stood, looking down. He extended his hand to Arkady, palm up. The brute placed Heinz's gun in it.

"It's not police issue," he said to himself, looking at the weapon. "In fact, the serial number has been filed off, so I'd say you probably picked this up illegally." The man made a tsk-tsk sound while shaking a finger at him. "Still, it doesn't mean you're not police." He pointed it at Heinz. "And since you're not carrying any identification on you, I'm going to have to rely on your good manners to tell me exactly who you are."

"You first," Heinz shot back, then bit his wayward tongue.

He smiled. "Well, that was either very brave or very foolish, but as the host, I will set the example. I am Vladimir Brezhnev, and this is my home," he looked around. "Well, one of them."

Shit!

"Now, please be so kind and introduce yourself."

Heinz thought fast, but decided he'd best keep as close to the truth as possible. "Martin Lintz."

"And are you police?"

"I am not." Heinz lowered his eyes, offering a cowed expression. "I'm a teacher of mathematics."

"Mathematics, is it? Herr Lintz," Brezhnev continued casually pointing the gun down at Heinz, "You seem to be quite a long way from Germany."

"Austria."

"Austria, then. How is it you think your daughter, whose home, I presume, is in Austria, would be here, inside my home, in Saint Petersburg?"

Heinz didn't have much wiggle room anymore. He could allow himself to vent his spleen and spill all the beans, letting Brezhnev know he knew exactly who he was; the Butcher, which would probably end in his death, or he could fudge a few facts, and maybe still get out of the situation alive. Birgitta would never forgive him if he didn't make it back home. He decided to fudge.

"She ran away. I tracked her here. I was told by the man who sold me the gun that this might be a good place to search. Apparently, he's been here before." He told the lie with a straight face.

Brezhnev stared at Heinz, weighing his words. He knew that Lintz hadn't told the complete truth, but the accounting of his actions upstairs by Arkady and Nestor, the concern they said he showed for the girls, and the man's own admission seemed to confirm, at least, the actions of a father desperate to find his child. He considered all options, but the Colonel-general's presence swayed him. With their dealings ongoing, he couldn't risk any scandal occurring while the man was under his roof. He would need to call in a favor.

"Arkady, please call the police and tell them we've caught a trespasser on the grounds. Let them deal with Herr Lintz."

Arkady turned to leave. Brezhnev stepped closer to Heinz, squatting low once again. He leaned in, extending his hand. In his palm was the Kseniya's room key card. "I expect that I will never see you around here again, yes?"

Heinz recognized the subtle move for what it was—they knew where to find him. "Nein, you will not."

"Very good." Brezhnev stood, turning away, then stopped. "And I do hope you find your daughter. Marlessa, did you say? A beautiful name. Quite unique." He strode out of the room.

Heinz breathed a small sigh of relief, and then began to fret about the next problem; the Russian police.

The guard stood at the doorway, rifle in hand, watching. It was unnerving, and there was very little time left before he would be answering more questions. Heinz worried that his passport might not hold up to an official investigation. He didn't have the same faith in HackTwice that Faust did. Of course, that was because he hadn't worked with her before, but he'd worked with Herman Faust for most of his life, so maybe he should simply leave his faith in the man, his friend, and hope for the best while planning for the worst. The Butcher was turning him over to the police, but he didn't seem at all concerned about inviting the police into his home/brothel, which meant whoever was coming, was on the Bratva's payroll. Knowing this meant that bringing up what he saw in that upstairs bedroom was moot. His rash actions hadn't saved those girls. By now, they were long gone, moved to another house where they would continue to be abused, raped, sold over and over again until they were no longer useful. Another piece of his soul died.

Twenty long minutes went by as Heinz racked his brain for a plan. There was no guarantee that he would be coming out of this situation alive. It could be that Brezhnev simply didn't want the murder to occur inside his home, didn't want the mess. An Austrian tourist dead inside his house would bring attention where none such was desired. An Austrian tourist found dead elsewhere was someone else's problem. An Austrian tourist who went missing, just another unsolved case.

A man of medium height and broad stature entered the room. His dark eyes pinpointed Heinz where he sat. He stopped, sticking his hands inside his overcoat pockets.

Heinz noted the stubble on his double chin. Apparently, the man enjoyed his food, but was loathe to use a razor. He looked like a fat, disgruntled bulldog.

"Is this the one?" He asked the guard in Russian.

"Da, this is the intruder."

Heinz caught about every other word, but he understood the gist of it.

"And what am I to do with him?" The bulldog seemed annoyed.

The guard's eyebrows lowered, taking affront on his boss's behalf. "What Gospodin Brezhnev pays you to do, Comrade. Take care of the problem!"

The policeman's nostrils flared. "The hassle isn't worth the paycheck," he grumbled.

"Take it up with the boss, then. I'll be happy to get him." The guard smirked.

The bulldog seemed to shrink in on himself for a moment before puffing out his chest and addressing Heinz. "You, let's go."

Heinz sat there, unmoving.

The guard laughed. "He's Austrian. Deutsch sprechen."

The cop sighed, then said in stilted German, "You there. Let's go."

Heinz stood. The cop stepped aside, indicating Heinz should walk ahead of him. Out in the foyer, the butler waited. As soon as both men were ready, he led the way through to a side door that came out to a separate covered driveway. It wasn't clearly visible from the street as it was partially hidden by three tall evergreen trees. It seemed ironic to Heinz that it smelled like Christmas in a Bavarian forest on a night when he might well find himself dead in a ditch somewhere in the former Soviet Union.

"Where are you taking me?" Heinz asked as he stopped just shy of the dark sedan parked under the carport.

The bulldog stopped, his dark eyes assessing the taller man. "To your car, Herr Lintz. I will follow you back to your hotel, the Kseniya, da?"

So, the man had already been informed. "And then what?"

"Get in." He offered no more.

Heinz hesitated, and then slid into the passenger side.

The bulldog got in, cranked the ignition, and pulled out onto the winding drive. At the gate, they waited as the wrought iron slid open, and then drove through. The car turned right, and then right again at the crossroad. A third right confirmed they were heading to the back alley where Heinz left his rental. They stopped.

"Get out. I'll follow you back."

Heinz stepped out, walked to the Volga Siber, and bent down to retrieve the keys from behind the wheel hub. As he got in and prepared to start the engine, he paused. A little voice in his head screamed, "Don't do it!" He took a steadying breath. There was no way they would blow up the car here right behind all of these homes, and so close to Brezhnev's residence. He swallowed, closed his eyes, and turned the key. The engine purred to life, humming low.

Air left his lungs in a whoosh. Relief flooded him, and he put the car in gear, reversing back down the alley. The bulldog cop did the same, backing out first, and just enough to allow Heinz to come onto the road. Then it was Heinz who led the way back to the hotel. It was quite a way to go to return to the Kseniya, and he wasn't out of the woods yet.

As he pulled onto the highway, he remembered his phone was stashed in the glove compartment. He reached in, fumbling around, and pulled it out, sliding it inside his coat pocket.

At this time of night, the highway was void of traffic. The windshield began to fog. Heinz turned on the defroster. As the haze cleared off the glass, snow began to fall. The asphalt ahead looked shiny. Black ice. In the rearview, the headlights that had remained right on his tail appeared closer.

"What the hell?"

The car tapped his bumper.

"Dammit!" Heinz hit the gas. "You sonofabitch!"

The sedan revved, and again, rammed into him. The Volga Siber lurched and slid. Heinz corrected the wheel, speeding up, frantically trying to remember which exit to take. By his calculation, he was still at least ten minutes away from his turnoff, and at this rate, he wouldn't make it. He eased to the right, and then let off the gas allowing the sedan to come alongside. When Heinz looked to his left, the cop was once again staring him down...over the sight of his gun. Heinz yanked the steering wheel hard to the left slamming into the sedan. The shot went wide missing the car, but the persistent police officer aimed again, firing. This time, the bullet shattered the driver's side window narrowly missing Heinz's head. The officer took advantage of the chaos and slammed the sedan into the side of the Volger sending Heinz skidding out of control.

He tried to turn the wheel in the opposite direction, letting off the gas and avoiding the brake, but the icy road did him in. The car went off the highway, over the embankment, and landed hard in the ditch below.

The sedan slowed down, rolling to a stop, and then slowly reversed back to the sight where the tire tracks blended into the dirt on the roadside.

The police officer stepped out of his vehicle and walked to the edge of the embankment. In the dark, he could see the taillights glowing in the ditch. He raised his hand, aimed, and fired two shots. The first missed, but the second one found its mark as the gas tank exploded. Satisfied, the bulldog returned to his car and drove away.

———————◆O◆———————

Flames licked the night sky as black smoke swirled, creating a hellish fog. The frozen ground was unforgiving, but a far better place to be than the inferno that was now his rent-a-car. Pain shot through his ribs with each breath, and consciousness threatened to flee. A fleeting thought had him reaching into his coat pocket. The mobile was still there. He tapped the screen with his finger, then found and hit the CALL button next to the contact marked EMERGENCY. It rang three times before an unfamiliar voice answered. Heinz's vision dimmed as he choked out, "I need help."

"Where are you?"

He coughed and winced. "I don't...know." He tried looking around, but a sharp jolt in his side from that action, and dizziness, robbed him of speech. Heinz tried to focus but failed. "Help...me..." Another coughing fit wracked his body painfully as the world faded to black.

Chapter 14

"Any word yet?" Faust poked his head into the small office two doors down from his own.

Elsa Kreiss looked up from her computer screen. She shook her head. "No, and I'm starting to worry. He didn't call last night, either, and you know how he is about checking up on me and Anno."

Faust stuck his hands in his trouser pockets, staring at the floor. "Hmm, yes, I know." He stepped inside the office and stopped short by the narrow window. "It hasn't been twenty-four hours yet, so we'll give it a little more time."

"Time for what? Who else do you have besides this one contact that you haven't told me anything about, Herman?" Elsa leaned back in her chair, watching the Direktor with concern.

"No one else, unfortunately. But I have operatives at my beck and call, and if need be, I can send one in." He turned to the window, muttering under his breath, "Hell, I was one. No one more qualified."

"But how would they even know where to begin? Your operatives, while I'm sure are more than capable, don't know Heinz like we do. They don't know the case or the history. And how on earth would they even begin to track down his alias?" Elsa stood. Her worry forced her to her feet, unable to remain still any longer. Something was wrong. She was sure of it. Every instinct she had said so.

"Elsa, you must understand that there are protocols..." Faust held up his hands.

"What protocols could there possibly be in this case, Herman? It's unsanctioned! You said so yourself. There is no contingency plan. No team waiting to be called in. It's just Heinz out there by himself with only some unidentified contact keeping tabs on him."

Faust stared at the redhead. His natural reaction to borderline insubordination from a fledgling agent was to put that person firmly in their place. Inexperienced officers did not question their superiors, but this was Elsa, and the long-dormant father inside of him recognized her tone for what it was, fear. She was scared for Heinz. Truth be told, so was he. He bit his tongue and counted to ten.

"There is always a contingency plan, Kreiss." He addressed her by her surname, trying to regain some control over an uncontrollable situation.

She walked to the window and stood next to him. "I'm sorry," she offered. "I spoke out of turn. But I don't know what to do. What do I do, Direktor Faust?" She backed off her verbal attack, ashamed for her outburst.

Faust averted his face, a half-smile on his lips. He reached over, placing a comforting hand on her shoulder. She was right. No one knew Heinz like they did, or the case history for that matter. And this wasn't state business, it was personal. Helping to send Heinz in made him responsible. He knew that from the moment Joseph guilted him into assisting in this hair-brained idea. His decision was made. "We wait until the twenty-four-hour period expires. And then, Elsa, we get on the first flight to Saint Petersburg."

She looked at him. "How?"

"Plan B," he said. Glancing down, he smiled at her. "I already had our faux passports and identification prepared days ago...just in case, *daughter*."

She blinked, then chuckled. "Daughter?"

"Yes, a father-daughter trip. Fitting, don't you think?" He nudged her shoulder.

Elsa threw her arms around him, hugging him tight. "You old softie!"

Faust rolled his eyes. "If you ever tell anyone, I'll have you hanged."

She smothered a laugh, then straightened. "Yes, sir."

He pulled his arm away, stepping back. "Now, you should go home and pack a small suitcase, enough for a couple of days because we won't have time for anything else. When you're finished, meet me back here. Oh," he said, as he walked to the door, "don't tell Lukas where you're going. Just tell him I have scheduled a training assignment for the next few days at the academy. If Heinz checks in before then, you'll have to stay in a hotel to cement the ruse. Of course, if you don't run into Lukas before then, you'll save the department some money and just go back home."

Elsa finished folding her jeans and sweaters. After placing them inside her suitcase alongside her thick socks, underthings, and toiletry bag, she zipped it up. She decided to wear her boots on the flight since packing them would be impractical. She'd already thrown in a pair of black running shoes and leg warmers. Saint Petersburg was the only place she could think of colder than Berlin, and she needed to be sure she kept warm while there.

Lukas came in as she lugged the suitcase out.

"Where are you going?" He stood inside the door with one eyebrow raised.

Elsa took in the sight of him wearing a dark gray suit that made his hazel eyes seem greener than usual, and smiled. "No need to panic. I'm off for a little training for a couple of days. Boss's orders."

He relaxed. "For a minute there, I thought you were leaving me." Lukas closed the door, and then walked to Elsa, taking the suitcase from her hand and sitting it down.

"And if I were?" She grinned as he wrapped his arms around her waist, pulling her in.

"I'd have to remind you why you should stay, of course." He ran his hands down her back until they rested on her bottom.

"I see. And why is that again," she asked, playfully running her own hands up over his chest and around his neck.

"Well," he gave her ass a squeeze, "I happen to know exactly what you like."

"Meh, I can train anyone to know what I like." Elsa gave him a saucy grin.

Lukas's lip twitched, but he fought the grin threatening to burst forth. "I suppose you could, but not many are as talented a student as myself," he ground his hips into hers, "nor are they nearly as well endowed with the proper tools for the job of pleasing you."

Elsa felt the tool in question grow hard against her. "Hmm, you mentioned tools, as in plural?"

A slow smile spread across his face. "How much time do you have before I have to let you go?"

"Oh, I think just enough. But no dilly-dallying. My Direktor is a hard taskmaster."

"I'm a rather hard taskmaster myself, woman," Lukas whispered before taking her lips in a scorching kiss. His tongue swept the inner recesses of her mouth as his hands worked to quickly unbutton and tug off her slacks. He noticed she wore her high-heeled leather boots beneath. "We'll leave those on, but nothing else!"

The rest of her clothing joined her pants in a pile on the hardwood floor. Before she could draw breath, Lukas had lifted her up, carried her to the sofa, and set her down. He threw off his jacket, pulled off his shirt, and knelt between her knees, pushing them apart. With one last smoldering look in his hazel eyes, he dove into her crevice, tongue first, and licked her into submission.

"You're right," she panted, "you're a keeper. Oh, yes, yes, yes!"

When she neared orgasm, he pulled back, and with one hand, freed his cock from his pants, positioned himself, and thrust home. Their lovemaking was frenzied and furious. Nails scratched, hair was pulled, and groins rammed together smacking hard.

"Oh, God, Lukas!" she screamed.

"Fuck, I love you!" he said, shooting his load.

Elsa's eyes popped open. He'd said it. He actually said it, but did he mean it? She glanced down. He was resting his cheek on her breasts, and she could only see the top of his head.

Her fingers caressed his scalp. She waited while he caught his breath. It gave her time to think.

"So," he said, "how long will you be away?"

"A few days. No more than three, I think." She spoke softly, absently running a finger around his ear.

He turned his head, taking a moment to lay a soft kiss on each breast. "I'll miss you."

Elsa smiled. In the afterglow of their lovemaking, she felt more strongly for him this time than she did any other time before. She still wasn't sure if what she felt was love. Something inside held her back. Perhaps it had to do with the suspicion that he was keeping a secret from her. "And I'll miss you. What will you do while I'm gone?"

"Nothing much. Just gallery business."

She remembered the message on his computer. "Anything else?"

He blinked and leaned up to kiss her lips. It was tender, sweet, and sexy. "Did you need something?"

"No, just asking."

He left her with one last kiss on the tip of her nose before pulling out and standing up. "Okay, good." He headed to the bathroom.

"Maybe you can spend a little time with your army friends while I'm gone. Maybe invite Dieter to come by."

He stopped and looked over his shoulder. "Maybe, but I haven't heard from him in a while." He continued to the bathroom and shut the door.

Elsa sat on the couch, still naked save for her boots, wondering why Lukas had just lied to her face.

Her phone pinged. She reached around to grab it from the table behind the sofa. It was Faust. The twenty-four-hour waiting period had run out, and he was expecting her immediately. There was no time to grill Lukas. She would have to put this on the backburner for now. Rising, she headed for the spare bathroom scooping up her clothing along the way. A quick clean up, and she was out the door. She didn't bother to say goodbye.

Chapter 15

Birgitta Mahler threw her purse down on the hall table as she stepped inside her flat. Her 7:00 p.m. appointment at Madame Denouve's had turned into four hours of interviews with more sex workers than she ever imagined in one place. Apparently, Minister Obermeyer enjoyed a great variety in his dalliances. Four of them were men, a fact that surprised her since the man went out of his way to behave as an overbearing womanizing chauvinist.

Out of the seventeen individuals she spoke with, only one set off her alarm. Bierkit Wiedner. Professionally, she was known to the minister as Marilyn, a cultured escort, however, Bierkit was originally a poor woman from a working-class family that came from the Rhein region near Frankfurt. She was thirty-two, but told clients she was twenty-three, and she looked it. Her youthful appearance was almost doll-like, and her figure was that of a 1920's cinema starlet, but it was her eyes that struck Mahler. For all their charm, the large, round, blue orbs fringed in thick false eyelashes lacked an ounce of warmth. There seemed to be no soul inhabiting the doll-like body. When asked questions, her answers came across as truthful and unrehearsed, but there was something not quite right. Mahler just couldn't put her finger on it. She'd made a tick in her notebook and intended to run a more detailed background check on her in the morning. Then, something else occurred.

On the way to her car, Salome stopped her.

"Leaving so soon?"

Mahler turned from opening her car door, surprised. "So soon? I've been here longer than I cared to be already." Exhaustion and irritation crept into her voice, an unusual breach of her usually stoic persona.

The woman sauntered closer, stopping to rest against the car door, effectively preventing Mahler from opening it. Salome stared hard at the detective, a sly smile on her painted lips. "Did you find what you were looking for?"

Annoyed, Birgitta took in a slow, steadying breath before replying. "I cannot discuss an open investigation."

Salome leaned in, reaching out to touch the lace at the collar of Mahler's black cocktail dress. It was Asian in design, fitted, with cap sleeves and a mock turtleneck of black lace. Birgitta had paired it with a multi-colored silken pashmina, mid-height black pumps, and a small red clutch bag. It was as close to an elegant after-five outfit as she owned, and one she'd worn on only one other occasion, her third official date with Joseph.

"He's rather a bastard to them, you know."

"Who?" The statement caught Mahler off guard as the woman continued to invade her personal space.

"The minister. He's a bastard to them all...when he's here. The only time he's kind is when he takes them out on dates outside these walls."

This was news. "He takes them all out?"

Salome smiled. "Nein, only his favorites."

"I thought they all were his favorites." Mahler held steady, allowing the slinky Salome to be drawn further in. As long as she was offering information, she would not be immediately rebuked for her invasion of personal space.

"Those you interviewed are simply the number of them he's sampled, but his favorites are the ones he comes back for time and again."

"And who are the lucky ones?"

Salome took one step closer, now merely inches from Mahler. She leaned down bringing her lips close to the detective's ear. "What will you give me if I tell you?"

Birgitta felt her spine stiffen. She'd heard those words before, but they'd always come from men. Having a woman speak them seemed very wrong to her, like women shouldn't be sexually harassing other women. It was like breaking a rule, one where women were supposed to have each other's backs. She swallowed.

"What do you want, Salome?" Birgitta kept the discomfort she was feeling out of her voice.

The answer she expected never came. Instead, the woman replied, "To go home."

The three simple words carried a strong note of sadness.

Mahler looked up. "Home? Isn't this your home?" She glanced back at the mansion.

The cat-like slyness previously inhabiting Salome's eyes was gone. In its place was despair. "Of course not. Would you live here?" She cast a sideways look at the house, and then returned her gaze to Mahler. "I was brought here three years ago under a false promise to model. As you can guess, that is not what happened."

Confusion marred Mahler's brow. "Then why not leave? Can't you go home?"

"One cannot travel without a passport."

"Who has your passport? Madame Denouve?" Birgitta felt anger rising.

"No. She's simply the face of the business." Salome's voice dropped to a whisper.

"Then who, Salome?" Mahler leaned in closer.

"I don't know who. All I know is that someone else, someone with connections within the ministry owns this house and two others. When I left Kiev, I didn't have a passport, but one was provided quickly, bypassing the usual application process. Once I got here, I was told I'd be staying in this house, and when jobs came available, someone would come and get me. Those jobs never happened. Instead, I was prostituted out, but only after being *trained* by Madame." Tears welled up within Salome's dark eyes. "I was raised in a good family, Detective. We went to church every Sunday. My parents," she faltered, sniffing. "My parents would be so ashamed. They probably think I'm dead by now. I haven't spoken to them since I left. I'm not allowed to call. My activities are always monitored. Please, please help me." She grabbed Mahler's hand, holding it tight.

Birgitta's heart lurched painfully. Suspecting the truth about these so-called *legitimate* brothels was one thing, but knowing the dirty truth was another. She knew in that moment she would do all she could to get Salome back home.

"I will help you, but I need your help as well. First, tell me who these favorites are of the minister's, and then I have another question."

Salome lifted Birgitta's hand and kissed it. "Thank you! I knew, you know, when I first met you that you were not like the others that have come through the door. I'm sorry if I made you feel uncomfortable. I just needed to make sure what kind of person you are. You understand?"

Birgitta nodded.

Salome sighed, then swallowed hard. "His favorites..." she paused, "are Karl, the blond one with the dark eyebrows. You remember?"

"Yes. He was the third male of four. Okay, and who else?"

"Marilyn. He adores her. It's those two that he takes out almost exclusively."

"Okay." Mahler made a mental note. "You said 'almost exclusively?' What do you mean?"

"Oh, well, he only takes those two out on dates outside of the mansion, but they are not exclusive with him."

"Well," Mahler chuckled dryly, "I would imagine not. After all, they work here, so must see other clients."

"No, I mean that from time to time, I've seen both of them leave with his assistant."

This surprised Mahler. "Herr Oppel? Does he pick up and deliver to the minister as well?"

Salome shook her head. "No, I don't believe so. He sees them on the minister's off nights."

Birgitta blinked. "Both of them? At the same time?"

Salome nodded. "Yes, sometimes. Mostly Marilyn though."

"That's rather..." Mahler searched for a non-offensive term, "quirky?"

"I suppose, but what's strange is that you won't find the appointments listed in Madame's ledger."

"I see." But Mahler didn't, not quite, anyhow. Still, it was yet another twist in the mystery.

"You said you had another question," Salome reminded her, bringing Birgitta back to the moment.

"Oh, yes." Mahler grew serious. "When I was here earlier, I saw a man leaving. Tall, rather good-looking, hazel eyes, drives a Mercedes."

Salome smiled. "Herr Trommler?"

"I suppose," she prevaricated. "Is he a regular?"

"Why? Are you interested?"

"What? No," Mahler sputtered.

"Hmm." The cat-like slyness returned to Salome's eyes. "Well, I don't know much about him except that he's new, and some kind of art buyer."

"Does he see anyone in particular?"

"That sure sounds like interest to me, Detective."

"I'm simply curious."

A slow smile spread across Salome's lips. "If you say so. I do know he's visited with Ekaterine a few times. She's old. Probably in her forties by now, but the older clients seem to like her."

Mahler choked. "Forties are not old, Salome!" She thought about her own age, and Joseph's. Were they old now? She shook herself. "Didn't you mention her earlier today? The one that Herr Oppel was with?"

The woman shrugged. "Yes. Herr Oppel has eclectic tastes. He is a strange little man."

It was a lot to take in. It was disturbing enough that Lukas was visiting a brothel, but now she discovered that he was carrying on with an old harlot, at that. It didn't make any sense, and it was only recently that he'd begun frequenting the place. Mahler felt like she was on information overload.

She looked at Salome. "Thank you. I know you're risking a lot by telling me all of this." Mahler reached for the door handle. "I'll need your information."

Salome slipped her fingers into the cleavage of her dress and pulled out a folded square of paper. "This is me. My real name, my birthdate, my home address, name of my parents, and their phone number." She placed the paper in Mahler's hand. "Thank you, Detective. Thank you from the bottom of my heart."

The sincerity in her voice touched Mahler. "Don't thank me yet. I have to devise a plan to get you out of here first." She stepped into her car, sliding into the seat. "Oh, and of course this means I'll have to bust up this brothel and arrest the Madame." Conviction colored her words.

"As long as you get me out first, you can burn this damned house to the ground for all I care."

Salome stepped back and closed the car door.

Mahler started the engine and drove slowly out of the winding driveway to the street. By the time she'd arrived at her flat, and tossed her purse onto the hall table, it was past midnight. She couldn't even remember the ride home, and now, she had to get up in less than five hours to pick up the minister for another fun day of babysitting the bastard. She was tired, irritated, worried, and needed to talk this all out, but the one person in the world with whom she could confide wasn't here. She couldn't even call him. It was too late, and he hadn't even answered her last text, which was unusual. Perhaps that would change in the morning, but for now, she would have to figure this one out on her own.

Chapter 16

It was late afternoon when '*Gerald Zimmerman*' and '*his daughter, Greta,*' landed in Saint Petersburg. The bustle of the airport slowed them down at the Customs counter. They eventually made it through the checkpoint, but not without receiving an interrogation of old-school KGB proportions. The gentleman verifying their passports had asked both no less than ten times why they were entering the Russian Federation, and who they might know within its borders.

"Who do you know in Saint Petersburg?" The man's cold, brown eyes held Faust's without blinking, an old interrogator's tactic meant to intimidate. His balding pate was only partially covered by the thin comb-over of his graying brown hair. An equally sparse mustache sat atop his thin lips which remained pinched.

Faust remained calm, providing the same answer each time. "We know no one here. It's simply a father-daughter vacation. You see, my wife," he paused, then tilted his head at Elsa, "her mother, recently passed. My dear Helga always wanted to visit this beautiful city, but we just never found the time, you understand. This is as much for her as it is for us, a time to both grieve, and celebrate her life."

Elsa bowed her head, sniffling once.

The security agent's face never changed. He kept looking back down at the passports as if something of keen interest suddenly appeared where it had previously been hidden. He asked the same two questions many times, re-ordering the words. Finally, he glanced at Herr Zimmerman and his daughter one last time, and then stamped the appropriate pages on their documents. "Enjoy your stay." With that, he dismissed them both.

"I think my ass is sweating," Elsa muttered.

"What's that?" Faust raised one bushy brow.

Elsa chuckled. "Nothing. Just something I remembered Frau Kluge telling Birgitta and I last week at our dress fitting. She survived the Nazi SS interrogations during the bombing of Berlin."

"I see." He didn't. "I'll never understand women no matter how long I live. How do you go in for dress fittings and end up discussing old wars? This is why I never ask Helga about her day. God knows she tells me anyway, but at least I can always say I didn't ask for it."

They stepped outside, searching for a taxi. Elsa laughed. "Well, *papa*, I'll remember that when next you ask me for a report."

They spotted an available cab and approached quickly. "Don't you dare give me sass, *daughter*. When I ask for a report, a report I expect. Pronto! Now, hop in. Time's wasting."

Elsa slid into the leather interior of the vehicle. "And where, exactly, do we begin?"

"At the nearest hotel. We have to settle in, after all." He addressed the driver. "Sprechen Sie Deutsch?"

The man shook his head in the negative.

"Great," Faust mumbled before switching to Russian. "Blizhayshaya gostinitsa, pozhaluysta. Prilichnoye odin." (*"The nearest hotel, please. A decent one."*)

The driver nodded, and put the car into drive, steering out into traffic. Elsa leaned back in the seat; arms crossed over her chest. She was glad she'd worn her leather boots. It felt colder in Russia than in Berlin. She glanced at Faust. "I'm very impressed, *papa*. I had no idea you had such a command of the Russian language."

He settled in, chuckling. "A story for another time, my dear."

"And after we get checked in to the hotel, then what?"

"Then, the real work begins. I have some points of interests we'll be visiting thanks to my personal guide," Faust replied carefully. He pulled out a folded guidebook of Saint Petersburg. Flipping it open, a map of the city was revealed with gold stars at all the usual tourist attractions. But it was the red X's that caught Elsa's attention. They were hand-written, with notes. Numbers accompanied each large, red X. Longitudes and latitudes.

"One day, you'll have to tell me more about this personal guide of yours," said Elsa.

"One day." Faust pointed them out, the two looking for all the world like exactly who they were supposed to be, a father and daughter on vacation. First time tourists. "This point looks closest to the airport." He handed the booklet to Elsa, and reached into his pocket, pulling out his cell phone. After searching for the right application, he entered the coordinates. "Yes, the closest to where we are now." He leaned up to speak to the driver. "Is there a hotel in this area?"

Faust pointed to the map on his screen. The driver slowed down at a light and glanced over. "Da. The Kseniya is there. It is decent. You wish to go there?"

"Yes. Take us there." Faust sat back, tucking his phone back into his pocket. "So, that's the hotel," he told Elsa.

She nodded, keeping her thoughts to herself. If they showed up at the hotel and Heinz was there, then she was sure they'd feel quite foolish, but at last check, right before landing, Faust still had not received any updates on her mentor. The inside contact hadn't checked in at all. It had now been more than thirty-six hours since the last report.

The ride to the Kseniya took less than twenty minutes. The driver helped to unload their bags from the boot of the cab, and after receiving payment, left them on the front doorstep. Inside, the ambience took a nosedive. The dark interior looked like an old, cold-war memory. The faded wallpaper was peeling off in the corners, and the dark wainscoting had several deep scratches. The Hunter green shag carpeting had lost its shag ages ago and now appeared like the matted coat of a wet, stray dog. It smelled nearly as dirty. Elsa wrinkled her nose.

"So, this is what passes as decent, eh?" She lugged her suitcase to the counter. A gentleman with faded blue eyes and pale blond hair greeted them. Faust stepped forward.

"We'll need two rooms, please, for me and my daughter." He handed over his passport. Elsa did the same.

"For how many nights?" the man asked.

"Three, please."

The man looked at their documents before making a copy.

"Oh, and a friend may be staying here as well. An Herr Lintz? Martin Lintz?" Faust asked in a friendly tone.

The man paused, glancing up at them. "Herr Lintz has already checked out. Just last night."

"Oh," Faust looked at Elsa. "Did he say he was returning home?"

"I don't know, sir. I was not the one on duty then."

"Might I speak to the person who was? He is a rather dear friend, and we were hoping to meet up." Faust continued agreeably.

"The owner is out. I'll let him know as soon as he returns." The blond man finished checking them in, and then handed over two keys.

Elsa took hers and noticed the man shook his head slightly at someone behind her. She turned and caught sight of a short, round, older woman with dark hair, and a distracting mole before that woman ducked around the corner. She sent a look to Faust who calmly palmed his key and turned to pick up his suitcase. He looked in the direction Elsa faced, but saw nothing. Together, they walked to the lifts. Once inside, Elsa shared what she'd noticed.

"Something is, indeed, not right. They know something, but for now, we'll settle in and plan our next move." Faust chewed the inside of his cheek, an old habit born of nerves and frustration. It helped him think.

"And what about the owner?" Elsa asked as the floor bell dinged indicating they'd arrived.

"We will have to tread carefully. If they are already suspicious of us, then we may have to change hotels quickly. We can't have the local police sniffing around...or worse."

"FSB?" She asked, referring to Russian Federation Intelligence as she walked down the hall toward their rooms.

"Exactly. We can't afford to tangle with those old KGB bloodhounds. We're going to have to move fast, Kreiss. No time to waste. Go set your things down, do what needs doing, and meet me here in the hall in fifteen minutes."

They parted, each entering their respective rooms which were fortunately side by side.

Inside her room, Elsa quickly put away her suitcase on the old-fashioned luggage stand. She didn't bother to unpack. She simply grabbed her toiletries, used the restroom, refreshed herself, and then took a moment to check her mobile. There were no messages from Lukas, but there was one from Birgitta.

"*I need you to go by the bakery and try some samples for the groom's cake. Joseph likes raspberry filling, so anything along those lines is fine. Pick the one you like most. I'm still tied up with the case Levitz pushed into my lap. Thank you, Elsa. I appreciate you. B.*"

Elsa pursed her lips. "Scheisse." She hadn't told the bride-to-be she would be temporarily out of pocket. Her fingers began texting a message to her brother. "*Anno, I need your help...*" She explained the situation as best she could without revealing her mission, and finished with, "*No excuses. Remember, I own you! Love, your only sister. P.S., Message me after. I need to know the job is done.*"

Grabbing her jacket, Elsa slipped her phone, room key, and wallet into her coat pocket, zipping it shut, before pulling the coat on. She stepped out into the hall, finding Faust already waiting.

"Typical. Always waiting on a woman," he said, pushing off from the wall where he leaned. "Let's go. We can rent a car not far from here, I'm assured. The front desk may be hiding some information, but they are very forthcoming otherwise."

Faust led the way, and together, they left the hotel, walking five blocks east to the car rental agency. There, they checked out a silver Volga Siber with GPS navigation. After figuring out how to change the language to German, Faust instructed Elsa on how to enter the coordinates on the map. "Label them by number and mark that number on the map so we don't accidentally make two trips to the same spot. Some of these may be nothing of importance."

Elsa leaned up and began inputting the various coordinates. When she was finished, she picked the second one on the map and pushed the button to begin.

"*You have arrived at your destination,*" it said.

Faust raised an eyebrow. "Well, now we know Heinz rented a car." He looked back to the young woman at the counter inside. "Stay here. I'm going back in to see if he returned it."

Elsa watched as Faust exited the car and walked back inside. She could see his back as he stood at the customer counter through the plate glass window. White flakes swirled, obstructing the view. The snow had begun to fall in earnest, landing on the hood, and melting from the heat of the engine. A large truck pulled into the parking lot. It was towing a chunk of burnt metal. Elsa's eyebrows pulled together as she realized it was the charred remains of a car.

The tow truck parked near the office, drawing the attention of the two people inside. The rental attendant's eyes grew wide. Faust followed her line of sight, blinking. As the attendant ran outside screaming questions, a police cruiser pulled in behind the tow truck. Faust stepped out onto the curb, hands in his pockets. Elsa hit the button to lower the window, listening, but her Russian was wanting.

A short, wide man with a round face that reminded her of a pug stepped out from behind the wheel. He approached the young attendant, flashing his badge. After a heated exchange, the girl grew quiet. Her expression changed, turning from angry to fearful. The police pug pointed at her, his finger inches from her face. Her eyes dropped. "What a bully!" Elsa muttered, angered by the pug menacing the young woman. The officer redirected his short, fat finger to the office. The attendant immediately ran inside, behind the counter, where she typed rapidly on her computer keyboard. She then turned to grab the paper coming out of the printer behind her, and ran back outside, handing it over to the bullying cop.

Faust kept his head low and made his way to the car. He slid behind the wheel and put the window back up.

"What was that all about?" Elsa asked.

Faust looked straight ahead, seeming to take a moment before answering. His face was conspicuously blank. He cleared his throat. "Kreiss, there's a new development."

"Well, what is it?" Her anxiety increased.

Faust slowly turned his head towards her. "Elsa," he began, "I think Joseph may be dead."

Elsa froze. She blinked twice, and then, "What do you mean? Why do you say this?"

Faust gripped the wheel, his knuckles turning white. "That policeman there," he nodded in the bully's direction, "I heard what he was telling the attendant."

"Which was what? What, Herman!" Elsa felt fear rising.

"He told her that there's been a terrible accident, one of their customer's cars was found on the side of the road burnt to cinders. He ordered her to print out the customer information, and then delete the history. He threatened her. That's why she was moving so quickly."

"But how do you know it has anything to do with Joseph?" Elsa was angry, and on the verge of losing control of her emotions.

Faust closed his eyes. "Because, my dear, he told her that Martin Lintz would not be coming back to settle the insurance claim."

Elsa exhaled, suddenly unable to breathe. She felt like a boxer had just punched her straight in the gut.

"Elsa…" Faust reached over to take her hand.

She snatched it back. "No! No, he's not dead! He's not! We have to talk to that policeman." She began to unbuckle her seatbelt.

Faust reached again, grabbing her hands, and stopping her. "We can't! Kreiss, get hold of yourself! That's an order," he barked in his most authoritative voice.

Elsa ceased moving. She panted, trying to regain control of the anxiety overtaking her, and crushing her heart.

Faust's grip on her hands loosened, becoming gentler, more comforting. "Don't you see? He ordered that poor attendant to erase any history at all of a Martin Lintz renting a car there, under threat to her life." He looked at Elsa, waiting for her to put it all together.

"He did it. He's involved, and he did it." She turned her wide, green eyes on him.

"Yes. And if he is involved, if he's the one who did the deed, then he's connected to whomever Joseph was investigating, which means Heinz found something. Or someone."

"What do we do?"

"We follow him. We need to know for which precinct he works, first of all. Then, I'll try to get in touch with my contact again. If that fails, there's always Plan B."

"This is Plan B! What is it with you and Plan B? We need a Plan C." Elsa's voice broke.

"Yes, well…" he chewed the inside of his cheek for a moment, then pulled out his mobile, aiming it at the policeman who was heading back to his car. Faust clicked the camera shutter three times in quick succession. With just a few keystrokes, he sent the pictures off. "Plan C. Happy?" He put the car in gear, preparing to follow the police cruiser.

"That depends. What did you just do?"

"I sent the pictures to my favorite hacker. HackTwice will run them through facial recognition software. We should have some kind of answer soon. In the meantime, buckle your seatbelt. This just became ten times more dangerous."

Elsa snapped the belt into the clip, and then reached into her pocket, pulling out a small notepad and pen. She began writing down the license plate number on the police cruiser, and then scribbled notes, being as detailed as possible.

Faust glanced over. "What are you doing?"

"Getting it all down." She looked around, adding in landmarks as they passed.

"Picking up Mahler's habits?" He raised an eyebrow.

Hearing her name brought a lump to Elsa's throat. She swallowed hard. "She is thorough."

"That, she is."

"Herman, how will we ever tell her?" Elsa whispered the words, afraid to voice them at all.

"*We* won't." He continued looking forward. He just couldn't look Elsa in the eye, at the moment. It would break his heart. "*I* will. Before he left, Joseph gave me explicit instructions in the event..." He slowed down to turn right, following the police cruiser two vehicles back.

"...he didn't come back," she finished his sentence. Tears stung Elsa's eyes. She blinked them away. There would be time for that later. Right now, she needed to keep a cool head. And it wasn't easy with grief threatening to swamp her. She'd lost so much in her life. First, her parents, and then, almost losing her only brother. Now Heinz. It was too much to lose one loving father, but to have two torn from her felt like punishment. And she would have to tell Anno. It just wasn't fair. "Why the hell did he do this, Herman? Why come here after all this time?" Pain radiated in her tone.

Faust shook his head. "His damn sense of honor." Without thought, he reached over and took Elsa's hand. "Push it down, Kreiss. Push all of that pain and anger down. Save it and use it later. We don't know anything for sure. Not yet."

Mahler picked up the Minister and drove him to the Reichstag. From there, she settled herself in a chair outside of his office. Oppel was not yet in. He was running an errand for Obermeyer to set up a conference and wasn't expected for at least two hours. It gave her time to check up on the investigation. She called Niederlander in forensics.

"Anything yet on the Obermeyer emails?"

Jensen Niederlander chuckled. "Good morning to you, too, Detective."

"Don't be a smartass." She smiled into the phone. Jensen was practically still a kid, a computer genius recruited straight out of school after getting into more trouble than one teen should hacking into the school computers and failing the entire senior class as a prank. He was now the same age as her own son, Jan. Despite his sarcasm, Mahler was fond of him.

"You know I can't help it. Anyhow, I did find some interesting information."

"Spill it. I want to wrap this case up as soon as possible."

"I get it. Obermeyer is a dick. So, I traced the IP addresses on the emailed threats. Not surprisingly, they bounced around all over the globe. Most digital forensic examiners would've given up, but I pursued it and finally found the origin."

"Which is?"

"A business. Elite Worldwide. Its address says it's located in Switzerland, but the digital thumbprint was traced right back here in Berlin. The IP user is *roeliteww*. It's a laptop."

"What kind of business does it say it is?" Mahler flipped open her notebook and jotted down the information.

"It doesn't, at least, I'm not finding any description, but there are satellite offices mentioned, and the paperwork shows property ownership here as well, three locations." Jensen fired off the addresses one at a time, but it was the last one that grabbed Mahler's attention.

"Did that help?"

Mahler took a deep breath. "Yes. You did well, Jensen."

"Yeah, but then, I'm a genius." The sound of a bag rattling followed by the crunching sound of chips being devoured came over the line.

"You're a pain in my arse, is what you are." Mahler chuckled. "Anything new with the voice messages?"

"No. Could really be anyone. They're pretty generic. Whoever sent those went out of their way to mask the original tracks."

"Okay." Mahler stared at the IP user address. "Jensen, is there any way to see if this IP address has been used anywhere else?"

"You mean like on social media or something?" Mahler heard the tap-tap of fast typing. "Sure. Give me a little time to run it. If it was used to sign up for any accounts, I'll find them."

"Good. Let me know as soon as possible." She hung up.

The 'ro' in the address bothered her. That was Ritt Obermeyer's own initials. Here it was an election year, and the unpopular Minister of the Interior was suddenly getting weird, yet unsubstantiated threats. They were vague, and he seemed mostly unconcerned by them. Was it all a ploy to garner sympathy from the voting public? It wouldn't be the first time a politician used underhanded strategies to boost their polling points. Turn tragedy into sympathy, sympathy into votes. The bastard. If she found out this was the case, then she would personally see to it he was publicly humiliated, ending any hope whatsoever of re-election.

Mahler checked her texts. Still no message from Joseph. Now she was getting angry. He could at least take a moment out of his fun trip to answer her. She fired off another text.

"*Joseph, call me!*" She kept it short. When he called, she'd unload on him then. "If he's knocking back vodka and salted fish with tall, blonde, Swedish bimbos, I'm going to kill him myself," she muttered under her breath.

Chapter 17

"You! Heinz focused on the familiar face, shocked.

"Yes, me." Lana Karakova sat on the side of the bed.

"But, you are...how?" Heinz felt a tightness in his chest. He winced, taking short breaths.

"Be calm, Herr Lintz. I've bandaged your ribs, but the bump on your head worries me. You've been unconscious for almost nine hours." She leaned over him, placing a cool cloth over the bump in question. It sat, raised, on the left side of his head just behind his temple.

"I take it you don't really work in the tech field?" His sarcasm was strong.

"No more than you are truly Martin Lintz. But since I'm not privy to your given name, I will leave that for now. No, I do not work in tech. Actually, I'm a private investigator."

"A PI? I thought the Kremlin cornered the market on investigating its own people."

She smiled. "I sometimes take contracts from the government, but mostly, it is individual cases. I spent ten years on the police force before going into business for myself."

Heinz eyed the woman wondering how he could have been so duped. But he knew the answer. Her beauty, and his own smug self-confidence were the key. So sure was he of his own deception that he failed to realize the truth. Beautiful women didn't just walk up and invite themselves to dinner.

"I can see the wheels spinning in your head trying to figure it all out. It's really very simple. Being a PI for the last five years, I've developed quite a network both inside Mother Russia, and outside of her borders as well. Now and again, I'm commissioned to keep an eye on people who come into the country—agents, officers, and those who operate on the wrong side of the law. The LKA Direktor sent me your information, said you'd be here, searching for a missing girl. My job was to keep you in my sight, report back, make sure you didn't get yourself into trouble. Simple. Only, not so simple. You've managed to find trouble after all."

Heinz's nostrils flared. Herman! Herman had him followed, even after telling him he'd be on his own. He didn't know whether to be happy about it or royally pissed. He looked around the unfamiliar room. The beige walls were plain, save for a few landscape paintings. The faded curtains were open, letting in the morning light. There were no items on the dresser, and the room was bare except for the furniture.

"And where am I?"

She glanced around. "It's a safe house. I keep it for clients. Sometimes, it's necessary to hide them."

"How in the world did you get me here? How did you even find me?" It had only just dawned on Heinz that he was last in a ditch next to a burning rental car.

She laughed. "GPS tracking. It's on your mobile. I was given the coordinates by our mutual friend."

He raised an eyebrow. "HackTwice?"

"The one and only. As for how I got you here, well, it was no easy task. I had to haul your unconscious body to my vehicle and lift you inside." She rubbed her neck. "You're heavier than you appear."

Heinz watched the movement. "I'm sorry. Thank you."

"What, no flowery speeches? No owing me your life?" she joked.

"I'm not a flowery speeches man. But I do owe you one."

She straightened. "Yes, you do. And you can begin by telling me exactly why you're here, and how you ended up in that ditch."

"I don't think—"

"Listen, I'm a private investigator. Who better than me to help you find a missing girl? I think I've earned the right to know." Strength flashed in her eyes.

The sun coming in from the window lit them from within. Amber, not green as he had originally thought that night at the hotel restaurant. *Why am I even noticing her eyes*, he thought. Heinz contemplated her words. Finally, he began telling Lana Karakova about Marlessa Schubert. It was a long story, one in which he still held back disclosing his true identity, but by the end of it, she looked determined.

"Okay." She stood up.

"Okay?" Heinz watched her walk to the bedroom door.

"I'm going to make you some breakfast, and then, I'm going to leave you alone to rest. You need it."

"I don't have time to rest. And I need to get back to my hotel."

"That's not a good idea. They'll be there." She eyed him pointedly.

"The Bratva? I didn't get the impression that Brezhnev would bother."

"Not the Bratva, the police. That officer will be erasing all evidence of you from that room as soon as possible if he hasn't already. Plausible deniability. If it looks like you checked out, then your death does not need to be investigated. He's in the clear."

"I left my passport there."

"I can get you another, but it will take a few days."

"Son of a bitch!" Heinz pounded the mattress with his fist. "My money is there too."

"Then it's gone. He'll take it as a bonus."

Heinz looked at her. "How am I to get back without money?"

She smiled. "We'll think of something. For now, please take those pills there on the nightstand." She pointed at the two white pills sitting next to a glass of water. "They'll help you with the pain."

He reached over, careful not to move his torso too much, and popped the two pills into his mouth. A swig of water and they were down the hatch.

"I'll be back in a bit." She left, leaving Heinz with his thoughts.

He could hear her in the kitchen rattling dishes. He thought about all that had happened in the last eighteen hours or so. He'd messed up. The moment he'd decided to enter that house was his first mistake. Now he was injured and presumed dead by the Saint Petersburg police, and by the leader of the Russian mafia. If he persisted in trying to find answers, and was caught again, they would surely kill him, and make sure the job was done this time. Worse, now Lana Karakova was involved, pulled into this dangerous situation. He didn't like being responsible for her as well. What if the corrupt officer or the Bratva found out? They would kill her too.

And if he returned home too soon, with possibly cracked ribs and a banged-up face, Birgitta would know he had lied to her. He was a dead man either way.

Lana returned with a tray in her hands. She placed it over his lap.

"It's not much, just some hot cereal, toast, and coffee."

The aroma from the java perked his senses. He smiled. "It's fine, I'm sure. Thank you."

He picked up the mug and sipped the black brew. A slow sigh escaped him.

"Eat up. I want to make sure you're fed before I leave." She sat down on a chair by the wall.

"Where are you going?" Heinz picked up the spoon and lifted a bite of the hot cereal to his lips.

"To my office. I'm going to do some digging around on Brezhnev. I'll check out that address you gave me and see if there's any connection to our police. Your description of his lapdog should help."

"Bulldog. He looked like a bulldog." Heinz finished the cereal and munched the toast. He felt light and content. "I'd be happy to help you. I just need my clothes." He looked around, realizing for the first time that he was not wearing anything beneath the covers.

Lana stood and quickly took the tray from him. "I don't think so." She set it on the dresser.

Heinz felt lethargy invade his limbs. "What's wrong with me?" He tried lifting his hand but couldn't.

"It's just the medication taking effect." She tucked the covers up around him.

"You drugged me?" His speech slurred, and a scowl marred his forehead. "You said they were pain pills!"

She nodded, keeping her voice low and soothing. "They are, but also, they are sedatives. You need your rest. Now, just close your eyes. By the time you wake, I'll be back."

"Dammit, Lana. How can I possibly trust that you don't work for them too?" His eyes fluttered closed.

"Sssh. You will just have to have faith, Martin Lintz." She ran her fingertips over his scowl lines, smoothing them out. In just moments, he was sound asleep. "I know how hard it is to trust someone." She kissed her fingers and lightly touched his cheek. "Worry not."

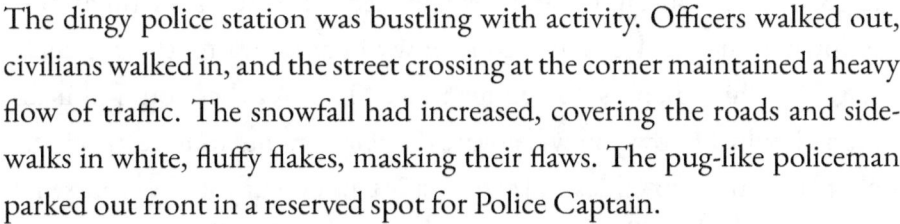

The dingy police station was bustling with activity. Officers walked out, civilians walked in, and the street crossing at the corner maintained a heavy flow of traffic. The snowfall had increased, covering the roads and sidewalks in white, fluffy flakes, masking their flaws. The pug-like policeman parked out front in a reserved spot for Police Captain.

"Of course." Faust pulled in across the street, watching from a safe distance.

"A Captain. A corrupt Captain. Great." Elsa wrote this down.

"Not just a low-ranking officer. He is in a senior position." Faust's phone pinged. He picked it up off the dash, looking at the text message. "Zakhar Sokolov," he said, reading. "Captain Zakhar Sokolov. Age fifty-three, married, three children. Earns a Captain's pay, but lives in a four-bedroom home far above his pay grade, and all his offspring attend private school out of the country." He held up the mobile, turning the screen toward Kreiss. "HackTwice is marvelous. I even have his banking records, account numbers, and oh, look at this," he scrolled down, "several official internal investigations against him..." Faust read quietly. "All dropped." He sighed.

"This hacker of yours operates far outside of the law." Elsa raised an eyebrow even as she made more notes.

"Sometimes, Kreiss, you have to tip-toe around the rules."

"That's dangerous thinking, Herman. Criminals think that way."

"Which is how you catch them. Think like a criminal. I know it seems counterintuitive, but you'll understand one day. The difference is the intention."

Elsa shook her head. "Still stinks. When you have to justify your actions, then maybe the actions are wrong."

Faust looked her dead in the eye. "Should we let Joseph just die out here if he isn't dead already or are you willing to bend a few laws to save him?"

That stopped her cold. She took a deep breath. "That's not fair, Herman—"

"No, it's not. Life isn't fair, Elsa. Criminals don't play fair. As one of the good guys, you can't always remain clean. You still sometimes must get down in the muck to fight. You know this already after the Ivchencko affair." He shifted and softened his tone. "The fact that you find it distasteful is why I know you will always do what's right. Your heart is in the right place, and your ethics will always stay true even if you find yourself in situations where you'll need to abandon them temporarily to save a life...or just survive."

He gave her much to think about. Elsa chewed her lip. "I'm sorry—"

"Don't be. You don't have to apologize to me for having a backbone. It's the one thing I truly appreciate about you."

She laughed. "Okay. So now what?"

"Now, we know who he is, where he lives, and that he's definitely on the take. We'll avoid Sokolov for now. Punch in the next destination. We need to follow the trail. Hopefully, we'll find our friend."

The third destination took them to a row of warehouses along the port. Faust drove through slowly, reading the numbers written in several languages along the way. The GPS informed them they'd arrived at their destination. Warehouse 214. "He found the warehouse. The time stamp that came with these coordinates showed he spent several hours here on his first two days."

"Staking it out, I imagine," Elsa offered.

"Yes. But what did he find?" Faust located a parking spot not far from the front of the warehouse. The doors were wide open. Inside, he could see crates stacked nearly to the roof, three vehicles, two medium-sized produce trucks, and one black limousine. "Odd. A limo in a warehouse?" He threw a questioning eyebrow at Elsa.

"Not what I'd expect."

"It's too bad we can't get a closer look." Faust was regretting not bringing along binoculars.

"I can." Elsa opened the car door, stepping out.

"Elsa, no! Get back in here right now!" Faust leaned over, trying to grab at her jacket.

She turned and leaned down. "Don't worry, Herman, I've been handling bad men for a long time. Just give me a few minutes."

"But you don't even speak the language! You'll give yourself away."

She smirked. "There's one universal language, Herr Direktor. No worries."

"Dammit!" Faust watched her flip her red hair back, and strut across the road, taking her time. She looked as if she were searching for something, or someone.

As she grew closer to the open doors of Warehouse 214, a tall, muscular man wearing a dark, fitted suit walked out. His build was intimidating, but the slow smile spreading across his lips revealed he wasn't the least bothered by the interruption.

Faust lowered his window, focusing in, trying to hear what was said.

"Hallo. Is this where Lukas works?" Elsa, smiling brightly, asked. She played up the confused and lost woman act. "I'm trying to find my boyfriend. Can you help me?"

The man's eyebrows came together. He shook his head. "What are you saying?" he asked, speaking Russian.

Faust heard him and muttered a prayer under his breath.

"Sprechen Sie Deutsch?" she asked.

"Nyet, sorry," he replied, laughing. Someone inside the warehouse spoke to him. The tall man looked over his shoulder, replying, "Just some bimbo. I can handle her."

Elsa, clueless, continued to smile at the man. He seemed to be falling under her spell, too, approaching slowly, grinning. Elsa mimicked smoking a cigarette, and the man reached inside his coat, pulling out a pack, and handing her one.

"Spasibo." She put the cigarette between her lips as the man flicked his lighter, igniting the tobacco.

"So, you know a little Russian after all, Da?" He chuckled, knowing she didn't understand him. "You're a beauty. What are you doing out here all alone?"

Elsa played along, replying in German, "You're eating this up, aren't you, big boy?" She fell back into her role. "Lukas. Have you seen Lukas?"

The man made a face, smiling. "Lukas? No, no, Konstantin." He laid his hand over his chest, looking down at her.

"Oh, you are Konstantin." Elsa touched his hand flirtatiously, then put her hand over her own chest saying, "Greta Zimmerman." She tilted her head.

The man's grin grew to salacious proportions as he took her hand, kissed it, and offered a somewhat formal bow. "Konstantin Petrovich at your service, Greta Zimmerman."

From a distance, Faust rolled his eyes at the display. "Oh, boy."

"And Lukas is?" he asked.

Elsa bit her lip in a comical display of feminine confusion as if she were trying to figure out how to communicate her next words. She glanced up, and then wrapped her arms around herself, puckering her lips in mock kisses, and said, "My boyfriend. Lukas is my boyfriend, you big, dumb, Russian!" She grinned.

Petrovich laughed. "Oh, I see." He took her hand again, pulling her in closer, and placing it on his chest. "You are wasting your time with this Lukas. What you need is a real man. Konstantin will take care of you, beauty."

Elsa turned coy, flicking the ashes off her cigarette. She took another drag, compliant. As the wordless flirtation played out, she glanced over his shoulder at the interior. There were three more men inside; one short, balding man standing near the first produce truck with a clipboard in his hands, one brawny bald man wearing a fitted suit similar to the one Konstantin wore, and finally, the third man who stood head and shoulders above them all. His dark gray suit complimented the salt and pepper of his short beard. He wore a black turtleneck sweater beneath completing the outfit. He was clearly the man in charge, and stood looking down at the short, balding man, speaking to him. The little man kept his head down, listening, and occasionally making a note.

Petrovich snaked an arm around Elsa's waist, pulling her in closer. She redirected her attention to the man, pushing at his chest.

"Hey, don't get too handsy, big boy." She kept the smile on her face, but her eyes said no.

Konstantin Petrovich did not like the look, and held tighter, causing Elsa to react in a way he was not expecting. She brought the high heel of her boot down on his instep. When he yelped, she brought her knee up straight into his groin. He released her immediately, clutching his jewels, bending over in pain. While this got her free, it also attracted unwanted attention.

The tall, bearded man turned, watching the commotion, and began walking toward them. When he cleared the door, Faust saw him and sucked in a breath.

Elsa backed away, chastising Petrovich. "That's not how you treat a lady, buster!"

The bearded man reached their side, and Elsa looked up, catching sight of herself in his blue eyes.

"My apologies for my employee's behavior," he said in perfect German.

Elsa blinked. She now curbed her words knowing this man, at least, understood her. "Yes, well, he got a little fresh."

The bearded man spoke softly in his native language to Petrovich who straightened up, and without looking at her again, walked back inside the warehouse.

"Can I help you?" The man offered.

Elsa dropped her cigarette, crushing it under her boot. "I was simply looking for my boyfriend, Lukas."

The man put his hands behind his back, casually standing, regarding her. "And where does your boyfriend work?"

"Here," she gestured around, "but I don't know which one." She straightened, showing not a flicker of fear, and maintaining eye contact.

"I see. Well, there is no Lukas working here. I'm sorry I cannot be of further assistance, Frau..." He let the inquiry trail off.

"Zimmerman. Greta Zimmerman."

"Frau Zimmerman," he bowed his head courteously, a half-smile on his lips.

Elsa noted the look in his eyes, part suspicion, part male appreciation. She relaxed her posture slightly, preparing to leave, when he reached out a hand, palm up. She hesitated, then placed her hand in his. He bent over, offering an old-world, gentlemanly kiss to her fingertips. It was what she would expect from a character in a novel like Anna Karenina or old Russian-themed movies like Doctor Zhivago. But that is not what struck her. It was the tattoos on his knuckles, and the one on the back of his hand once he released hers. This man was Bratva. This must be what Heinz discovered.

Carefully, she extracted herself. "Well, I've taken up enough of your time. Thank you for your help." She turned to leave.

"Aren't you going to check the other warehouses?" he asked.

She turned back. "No. I'll just call him. He'll find me. Thank you."

The man stood tall, smiling at her as she walked away. Elsa moved past the car where Faust was parked, continuing out of sight of Warehouse 214.

As soon as the bearded man returned inside, Faust started the engine, pulled out, and went in search of his protégé. He found her more than a half mile down the dock, waiting.

"Jesus, Kreiss! Are you trying to give me a heart attack? Do you know who that man is?"

She slipped into her seat, buckling the seatbelt. "I saw the tattoos. He's Bratva."

Faust blew out a breath. "You haven't been doing all your homework, Kreiss. He's not just Bratva, he's the head of the snake. He's the damned Butcher!"

"What?" She blinked. "That was Vladimir Brezhnev?"

"Yes, damn you!" Faust was angry. She'd put herself in danger unnecessarily. "Had you simply waited, we most likely would've seen him when they left."

"Holy scheisse!" she said, shaking her head. "Well, he doesn't know who I am. I used my alias, and he's not suspicious. You saw him. And it's entirely possible we wouldn't know who he was because he would've been inside the limo. Those windows are tinted. We would never have seen him. Now we know for certain." She turned to Faust. "You're welcome."

"Don't be a smartass, Kreiss!" Faust counted to ten in his head. He knew part of the reason why he was so angry was his worry for her safety. After he calmed down, he turned, looking at her. "Don't do that again, do you understand? That's an order." His bark had lost most of its bite.

Elsa had heard this tone before, from Heinz during the Ivchencko affair, and from her own father when she was but a girl. She knew what it meant. "I'm sorry, Herman. I won't do that again." She spoke softly.

He relaxed, clearly relieved. "So, that warehouse belongs to the Bratva. That makes sense considering the information in the ledger. And those trucks could easily carry anything."

"Like kidnapped girls," Elsa added.

"Yes, like kidnapped girls. You realize we'll have to follow them." He turned the car around, heading back in the direction of the warehouse. He pulled off to the side. "Can you do something with your hair? It's like a red flag waving."

Elsa raised an eyebrow. She lifted her arms and began plaiting her locks into a tight French braid. When she finished, she reached into her pocket and pulled out a knitted, black skull cap, pulling it on. "Better?"

"Much. Thank you." He put the car in drive, and they came within sight, waiting for one of the trucks to leave. They didn't need to wait long. Within half an hour, the limo pulled out, followed by the two produce trucks. One stayed with the limo, the other turned off in the opposite direction.

"Which one do we follow, Herman?"

Faust kept his eyes on the prize. "The one behind the limo. That's what Heinz would've done."

Elsa thought about it. "Agreed. That's exactly what Joseph would've done. Did do," she corrected herself, keeping her mentor in the present tense.

They shared a look, comforting each other in the silence. "Then let's go." Faust followed as soon as the one they now knew was Petrovich closed and locked the warehouse doors and climbed inside the limo.

Chapter 18

Lana Karakova stared at her computer screen, shocked. Hours passed as she followed one lead to the next. Port entry records had led nowhere. Whatever Warehouse 214 was used for secretly was a mystery, because publicly, it was listed as a Federation Army receptacle, and therefore, its import listings were classified. She'd then searched all records of Vladimir Brezhnev online, of which there were many. News articles in the thousands came up in her keyword search for Bratva, Brezhnev. Some were gossip, some actually touted his donations to various senior housing projects, children's educational programs, and even one to, of all things, a women's shelter. The rest covered his criminal activities, investigations, and most often, his acquittals, but there were a handful of articles that detailed his first few incarcerations beginning with the man's first murder, his own father, Kirill. This was the case that earned him his nickname, the one given to him by the press, and one he had wielded successfully as a weapon of fear since. The Butcher.

At age nineteen, Vladimir Brezhnev was convicted of the brutal murder of his father, noted drug runner, Kirill Brezhnev. Already, the young man had several arrests on record for possession with intent to sell, so when he was presented to the court as the defendant in a murder trial, his fate was already sealed. The crime described was cold-blooded. The nineteen-year-old viciously stabbed and dismembered his father while the man lay passed out drunk. His only explanation was that he was defending his mother, Olga, whom his father had beaten in a drunken rage, leaving the woman with a broken arm, two cracked ribs, and multiple contusions. He said his only regret was that he had not done the deed sooner.

In short order, he was sentenced to ten years in Matrosskaya Tishina in eastern Moscow, far from family and friends, but he made new friends inside. Unfortunately for Brezhnev, he also made enemies. Confinement was supposed to be rehabilitative, or so his judge stated at the hearing, but everyone in Russia knew that prisons were overcrowded, filled with child molesters, rapists, murderers, and worse. If one of them didn't kill you, the rampant diseases running amok like Tuberculosis would. If a person managed to survive incarceration, he or she always came out worse than they went in. The Butcher survived, and on the outside, thrived, rising in rank amongst his new family, the Brotherhood known as the Bratva.

As he grew older and took control, his status as a Godfather figure swelled. There were far less articles in recent years connecting him to crimes, and instead, more articles showcasing the man as some sort of upper-class citizen to be revered. Lana found this disconcerting. There were pictures of him escorting his mother to the opera, dining with upper echelon businessmen, and even several shots of him with high-ranking members of the Armed Forces of the Russian Federation and two members of the FSB. She sifted through the Yandex search engine. Brezhnev was standing in the background at a ceremony celebrating the military funding of a scientific medical research institute headed by Doctor Boris Nikilin, a leader in biomedical engineering. He was being congratulated by Colonel-general Dmitry Vasiliev.

"Now what is a mobster doing with a Colonel-general and a scientist?" she asked herself. She flipped through a few more images and backed up. One picture caught her eye. A pugnacious face standing out from the sea of faces. A face that, to her, reminded her of a pug, but to a man, would equate to more of a bulldog. She looked closely. Brezhnev was among five in the shot listed as magnanimous donors to the policeman's youth soccer league. The bulldog was listed as Captain Zakhar Sokolov, head of the league's precinct, and father to one of the boys who participated in the league each summer. "Aha!" She sat back, feeling a sense of triumph.

Switching to another computer, one set up specifically to hack into government sites, she typed a series of digits, then keyed in the Captain's name and hit ENTER. The screen changed, and then locked. She retyped the digital skeleton key and hit ENTER once again. A warning popped up, blinking red.

UNAUTHORIZED ACCESS. UNAUTHORIZED ACCESS. FSB ENCRYPTION HACK ATTEMPT. A new window opened, running a trace program. It wasn't hers.

"Shit!" Lana pulled the plug on the computer, unplugged the CPU, and carried it out to her car, stashing it in the trunk. She ran back in, shoved a CD in the backup drive of her mainframe, ran the program, transferring all data to the disc, and when she popped it out, keyed in a system-wide delete. Once she pushed ENTER, all data would be wiped, but this was an emergency. Somehow, Sokolov's personnel file had set off the alarm in the backdoor program she used to access police records. The FSB would be showing up on her doorstep, and she needed to make sure they found nothing incriminating. She hit ENTER. Her entire network of connections would be gone within thirty seconds.

She used that time to turn off the lights, lock up, and leave. She would need to swing by her home and pick up her son. It wasn't safe now. The FSB would use him to get to her, and she couldn't have that.

"Fuck!" She drove fast out of the parking lot, speeding down the road. "Dammit, Martin Lintz, you better be worth it!"

It was sundown by the time Lana Karakova arrived at the safe house. Heinz had already awakened and gone in search of something to eat. He found bread, cheese, and tomatoes, so made himself a sandwich. There was also coffee. He was standing at the stove heating the water in the old percolator when he heard a car approaching. Headlights filtered through the slats in the kitchen blinds. He stepped out of sight, eyeing the vehicle cautiously from the side. Two people emerged. One was a young man who appeared to be in his teens. He had short, dark blond hair that stood up in the back like alfalfa sprouts. He swung a backpack over his slumped shoulders. He looked angry. The other was Lana Karakova. The expression on her face alarmed him.

Heinz walked to the front door, opening it wide. "What's going on?"

"Who's this loser?" the young man asked, addressing Lana.

Heinz looked to her for translation. None was offered, but she responded back to the boy in her native language.

"This is Herr Lintz. I am helping him. Behave. I've already told you. This is no joke, Alexei!" To Heinz, she made introductions, switching to German. "Herr Lintz, this is my son, Alexei."

Heinz nodded at the boy who walked past him heading towards the kitchen. He watched the boy go, and then turned to Lana. "What's going on? Why would you bring him here?"

She stepped up onto the porch, looking him in the eye. "Something happened. We might need to leave. Step inside," she brushed past him in the narrow doorway, "and I'll explain."

Heinz felt her pass, like an electric current humming. He shook off the feeling and tried to ignore the lingering scent of her perfume. There were obviously more pressing matters than his traitorous libido. He swept his gaze around the darkening yard one last time, and then closed the door, locking it.

Inside the kitchen, Alexei sat at the table with earbuds in his ears, music cranked up loud on his Mp3 player. Lana glanced at the boy, and then tilted her head indicating the living room. She walked ahead, and Heinz followed.

"So what happened?" he asked as they entered the larger room.

Lana stopped, turning to face him. "I tripped an FSB alarm."

Heinz's eyes narrowed. "What, exactly, do you mean? Tripped how?"

She wrung her hands. "I spent the afternoon researching Brezhnev, and I finally found your bulldog. He's police Captain Zakhar Sokolov, by the way."

"A Captain? He's senior—"

"Yes, he's up there, which means he has quite a bit of pull. Still, his record shouldn't be classified. I've searched hundreds of police personnel records before today, and never once have I run into one that was FSB classified encrypted."

Heinz was still trying to put the pieces together. "Why would the FSB have this Captain's record classified? Do you think they're investigating him?"

Lana paced. "More than likely. It would be the only explanation. Still, triggering that alarm leads them to me, eventually. They'll backtrace. It will take a while. I have several routers in place that I go through, but with their manpower, they'll find me. Russians are very adept at hacking, Martin. I've wiped my main server and brought the CPU from my other computer with me. That's why I brought Alexei here. I have to protect him." She stopped pacing and sat on the dark brown sofa.

Heinz noted the anxiety in her amber eyes. His own anxiety inched ten notches higher. The last thing he wanted to do was put her in danger. That's why he wanted to leave earlier, to continue on his own. Now it was too late. She was involved, and he had no idea how to protect her from her own people. He walked across the short distance and sat down next to her, maintaining some personal space. He rubbed his hands together, thinking. "So now what? Is there any way they can trace you here?"

"This house is in a client's name, but I can't be certain they wouldn't pinpoint the connection."

"So, we might have at least twenty-four hours?" He looked at her.

"Perhaps." She turned. "I need to tell you what I found." Lana shared the information she'd uncovered highlighting Brezhnev's criminal career, his rise in the Bratva, and his newfound status as a community leader along with his connections to the military, the police, and more.

Heinz listened. His mind processed the information even as he silently wished Mahler were there with her calm, cool approach, and her manic notetaking. He'd come to rely upon her organized way of laying out the details. He was more of a 'go with your gut' kind of guy. It was one of the reasons they worked so well together. In that moment, he knew he missed her terribly. She was truly his other half.

"So, we know this Sokolov works for the Butcher. We know the FSB has their eye on Sokolov. We also now know that Brezhnev sometimes uses the police to handle his dirty work like he did with me. This means Sokolov knows full well what Brezhnev is up to inside that house, and he helps protect that bastard even as young girls are being kidnapped, raped, and sold. It's even possible this disgraceful fuck has seen Marlessa. And even if he doesn't have that information, he has access to it." Heinz's eyebrows came together as anger took over his features. "How any officer of the law, in any country, can condone such is beyond me. That piece of shit has children of his own from what you're telling me, and yet he lets this go on?" He looked at Lana.

"You have to remember; he may not be helping Brezhnev voluntarily. The man is a killer, Martin. He threatens and bullies to get what he wants. I'm willing to give him the benefit of the doubt."

"I'm not." He steepled his fingers, pressing them to his chin. As he sat, elbows leaning on his on knees, he grew more determined. "We need to have a word with Sokolov."

"No, Martin!" She sat forward.

"Then I need to. Do you have his address? Tell me you have it!" He begged with his eyes.

Lana saw the raw appeal in them, and wanted to resist, but his was a soul in torment, one that would not rest until he found his answers. She knew this, but it still pained her heart. "I don't have it."

Heinz's face fell.

Lana watched, and against her better judgement, said, "But I can get it." Her softly spoken words were filled with sadness.

Heinz felt the weight of them even as triumph filled him. He reached out, covering her hand with his. "Thank you."

Chapter 19

The day was nearly over. One more stop carting Obermeyer around, and Mahler would then be free for the evening to continue her investigation. She hadn't heard back from Jensen on the IP address yet, but she wanted to run more background checks on the sex workers she'd interviewed. She also wanted to look into the tax records of Madame Denouve's business. If even one item was off or missing, it would provide enough reasonable doubt to open an official investigation, which, considering the nature of the business, might also grease the wheels for a search and seizure warrant. If she could find a pathway forward in that direction, she'd be able to keep her promise to Salome, and any others who were being kept there against their will.

The last stop was a ribbon cutting ceremony at the new, improved park in Obermeyer's home district. Residents had come together to raise funds for landscaping, a jogging trail, a playground for the children, a dog run, and thirty newly planted trees. The local government had promised to match what was raised, and the community effort proved worth every penny. Mahler looked around as she followed Obermeyer from the car to the podium set up in front of the gleaming white, centrally located gazebo. A bright, red ribbon was tied around the structure, and ten other government and community leaders, including the mayor, stood ready as the press vied for position from which to take their pictures. A large crowd was assembled, filled with smiling faces. Some brought their kids; others had their pets in tow on leashes. A vendor was passing out balloons while an Oompah Band in full lederhosen played a lively polka. It was a festive occasion set to commence at exactly 4:00 p.m.

"Do you think you can stand back over there?" Obermeyer looked at Mahler, pointing over her shoulder to the far right of the podium. "I don't need police protection showing up in the press from this event. It makes people nervous," he said.

Or makes your voters nervous, she thought. "It's not an optimal position." Mahler scanned the area. The best spot would be to position herself on the gazebo. It would give her a vantage point, but to protect the budget-cutting bastard, she'd really need to be out in front of him. There was a sea of journalists between the community leaders and the crowd. The press moved about freely, but the crowd was being contained behind a green velvet rope. Several security guards were stationed on either end. The next best protective position was there. "I'll stand right there," she pointed to the center, "in front of the cordoned off area. That puts me in the best place to keep an eye out without being in front of any cameras." *I have no desire to be connected to you, either, Herr Minister.*

"I doubt we need to worry about anything here, Detective. These are my people. They love me." Obermeyer smirked, patting Mahler on the shoulder in a condescending manner.

She breathed slowly, fighting the urge to grab his hand and twist it painfully up behind his back. "I'll be over there." Mahler walked through the journalists, and positioned herself in front of the rope, dead center. Her short stature wouldn't cause any problems for those watching from behind.

Birgitta cast her eyes about. Five minutes to go. In front of her, a slender young man wearing a blue jacket and black baseball hat positioned himself, shouldering a DSLR camera. He was taller than her and blocked her view of the podium. Mahler shifted right, shooting an annoyed glare in his direction. It went unnoticed as the camera prevented him from seeing her.

The mayor stepped to the podium, lifting his hands to get the crowd's attention. The band ceased playing, and when everyone quieted down, he began to speak.

Mahler scanned the crowd, looking left and right. The mayor droned on about community pride, family, and German values. She shifted further right, turning slowly, skimming the sea of faces.

"And now, let me introduce to you one of our own, the Minister of the Interior, Ritt Obermeyer!" The mayor's voice was drowned out by the swelling applause from the crowd.

Obermeyer shook the mayor's hand and took his place at the podium. Mahler glanced in his direction, checking the order of those surrounding him. The Minister was smiling, waving, and taking it in. He raised both hands to gain control, preparing to speak. To her left, the tall, slim man with the heavy DSLR camera moved closer, pushing through two other photographers who were snapping pictures. He stopped, aiming the camera. Obermeyer began speaking. A shot rang out, slicing through the air, startling the birds from the trees. The Minister was thrown backwards, and the crowd panicked, erupting in screams.

Mahler pulled her gun, looking left and right, searching for the shooter. When the tall, slim man dropped the camera and ran, she thought nothing of it until she glanced down. The lens of the camera was smoking. She looked at the podium and saw that the mayor and community leaders were at Obermeyer's side.

"Call an ambulance!" she shouted. "I'm going after him!" Mahler took off, running after the man. She saw him ahead, slipping between the cars in the lot, quickly moving through and racing for the street. If he made it, she'd lose him. There were too many side roads he could duck down on the other side.

From the distance, the blaring of sirens grew louder. Help was on the way. Mahler made it through the parking lot, and was catching up when a bus drove past, cutting off her line of sight. She ricocheted left, running behind it. Throwing up her hand at the oncoming traffic, she dashed out into the road. On the other side, there was no sign of him. She looked left, and then ran right. The cross streets for the next three blocks were void of anyone even remotely similar. She'd lost him.

"Scheisse!" Mahler pulled out her cell phone and called dispatch. She gave them a detailed description, ordering an all-points bulletin. Several of the police cars broke off, making the rounds in the area, searching for the suspect. She returned to the scene.

As she arrived at the podium, the people helping Obermeyer parted, making room. He was lying on the ground, unconscious, a gunshot wound in his chest. The mayor was beside himself, but another gentleman with dark red hair seemed to be handling the situation. He'd pulled off the cloth covering the podium and used it to staunch the bleeding.

"What's the damage?" Mahler dropped down beside him.

The red-haired man looked up. "Not sure. The bullet hit the right side of his chest, which may be a good thing, but I have no idea how grave the injury is. Where the hell is the ambulance?" He cast his eyes around, clearly agitated.

Mahler laid her hand on top of his. "It's on its way. You're doing great. Keep the pressure on. You're a hero." She spoke calmly, attempting to soothe the man's frazzled nerves. "I'm Detective Mahler. What's your name?"

"Felix. Felix Kraus. I'm...I'm the parks and recreation architect. I designed the park," he said, babbling.

"It's beautiful. You did a great job." She patted his back with her free hand. To their right, what was left of the crowd of gawkers parted as the emergency medical response technicians arrived.

"What happened?" one of the emergency techs asked.

"Gunshot wound to the chest. A single bullet. Approximately twelve minutes ago. This man here applied pressure to help stop the bleeding. His name is Felix." She spoke in even spurts.

The paramedic, a man in his early forties with short, curly blond hair, pulled out several large gauze pads, and began lifting Felix's hand away, removing the podium cloth and replacing it with the pads with incredible speed born of experience. He spoke as he and his partner worked to stabilize the Minister.

"You've done a fine job, Felix. Thank you, we'll take over now."

Felix sat back, dazed. He appeared to be in shock. The paramedic exchanged a glance with Mahler who put her hands on Felix's shoulders, helping the man rise.

"Come with me. We'll need a statement from you. After all, you've just helped save the Minister, isn't that right?" She looked at the paramedic, who nodded.

"Precisely. A real hero."

Mahler walked Felix towards one of the police cruisers. She called the officer over and asked him to take Felix's statement. "And then get someone to check him over. The man is in shock."

The medical team ran an IV, put the Minister on a gurney, and before long, had him loaded into the ambulance. As they took off for the hospital, another arrived to handle those who'd been hurt in the stampede of bystanders. Someone was checking Felix's response to light and stimuli. The police took statements and pictures. A forensics team put police tape around the area. What was once a festive occasion to open a park only a short time ago had now become a crime scene. She dialed a number. The phone rang four times.

"Levitz."

"Captain, it's Mahler. There was an incident," she began.

"Is the Minister dead?" His tone was calm, but there was an edge to it.

"No, but that may change in the next hour."

He paused, surprised. "What happened?"

Mahler gave Levitz a detailed briefing.

"Get to the hospital, Mahler. Whoever did this will try again once they realize he isn't dead. Stay at his side. I'll put the fear of God into the forensics unit to lift any and all information off that camera-slash-gun. If there's a single fingerprint, we'll get it."

"Yes, sir." She hung up. After giving her statement to the first officer that arrived on scene, she left, heading straight for the hospital. It was going to be a long night.

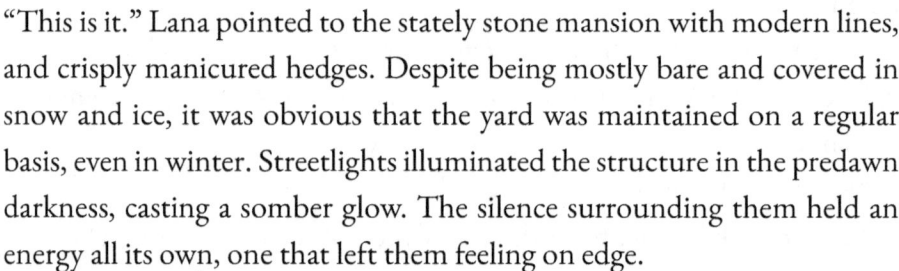

"This is it." Lana pointed to the stately stone mansion with modern lines, and crisply manicured hedges. Despite being mostly bare and covered in snow and ice, it was obvious that the yard was maintained on a regular basis, even in winter. Streetlights illuminated the structure in the predawn darkness, casting a somber glow. The silence surrounding them held an energy all its own, one that left them feeling on edge.

Heinz shook his head. "A police captain, and yet he lives like a celebrity by the grace of his own criminal compliance. Bastard! Has he no shame?"

Lana watched his face. "Not everyone possesses nobility of character. Not here. Corruption is widespread in the police units."

He glanced at her. "We have our own, as well, although I haven't seen it be as blatant as this."

"Or maybe you just haven't had cause to really see it."

"Maybe. I sure as hell hope it isn't this bad." Heinz pulled out the Sig Sauer Lana had lent him. It felt good to have one in hand. He checked the clip, and then slipped it back inside the body holster just inside his coat.

Lana sighed. "I don't suppose I can talk you out of this suicide mission?"

"It's the only way. We discussed this already."

She looked away. Heinz sat, patiently waiting. Finally, he said, "I'll be all right, Lana."

"Will you?" she asked, still looking out the driver's side window. "You thought so the last time and look what happened." She turned to face him; her amber eyes filled with worry. "And what about me and Alexei? The FSB will not be kind when they catch up to us, and they will catch up to us."

Heinz hated seeing the fear in her eyes when she spoke of her son. It wasn't fair, he knew, but he was limited in what he could do to help her. He reached out, taking her hand. "Lana, follow the plan. As soon as I get out of this car, go get Alexei, and leave that house. You have the fake passports for both of you. Drive to the Finnish border, and once you pass the checkpoint, keep going until you reach Sweden. Get to Stockholm, and then contact HackTwice. Tell her I sent you.

"I still can't believe she's a she." She shook her head. "But how will you get out, Martin? You have no papers." She gripped his hand, pain in her eyes.

Heinz was not unmoved, but he pulled back. "Don't worry. I'll find my way."

"But there was no time to get your passport made. You won't make it without one!"

"Lana!" He spoke over her rising anxiety. "I will get out. Don't think any more about it. I have the cell phone, HackTwice's number, the money you lent me, and the gun. I will get in, get my answers, and then I'll be right behind you. Now, go." He pulled back quickly, climbing out of the car.

Lana stared at him; her eyes moist with unshed tears. Heinz stood beside the car, waiting. When she hesitated, he reached out, tapped the roof, and turned, walking away. He knew it was the only way she'd leave. The early morning light was just breaking across the horizon, turning the black skies a dull gray as the cloud cover hung, threatening more snow.

As he walked away, he heard her shift the car into gear and drive off. Each step he took towards Sokolov's house became louder in his ears. His plan was simple. Break into Sokolov's garage and wait for the man to come out. The element of surprise was on his side, but he didn't have much time.

Heinz bent low, keeping to the line of shrubbery, moving quickly. The crunching of snow beneath his soles broke the silence. He made it to the side of the house near the garage. Slipping around back, he sought a door. He found one, but the double locks made breaking in impossible. He couldn't very well shoot holes in them. That would defeat the purpose, and he had no silencer for his gun. There was a small window to the left of the door. Just enough room for him to enter if he could manage to open it. He looked around, making sure he was still alone. All was quiet.

He began feeling around the edges. It was the type of window that opened out, similar to the kind commonly found on houses back home in Germany. This one was old and cracked. The break began at the top and ran in a zig-zag pattern diagonally to the opposite side on the bottom. A chip in the crack proved that an opening did exist. Heinz looked on the ground around him. He needed something slim and strong to slip into the crack. If he could pry it out, the glass would break and fall to the soft, snow-covered ground outside. Then, he could reach in and flip the latch.

He scuffed the toe of his shoe into the snow, clearing it away. After a moment, he noticed a glint by a flower bed two feet over, bordering the far side of the terrace. Heinz dropped down and cleared the dead leaves and snow away with his hands. Luck was on his side. It was a gardening trowel left out and forgotten.

"That will work." He grabbed it, rising, and headed back to the window. The sky was lighter now. He needed to move fast.

He slid the tip of the trowel into the chip in the crack and carefully pried out the glass. The sound of it cracking was like a whip. A chunk flew out, bouncing off his coat and hitting the ground, breaking. But at least the ground muffled that sound. He had just enough room to put his hand through. Finding the latch, he lifted it and pulled the window open. Within moments, he was up, over, and inside the cold garage. Now all he needed to do was wait.

He didn't have to wait long.

No sooner had Heinz climbed into the backseat of the tan colored luxury model Lada Priora parked inside the icy stone and concrete garage when the side door leading from the interior of the house opened. Sokolov walked down three steps, and, switching his coffee thermos to his left hand, unlocked the vehicle. He fell into the driver's seat and set his thermos into the cup holder. Whistling to himself, he cranked the ignition and reached up to hit the button to open the garage door. The whistle died on his lips as cold steel jammed against his temple with an ominous click.

"We have some unfinished business, you and I." Hienz leaned over the seat, close enough to see the surprise and fear enter Sokolov's eyes.

"You survived." The police captain's eyes shifted right. "I wondered. We did not find a body. Still, I'd hoped you'd merely crawled out into the open somewhere and expired from exposure."

"Sorry to dash all your hope, asshole."

"How did you find me? Who's helping you?" Sokolov's left hand lowered.

Heinz wrapped his left arm around the man's thick neck and pulled backwards, cutting off his air as he tapped Sokolov's head painfully with the Sig's barrel. "Keep your hands where I can see them, Captain. How I found you is not important. What is important is that you answer my questions."

Both hands lifted, resting on the steering wheel. "And if I don't?"

An evil smirk curled Heinz's lip. "If you don't, I'll put a bullet in your head where you sit, and no one will be the wiser."

"My people will find you, Herr Lintz." Sokolov threatened.

A chuckle escaped Heinz. "Herr Lintz does not exist...or haven't you figured that out yet? And here I thought being a police captain meant you were a smart man. No?" The man clamped his mouth shut. Heinz continued. "Yes, I know all about you, your connection to Brezhnev, your corruption. You're a disgrace to law enforcement, Sokolov. You're a paid thug for an evil bastard who kidnaps children and traffics them to perverts, rapists and criminals!"

Heinz's voice rose heatedly with every word. Sokolov sputtered, "You don't understand. It's not what I wanted—"

"Shut up! You sold out, you pig! I don't want to hear your excuses. You are the law! It's your job to fight criminals, not work for them. You are weak, and your weakness allows little girls to be taken from their homes and raped over and over again until they are no longer young and beautiful.

They are strung out on drugs, beaten, molested, gang-banged! And then they are killed. You have children of your own, Zakhar Sokolov. Is even one of them a daughter?" Heinz drilled the man mercilessly.

"Yes," he choked out. "I have a daughter, damn you! Why do you think I complied? That bastard threatened my Cristina. When I tried refusing, he took her! I couldn't find her for days."

A look of surprise crossed Heinz's face. Still, he was skeptical. "Are you lying to me?"

"No! I couldn't find her. During that time, Brezhnev told me I had seventy-two hours to decide if her life was worth my defiance. I did it for her. Have been doing it since. He holds the cards. Has all the connections. The police cannot touch him anymore."

"If that's true, why does he still need you?"

Sokolov shrugged. "He still needs someone else to do his dirty work for him now and again. Someone with legitimacy."

"Are you fucking kidding me? Legitimacy, ha!" Heinz pushed the gun into the man's temple. "And what about your daughter? What happened to her? How does Brezhnev still have a hold over you?"

Sokolov slumped. "He still has her, sort of." The defeat in the man's voice was genuine. "He sent my Cristina to boarding school in Vienna. He pays for her education. She has no idea, of course, and explaining this to her mother," he sighed, "she knows. My wife, Daka, she knows, but not completely."

Heinz had not expected any of this. He felt some of the wind go out of his sails, but his resolve bolstered. Sokolov was still dangerous to him. The man was beholden to the Butcher and would do anything to clean up the mess Heinz being alive now presented. Sokolov would kill him to protect his daughter's life. The captain was a cornered animal, and cornered animals were deadly.

"I understand, but you must understand this. I came here for a reason, to find a missing girl."

"Your daughter. I know, I was told." Their eyes met in the rearview mirror.

Heinz did not feel it necessary to divest the white lie. As far as he was concerned, Marlessa was part of his family, his own Ingrid's best friend, and that made her his responsibility. "Then you know what I am going to ask. Man to man, Sokolov, father to father."

"What is her name?"

"Marlessa Schubert."

"And how long ago?"

"Eight years."

The captain's eyes turned sympathetic. "Herr Lintz, whatever your name is, I'm terribly sorry, but," the tone of his voice lowered, softening, "they never last that long." He gave an almost imperceptible shake of his head.

"But you must know something! Anything! Where was she taken to? For how long? When did she..." Raw emotion colored Heinz's words.

"What did she look like?"

"Blonde hair, long blonde hair, and blue eyes. Five and a half feet tall, petite. She had a birth mark on her right shoulder. It was shaped like a heart."

Sokolov's eyes widened. "A birthmark, you say?"

Heinz noticed. "Yes, why? She's alive? Where?"

"No, no. I have not seen her, but..."

"But what? Spit it out, or so help me!"

"There's a child, one of the whores that works in the house, Valentina, she takes care of a little girl. She's three. I always thought it strange, what with all that goes on in that house."

"A child? Inside that house?" Heinz's mind began running amok. "What about this child?"

"The birthmark. She has a birthmark like you described, it's on her right shoulder. I've seen it, during the summer when she was running around in a sundress. Brezhnev picked her up and showed her off. He said, look at my little Cupid. She wears her heart on her sleeve all the time. He called her Nikola."

Heinz forgot to breathe. *A child!* "What happened to her mother?"

"I guess she died. I've never met the mother, only Valentina takes care of her."

"What does she look like?"

"She has curly blonde hair, and blue eyes, I think."

It was a lot to process. It was also more than Heinz expected to learn. He'd hoped to discover, by some miracle, that Marlessa was still alive, but if nothing else, he hoped to get some closure even if he discovered she'd died, but a child was nowhere in his thinking. A child was a miracle in itself, and if it was her child, he had to save her.

"Sokolov, you're going to help me."

"I don't think I can," the man began.

"Of course you can."

"No, you don't understand. It's too late." He cast his eyes in the rearview mirror.

"What are you doing? What are you talking about?" Heinz looked in the mirror and then turned to stare out the back window through the open garage door.

In the driveway sat two black sedans. The passenger doors of the closest one were open. Standing on either side of the Lada Priora's back doors, with guns pointed at his head, were two large men, each with telling tattoos on their hands and faces.

"They keep me under surveillance. You were doomed the moment you got into this car. I am sorry, Herr Lintz. Much like your name, soon, you will no longer exist." Sokolov reached up, lifting Heinz's arm from around his neck. He stepped out of the car, moving out of the way of the Butcher's men.

Chapter 20

The phone on the dash pinged. Faust picked it up, reading the text.

"It's his house."

Elsa looked at him. They'd been sitting outside of this house all night, watching and waiting. She was cold, tired, and needed to pee. When they'd arrived yesterday evening, the limo pulled through a wrought iron gate, and up to a large manor where the occupants exited, entering through the grand double doors. The second produce truck that followed them drove around to the back, out of sight. Faust pulled over down the block, just within sight. After that, he fired off a series of texts to HackTwice to investigate who owned the home listed at these coordinates, not that they didn't already have an inkling. They were hoping for a little more information than just confirmation the home belonged to the Butcher.

"Is that all?" Elsa chewed a handful of peanuts.

"No, actually." He shifted in his seat. "The address is also listed as a satellite office for the FSB. That's very interesting."

"So, he has connections within the Kremlin itself?" Elsa's eyes darted around the vacant lot near where they were parked. Several bushes lined one side, and a copse of thick pine trees created a wall of cover between the car and the bushes. "Herman, if I don't relieve my bladder, I'm going to piss all over the seat." She looked back toward the house. "No one is up and about. I won't be but a minute."

Faust nodded. "Be quick. I need to as well, but I can just go behind the car. No one cares about an old man walking."

"I'd argue that, but it will have to wait." Elsa slipped out of the car quietly, and dashed across the lot, gaining the trees. She made her way from there ducking under branches laden with thick snow. The cold did not help. As she arrived at the wall of bushes, she picked out an opening. As she unbuttoned and unzipped her jeans, she heard the car door open and close softly. Herman would do his business, and she would manage hers. She'd barely squatted down before she let loose. The relief was intense. Still, it was freezing, and she was afraid if she didn't hurry, she'd have icicles hanging off her ass.

She stood, pulling up her pants, and was just buttoning them when a click alerted her she wasn't alone.

"Turn around slowly, Greta Zimmerman."

Elsa heard the unfamiliar Russian words but recognized her faux name. She raised her hands, moving with caution. She came face to face with the business end of a Lugar, pointed at her by Konstantin Petrovich.

She blinked, then smiled. "Well, hallo!" She played dumb.

"Quiet!" He did not take the bait.

Elsa muttered to herself. "I guess you're still sore over my knee slamming into your balls."

Neither understood the other, but the intent was clear. She'd been caught. Her mind raced, thinking of Faust.

"March!" He indicated she should step forward and walk ahead of him. When she did, he moved in close behind her, shoving the gun into her back.

At the street, she saw the other thug Petrovich had been with at the warehouse, the slightly shorter one with a bald head. The man was bursting with muscles, and he had Herman bent over the boot of the car with his arm shoved up behind his back. Faust looked pained, but his eyes contained resolve. He was trying to remain calm for her, she knew.

When they drew near, Faust said, "They've made us, as you can see."

"I figured that out, thanks. Are you okay?"

"Shut up!" The bald one barked the order.

"They want us to be quiet," Faust translated.

"Walk. This way!" Petrovich pushed Elsa forward. The other thug pulled Faust upright and followed.

"They're taking us to him," Faust whispered.

"What do we do, Herman?" Elsa asked, unafraid to speak despite her worry.

"For now, we have no choice. Don't worry. I'm working on Plan B."

Elsa bit her lip. If this new Plan B was anything like the others, they were in for far more trouble.

Petrovich kept the gun at her back as Elsa navigated the icy street. At the gate, the guard let them in. He barely glanced their way, keeping his eyes averted as he returned to the small enclosure where he kept watch over the entryway. It was a long walk up the icy driveway.

Elsa noted they were taken in through a side door and guided down a narrow hallway before being pushed roughly inside a luxuriously appointed office. The walls were covered in cherrywood. Crown molding topped those walls, and plush crimson carpeting softened the floor. There was a large, masculine desk of dark red oak in front of the wide, multi-paned window. Sitting behind that desk was a man wearing a bronze-colored silk robe with gold quilted lapels. Even in pajamas, the Butcher still projected an aura of menace mixed with the casual elegance of the rich and powerful. He looked up from the newspaper he was reading, a barely perceptible look of surprise flashing in his eyes. It was masked quickly. His lips spread into a thin smile.

"Please have a seat." He spoke in near-perfect German and pointed to the two tufted leather chairs facing the desk.

Petrovich nudged Elsa, who moved forward, taking a seat. Faust was also pushed into motion, but he waited until she was seated before taking his own.

"Frau Zimmerman, just what are you doing here, and so early in the morning?" Brezhnev's deceptively soft tone belied the danger lurking in his cold, blue eyes.

Elsa began to answer when Faust spoke up. "It's my fault. We got a little lost..."

Blue eyes zeroed in on Faust. "I don't believe I asked you." He turned back to Elsa. "Are you now going to tell me this is the 'boyfriend' you were looking for at the dock?"

"No, of course not. This is my father." She kept her answer simple, sticking to their aliases.

"I see." Brezhnev sat back, staring steadily at the red-haired woman. "And you and your father just happened to get yourselves *lost* across the street from my home." It was a statement, not a question, so she didn't answer. "How convenient." Brezhnev stood, coming around to the side of the desk. He held his hand out to her. "Come with me. There's something I think you should see. I believe you may be able to shed some light on it for me."

"She goes nowhere without me!" Faust rose, but the muscular goon pushed him back down into the chair.

"Calm yourself, old man." Brezhnev sent a look to his henchman. "If he moves, shoot him."

Elsa cringed. She kept her face neutral, but there was real fear in her eyes now when she glanced at Faust. He offered her a reassuring nod.

"Come, my dear." Brezhnev waited for Elsa to place her hand in his.

Tamping down her own trepidation, she complied. He stepped forward on gold-slippered feet. Even his pajama bottoms were bronze silk. He spared no expense, it seemed.

"Where are we going?" Elsa dared ask.

They walked through the narrow hallway to a much larger hall of marble flooring with gold wainscoting. Above that, the walls were covered in rich damask wallpaper and decorated with priceless works of art. She wondered briefly why criminals were so devoted to art even as they were committed to killing in cold blood.

"So much excitement this morning. I haven't even had time to dress. At least, in your case, it was a pleasant surprise. A beautiful woman is never unwelcome."

She chose not to respond to his statement, especially since he hadn't answered her question. They continued through the house, entering a wing off to the east. It was colder in this section and appeared as if it was not used often. He led her up a staircase, two flights. When they reached the third-floor landing, they proceeded down the hall to a room at the far end. It was there, he gave a perfunctory knock before entering. He held her hand in a gentlemanly fashion the entire time.

"This is what I'd like your input on...Officer Elsa Kreiss."

The words hung on the air, exploding like a grenade. Elsa stopped breathing even as her eyes took in the man tied to the bed, one eye swollen shut, and lip busted open, bleeding.

"How?" was all she could say, still trying to control her inner turmoil.

Brezhnev snorted. "How, indeed. I found you once before, as you may remember. I have an entire file on you, pictures included. Did you think I would not know who you are? Now, tell me, truthfully please, what you are doing here. I can see you know him. And don't try telling me he is your boyfriend or your father."

Heinz looked up at Elsa through one eye, surprise evident on his face. He shook his head "no", but she turned away, ignoring his plea.

Brezhnev crossed his arms over his chest, waiting. "He is my mentor, Kommissar Joseph Heinz. And the man downstairs is my superior, Direktor Herman Faust of the LKA. We came here to find Joseph, to bring him home."

"Tell me why he is here?" He pointed at Heinz.

"To find out what happened to Marlessa Schubert. She was his daughter's dearest friend, and she disappeared eight years ago. We found a ledger on the Vledelets. Yuri Ivchencko kept precise records, and her name was in that book. He is the one who took her and brought her to your warehouse." Elsa's voice became sharper as she spoke, and her last words were accusatory. Her green eyes shot sparks at Brezhnev.

His face went rigid. "Careful,' he said, his voice low.

"I don't know why you're acting offended. You're the Bratva's leader. Your organization traffics young women and girls. Why deny it now when we both know it is the truth!"

"Elsa!" Heinz spoke, trying to stop her from getting them killed.

"Nein! I will not hold my tongue. We're here. He knows. The jig, as they say, is up. You want answers? I want answers." She refocused on Brezhnev. "Tell us, Butcher, what did you do to that poor young girl? Where is she now?"

The man reached out, grabbing her hand painfully. He yanked her out of the room.

Heinz struggled with his bonds, shouting, "Elsa! Don't you hurt her, you bastard! I'll kill you!"

She could still hear Heinz raging as she was pulled back down the hall, and down one flight of stairs.

On the second floor, they turned left, heading for a set of double doors. He threw the doors open and pushed her inside. It was a spacious suite. A tall, blonde woman standing at a mirror brushing her hair swung around, startled. Upon seeing Brezhnev, she immediately lowered her eyes, staring at the floor.

"Gospodin, how may I serve you?"

"Valentina, this is Officer Elsa Kreiss." His voice held an edge of anger. "Show her what is left of Marlessa."

What is left of her? Elsa felt horror rise inside of her. She waited, fearing what she was about to see.

The woman called Valentina stiffened. She set her brush down on the vanity with a shaky hand and walked slowly toward a partially closed door located in the corner of her own room. She slipped inside. Elsa waited in silence, tension vibrating all around her.

The blonde woman reappeared, carrying something in her arms. As she moved closer, Elsa could see it was a child. She had curly blonde hair and was sound asleep.

Elsa stood stock still, shocked. "But this is a child." She looked at Brezhnev.

He gave her a dark look. "Yes. Her child."

"And where is Marlessa?"

"This is all that is left."

"Are you saying she is dead?" Elsa pressed for confirmation.

"As I said, this is all that is left. Marlessa Schubert is dead."

Elsa turned back to the sleeping child. Reaching out, she touched a curl. "What's her name?"

Valentina answered, "Nikola."

"And just what the hell are you going to do with a child in a place like this? Are you selling her too?" Anger returned as Elsa's temper flared.

"You are pushing my limits, Elsa Kreiss." He stepped closer, towering over her. "You would be wise to hold your tongue from here on out."

Once again, he grabbed her hand, and yanked her out of the room, practically dragging her back down to the office. The relief on Faust's face was telling.

"Petrovich, watch over our guests." He turned to leave.

"Where are you going?" Elsa asked.

Brezhnev paused, looking over his shoulder. "To get dressed, and to decide what I am going to do with you." He left.

Elsa's stomach flip-flopped. The muscular goon took up post outside of the office while Petrovich stood just inside the door, hands crossed in front of his body as he stood at attention, watching them.

"What happened?" Faust asked, aware that Petrovich did not understand.

"Joseph is alive, Herman." She felt a wave of emotion rise threatening to spill out of her eyes and down her cheeks, but swallowed it down, taking a deep breath.

"What? How do you know?"

"He's upstairs, on the third floor of the east wing. He's hurt. It looks like they beat him badly, but he's alive."

Faust blew out a breath. "Thank God."

"But that's not the worst of it. Brezhnev knows who we are." She paused. "Well, he knew who I was all along, so he extrapolated from that. He knows all of our identities."

"Dammit! Elsa, this is not good." He rubbed his hands together.

"There's still more." Her voice lowered.

"What? How could there be more?"

"The Schubert girl..." she began.

"Don't tell me she's alive in this house too? God, Kreiss, it has been eight years!" He sounded incredulous.

"No," she said, "no, she's not alive. I don't know the details of her death, but Herman, she had a child. That child is upstairs now. She can't be more than three years old." Her voice caught.

"Jesus, he's not..." he let the question hang.

"I don't think so. He became very angry when I asked."

Faust covered his face with his hands. "It's a wonder he didn't kill you on the spot." He looked up. "Elsa, you must be more careful. He's not a man you can control. He's very dangerous."

"I'm aware of that. I just," she bit her lip, "it's a child, Herman. A toddler. If he was selling her out, I wouldn't hesitate to tear his testicles off and feed them to him."

"I understand, but I need you to keep a cool head. We have to think of a way out of this mess or else we're all doomed."

A full half hour passed before Brezhnev returned. His silken pajamas were replaced with a tailored Italian suit in slate gray accented by a black cashmere turtleneck sweater beneath, and a pair of polished Prada Spazzolato Captoe Oxfords. There wasn't a hair out of place.

The Butcher walked behind his desk and sat down. He gestured to a henchman waiting in the hall. "Bring them in," he ordered.

The man left. Elsa kept her hands in her lap, staring Brezhnev down despite her fear.

"So, what have you decided to do with us?" Boldly, she pinned him with her green eyes.

A smile spread across his lips. "You are quite spirited, my dear. Truly, you live up to the reputation of redheads. A real firebrand." His smile disappeared. "But you've caused me a problem, and for that, I must decide upon a solution." He turned to Faust. "Her, I understand. She's a woman, and as such, is ruled by her emotions. It is expected that one such would have the heart of a lion when it comes to the young women who end up being employed in homes like my own," Elsa began to protest his reference to employment, but he held his hand up to stop her, continuing speaking to Faust, "but as for you, a high-ranking Direktor of the Landeskriminalamt, no less, and Kommissar Heinz, I am baffled. Surely your being here is not on the order of the German State?" He raised his eyebrow.

When Faust remained silent, merely offering a steely stare, Brezhnev nodded. "I thought not. This leaves me with somewhat of a dilemma. You see, on one hand, I can easily kill you all since I'm sure now you've not told anyone of your true whereabouts or mission." He paused, reflective. "On the other hand, I've learned only this morning that your being here has caught the attention of the FSB, and while I do have some influence in that direction, a dead German State LKA Direktor, a KriminalKommissar, and," he looked at Elsa, "a lovely new Schutzpolizei..."

"Landespolizei," Elsa corrected.

Brezhnev raised an eyebrow. "Oh? Congratulations on your promotion. The Ivchencko arrests?" he inquired.

Elsa nodded.

"You obviously made an impression. I know I, myself, was impressed with your intelligence in coming to the conclusion that turning Yuri over to me was in everyone's best interest." He cleared his throat even as Faust's face registered the absurdity of the conversation happening between the head of the Russian mafia casually considering killing them, and his prisoners, as it were.

"You were saying?" Faust prompted

"Yes, as I was saying, the three of you are a problem. You see, you've compromised my police contact. Sokolov has been," he paused, "valuable to me. Now, since someone has been digging around in his personnel file, the FSB is alerted."

"I don't understand," said Elsa, "if the FSB is working with you, why do they care about your connection to Sokolov? Everyone is already compromised in this web of corruption. Why worry over who looks into Sokolov's file?"

Brezhnev leaned back, crossing his ankle over his knee as he regarded Elsa. "It's etiquette. Like the wife of a rich man knowing he is having an affair with the help. It's politely ignored...until such time as it finds its way out into the open. That is the point at which it becomes a problem. My affairs are now out into the open. My inside informant at the Kremlin tells me Sokolov kept an encrypted file on me detailing every single job he performed at my request. A sort of death insurance policy for his family's honor. Your Kommissar's supposed roadside death included." He pinned Elsa with a glare. "Quite inconvenient. This creates a public relations nightmare for my business dealings with the FSB and, in particular, Colonel-general Vasiliev." Brezhnev sighed. "He is a man of particular tastes. Sokolov has kept a file on him, too, this one at my request, for a year. This is my own insurance policy, but now that your meddling has outed him, Sokolov has become a liability to both the FSB, and to me."

Footsteps behind them alerted Elsa and Faust. They both turned. The henchman returned pushing a stumbling Heinz, and the police captain, Sokolov, into the office. Heinz collapsed just short of Elsa's chair. She reached out, helping him sit upright next to her.

"See? Women and their soft hearts." Brezhnev stood. "Now, I have to fix this mess before any more damage is done."

Heinz concentrated on his breathing, holding his left side. He was sure a rib or two was cracked. Faust reached out a hand to grip his shoulder. Elsa kept her own hand on the back of his head, offering as much comfort as she could under the circumstances. It did nothing to ease his guilt in knowing it was his fault they were now embroiled in his mess, and that they may all be dead within the hour.

"Why?" he wheezed out.

"Why what?" Faust asked.

Heinz cast his eyes sideways at his friend. "Why did you come here? And for God's sake, Herman, why did you bring Elsa?"

"Hey! I'm right here," she protested. "You can address me directly." Irritation flashed in her eyes.

Faust sighed. "Did you think I'd really let you waltz into the Russian Federation all by yourself without keeping tabs on you?"

"You said once I was here, I would be on my own!" Heinz winced, pained by his growing anger and frustration.

"I lied. Get over it," Faust said. "You're my oldest friend, Joseph. There was no way I wouldn't come for you when my contact failed to check in. As for why I brought Kreiss," he glanced at her, "she nagged me."

Elsa half choked on a combination of outrage and indignation. Now really wasn't the time, she knew, for any of this.

"What happened to my contact, by the way," Faust whispered.

Heinz inhaled slowly, trying to ease the agony the action caused. He kept his voice low, noting that the Butcher was speaking to his subordinates behind them. "She was compromised, but she should be crossing the Finnish border as we speak. She'll be okay."

Faust felt some relief. Ms. Karakova did not deserve to be caught up in this dangerous situation. The private investigator came highly recommended through HackTwice who'd run a most thorough background check on her. All Faust needed at the time was someone who could identify Joseph, keep an eye on his whereabouts, and report daily that his friend was still alive. He knew the woman had previously been in law enforcement, so she had a particular ethical code that Faust could relate to, and he knew she had a son. Now, Karakova and her son were running for their lives, away from the country of their birth, and would not be able to return home again. For that, he felt guilty. "I'm glad to hear she will be safe."

"Herman, you need to get Elsa out of here. I'll make a bargain with Brezhnev—"

"You will do no such thing! We are not leaving you," Elsa whispered.

Heinz looked at her. He reached out, taking her hand. "Listen to me. You must live. Anno still needs you, and you have Lukas."

"And you have Birgitta," she said. "What about her? And what about the child?"

Caught off guard, Heinz's eyes popped wide. "Child? What child?"

"The one upstairs." Elsa pointed a finger at the ceiling.

The look on his face registered shock. "She's here? In this house right now?"

"You knew?" Elsa raised a delicate brow.

"Not until this morning. Sokolov spilled the beans. You've seen her?"

Elsa bit her lip. "Yes, after I saw you in the room. Someone called Valentina is caring for her, but this is no place for a child, Joseph. We have to get her out of here. We just need a plan." She looked at Faust, her eyes pleading with him to think of something. The man shrugged, appearing stumped.

Breshnev returned his attention to them. Petrovich grabbed Sokolov by the arm and began pulling him out of the room. Having felt relatively secure in his position as the Bratva's police informant thus far, the change in treatment surprised Sokolov.

"Gospodin, no! I am still your man. There is no need for this. I won't tell anyone anything, I promise!" Sokolov resisted the goon's force, pleading for his life.

Vladimir Brezhnev stood unmoving; his cold eyes unblinking. "Do not worry, Comrade Sokolov. Your daughter will be immediately returned to your wife. Of course, this means our deal is off, and Mrs. Sokolov will have to make new educational arrangements for her, but the sins of the father will not be visited upon the daughter. And of course, you will not be telling any tales. Did you think I wouldn't find your file on me? It has been destroyed already, by my own inside man."

A second henchman stepped in, grabbing the captain's other arm. Together, they dragged him away.

"No! No, you don't have to..." Sokolov's voice carried down the hall, fear pouring out in every desperate cry.

Brezhnev walked to Elsa's side, once again offering his hand. This time, she refused to take it. "Suit yourself, but please, come to the window." He backed up, giving her room.

She stood, inching around the desk, and approached the multi-paned window. Brezhnev came up behind her. Outside, Petrovich and the second man marched Sokolov to a clearing in the yard. It was covered in snow, marred only by their footprints. Behind them, another thug with dark hair and a short beard approached. He carried an assault rifle slung over his shoulder, and in his hand, a 9 mm outfitted with a silencer. When he came around to stand in front of them, Sokolov saw the gun and began to scream. Petrovich punched him in the side of the head, knocking the short, portly police captain to his knees. He remained there, sobbing now, and holding his head in a protective manner. The dark-haired man moved into position over him, aiming the handgun. He glanced up at the window. Brezhnev nodded once.

The gun fired four times; two shots in the head, and two in the chest. Sokolov was dead, his life blood staining the pristine white snow a dark crimson.

Elsa felt her stomach clench into a tight knot. Her mind raced even as she fought to keep the bile down now threatening to rise.

Next to her, the Butcher remained still, breathing deeply.

"Is this your solution for us as well?" she whispered.

"There can be no other." He turned his head, catching her eye.

"I beg to differ." Her voice strengthened.

He raised one eyebrow, surprised. "Do you?"

Elsa turned, facing him fully, eyes determined and spine stiff. "Yes. You owe me." Slowly, without breaking eye contact, she pulled a folded envelope out of her coat pocket. Reaching out, she handed it over.

Brezhnev took it, unfolding the parchment, and extracting the letter inside. He recognized the missive he'd sent so many months ago. Finally, he looked up. "So, you're calling in your marker."

From the other side of the desk, Faust and Heinz sat confused, watching them, waiting to see what the Butcher's next move would be, ready to spring into action, to go down fighting.

"I am. I had no idea I would need it. Didn't even know what you looked like until yesterday, but I figured if we ran into trouble, I could call on you for help. What I didn't count on was you being that trouble."

He refolded the paper, handing it back. "My offer was for you, not anyone else." His steely gaze rejected her claim.

Elsa lifted her chin, straightening her back as she stood her ground. "Then you should have been more specific when you wrote this. I'm calling in the favor, and it's for us all." She swung her red-tipped fingernail in a circle. "Me, Heinz, Faust," she took a deep breath, "and Marlessa's child."

A short bark of laughter erupted from Brezhnev. "My God, you have balls, woman!"

Elsa narrowed her green eyes, placing her hands on her hips. "Yes, and I wear them on my chest. I believe mine are bigger than yours, *Gospodin*!" Elsa let her inner dominatrix out, injecting as much authority into her voice and posture as possible without going too far. She refused to back down. Their lives depended on this working.

"And just how is this solution you're proposing benefiting me?" He stepped closer, nostrils flaring as he peered down at the feisty redhead.

Elsa held his gaze and held her ground. "How is it not? We leave. We were never here. No mess. No interference in your business. No bodies to dispose of, and no more child in the way. It's a win-win for us all."

"And just how do you propose leaving the country with the child? She has no papers. Have you even thought of that? The minute you try, you'll trigger security, causing me more problems."

"I thought about that." The corner of her lip lifted in a self-satisfied smirk.

"And? Please, Frau Kreiss, I'm breathless with anticipation." Brezhnev's words rang with sarcasm.

"You're going to smuggle us out on one of your ships."

He paused. His blue eyes went wide with surprise.

"Well, why not? You smuggle people in all the time. Getting someone out should not be a problem." She continued, "Remember, Brezhnev, no international incident on your doorstep. No dead German cops. No more barriers in the way of your business with the Colonel-general and the FSB. That should be more than worth the effort as I'm sure you stand to profit greatly from whatever corrupt scheme you're running."

The two stared each other down. The silence was deafening. Heinz and Faust sat, hardly breathing, watching the exchange.

The mafia boss stood tall, hands clasped behind his back, considering her words. After two long minutes, he relented. "I will get you out." He moved to his desk, picking up the phone, and dialing out.

Faust quietly sent a prayer of thanks heavenward. Heinz caught Elsa's eye. There was both censure and pride dwelling within his as he gave a slight shake of his head.

Heinz rose slowly and painfully with a small assist from Faust. He walked to his protégé and placed an arm around her shoulders, hugging her. Together they looked out into the yard at the dead Russian officer, both knowing they'd escaped death only because Elsa managed to convince a killer that keeping them alive was not only in his best interest, but also that his honor demanded he deliver on a promise made. Now, they had only to wait, and hope they got out safely, and in time.

Chapter 21

Birgitta Mahler's eyes slowly opened. She focused, looking around the room. Next to her, a monitor beeped rhythmically in time with Minister Ritt Obermeyer's heart. It was still beating. The man had been rushed into surgery to remove the bullet from his chest and repair the damage. After being moved into a room in surgical intensive care, Mahler had settled herself in for the night, falling asleep in the wee hours of the morning slumped in the world's most uncomfortable chair.

An IV pole supported bags of saline, antibiotics, and blood. Obermeyer lost quite a bit from both the initial gunshot wound as well as during surgery. A nurse had already come in to hook up a second unit of O-Positive after midnight, and again around 4:00 a.m. It was after that Mahler's eyelids refused to remain open any longer. She didn't feel too bad about it since Captain Levitz had sent over two officers to sit outside the door. If anyone had approached other than the medical staff approved by the department, they would have alerted her immediately.

She sat up, stretching her arms over her head, and then cracking her neck by turning it first left, then right. There was a kink in the muscles from her uncomfortable sleeping position. Standing, she moved around to get the blood circulating. It helped. She pulled out her phone to check messages. Still no reply back from Joseph. Now she was angry. It had been more than twenty-four hours since she'd last heard from him. Quickly, she fired off a message, and another to Elsa. If anyone had heard from him, it would be her. Joseph checked on the young woman like a helicopter parent. It was nearly 7:30 a.m. so she knew Elsa would be up, and on her way into work.

She decided to seek out a cup of coffee while she waited on her maid of honor's reply.

Outside the room, two tired-looking officers lifted themselves off the wall they were leaning against, trying to appear alert.

"I'll be back in a minute. Getting some coffee." She nodded to them as she passed, then stopped. Looking back, she asked, "Can I bring you a cup?"

The taller of the two smiled. "That would be wonderful, thank you, Detective."

The shorter one declined. "Never touch the stuff. But thanks."

Mahler raised one eyebrow and turned, continuing down the hall. "Suit yourself. Be right back."

The patient lounge was located at the end of the hall near the elevators. Inside, a flat-screen television mounted on the wall ran the news. There was no one inside, but she did find a coffee vendor. Digging some coins out of her pocket, she dropped in enough to pay for two cups. Within moments, she had two steaming black coffees in hand. Nearby was a table stocked with swizzle sticks, sugar, and creamer. Hospital issued condiments, but it would do. She added in one sugar and one creamer to her own, stirring the contents. Not knowing how the officer liked his java, she simply grabbed a handful of sugar, creamer cups, and a swizzle stick along with a few napkins. He could fix his own. She sipped hers, taking a minute to appreciate the relative silence. It wouldn't last. She needed to get back to Obermeyer.

As she turned to leave, the on-air anchor interrupted the morning program with breaking news.

"Last night, Minister of the Interior, Ritt Obermeyer, was shot while attending a ribbon cutting ceremony to honor the new Timberland Park in his neighborhood. Word on his condition has been tight as both the government and the police have offered very little information. This morning, a woman connected to Obermeyer was found dead in an Omni Hotel room located in the Kurfürstendamm district. The woman has been identified as Bierkit Wiedner, a high-end escort known to her clients only as Marilyn. The cause of death has not been determined but following on the heels of the attempt on the Minister's life raises questions that the public would like answered. We will keep you updated on this developing story." The newscast went to a montage of images showing Obermeyer and Marilyn together on several occasions ranging from state functions to personal dinner dates. Mahler was not happy.

She set the cups down and called Captain Levitz. On the second ring, he answered. "I suppose you've seen the news?" His dry sarcasm did not sit well with her.

"I have. When were you going to tell me?" she snapped.

"Calm down, Mahler. I only just found out myself thirty minutes ago. It's not our borough. The news came down through the wire, and I've been trying like hell to gather as much information as possible first before alerting you."

"And what have you discovered?"

"Not much yet. The woman was found by a maid who came in to clean the room. There are no obvious external wounds reported, and no blood. It could be an overdose, possibly foul play or even natural causes. Until the coroner makes an initial assessment and then performs an autopsy, we don't know."

"Who was she with?"

Levitz sighed. "That is the strange part. The room was rented in her name, but the manager swears someone else picked up the key. He said it was a petite blonde woman."

Mahler snorted. "Marilyn was a petite blonde woman, Captain. How does the manager know it wasn't her?"

"He was quite sure in his statement. The investigators did show him her picture, and he swears it wasn't her. He said this woman wore dark sunglasses and didn't speak much. We're trying to get copies of the hotel's closed-circuit cameras now. The manager says that they keep a camera trained on the front desk from two angles at all times. There should be an identifiable image of this mystery woman. I'll let you know as soon as I know. How is the minister?"

"Still alive. I'm on my way back to the room now. I was getting coffee."

"Get back in there. He's your responsibility. I'll call you soon." Levitz hung up, leaving Mahler shooting daggers at the now dead phone line through narrowed brown eyes.

She wasn't happy with this new twist at all. Worse, Elsa still had not called her back or sent a text. No one was answering her calls, and everyone seemed to be hiding something.

"Well, someone is going to give me some answers," she mumbled, dialing.

The phone rang five times before a sleepy, sultry voice answered. "Yes? Who is this?"

"Salome, it's Detective Mahler. I need your help."

There was a brief pause. "You realize it's still dark outside, don't you?"

"Actually, it's not. It's nearly 8:00 a.m. I'm sorry for disturbing your sleep considering the hours you keep, but it's important. Something has happened."

Mahler could hear the bed creak on the other end of the line. Salome inhaled deeply, trying to wake up.

"Okay. What has happened?"

"You saw the news last night?"

"About the minister? Sure. Everyone was talking about it until Madame Denouve cracked the whip and told us to get back to work. She forbade us from discussing it with anyone, as if we would. Generally speaking, we don't talk about one client with another."

"So, it was business as usual last night?" Mahler inquired.

"Pretty much."

"And was everyone in last night?" she pressed.

"What do you mean by 'in'?" Salome's voice slurred slightly, still on the edge of sleep.

"I mean, were all the employees present? Did anyone go out?"

"Oh, I see. Well, yes and no, I guess. Karl was out for the afternoon. He didn't take any new clients, as far as I know, so I don't know what he was doing. I didn't see him return, but I suppose he did. I was busy last night. Oh, but Ekaterine had another visit from your Herr Trommler."

Lukas was there again? My God! Mahler knew she would need to deal with this soon. The longer it went on, the more she felt like she was betraying Elsa by not informing her of his infidelity. "How long did he stay?"

"So, you *are* interested in him! I wonder why?" The cat-like purr rolled off Salome's tongue.

"Salome..." Mahler admonished.

"Okay, okay. I suppose he was here for about half an hour. Not long enough to truly enjoy what we offer, but enough time to bust a nut with the old gal. He really is very handsome."

Birgitta snorted. "Anyone else?"

"Well, Marilyn went out after 9:00 p.m. I don't know who she was meeting. I haven't checked the book."

"Can you look for me? It's very important."

"Why? What's the big deal? What did the little hellcat do?"

"She's dead, Salome. She was found this morning. That's all I can say for now, and I need you to keep this to yourself. It's an open investigation, you understand?" Mahler put every ounce of authority into her voice.

There was a long silence on the other end of the line. Finally, "You're not joking, are you?"

"No, I'm not. I need you to see who she was meeting last night and call me back. Don't tell anyone, not even Madame Denouve. I don't know who can be trusted right now."

"But you're trusting me," she said. There was something new in the woman's tone. Astonishment, and a quiet respect.

"I am. Can I trust your discretion, Salome?"

"Yes, Detective," she answered, her words assuring, "yes, you can."

"Good. Call me as soon as you have that information. Thank you, Salome." Mahler ended the call.

She checked her text messages. Still no answer from Elsa or Joseph. Anger bubbled to the surface. She refocused on the case and fired off a quick text to Jensen Niederlander. She needed information and hoped he'd found more about the IP address. Things were quickly spinning out of control, and she knew she had to get it all in hand before everything came to a head. She knew, also, that she would have to confront Lukas. It was going to be damned awkward, uncomfortable, and ugly, but his indiscretion couldn't be allowed to continue. He had to choose. She wasn't going to give him any other choice.

At the house in Reinickendorf, Salome made her way downstairs and across the foyer to the small office she used assisting Madame Denouve. The Madame was not yet up and about. For that matter, most of the house still slept. They wouldn't rise until much later in preparation for the night ahead. Salome intended to use the quiet time to find out just who it was that Marilyn met with last night. Time was running out before police would show up at their doorstep with questions once they connected the dots between Bierkit Wiedner, aka Marilyn, and the high-end escort service.

Inside the office, she flipped on the light, closing the door quietly. The leather-bound book was locked away in her drawer. Only she and Madame Denouve had a key. Sitting behind the desk, she inserted her key and unlocked the drawer, sliding it open. Salome didn't remember making an appointment for Marilyn for last night, so the only other person who could have would've been the Madame.

She found last night's column and ran her finger down the list of names until she found BW, the initials for Bierkit Wiedner/Marilyn. No appointment listed, which was odd.

There was no arranged rendezvous with the minister or anyone else. And still, Marilyn went out. She closed the book, placing it back inside the desk drawer, and locking it. Pulling out her cell phone from the pocket of her robe, she called the detective back. It rang twice and went straight to voicemail.

"Detective Mahler, it's Salome. I have that information for you. I found no appointments listed for Marilyn last night. I'm sorry I couldn't be of more help. Please let me know if there is anything else I can do for you."

She ended the call. No sooner had she walked out of the office when the doorbell chimed alerting her to visitors. Time had run out. The police were outside, and the Madame was not going to be pleased with the attention Marilyn's death would bring to her business, and neither would the owner. Taking a deep breath, she mentally prepared herself for the next few grueling hours. Salome threw her shoulders back and sauntered to the front door, opening it wide, and smiling her most inviting smile at the officers standing before her.

"Good morning, gentlemen. And how may I help you?"

The taller of the group stepped forward, stern-faced, and held out an official document. "We have a warrant to search the premises. Please inform the owner immediately." The officers pushed past, filing into the large foyer. Salome stood holding the papers. With calm deliberation, she marched upstairs to Madame Denouve's boudoir.

Chapter 22

A full day passed inside the home of Vladimir Brezhnev. Heinz, Elsa, and Faust were treated cordially, even fed as the Butcher made his arrangements. All went well until Colonel-general Vasiliev showed up with a small entourage of FSB agents in tow. The three were quickly escorted upstairs to the corner room on the third floor where Arkady locked them in. Brezhnev made sure to hide their whereabouts. His men had already disposed of Sokolov's body, cleaning up the mess outside with the help of a fresh afternoon snowfall.

"What do you think is going on down there? Elsa asked.

Heinz shrugged, careful not to move too much. "I imagine the Kremlin is none too happy with Brezhnev's police mole being investigated. They will be even less pleased when they discover he's gone missing. I wonder if the butcher will tell them the truth, that he assassinated the man in cold blood?"

"I don't think he would be so foolish," Faust added. "But I do feel rather guilty about it. Despite the man being corrupted, he was an officer of the law and a family man. I'd prefer to have seen him prosecuted, not executed."

"Why do you feel guilty, Herman?" Heinz asked.

"Because I had HackTwice dig up information on him. I really thought my hacker was better than that, but I suppose everyone has an off day. It's just that most people's off days don't end with a bullet in someone's head."

Heinz sat forward. "Nein, Herman. You are not responsible for this one, and neither is HackTwice. It was Lana Karakova. She's the one who triggered the alarm. That's why she had to get out of the country. The FSB will eventually trace the hack back to her. If it's anyone's fault, it's mine. I'm the one who asked for help."

Faust looked surprised, and then alternately relieved and worried. "So that's what you meant when you said she'd been compromised?"

"Yes, and I'm sorry for it. She's a good woman." Heinz sighed.

"Guys, I don't think recriminations are the best way to spend our time right now. We need to keep as far ahead of this as possible. Stop being self-indulgent. You can cry into each other's beers once we get home, but for now, we have to remain sharp." Elsa cracked her verbal whip. "Now, we really need to bind your ribs, Joseph. Sit up." She helped him sit straighter on the bed and stuffed a pillow behind his back. "Herman, help me tear this sheet into strips." She pulled the top sheet off the bed, yanking from beneath Heinz, and handed it to Faust.

"Using what? I have no knife on me. They stripped us of our weapons, Kreiss."

Elsa reached inside her sweater and pulled out a small Swiss army knife from between her breasts. "Will this do?"

Faust chuckled. "He never even searched there, did he?" he replied, referring to Petrovich.

"No, he did not, and yet his eyes were glued to my cleavage the whole time. Men."

Heinz struggled not to laugh. It was the first time in days he felt any humor whatsoever. "Please, you two. My ribs."

Faust cut strips, ripping the fabric. "One more reason for Brezhnev to want to kill us. Destruction of property. Feels pretty good, actually."

"Hand them over. I think three or four should be enough." Elsa proceeded to lift Heinz's sweater and t-shirt over his head. He grumbled a few times, but not nearly as much as when she began to bind his torso, expertly tying off the knots.

"You're rather good at that," Faust noted.

"Years of experience hog-tying bad men, Herman." She grinned. Stepping back, she admired her handiwork. "Better?" she addressed Heinz.

He moved his arms cautiously, then took a breath. He smiled, but there was a hint of pain still in his good eye. "Yes, actually much better. Thank you, Elsa."

"You're welcome. That should hold until we get back home." She turned to Faust. "One problem down."

"Indeed. And now we need to figure out how in the hell we're going to travel with a toddler." Faust put his hands behind his back, pacing.

"If we can get our damn phones back from Breshnev, we need not travel too far before we can make better arrangements suitable for a child." Elsa walked to the window, moving the curtain aside and looking down into the yard. Two guards walked the perimeter of the house. She knew more were stationed further out.

"It won't be easy no matter our arrangements," Heinz said, getting to his feet to join Elsa by the window. "The child doesn't know us. She's going to be upset; being taken from the only person she knows. Not to mention, she's just a toddler. At her age, patience isn't in her vocabulary yet."

"You're the one with the most experience with children, Heinz." Faust pinned him with a stare. "This is your call. I know you want to return her to the Schubert girl's parents, but what if they don't want her? Consider that. It's entirely possible they will reject the offspring resulting from Marlessa's repeated rapes. Then what?"

It was a hard question, one that had reared its ugly head in the back of Heinz's mind a few times already. He stared down into the yard, quietly contemplating the situation. Finally, he turned to Faust. "If that is the case then I will raise her myself."

Elsa's jaw dropped. Faust stood regarding his friend, unfazed.

"I figured as much," he said. "And what about Birgitta? Does she not get a say in this? It affects her too."

"Of course she does." Hienz walked back to the bed, sitting down carefully on the edge. "I'm sure she will agree if it comes down to it." He did not appear entirely convinced.

Elsa closed her mouth and crossed her arms over her chest. "Well, if it's a problem, then I'll take her."

Faust rolled his eyes. "And what about Lukas?"

She watched Heinz closely. He'd suffered eight long years. Guilt over not being able to protect and rescue his daughter's best friend had taken a toll on her mentor. She knew how big his heart was beneath all his bluster. He'd nearly lost everything beating himself up and now he had the chance to make some small part of the tragedy right again. After everything he'd done for her and her brother, she could not pass up the opportunity to help him in return. If that meant adopting a little girl to save her from being prostituted out when she grew older, then that's what she would do. No question. She'd do it even if it didn't have anything to do with Joseph.

"If he has a problem with it, he can fuck off," she said. With that, she joined Heinz on the edge of the bed, placing her arm around his shoulders. "We can't leave her here. She'd end up like her mother, and you know it."

Faust raised his hands in surrender. "I wasn't suggesting we leave her here. I'm no monster. I am simply pointing out that raising a child is a full-time job, not one a middle-aged, newly married couple could take on with any ease. And you are middle-aged, Joseph, so hold your protest," he said, pointing at Heinz who already offered a rude hand gesture in response. "And you, Kreiss, are single, and have a demanding job that puts you in danger more than is healthy. Imagine how upsetting that would be for a small child. You'd have to hire a full-time nanny, and that's expensive. A child needs stability."

"What the hell do you suggest? Should her grandparents reject her, we're supposed to put her in state care?" Elsa was fuming.

"No." Faust found the chair in the corner and sat down. His knees popped as he bent, finally relaxing into the seat. "I'm saying it will take someone with plenty of spare time on their hands. Someone with some experience with children." He sighed, placing his hands on the chair's arms. He glanced away, looking at the wall. "I'm saying Helga and I would take her…if she has nowhere else to go."

A half smile lifted the corner of Heinz's mouth. "Well, I guess that answers the question of what you'll do in retirement, old man."

"Yes, I suppose it does." An answering smile twitched on Faust's lips. "That is, provided we make it home without getting killed or captured."

"There is that." Elsa sent her superior an apologetic look. "You really are something, you know that, Herman?" She looked at Heinz. "And so are you." With that, she leaned over, placing a kiss on his cheek. "My heroes."

"I think the real hero here is you," Heinz said. "You've saved us, but I still don't understand what that was all about downstairs."

"I do," Faust stated, looking at her.

Elsa regarded them. "You did say I might one day have to bend the rules, that I'd have to fight dirty."

Faust nodded. "I see my lesson came late. So that's what happened to Ivchencko."

Heinz finally understood. He looked at Elsa. "You. It was you? You told Brezhnev where to find Ivchencko?"

Elsa looked away and then turned to face her mentor. "Yes. It was the only way I could keep you all safe."

"That wasn't your decision to make, Elsa. Why didn't you come to me? I would have helped!"

"There was nothing you could have done. Ivchencko was hellbent on revenge. He wouldn't have stopped until he killed one or all of us. And even if he failed, even if he'd been captured and taken into custody, his arrest would have exposed Brezhnev who would then have gone to any lengths to not only silence him, but exact revenge for his losses on the officers involved. I did what I had to do, Joseph." Emotion colored her words and begged for understanding.

Heinz gripped her hands. "I would have done anything to protect you from making a deal with that devil, Elsa. Anything. Why are you so hard-headed?" He pulled her to his side, hugging her.

"I know," she said, her voice muffled against his shirt. "But I'm not sorry. It saved us today."

"Don't ever do that again. Please!" Heinz held her, staring over her head at Faust who sat in silence regarding them. The fathers inside both men had been rattled to the core. Each knew that no matter how much they might wish otherwise, there was only so much they could do to protect her, and knowing their limitations caused fear to invade their hearts. It was a familiar fear, one that reared its ugly head time and again in their personal lives and their professions.

An hour passed while the three of them sat in silence. They were exhausted, both physically and mentally. Heinz, at Elsa's urging, laid back against the headboard to rest. Faust stayed put in the overstuffed chair, and Elsa stretched out across the foot of the large bed. They were dozing lightly when the sound of the door unlocking woke them.

Arkady stepped in. "Time to go." His hand twitched over his gun holster. It was obvious he wanted to have it in hand, pointed at them, but it appeared Brezhnev had given alternate orders.

Faust stood, and Elsa helped Heinz rise. Together, they made their way down three flights of stairs to the office. Inside, the Butcher leaned upon his desk, waiting. The little girl, Nikola, sat in one of the two chairs facing him, sucking her thumb, fresh tears still rolling down her soft cheeks.

"I've had to expedite your travel arrangements. My ship leaves in two hours for Stockholm. You will be on it, down in the cargo hold. I've had my cook prepare a basket of food and necessary items, mostly for the child." He looked at the girl, a small smile on his lips. "We leave in five minutes, so prepare yourselves. A bathroom is across the hall." He looked at Elsa, clearly addressing her. "Make sure she goes. It's a long ride to port, and the crossing takes thirty-six hours."

Elsa stepped forward, approaching the small girl. She smiled and held out her hand. Breshnev spoke, switching to the only language the child understood.

"Go with Elsa. She is going to be taking care of you."

Nikola sniffed, and wiped her nose on her sleeve. She seemed to shrink further into the chair, but Elsa didn't give up. She took another step, and finally, the child put her tiny hand in hers. The two walked across the hall to the bathroom leaving the men in the office.

Brezhnev looked at Heinz. "I assume you will be returning the child to her grandparents?"

"Yes. It's where she belongs." Heinz eyed the man, barely containing the anger in his voice.

The Butcher nodded. "And what will you tell them?"

"The truth, of course."

"Then you should know all of it." Brezhnev walked behind his desk, sitting down. He indicated Heinz and Faust should do the same. "Her mother's life did not end well."

"How could it? Look where she was!" Heinz's voice dropped low, rage seeping into his words.

"I won't apologize for it. Many of the girls who come here adjust and do very well. Some even come here of their own accord knowing full well what they're walking into," he began.

Faust interrupted. "But too many have no choice at all. You have them kidnapped. You're a fucking monster."

"Be careful, old man. Retirement may not agree with you after all." The subtle threat hung in the air between them.

"Finish your story," Heinz said.

Brezhnev's eyes shifted back to him, although the muscles around the blue orbs remained tight. It was evident Faust's condemnation rankled. The Butcher did not like being called a monster, but monsters rarely did.

"As I was saying, Marlessa's life did not end well. It was a difficult birth, especially since we were unaware of her pregnancy for so long. She hid it

well. Some of the other women helped her in that regard. Had I known;
I could have prevented what came next. She was the Colonel-general's
favorite for many years, despite the fact that she'd grown older. He doesn't
usually stick with any of them once they've passed the age of eighteen, but
he'd grown strangely fond of her. His attention waned for the most part.
Oh, he still liked to break in the new, fresh girls, but he visited Marlessa
from time to time. The thing about Vasiliev is that he likes to think the
girls are his exclusively. You see, he has quite a temper. When he discovered
that Marlessa was pregnant, he beat her. It was brutal. The man does
not tolerate betrayal, and that's how he saw it. I barely recognized her
face, and the bruising on her body ruined her beyond all hope of ever
being productive again. She was barely conscious but kept saying, "save my
baby." That's when I knew. The child was a month premature from what
Valentina tells me. She never knew her mother. Marlessa died that night,
whether it was from complications from her beating or from childbirth,
I do not know. As you can understand, I could not take her to a hospital.
Valentina and my housekeeper helped bring the baby into the world, and
she survived. Once we knew she was not going to die, I named her. She
has been here in this house since. It's the only home she's ever known, and
Valentina is the only mother she knows. She's inconsolable now that I've
taken the child from her. If she doesn't snap out of it, I'll have no use for
her." Brezhnev concluded his story, leaving Heinz and Faust stewing in
their outrage and anger.

"Faust is right. You are a monster," Heinz whispered. He cleared his
throat. "I hope in time the child forgets this place and everything and
everyone in it. The only small bit of gratitude I feel is to Valentina for caring
for her. Just remember," he pinned Brezhnev where he sat with a cold stare,
"if you harm Valentina, there won't be a hell hot enough for you. Even
you must have a mother." He spoke carefully. "I see that you do," he said,
noting the muscles twitching around Brezhnev's eyes. "Then let Valentina
go. She's more than served her purpose. Send her back home."

The two men stared each other down, neither blinking.

Elsa came back in, Nikola at her side. "We're ready."

"Then let's go." Brezhnev stood, coming around the desk. He stopped by Heinz. "Oh, and the FSB found their security leak. They picked her and her son up near the Finnish border. One less problem for me. Shall we?" He walked out of the room, leaving Heinz choking on rage.

Chapter 23

Captain Levitz sent relief. Edelmann showed up bearing the good news. "I'm here for the next eight hours, so go home and get some rest. Captain's orders."

Mahler nodded wearily at the ginger-haired officer. "Call me if his condition changes."

"Will do." Edelmann took over at the minister's bedside. "Looks like he'll be sleeping most of the day anyhow."

"Yes. The nurse has already come in and changed out his intravenous fluids. The doctor should be around soon. Take notes. I'll expect a full report when I come back."

Edelmann chuckled. "Yes, Detective. No worries."

She picked up her keys and cell phone from the table and walked to the door. Pausing, she turned back. "Did the Captain have any news? Anything at all?"

"Not yet. My understanding is they are waiting on ballistics and forensics. Fingerprint matches and such."

"What the hell is taking them so long?" Irritation colored her words.

The officer shrugged and glanced down at the minister. "Budget cuts."

Birgitta looked at Obermeyer's sleeping form. "Bastard," she muttered.

"Have a good sleep, Detective." Edelmann pulled a rolled-up newspaper from his coat pocket, preparing for a long day.

"Thanks. Wiedersehen."

It was a long walk out of the hospital and through to the parking lot. Mahler was weary to the bone, and yet her mind was running ninety miles a minute. The cell phone buzzed in her hand indicating a new message. As she sat in the front seat, she listened to the voicemail from Salome. It didn't make sense to her that Marilyn would be going out on her own last night, but then, at the moment, not much made sense.

"Dammit. Why can't things be simple just once?" With that, she started the car and pulled out of the lot. The facts flashed through her mind. The Minister of the Interior had been receiving death threats via email, standard mail, and voicemail from an unidentified person. Obermeyer seemed more irritated by it than concerned, until he was shot last night. The deeper she dug, the messier the whole sordid mess became. They needed that information from ballistics and forensics. They needed to discover who Marilyn met in that hotel room, too, as well as get a concrete cause of death from the coroner. That one would take time, of which they had very little to spare. There was still the odd detail of the other woman checking in who resembled Marilyn. Mahler knew she would not be satisfied until she viewed the hotel's surveillance tapes personally. Then there was the IP address and the unidentified owner of Madame Denouve's business, not to mention she'd promised to help Salome. And there was Lukas. How in the hell he was smack in the middle of it all made no sense whatsoever. As far as she knew, there'd been no new death threats which seemed par for the course if the suspect believed that he or she had hit their target yesterday. So much to consider, and she was too tired to put the pieces of the puzzle together at the moment. She needed sleep.

"And when I wake, there damn well better be a message from you, Joseph!" She yelled this last as she rolled to a stop at a traffic light. The man in the car next to her stared hard. When she calmly flipped up her middle finger at him while flashing her badge, he quickly faced forward.

Muttering to herself, Mahler berated the thin air. "I'm getting married in a few weeks, and I can't even enjoy myself. Babysitting a budget-slashing whoremonger, mixed up in an assassination attempt, witnessing Lukas's cheating, and my maid of honor and husband-to-be are both MIA! This is not how it's supposed to go. Not at all." Birgitta grumbled, putting the car in gear as the light turned green. "Things had better change soon or Bridezilla is going on a rampage."

<hr/>

She felt like she'd no sooner laid down when her phone rang. Bleary-eyed, Mahler reached over to grab it off the nightstand. The time said she'd been knocked out for three hours. The phone number identified the caller as Niederlander.

"Tell me you have news," she grumbled into the speaker.

"I have news," he chuckled. "Someone didn't get any sleep, I take it?"

"I was sleeping. You woke me, so it better be good."

Jensen Niederlander sobered. "Sorry, Detective. I know you had a long night. I got a hit on that IP address on an obscure social media site."

"Yes?"

"It belongs to a Rudolf Oppel."

Birgitta sat up. "Say again?" She rubbed her eyes.

"Rudolf Oppel. Does that help?"

Mahler sat thinking. RO was Ritt Obermeyer in her mind. She couldn't quite believe that it escaped her that RO could also be Rudi Oppel. He was annoying and unpleasant, but she hadn't pegged him as a criminal mastermind, much less as someone who would own brothels. "That doesn't make sense," she muttered. "What was the social media site?"

Jensen's fingers clacked over his keyboard, the sound transmitting over the phone line. "It's a dark site for people with all kinds of weird fetishes. It's billing itself as Benders & Enders. Kind of a dating site for those whose sexual proclivities go beyond the usual."

"He has a profile on this site?"

"Yeah, but not under the name I gave you. That's what showed up on the account, but the profile members see is for a *Rachel*. I can send you a screen shot."

Mahler's eyebrow shot up. "Rachel? Are there pictures?"

"Oh, yeah. I suppose if I were drunk enough, I might be fooled. God, I hope that never happens," he said. "Hold on, I'll shoot it over to your phone."

"Okay." She waited until her phone buzzed, indicating a new text had arrived. When she opened the file, her eyes bugged. There he was, or she was. Rudi Oppel, the slim, elegant gentleman she'd met was fully made up from lipstick to fake eyelashes, wearing a tight red dress, nylons, stilettos, and a blonde wig. He/she was standing in the half light of a lamp in a well-appointed bedroom casting a seductive gaze at the camera. Niederlander was right. Under the right circumstances, he could fool someone. Like a hotel desk clerk checking him in late at night under subdued hotel lighting. His entire look was very similar to the now deceased Bierkit Wiedner, also known as Marilyn. This changed everything.

"Jensen, I need you to dig up everything you can on Rudolf Oppel. Get it to me as quickly as possible. I'll start you off in the right direction. He's the undersecretary to Obermeyer. Got that?"

"I got it, and holy crap! Damn, Detective. Working with you is never boring. I'll get right on it and get back to you as fast as I can."

"Good. Thank you." She ended the call and sat on the edge of the bed. Oppel was the woman in the hotel video surveillance. Her instincts were certain, but she needed confirmation. She called Levitz and forwarded the text message. He'd seen the video. He'd know right away when he opened the copy of the screenshot. Mahler relayed all the information Jensen found, and what she knew.

Captain Levitz put out an APB to all units. Oppel was to be brought in immediately for questioning, and his home searched, including all computerized devices for evidence.

"Stay put, Mahler. I've got people on it. I'll call as soon as I get word we've got him. Go back to sleep." He hung up.

Birgitta stared at her phone. "Go back to sleep? That's not going to happen." She knew sleep would not return anytime soon. She really wanted to talk to Joseph. He still had not messaged or called. Frustrated, she dialed Faust's cell. It rang four times before hitting the voicemail. Angry, she tried his office. His secretary, Lora, answered.

"He's on a training exercise, Detective. Can I take a message?" Lora explained.

"Training?" *Herman?* "Sure. Yes, please have him call me as soon as possible." She started to hang up and stopped. "Wait! Lora?"

"Yes, Detective?"

"Can you connect me to Officer Elsa Kreiss?" Since her maid of honor hadn't responded, she decided to hunt her down. She hadn't even congratulated her yet on her promotion, having only heard of it in her last call from Joseph. It seemed like a lifetime ago already.

There was a pause. "Officer Kreiss is also out on a training exercise," she replied.

"Both of them?" She sighed. "Trying to train up the new agent?"

"I believe so." Lora added, "Shall I leave her a message as well?"

"Yes, I suppose. Any idea when they will return?"

"I couldn't say. The Direktor left it open."

That was unusual. Generally, training was a set curriculum. The more she thought about it, the stranger it seemed. It was not normal for the Direktor of the LKA to personally oversee the training of a new agent. Mahler didn't think that even Elsa's status as a personal friend of a friend would warrant such attention. "Thank you, Lora. Please leave them both a message from me." She hung up and made a mental note. Before she had time to second guess her actions, she called Anno. A brother would know where his sister was, surely.

"Anno, it's Birgitta."

"Oh, hallo. What's wrong?" Anno sounded like he was in a hurry.

"Wrong? Why would anything be wrong?" she asked.

"Well, you don't usually call me. The few times I've heard from you have always been bad news." He chuckled. "But if nothing is wrong, I'm happy. What can I do for you?"

"I'm sorry, Anno. I had not thought about that before. Anyhow, I'm trying to track down your sister."

"Aren't you always?"

"Seems that way."

"She didn't tell you?" he asked.

"Tell me what?"

"About her training. Old Faust sent her on some training exercise."

"Oh, that. I only just found out, actually. Have you heard from her?"

"Not since a couple days ago. Oh, and I picked out the groom's cake. It's a chocolate ganache with a raspberry filling. Hope that's okay. It was delicious. She did say Joseph prefers a sweet filling in his cakes."

This was news to her. "Two days ago?" She hadn't heard from Joseph for three days. And now both Elsa and Faust were on some unnamed training exercise together. Something wasn't right. Her instincts were twitching all over the place. "That's fine. Thank you, Anno. Please have her call me if you hear from her."

"I will. Oh, and Birgitta. I heard from Sarah. She's coming to the wedding."

She could hear the excitement in his voice. Since he'd first met Sarah Brown, Anno had had a crush on the American woman whom they'd all come to know three years ago when that wretched Dutch pedophile, Peter Knudson, kidnapped him. Thankfully, they were able to rescue the boy before any harm came to him, and she still wasn't sorry that the monster had been fatally shot in the rescue.

"That is wonderful news. I'm looking forward to seeing her again. Is she bringing a date?"

"What? Birgitta! Bite your tongue," he laughed. "No, she didn't mention a date. Maybe this will finally be my chance. I'm a grown man now, after all."

She rolled her eyes. Anno was only one year younger than her own son, Jan. Both were currently attending university. "Whatever you say,

Anno. Okay, I must go. Give her the message for me, and call if you need anything."

"Okay. Take care and see you soon."

As she sat there, she knew there was one more important task to tackle. She needed to see Lukas. Mahler got up and headed to the shower. An hour later, clean, dressed, and ready to beard the lion in his den, she headed out.

Chapter 24

The day dragged on as officers combed through the house in Reinick-endorf. Madame Denouve remained cool and aloof, cooperating only as much as was legally necessary. She made a call from the phone in her sitting room before they were herded into the salon. Salome noticed, but was not privy to whom she'd called. The old woman stayed tight-lipped.

"So, what are we to do about tonight?" she asked, wondering how in the world they were to inform their patrons. If the police were still on site when they arrived, they'd likely never come back again. Their presence was bad for business.

"What can we do? We are cut off from using our own phones since they've confiscated them, cut off from entering the office. We have no way to forewarn tonight's appointments. This is a disaster. Damn that Marilyn! Interfering in my business, even in death."

Her last words made no sense but listening to the Madame rant coldly about her deceased employee made Salome's blood boil. She didn't care for Marilyn either, but that didn't mean her life did not matter. Treating someone's demise as an inconvenience showed a lack of soul as far as she was concerned. It bolstered her own desire to get away from them all. She was reaching the point of desperation, and fervently hoped the detective was a woman of her word or else she'd end up just like Marilyn. Dead, with no one caring one whit about her passing.

As police moved in and out of the house like busy ants, a black van pulled up in the driveway followed by an army Jeep. Men in black uniforms and face masks stepped out of the van. One approached the officer in charge, and their exchange turned heated. The officer stormed off, shouting at his men to stop what they were doing and to leave.

"What's going on?" Salome asked Madame Denouve.

"Looks like the police have been pushed aside, but for who, I could not say. They look like Special Forces, but why? What did that foolish bitch get herself mixed up in?" Her silver brows furrowed.

Salome knew she referred to the deceased Marilyn. She was just as confused. Two of the black-masked men entered the house, and one passed her heading up the stairs. He glanced at her briefly, his hazel eyes touching on her own before he looked away, bounding up the stairs. She turned to watch as he entered Ekaterine's room. Something about him felt familiar, but she couldn't think why.

The other man entered the office. After twenty minutes passed, he came back out carrying a stack of files and the leather-bound appointment ledger. He gave instructions to another officer standing outside on the front porch to retrieve the safe from within the main office. Madame Denouve was then escorted outside where she was placed in the back of the Jeep. The man who'd taken the files from the office approached Salome.

"Are all the residents of the house here? Is anyone missing?" His dark eyes probed her own demanding answers.

"I don't know. I'd only just awakened before you arrived," she answered.

"Come with me. We will check every room. If anyone is unaccounted for, I want that person's name. Understand?"

"Yes. I understand." Salome felt his hand wrap around her upper arm, directing her up the stairs. Together they checked each room, ejecting the stragglers from the bedrooms, and sending them downstairs to the salon. Everyone was present except for Marilyn and Karl.

The masked officer did not show surprise at Marilyn's absence, but asked questions about Karl; when she'd last seen him, what was he wearing, who did he entertain?

"I don't know what he was wearing last or who he was with. You confiscated the appointment book. You can answer your own questions. As for when I last saw Karl, it was early yesterday. I passed him in the kitchen. He was leaving as I came in. We didn't speak, so I don't know what he did after that or where he went. We're all responsible for our own schedules." Salome kept her answers short, feeling cornered.

"What about you? Where were you last night?" He pressed her for information.

"I was here. It's in the book. You can confirm that."

"Don't worry, I will." His tone was ominous. "Was Minister Obermeyer one of your clients?"

"Herr Obermeyer?" This threw her. "I thought this was about Marilyn?"

"Just answer the question. Did you service the Minister?" Brown eyes bore into hers.

Salome pulled her robe tighter, still not having yet dressed. The police raid prevented all of them from being properly attired. "Herr Obermeyer was a client of mine only once."

"Really? Either you're lying or something is wrong with you."

"I am not lying, nor is there anything wrong with me. The Minister has particular tastes. I am not his type, thank God." She muttered the last.

The officer chuckled mirthlessly. "Who did he indulge his particular tastes with?"

"Marilyn was one of his favorites." The man nodded. "And Karl was his other regular."

"The one who is now missing?" He gestured to the officer outside, gaining his attention. That one walked over, joining them.

Salome nodded.

He turned, addressing his comrade. "Pull the file marked 'Karl.' Put out a BOLO on him. We need to bring him in as soon as possible."

"Yes, sir." The officer left, jogging outside to the black van.

The one interrogating her directed her to a chair. "Stay put."

"Where else would I go?" she snarked.

"Don't be smart." He walked to the stairs, taking them two at a time. At the top, he turned and entered Ekaterine's room where the other masked militant went earlier. He still had not come out, and neither had Ekaterine. Salome watched, curious as to what was going on, and why the woman had not been forced from her room like everyone else. The questions about the Minister made her think of Detective Mahler. She wondered if these men were part of that investigation but considering the way in which Mahler approached Madame Denouve's business, it didn't seem likely. Mahler was discreet and investigating at the request of Obermeyer. At least, that was her understanding. These men were anything but discreet with their early morning raid, and the warrant presented by the first group of police cited the sudden death of Bierkit Wiedner, aka Marilyn, as the catalyst for the search. How the death of one prostitute could prompt two conflicting searches, one a special operations tactical squad, to come and toss the premises of a legal bordello made no sense at all.

Salome wanted to call Mahler, but her phone had been taken along with the rest. She still had her business card. All she needed was access to a phone. Across the hall, the others sat whispering among themselves, gossiping. Madame was still sitting in the back of the Jeep outside. The officer from the front porch was still standing by the van, and the two upstairs had yet to come out. Carefully, she stood, trying to remain calm and cool. There was a powder room down from Madame's office. One door beyond was a small reading room. It wasn't used much by anyone except Madame. It was her quiet place, but there was a phone, the one she'd used earlier to make her own call. If she could get to it, she could call the detective.

Acting casually, Salome walked to the door of the powder room. If anyone asked where she was headed, it would be her alibi. Once there, she glanced over her shoulder, checking to see if anyone watched. She was in the clear. Five more steps had her inside the small library with the door closed. She ran to the phone.

There was no answer to her knock. Lukas was not at work, where she'd first checked, nor was he at home. The assistant at the Georg Nothelfer Gallery said Lukas had not been in at all that day, and had, in fact, been absent quite a bit lately. Bitchy employees tired of being left to run things were the best sources of information.

She was about to use less than ethical measures to hunt him down when her phone vibrated in her pocket.

"Mahler," she answered.

"Detective," a voice whispered low, "it's Salome."

"Why are you whispering?" Birgitta stepped into the elevator, heading back down to the garage.

"Because we are being raided!"

"Raided? By the police? What for?" She knew police would be going around to the residence in Reinickendorf to speak with Madame Denouve regarding the death of Bierkit Wiedner, but over-dramatizing it as a raid seemed a bit stretched. "I'd hardly call routine questions a raid, Salome."

"There is nothing routine about this, Detective. There is an entire special forces team here tossing the place."

This stopped Mahler in her tracks. "What do you mean? Special Forces?"

"Yes, men in masks. They arrived in a black van along with an army Jeep. They have the Madame in the back of the Jeep now, and the rest of us herded like criminals into the salon. I snuck out to call you. They've confiscated our phones! They're asking about the minister too."

The panic in Salome's voice set off her own alarm bells. "Salome, I have to make a call. Don't talk to anyone if you haven't already. I'll be in contact." She hung up and immediately dialed out.

"Captain, it's Mahler. What do you know about a raid on the brothel in Reinickendorf?"

Levitz paused. "What raid? All that is ordered is a simple bench warrant for the deceased's residence. Just routine investigation into Wiedner's death."

"That's what I thought." Over the next few minutes, she filled her captain in. By the time she was finished, he was on the horn to higher ups to gather information and simultaneously gathering a squadron of available officers.

"Meet me there in twenty minutes." Levitz's no-nonsense voice gave the order.

Mahler left the apartment complex, driving quickly to the other side of town. Traffic flowed with only one minor hiccup in the off-rush hour. She pulled up to the house amid five police vehicles. An angry Captain Levitz stepped out of the lead car, storming like a bull inside the house. Birgitta followed, trailed by two of the four remaining officers outside.

"Who is in charge here?" Levitz bellowed.

Two military battle-dressed men stepped out of a room at the top of the stairs, looking down into the foyer. Seeing Levitz, they made their way down, coming to a stop in front of him.

Mahler glanced at them both, first one, and then the other. Her perusal stopped when she met the eyes of the second masked man. Something about him seemed familiar. His gaze darted away from hers, focusing on Levitz. The masked man in front of him spoke.

"I am."

"And just who the hell are you? Don't lie. I've already checked every law enforcement agency, and the only warrant for this residence is for local police. Nowhere in it is there authorization for a military operation, so how about explaining why you're here and interfering in police business." He shook a copy of the bench warrant at the man.

"You're out of your element, Captain. This is none of your concern."

Levitz was taken aback. He'd yet to identify himself. "I see you already know who I am," he countered. "Now be so kind as to enlighten me as to who the hell you are." The captain's voice dropped deceptively low.

"Come with me." The man led Captain Levitz off to the side. The two spoke quietly amongst themselves, leaving the rest to stand in awkward silence.

Mahler stared at the masked man before her. He kept his head turned away as she studied him. He was dressed head to toe in black combat gear. The mask covered his head and face leaving only holes for the eyes and nose. It was something about his eyes that grabbed her attention. While she continued watching him, movement at the top of the stairs caught her eye. She glanced up and saw a red-haired, older woman step out, being led down by yet another masked man. She recognized her as Ekaterine, the old prostitute Oppel had visited the first time she'd stepped foot inside this house. She was also the woman Salome said Lukas favored, but for the life of her, she couldn't figure out why. The woman was nearly old enough to be his mother and had seen better days. She knew it was an unkind thought, but accurate.

As she reached the bottom of the stairs, Ekaterine turned a smug smile on the masked man still standing in front of Mahler. He offered an almost imperceptible nod to the woman, and then it all clicked into place.

"Lukas!" Mahler hissed out his name.

The masked man turned halfway in her direction, and then stopped himself. He glanced sideways, eyes narrowed, and began walking away.

Mahler reached out, grabbing his arm and leaning in. "I know it's you! Don't you dare walk away! You have a lot of explaining to do."

"Be quiet!" he whispered harshly. "Now is not the time." He pulled away and walked off, leaving her standing there fuming.

Birgitta looked around. Her people and their people faced each other, neither giving way as Levitz and their leader argued quietly in the corner. Her captain's face was red, a sure sign he'd surpassed his usual calm command of a situation. Finally, they broke apart.

Levitz approached Mahler, nostrils flaring. "Come." He raised his hand indicating his team should follow. "I'll explain outside," he told her.

On the lawn, Levitz turned, opened his mouth, and then stopped, closing it again. He seemed to be forcing himself to breathe steadily and gathering his thoughts at the same time. When he spoke, it was with the measured cadence of a man frustrated by circumstances beyond his control.

"We seem to have bumbled into an Intelligence operation. Honestly, I don't even know which branch because apparently, it's above my goddamn pay grade!"

Mahler stiffened. "Intelligence? Which part of this has anything to do with State Intelligence? Wiedner was a legal prostitute as far as we're aware."

Levitz rubbed his chin. "Perhaps, and perhaps not. The only thing that Captain Kelner said was that they are investigating an illegal sex trafficking ring."

"Dieter? That was Dieter?" Mahler pointed back at the house. Of course it was. Wherever Lukas was, Dieter followed, and vice versa.

"I take it you know him," he stated, not asking for confirmation.

"I do. He was involved with us in the Ivchencko affair."

"I see. Yes, I think I recall reading his name in the report. Well, now at least I have a clue as to how deep this runs. The point is, we have to hang back. This is their fucking mess now."

"What? No! Forgive me, Captain, but we're balls-deep into this rabbit hole. We have a responsibility to the public to find the shooter, and the person who murdered Marilyn."

"Our responsibility is to the chain of command, Mahler. We're out-ranked and outmaneuvered at the moment."

"But we have information that they don't. We have Oppel." She pointed out their advantage.

Levitz stood with hands on hips, mulling over what she said. His training said follow orders, but his gut screamed solve the case. "What are you suggesting?"

"That we make a deal with Captain Kelner. Offer our intelligence in return for being included in the investigation. Tit for tat."

Eyes narrowed, and jaw grinding, Levitz considered the detective's idea. "He won't go for it. He all but shut me out. What makes you think he'll listen to you?"

Birgitta's lips spread into a thin, mirthless smile. "Leave that to me."

She turned, marching back inside the house. Locating Lukas in a sea of black masks was challenging, but he gave himself away when he turned an angry glare in her direction.

"Just the man I was looking for." She cornered him. "I have an offer for you, Lukas, and you'd better think it over carefully because your future happiness depends upon your answer."

"What are you talking about?" he demanded.

"Ekaterine. Are you listening?"

Kelner joined them, standing next to Lukas. "What about her?"

Mahler glanced at the man. "Hello, Dieter. I'm referring to this cheating bastard." He froze, surprised she knew his identity, as she focused again on Lukas. "We both want to find Marilyn's killer."

"So?" Dieter answered.

"And I am tasked to discover who has been sending death threats to the minister. They're connected."

"Did you just call me a cheater?" Lukas asked.

Mahler looked him straight in the eye. "I did."

"With who?" he asked, voice rising.

"That old whore, Ekaterine. Don't lie now. I saw you leaving here with my own eyes four nights ago, and my own source tells me you've been visiting her often beginning recently. Honestly, Lukas, how could you do that to Elsa? What kind of man are you?" Anger sizzled in her voice, growing more heated with each word she spoke.

Dieter began to laugh, his chuckles shaking his shoulders. "Lukas? Cheating with that woman?"

Mahler pulled herself up to her full height of five foot four inches and raised her chin. "Apparently, you do not have all the facts, Captain," she fumed.

Lukas squared his shoulders, staring down at her. "No. Apparently, it is you who do not have all the facts, *Detective*!" His voice dropped low. "Ekaterine is working for us. She's my source in this investigation. That's why I was here, and the only reason you saw me. The *only* reason! And just what in the hell were you doing here?"

Birgitta paused. Her mind flashed back over what she knew, or thought she knew. But another thought hit her. "Does Elsa know you're still in?" she asked.

Dieter answered for him. "She doesn't, and we want to keep it that way. Maintaining the outward appearance of a civilian status is what makes Lukas so valuable. So, Detective, I need to know right now that you will not out him."

She locked eyes with Dieter. Mahler knew she'd erred, and badly. It wasn't like her to make such mistakes as she was usually both methodical and cautious in her assessments of any and all situations. She relented. "I will say nothing. You have my word."

The captain relaxed his stance as well. "You were saying that Wiedner's death and the minister's death threats are connected. Tell me what you know."

She stiffened her resolve once again. "Guarantee to include me in your investigation and I will."

"Birgitta, we don't have time for this—" Lukas began.

"Then stop wasting it. Yes or no?"

The two men stared at each other, silently communicating. Finally, Dieter extended his hand. "Yes, but only you. No other police agencies, and you cannot relay any information back to your captain until we solve our case."

Mahler nodded, and clasped hands with him. "Agreed."

"So, what have you got?" Lukas asked.

She pulled out her cell phone and showed them the information she'd received on Rudi Oppel, explaining what she knew.

"Tell Levitz that as soon as he's brought in, we need to know. No one is allowed to question Oppel except myself or Lukas. No one. Understood?" Dieter commanded.

"I'll let him know. Oh, there's one more thing."

"Yes?"

She turned to Lukas. "Salome."

He nodded. "What about her?"

"I promised to help her. She's been held here against her will. Her passport was confiscated as soon as she arrived in Germany. She said that's the case for many here."

"Ekaterine said something similar," he replied.

"She wants to go home. Can you help me to help her? Surely her passport is among the many files and boxes you've carted out of here."

Dieter sighed. "As soon as we've gone through everything, I'll see to it. All passports will be returned."

"Thank you. Now, I've shared my information. Quid pro quo. Tell me about this trafficking ring you're investigating."

Lukas answered. "It's more like a vast, complicated network. Our own government has been complicit. Seems the Minister's office has been clearing undeclared cargo coming in from Saint Petersburg. It's arriving on commercial carriers but marked as military munitions. We conducted a raid a month ago on one of the ships and found two tons of uncut heroin along with human cargo."

Dieter cut in. "The heroin is produced in Russia, but the poppies it's created from are grown in Turkey. The two countries had a deal to profit from the drug trade until Turkey decided to renege by demanding higher payment for their product. President Arslan got greedy. Payback began with the death of a Turkish ambassador. Then Turkey shot down A

Russian SU-24 on the Turkish-Syrian border. Following that incident, Mishin and his criminal network set out to bypass Turkey altogether by making a deal with a crime syndicate in Laos, but that fell apart when the Laotian syndicate clashed with the Bratva. Some prison yard drama we believe was orchestrated behind the scenes by Arslan at the same time he put his coup for power into motion. They are still retaliating against each other with Turkey picking off Russian diplomats, but in the meantime, they've struck up a tenuous cease-fire on the opioid deal. The drugs are still coming in, although we're now tracking each shipment to see where it all ultimately lands, but there is also this trafficking ring. When these same ships leave the port in Hamburg, we know they contain human cargo, just like the situation with the Vledelets and Ivchencko. Only now, it's far more sophisticated. These ships are escaping inspection. Oh, the paperwork says they are all inspected, but it's fraud, and the fraud is coming down from the minister's office. Port trade is their purview."

Mahler nodded, taking it all in. "So, you've been tracking Obermeyer's movements."

"We have. They led us here. I sent Lukas in to cultivate a contact. That's why he has been seeing Ekaterine. The old whore has been trapped here longer than Salome. She's a German national, born and raised until she was eight outside of Potsdam. She was kidnapped and taken to Saint Petersburg where she was groomed for the sex trade. When she was no longer a child, they sent her back to work in one of the houses here," Dieter stated.

"Good lord!" Mahler was appalled.

Lukas placed his hand on her shoulder. "And Birgitta, that's not the worst of it. She told me that the man responsible for turning her out is none other than the Butcher. She said she lived for six years in his house, passed over first to his henchmen, and then to some of Russia's top government and military men."

Her hand rose to cover her mouth, an involuntary reaction to the horrors he described. "The Bratva and the Kremlin are in bed together?"

Dieter nodded. "As far as we can tell, there is very little difference between the Russian government and organized crime. As long as they can profit, there are no moral barriers. And with Russia being on the receiving end of harsh sanctions from the United States and the European Union, they will take money wherever they can get it. This is how Mishin is building up his military."

"This is beyond complicated, Dieter. Just exactly what is your goal here?" What he'd described extended so far beyond what Mahler expected, what she dealt with daily. It was damn near incomprehensible in scope, a global web of corruption.

"Our goal is simple. We find the person responsible within the ministry for allowing these ships into port and arrest him. We shut down the Russian's drug and trafficking ring in our country. Then, we share our intelligence with our allies so they can protect their own. If we can cut off all financial avenues that the Russian Federation has developed, we cripple their power base and protect future kidnapping victims. It's the best we can hope for. Starve the beasts, both their government and their criminals. One and the same, of course."

Mahler felt overwhelmed. She took a moment to think. Turning to Lukas, she reached out, touching his arm. "I'm sorry I accused you of cheating. I should have known better."

He nodded. "Thank you. And yes, you should have." He blew out a breath, half laughing. "I thought it was pretty obvious how I feel about Elsa, but maybe I need to step up my game."

Birgitta smiled. "It couldn't hurt."

"You're just saying that because you have wedding fever. How is Heinz, by the way?"

"I wish I knew. I haven't heard from him in days. I'm about to hop a plane to Sweden and kick him in his arse."

"Sweden?" Lukas asked, surprised.

"Yes, didn't Elsa tell you? He's attending seminars required for promotion. Of all times, too, to do this to me right before our wedding." She pushed a stray hair back behind her ear.

He shook his head. "No, she didn't, but then, she's been busy with her own promotion. She's off training for a few days. Faust sent her."

"Yes, I heard. He's with her, apparently. I called his office today, and Lora said they were both out until further notice."

"That's unusual," Lukas replied.

"I thought so, too, but who knows? Between preparing for the wedding, and this case with Obermeyer, I've been a little busy."

"So, Heinz is out of the country, Elsa is away at training, and Faust is gone too?" Lukas stood, hands on hips, staring down at her.

Mahler noted his stance. "Yes, that's what I just said." Her eyebrow rose a fraction, questioning him.

"And this doesn't strike you as strange?"

"I just said it did. What are you saying?" The two stood staring at each other.

Dieter spoke up. "He's saying they're up to something, something they didn't want anyone else to notice, of course." He shook his head and walked away, leaving Mahler and Lukas to figure it out.

Chapter 25

The trip to the dock took nearly an hour as snowfall caused traffic delays. Elsa held Nikola on her lap, bundled in a fuzzy pink coat and wrapped in a blanket for warmth. The child fell asleep ten minutes out with her thumb in her mouth. Heinz sat next to her, and Faust and Brezhnev shared the seat across from them in the back of his limousine.

The sun set, providing the cover of darkness.

"As soon as we arrive at the warehouse, Petrovich will lead you down to the ship." Brezhnev briefed them as they sped down the highway.

Heinz eyed the man, still simmering in anger. Guilt swamped him. He knew that Lana's troubles were only just beginning, and the fact that she'd been sucked into this mess along with her son because of him caused no end to his anguish. "What will become of Frau Karakova?"

The Butcher turned cold blue eyes in his direction. "It is Gospojah here, Kommissar, and Gospojah Karakova is in for a very unpleasant time. The FSB are only removed from their former counterpart, the KGB, by a change of name. Public relations, you understand. She has aided a foreign spy. They do not look kindly upon such betrayal. I imagine they will first interrogate her until they're satisfied she has confessed all and has nothing more to offer."

"And then what?" Heinz counted to ten in his head.

"And then her usefulness will end."

"What do you mean by that?"

Faust caught Heinz's eyes, mentally urging him to calm down.

Brezhnev smiled, just a thin spread of his lips. "I think you know, Kommissar Heinz."

"What of her son? He is innocent in all of this? Will the Federation murder a child?" Heinz's voice held a sharp edge. He leaned forward. "I know that the sanctity of life means precious little to your sort, but even you must condemn killing an innocent child. Are you so far gone, Brezhnev?"

The Butcher sat forward, meeting Heinz in the space between seats, elbows resting on his knees. His eyes narrowed as his nostrils flared. "I do not concern myself with matters beyond my control. If you're asking if I disagree with killing a child, the answer would shock you. I learned long ago very few people care if another lives or dies. It's all about self-preservation and survival. Even those who claim to care, try to protect others, have their limits. When those limits are tested, they invariably choose their own safety over that of others. It's human instinct. Would I prefer my government be more lenient where children are concerned? Perhaps. I've seen many lost in sacrifice to Mother Russia's ambitions, but that really isn't the question. What you're asking is will I do anything to stop them. The answer is no. Be happy that I am helping you all now, that I've granted the magnanimous favor of allowing you to take Nikola." He sat back. "I am a man of my word, if nothing else, and I am following through on my own promise to Officer Kreiss despite the very real threat to myself, and my business, by doing so."

Faust and Elsa watched the exchange, both on pins and needles as the tension inside the limo grew. The vehicle slowed, turning onto the side road that led to port. Heinz was about to reply when the silence was interrupted by the ringing of Brezhnev's mobile. He pulled it from his pocket. As he read the caller ID, his brow creased.

"Yes?" He answered, listening. "How long ago?"

Faust and Heinz locked eyes.

Brezhnev exhaled, anger evident on his face. "Thank you for the information." He hung up, and reached forward between Elsa and Heinz, tapping the divider between the front and backseat. The tinted glass slid down.

"We have a problem. Head for the far end of port. Take the alley. Petrovich, call Captain Lukin. Tell him he's about to get a visit from the Colonel-general, and to say nothing of our arrangement. Remind him of his obligation."

Brezhnev sat back and looked first at Faust, then Heinz. "Someone has tipped off Vasiliev. He knows you're here, and he knows I'm helping you." He fired off a succession of harsh words, cursing colorfully.

"What? How?" Elsa asked, surprised.

"Valentina. It had to be her. She's the only one within my house that knew, and the only one who would betray me to Vasiliev."

"But why?" Heinz looked at the angry man across from him. He knew just how dangerous the Butcher was. It did not compute why anyone would be so foolish as to purposefully aggravate him, even though he'd only just done so, himself.

Faust broke his own silence. "Because of the child."

Elsa hugged the girl closer.

Brezhnev looked at the little one, and then his gaze traveled up to lock eyes with Elsa. "Women," he replied with derision. "Always reacting instead of thinking. Always causing a problem."

Anger bubbled over inside of her. "Men! Always causing women problems. Of course she betrayed you. This child is all that she had. She loves her. In her mind, she has nothing left to lose after everything you've taken from her. Blame your own monstrous nature, not the victim you enslaved!"

He moved fast, slapping Elsa across the face. Heinz pushed himself between them, grabbing the Butcher's arm, yanking it forward and twisting it around behind the man's back as Faust snaked his own around Brezhnev's neck, squeezing.

"You're all dead if you do not let go of me now," he choked out, his face red as he struggled to breathe.

Elsa turned her head sideways, noticing the barrel of a gun next to her face pointed at the back of Heinz's head. Petrovich's hand was steady, his finger already pulling the trigger back.

"Stop! Everyone stop. The child!" She held the girl protectively even as her ears still rang and her cheek stung from being struck. Nikola whimpered, frightened.

Faust noticed the gun, and he loosened his grip, releasing Brezhnev who threw Heinz off, sending the injured detective back into his seat. The Butcher held up his hand.

"Cease. Make the call, Petrovich. We don't have time for this now. And tell Lukin to ring me as soon as the Colonel-general and his men leave the ship." He straightened his coat and jacket, fury lighting his blue eyes as he pinned Elsa with a glare. "You see? No control over your emotions. This is why you are the inferior sex."

Elsa bit her tongue. Inside, her blood boiled, and her fingers itched for the grip of a cat-o-nine tails. Mentally, she was already flaying the skin from his back.

Heinz moved closer to Elsa, placing himself between her and Brezhnev. "If you ever touch her again, I will kill you. Your man won't have time to save your ass before I do." His threat rang with truth, his meaning clear.

The two men remained locked in a stare-down, neither giving in.

The limousine came to a stop. Petrovich leaned over the seat, looking back at them. "We're here. Now what?"

Brezhnev looked out the window, and down the dock. "Now, we wait. There is nothing aboard that ship as of yet. Our protocol remains in place. No illegal cargo loaded off the dock."

"Then how do you plan to get us on board?" Heinz asked.

Brezhnev pointed toward a smaller pier along a rocky shoreline. "There. We keep several small fishing vessels tied there off the main dock. Petrovich will accompany you out to the Morskoy Drakon. The crew will throw down a ladder."

"So, we climb up?" Elsa's eyes widened. "I'm carrying a child!"

"You wanted to take her. You'll figure it out," Brezhnev remarked.

The darkness lit up down the dock as a line of military Jeeps drove in turning toward the section where Warehouse 214 was located. Half of them split moving off to where the Morskoy Drakon was docked. The sounds of the engines were loud enough to reach them where they sat under cover of night waiting. The line of military vehicles came to a stop. The Colonel-general got out, flanked by three soldiers carrying what appeared to be Vityaz-SN submachine guns, the Kalashnikov variant, standard for all Russian military, and deadly. They tried entering the warehouse through the front but failed to bypass the electronic lock. One of the men went around the side. Shots rang out, followed by a bang. Within minutes, the large front door was sliding open, and Vasiliev and his men were inside. They tore through like vandals before exiting and heading down on foot to the ship. The Colonel-general looked angry from where they sat, watching.

"Out of curiosity, what will you do now that Vasiliev knows of your betrayal?" Faust asked, his face a study in German stoicism.

Brezhnev turned, quiet fury in his eyes, and looked at the Direktor. "Generally, it would not be good. However, I am not without my own leverage. The Colonel-general has secrets that would not only end his career, but his life if ever they were made known to the public."

"You could have simply decided to turn us over to him at any time. Why didn't you?" Heinz pinned the man with a glare, still simmering in his own anger. He did not want to let it go. It was his edge, and he needed it right now to bypass his physical pain, to stay sharp. He knew through his own experiences that their situation was unstable and could go south at any moment.

The Butcher lifted his chin. "Before Vasiliev knew I was helping you, it did not suit me. We are partners in business, Kommissar. It does not mean that I like the man. But now that he knows, it would be seen as a sign of weakness if I turned you over, that he holds the power, and that does not suit me either. As you must understand, in my position, power is everything. Any blood in the water, and the sharks come out. I run the

Bratva like a well-oiled business organization. It takes great strength to keep everyone in line, to keep the machine turning a profit. Without my leadership, the factions would be fighting each other over scraps. There would be gang wars on every corner. Believe me. Had it not suited my needs, you would all be dead now. Vasiliev is trying to gain the upper hand. He is reacting to the information handed him by Valentina in the same manner that women," he looked at Elsa, "react all the time, rashly and without forethought. He thinks he's making a power play that will put him in control of our arrangement. The man is impulsive. I've known this from the beginning. It was how I lured him in, using his own sick desires, his own lack of control to bind him to me and to the Bratva. All I had to do was dangle a young, juicy carrot before him. And now, all I need do is wait until he runs out of steam. He will find nothing, and then he will leave, most likely to seek me out in my home. When he cannot find me, he'll begin to worry, and when he worries, he'll make more mistakes. In the interim, I'll leak bits of information to the press. Just enough to send a clear message to the Colonel-general that he is treading on thin ice. He will be brought to heel. All I need do, Kommissar, is wait."

His cold, calculated speech left them thinking hard in the quiet interior of the limousine.

"You really are a dangerous animal." Heinz spoke low, eyes filled with disgust.

"Yes. Try to never again forget that." Brezhnev's thin smile sent a chill through him.

They sat in silence for half an hour. Finally, Brezhnev's phone rang. The captain gave the all-clear as Heinz, Faust, and Elsa watched the line of military vehicles leave the dock.

"See? A waiting game. And we are only a little behind schedule." The Butcher stepped out of the limo and extended his hand to Elsa. She refused, struggling to exit, holding Nikola who clung to her. Heinz and Faust exited the other side taking the basket provided by the cook at Brezhnev's house.

Petrovich led them down the pier to a short set of stairs that descended to a smaller dock. A fishing boat was tied to a pylon, bobbing on the waves. He climbed aboard first, making his way to the tiny wheelhouse where he started the engine. Faust stepped in and reached up for the child. Elsa handed her down, which was not easy since Nikola did not want to let go. Heinz stood on the dock next to Brezhnev, the cold wind whipping his short hair. Frozen sea spray stung the cuts on his lips and eye reminding him that the Butcher possessed very little mercy, but he knew he had to try.

"I am not in the habit of asking criminals for favors, Brezhnev." Heinz looked the man in the eye.

The corner of Brezhnev's lip lifted sardonically. "And yet you are going to ask."

Heinz stared at his nemesis. Hate filled him for all the girls this man had forced into sex slavery, for every single one that died at his hand, but he needed to push that aside. "Save her."

"I can't."

"You can. You know you can. You already have the Colonel-general's number. You know how to manipulate him. She's one person, one small fly in the ointment, and she was only there because I begged her to help me. She is innocent in all of this. Save her."

"Manipulating him for my own gain is one thing. Doing so for you is another. You've already caused me problems, Kommissar. Even if I could save Ms. Karakova, why would I?"

On the boat, Faust helped Elsa get the child settled inside the wheelhouse. He glanced back at the two men on the dock, waiting. Heinz noted his friend's scrutiny, turned, and began climbing down into the vessel. With his back to Herman, he returned his attention to Brezhnev.

"A favor for a favor. On my honor," he whispered.

Brezhnev remained quiet as he stood, hands in the pockets of his overcoat, watching Heinz. With a barely discernable nod, he squatted down to the detective's eye level. He stuck out his hand which was reluctantly clasped in return. "And I will collect." With that, the leader of the Bratva rose, walked back up the pier to his waiting limousine, and left.

Chapter 26

Returning to the hospital after her confrontation with Lukas left Mahler on edge. While she was happy to discover he hadn't been cheating on Elsa, she was burdened with yet another secret; Lukas Trommler was an active-duty Special Operations agent for the Military Counterintelligence Service, or MAD, working directly with the Bundesnachrichtendienst (BND). The last they all knew was that he'd spent four years in the Marines ending his time as Kapitänleutnant Trommler. Of course, when Joseph asked him point blank why he'd processed out of the military, Lukas had answered, "That's my business." No one questioned him beyond that. They'd all simply assumed that since he worked at the gallery, he was a civilian. Now she found out that was only a ruse, and the man was, in actuality, a military intelligence agent, a true-to-life James Bond figure. She was now tasked with the responsibility of keeping this secret.

Stranger still was what Dieter shared. The BND had received a very specific request to investigate the office of the Minister of the Interior along with a file listing port authorization for ships that were never listed on the dockets, and exports that did not match up to any state inventory or businesses. There was also a separate file outlining ministry funding that did not add up. The files had been given over to agents to investigate who discovered the military munitions on the first 'ghost' ship they raided. This led to coordinating with MAD, which landed the investigation in the laps of both Dieter and Lukas. They'd been following the trail since, one which led to the house in Reinickendorf, and the cultivation of Ekaterine as an inside source.

What they didn't know was who tipped off the BND or why. And now that Mahler had put them onto Oppel's trail, it was all beginning to make sense, everything except for the threats to Obermeyer's life. If the minister was not the one responsible for authorizing the incoming and outgoing illegal cargo of drugs and kidnapped women, then that left Oppel who would not want to rock the boat and draw attention to his activities. Only a lunatic would be so stupid.

All these thoughts weighed on her as she walked down the hall and into Obermeyer's room. It was time to relieve Edelmann. The ginger-haired officer stood as she stepped inside. He seemed flustered. Mahler's eyes bounced from him to rest on the head of a woman sitting at Obermeyer's bedside. She had long, chestnut brown hair, highlighted naturally with invading silver strands. The sleek style was simple, parted in the middle and ending midway down her back. The woman turned her head to see the new arrival. Mahler recognized her straight off.

"Vera Wolf."

The woman stood to her full height of five foot, eleven inches, turned, and extended her hand. "Yes, and I take it you're Ritt's night bodyguard?"

Birgitta cringed inwardly at the incorrect reference, but outwardly, she remained calm. "Detective Mahler," she answered as she clasped Wolf's hand.

"My apologies, Detective." Vera Wolf's large brown eyes held both intelligence and humor. They were also shrewd. As the leader of the opposition party to Obermeyer's, she'd successfully campaigned for many of the programs currently benefitting the German people, but they weren't enough. Most of them had been crippled by compromise with the conservatives making them far less effective than they could have been. Still, she did what she could. Mahler admired her for it, but that admiration was now tainted with the knowledge that Wolf had been having an affair with Obermeyer, a man obviously lacking any morality or decency. He was a corrupt soul even if that corruption did not, so far, seem to extend to his misuse of ministry authority and complicity engaging in the trade of drugs and human trafficking.

"It's an honest mistake." Mahler nodded to Edelmann. "I'll walk you out." It was clearly an order. He said goodnight to Vera and made his way to the door where he waited for Mahler to precede him.

Outside in the hall, she pinned him with a hard stare. "I suspect you have much to tell me."

Edelmann ran a hand over his chin. "I do. I guess the first part should be his medical update. The doctor came around. Obermeyer is doing well but being kept sedated for the time being. They don't want him moving around for the next few days while that surgical wound heals. They had to repair an artery, and don't want the stitches to tear, so he'll be out of it mostly until they deem him stable. Other than that, he's fine. Should recover nicely."

Mahler waited patiently. "And?"

He grimaced. "Wolf showed up about two hours ago."

"What part of no visitors escaped you?" She berated him quietly.

"I understand the concept, believe me, but I received a call directly from the BND instructing me to allow her in. I'm just as surprised as you," he said when he noticed Mahler's usually stoic face showing surprise. "What was I supposed to say to that? I called Captain Levitz, and, well, he cursed a blue streak and then told me to let her in."

Mahler pursed her lips. "Yes, well, he's had that kind of day. Okay, I get it." She patted him on the arm. "Go home. Get some rest." She dismissed him but then turned back. "Thanks, Edelmann, for coming in this morning. I won't forget it." She mentally noted his dedication. Hans Edelmann was proving to be the best kind of officer; one she could rely on. When this was over, she planned to write up a recommendation for him to Levitz. He deserved to be advanced up the ladder. If he could prove himself in training, he'd make a fine detective.

Vera Wolf met Mahler at the door.

"Leaving?"

The towering woman looked down at Mahler. "Yes. It has been a long day."

"It was nice of you to visit the minister."

The woman cast a glance back at Obermeyer. "I'm not sure he would agree," she said softly.

Birgitta watched her. Her words implied affection, but something was missing from her eyes. Perhaps it was as Rudi Oppel said, sour grapes over being dumped.

Wolf collected herself, stepping through the doorway into the hall. "Watch over him, Detective. He's had quite the close call."

"Yes, he has."

"Any news on the shooter? Have you caught him yet?"

"Him?" Mahler asked. Although the news had been running the story of the minister's shooting on all stations, details of the incident had not been released because of the ongoing investigation.

"I assume it was a *him*. Aren't most shooters male?" She placed her suit jacket over her arm.

"In most cases, yes. But we will not know until we know. We're working on it. When was the last time you saw Obermeyer?" Birgitta threw in the last question. She'd been led to believe the affair between Wolf and the minister had been over for some time. If her assumption was correct, it was curious that the woman would take time to visit him in the hospital.

A small tug lifted the corner of Vera's lips. "I'm not sure. At least a month or so. Work, you understand." She stepped back. "And work continues. I have meetings in the morning, bright and early. The party has much to do over the next few weeks before the elections. Do you vote, Detective?"

Mahler noted the change in subject. "Of course."

"Then I hope we can count on your support. The Women's Alliance is a huge advocate of law enforcement, especially women in law enforcement. I understand there have been budget shortfalls. Our officers should not be left without the funding needed to safely perform their duties. We are campaigning on increased funding for all our law enforcement agencies and first responders."

The scorned woman turned into the politician right before Mahler's eyes. This was the persona she was familiar with, and she was saying all the right words. Her passion was apparent. It shone in her eyes. For Birgitta, it was telling. Wolf's feelings for her work were honest and obvious. Her feelings for Obermeyer were murky and much harder to define. It made her wonder why she bothered to visit him.

"Your support for us is most appreciated, Frau Wolf."

Vera smiled. "Anytime, Detective. Please feel free to reach out to me with any concerns. Perhaps we can tempt you to join us sometime?" She left the question hanging.

"I'm afraid it would be considered a conflict of interest and against our code of conduct. We must remain objective at all times." Mahler's eyes slid involuntarily toward Obermeyer's sleeping form.

Vera's eyes followed. "I understand," she said. "Still, sometimes we must break a few rules to advance democracy." She turned. "Goodnight, Detective Mahler."

Birgitta watched her go. Something inside her felt off. It was Wolf's parting remark. It struck a nerve, one that continued to tingle. It seemed an odd thing for the woman to say, inconsistent with her public persona. Still, the entire day had been strange, and she was tired. More had been revealed in the last twenty-four hours than a person should have to deal with. There were secrets around every corner, and conspiracies crawling out from every rock. Mahler filed this one away, but mentally, she stuck a red tab on it.

Inside the room, the minister slept on, sedated. She was thankful that at least the department had managed to keep a lid on Ritt Obermeyer's death threats. The less the public knew, the easier it made investigating the case. When seeking a criminal, you don't want them to know you're on their trail.

The next morning was a game changer. Mahler's phone rang at 0700 sharp, just as Edelmann walked in to relieve her. It was Captain Levitz, and he was in a foul mood.

"Have you seen the headlines?" He yelled, firing off several choice words to everyone and no one at the same time.

"I've been at the minister's bedside all night. How could I possibly have seen a newspaper yet?"

Edelmann shifted, fidgeting. He could hear their captain yelling from where he stood. He reached out, handing a folded newspaper to her. Birgitta opened it, read the front page, and felt sick.

ATTEMPTED OBERMEYER ASSASSINATION A RESULT OF BIZARRE LOVE TRIANGLE!

The article featured images of Obermeyer out on the town with Marilyn, and a mugshot of Karl Eugene Gephart from a previous prostitution arrest. The author outlined the relationship between the minister and the two sex workers, cited Marilyn's murder, and noted that Karl Gephart was wanted for questioning, but nowhere to be found. Mention was made of the recent death threats, the department's involvement in protecting the minister, and the investigation into who was sending them. The only person not mentioned was Rudi Oppel. It was a leading story, one that suggested a rivalry between Marilyn and Karl for the minister's affections. This was news to Mahler. Salome had stated that both were the minister's favorites, but nothing about one being jealous of the other.

"Heads will roll!" Levitz ranted on. "Discretion, Detective! It wasn't a suggestion. Who knew about this?"

Birgitta's gut clenched. "The only persons I've spoken to regarding the threats are Madame Denouve and her assistant, Salome, and only in regard to my soft investigation. No details. This article has details that no one else could possibly know." She neglected to include Lukas in her statement. She knew he would not speak to the press. She also knew she had not given any of these details to him. This was someone else. "Captain, the only other person who could possibly know any of this is Oppel," she said.

Edelmann cleared his throat.

"What?" Mahler looked at him.

The ginger-haired officer gave her a wide-eyed look. "And the perpetrator."

"What's going on? Mahler?" Levitz barked into the speaker.

"Edelmann makes a good point, sir. Besides Oppel, the only other person privy to this much information would be the person we seek, the one who's been sending these threats." She gave Edelmann a thumbs up, mouthing the words, "Good job," to him.

"Then before you retire for the day, I suggest you visit the offices of the Berliner Zeitung and speak to," Mahler heard Levitz rattling the paper as he paused to read, "Herr Wolfgang Hachmeister. I don't care what bullshit he cites about protecting sources. I want a name!" Levitz hung up.

Mahler took a deep breath. It was going to be a long morning. She was not looking forward to locking horns with a reporter. They were notoriously closed mouth when it came to speaking with law enforcement, seeing them all as the enemy of a free press.

"So, what's the verdict?" Edelmann waited for her to gather her reserves.

"I am tasked with discovering the article's source." She looked at the paper again. "I'm just not sure how I'm going to accomplish this."

He offered a sympathetic look. "We are not islands, Detective. We cannot always stand alone. Sometimes, we need help." He patted her shoulder and stepped past her, into the minister's room. "Did the nurse at least bring breakfast around? The minister won't be needing his, and I missed mine."

Mahler smiled. "I'll ask her to send you a tray on my way out. And thanks, Edelmann. You are fast becoming my favorite person." She picked up her handbag, heading first to the nurse's station to make sure the officer was taken care of, and then she drove straight to the house in Reinickendorf. She knew exactly who might be able to finagle information out of Herr Hachmeister. Her very own Mata Hari.

Chapter 27

They were fourteen hours into a thirty-six-hour journey by ship. It was cold down in the cargo hold. Heinz paced back and forth, feeling every single one of his forty-eight years. The pain in his ribs seemed sharper in the cold and damp despite the tight binding around them. They were well on their way back to Stockholm, and he knew he should be feeling grateful, but instead, he was worried.

He was due back in Berlin in five days according to the elaborate lie he'd woven for Birgitta. The bruising on his face and body would not be gone by then, and if he, indeed, had cracked ribs, he would not be able to hide that fact from her. There would be questions, and he knew he could not complicate his lie further by adding to it. Realizing this, he knew he'd rather endure another beating than face the woman he loved and tell her what he'd done. Somehow, he didn't think she'd be forgiving, not even in the face of the fact that he'd finally found answers. Not even for the fact that because of his drive to solve the case, he was bringing a part of Marlessa Schubert home to her parents. He glanced at the child.

Nikola was sitting next to Elsa, playing with a pink, stuffed rabbit. The toy had been placed inside the basket of food by Valentina with a note. Faust translated it for them.

My darling Nikola,

You will no doubt grow to forget all about me, but I promise, my love, I will never forget you. You were my ray of sunshine in a dark world. You were the daughter I always wanted, and I loved you more than anything in this life. I will continue to love you even after. I knew your mother. She was my dear friend. We were both taken at the same time by the same evil man. I know someone will explain more of this to you when you are older, but I want you to know, she was strong. She never gave up. Marlessa wanted you, and she fought so hard to be here for you, but her body could not hold out. From that day, I promised to care for you, and I did the best I could. I know letting you go was the right thing to do. It was the only way I could save you from all of this. Be well, my darling. Be strong and do something marvelous with your life. I love you.

Valentina Yefremova

The missive was once again tucked away inside the envelope with the child's name written across the paper with a flourish. Heinz would give it to the Schuberts and let Marie and Anton decide when to share it with Nikola.

"Your pacing is making me tired, Joseph," Faust grumbled at him.

"My apologies, old friend." Heinz stopped and stood staring down at Faust.

"Worried?" he asked.

"Yes. Not sure what I'm going to say."

Elsa looked up. "I can imagine it's going to be quite a shock."

"Yes," he acknowledged.

"But a good one, of course. Who wouldn't fall instantly in love with this little angel?" Elsa smiled at the blonde-haired girl, who grinned back, completely unaware of how drastically her life was changing for the better.

"What?" Heinz blinked. "No, that's not what I meant—"

"He means Birgitta," Faust interrupted, answering for him.

"Yes, that." Heinz nodded.

"Oh, I see." Elsa looked from one to the other. "Well, you can't go wrong with the truth. And yes, she's going to be pissed. There's no doubt about that, but I think she will understand."

Heinz remained agitated. A few beads of sweat popped out on his forehead despite the chill. "Yes, but will she forgive me before or after she calls off our wedding?" He began pacing again.

"Stop dwelling on it. You'll make yourself crazy." Faust stood, and joined his friend in his pacing, trying to work out the kinks from sitting too long. He reached around to rub his back. "I'm too old for this, you know."

Heinz clapped him on the back as they passed rows of containers, many of which he knew were filled with heroin. When they'd arrived at the Morskoy Drakon, several other smaller vessels were lined up to deliver the illegal cargo. A large crane lifted the containers onto the ship, dropping them down into the hold. Elsa managed to climb the rope ladder carrying Nikola who had been strapped to her back using a fishing net provided by Petrovich. It was the best they could do. Faust climbed up behind her keeping an eye out to make sure the child didn't fall, and Heinz struggled up one rung at a time with his beaten body. It was slow-going and painful, but they made it.

"What are you complaining about? I imagine Helga will never know the truth about where you've been the past few days," Heinz grumbled.

"Of course she will. You're telling Birgitta, aren't you? I can smell the shit sandwiches already."

"Only because I won't have a choice. Look at me? It's not like I can hide my injuries." He limped along.

"Maybe you don't need to tell her." Elsa spoke up.

Both men turned. "What do you mean?"

"Well, I'm not one to advocate a lie, but this was more in the line of duty, and does fall under the rules governing LKA operations, does it not?" She looked at Faust.

A slow grin spread across his face. "It does. I knew I hand-picked you for a reason, Kreiss."

"What?" Heinz waited.

"LKA operations fall under a gag rule, or so I've been told by my superior, so we are not allowed to speak of them. Why can't your injuries have occurred while in Sweden?" She raised an auburn eyebrow.

"At a conference for A16 advancement seminars?" Heinz appeared skeptical.

"Hear me out, Joseph. You've been on what she basically looked at as a mini vacation. Aren't there any activities in Stockholm where you could get hurt? Surely there is something stupid you might have done, given the chance, or offered the encouragement. Think, man!" She prodded him with her words.

He hesitated, thinking, and then, "Well, she did warn me to not get drunk with Swedes..."

Faust laughed. "And we all know the rivalry between Swedes and Germans when it comes to drinking. Joseph, I do believe you got yourself into a bar fight." He clapped Heinz on the back who grimaced. "Oh, sorry, my friend!"

Heinz took a breath. "It's okay. Just don't do it again." He looked at Elsa. "This means, as far as everyone knows, I simply stayed in Stockholm for the scheduled period of time, and will return to Berlin on schedule, picked up by Herman." He rubbed his chin. "In the meantime, I can take Nikola on to Potsdam and deliver her to the Schuberts, hide in a hotel for a few days. I might not look quite as bad by then, and I can visit a doctor while there."

"There you go. Problem solved." She smiled.

"I guess this means I owe you one if it works," Heinz added.

"You don't owe me a thing. Just never do anything this hair-brained again or I will personally hog-tie you and deliver you to Birgitta myself. And I did this as much for her as you. She doesn't need any more stress before her wedding." She stood and approached her mentor. "You just do everything in your power to make her happy and be happy yourself now that you've put your ghost to rest."

Joseph Heinz looked at the young woman he'd taken under his wing for the past three years and smiled. "You know, I..." He stopped, swallowing.

Elsa grinned, reaching out to hug him gently. "I know. I love you too."

Faust rolled his eyes. "Yes, yes. I love you's all around. You've saved more than one marriage today, Kreiss. Good job."

The Berliner Zeitung staff had quite a show that morning. Salome looked every bit the sexy supermodel in her bronze, silk sheath dress that ended mid-thigh, and her black leather, knee-high stiletto boots. The dress had long sleeves, and the scoop neck managed to stay above her nipples, but only just barely. If she leaned over far enough, they peeked out, winking flirtatiously. It was Mahler's secret weapon to loosen Wolfgang Hachmeister's lolling tongue. The woman's almond-shaped brown eyes smiled down at her.

"Think it'll work?" She did a small turn in the foyer when Mahler picked her up.

Birgitta grinned. "If it doesn't, he's gay, and I'll have to return with Edelmann in tow."

Salome laughed. "Well, I'm happy to help, and it's nice to get out of here."

"I have it on good authority you'll be getting your passport back soon," Mahler said. "What are your plans after?"

Her eyes went soft. 'I'm not sure about the future yet, but I'm looking forward to seeing my family again. I miss them. My mother and father haven't seen me in years, and my younger sister and brother, I have no idea what's going on in their lives. I just want to see them, and then I can think about the rest later. I'll be with my family. It will all be okay." She sat in the car now, wrapped in her leather Trench coat, looking out the window as they merged onto the autobahn.

Mahler understood. The most important thing to these women was to get back home, get back to loved ones.

When they arrived at the offices of the newspaper, they marched in, "tits up" as Salome put it.

"Always put your best assets forward, Detective, and show no fear. This is my advice. It has worked for me. Never let anyone see you are less than one hundred percent in control and confident."

Birgitta chuckled. "It certainly does work. You intimidated the hell out of me when we first met."

Salome cast a sly glance sideways. "I was testing you."

"I know this now."

"But there is something you don't know."

"And what is that?" Mahler lifted one eyebrow.

"I was half serious. You are a very attractive woman. I wouldn't have minded if you'd failed my testing of your character just a little." She looked ahead, grinning.

Birgitta's eyes popped, and just as quickly, she wiped the surprise from her face. "I don't know what to say to that."

"You don't have to say anything. I see the engagement ring on your finger." Salome looked at the princess cut diamond set in white gold. "I hope he knows how lucky he is."

Mahler looked at her ring. She smiled, and then remembered she hadn't heard from Joseph in days. Her smile disappeared. "I'm beginning to wonder." She clipped off the words as they reached their destination. Herr Hachmeister's office door was open. He sat behind his desk typing away on his computer unaware he was about to be ambushed by both brains and beauty. He would give up his source one way or the other before the hour was up.

She looked at Salome. "Ready?"

Salome squared her shoulders, her breasts proudly displayed in draped bronze silk. "Ready."

Together, they entered the den of the beast, prepared to slay this journalist by wit or by tit. There would be no prisoners taken.

Hachmeister proved a worthy opponent when questioned, but he was still a man, and Salome knew how to make a man spill his secrets without realizing he had. Birgitta thought she would make a marvelous spy. Her own hard-hitting inquiries erected the man's defenses, but her counterpart's compliments made him erect in other areas. It was almost embarrassing. Wolfgang literally had a boner, his jeans taught over his crotch, as Salome leaned forward, begging him with ruby-red lips to help them catch a killer, the person who may very well have murdered her friend. It was a tad over-dramatic, but Salome was now fully immersed in her character. The man, who was in his early thirties, and should have had a bit more control over himself couldn't keep his eyes from zeroing in on her now exposed nipples.

Mahler understood. Hachmeister had 'nerd' written all over him. His slight physical stature, thick glasses, and lack of style spoke to a man who'd spent his life in books, fantasizing. He'd probably never seen a naked woman outside of a magazine, and now one was right in front of him, reaching a hand out to touch his knee in a beseeching manner. She watched it play out, and then wished she hadn't. As soon as Salome's fingers touched just above his knee, grazing his thigh, Wolfgang shuddered, wetting himself as he involuntarily orgasmed.

"No worries," she said, coming off the chair she sat upon, and sinking to her knees before him. She continued to massage his thighs, just out of sight of anyone walking past the door. Mahler shifted right to help further block any curious eyes. "Just give us a hint. I'll offer some names, and you just nod yes or no. Then you won't be betraying your source. We will simply figure it out. Okay?" Her hands traveled up, closer to the dark stain at the vee of his pants. Amazingly, he was growing hard again.

Mahler kept her eyes up, not wanting to watch the man have both his first and second sexual encounter with a professional escort. It was probably the experience of his life, but it didn't come free. He would pay with information.

"Now, was your source a man named Rudi Oppel?" Salome's hands moved up and down his legs as she introduced the names of possible leaks.

Wolfgang squirmed, sliding down a bit in his seat. "I've never met him, but I do know who he is."

Salome removed her hands. "Tsk tsk. You need only nod yes or no."

"Oh, I'm sorry." He shook his head in the negative. Salome leaned closer between his knees, and resumed touching his thighs, her breasts swaying as she allowed them to come into contact with his legs.

"Okay, then. How about a blond man named Karl?"

The journalist again shook his head "no." Hands moved further up, making circles with her manicured fingernails.

"Any special forces types? Law enforcement?"

Mahler waited. This one could be key. Still, Hachmeister offered a negative reply. Salome looked at her. She was running out of names.

"Is it a male?" Mahler added.

Negative reply, and Salome's hands did not advance. Beads of sweat popped out on Hachmeister's forehead as his erection strained the threads of his pants.

Salome returned to her questioning. "Is it a female?"

A strong nod "yes" was accompanied by short, panting breaths. He was giving Salome clues with his eyes to keep asking, or maybe it was to put him out of his misery. At this point, Mahler wasn't sure.

"Okay, and is this woman someone we might know?"

Again, a nod for yes. He was squirming hard in his chair.

"Is she famous?"

Wolfgang's head nodded.

"Famous as in celebrity?"

Back to a negative shake.

"Not a celebrity, but she would be known to us. A public figure?"

Nodding again. Hachmeister's hand waved at Salome to keep asking. The man licked his lips, mouth agape. He was pretty far gone now, and her fingertips were merely an inch from touching his tent pole.

She looked at Mahler. "Someone in government?"

He looked at Mahler, nodding.

Salome took it home. "Do you know her name?"

He nodded yes.

Mahler stared at Hachmeister, voicing her suspicion. "Is her name Vera Wolf?"

He stared back, reluctant. Salome's hands stilled, and he looked pained. He was biting his lip, having an internal struggle between his journalistic integrity, and immediate need. Looking around, he seemed to come to the conclusion that his integrity had already gone out the window. He nodded once, and then looked at the woman between his thighs, need shining in his glazed blue eyes.

Salome stood, leaving him high and dry. "Thank you, Herr Hachmeister. It has been no pleasure."

"What? Wait! You can't just leave me like this…" He stopped himself, sitting up straight, clearly uncomfortable. "Get out. Get out of my office!"

"Have a wonderful day, Wolfgang." Birgitta turned and left, followed by Salome. They could still hear Hachmeister cursing as he got up and slammed his door shut.

"Probably going to finish himself off," Salome laughed.

"You think so? Here?" Mahler was shocked.

"Why not? He was willing to let me do it for him here. What's the difference?"

"I don't know anymore." They headed down the elevator. "But now we have the source, thanks to you and your impressive skills. My God, you could turn governments on their ears." What she needed to find out next was how Vera Wolf knew these details. The only logical answer was that she was the one making the threats, but this didn't seem to fit with who the woman was. She had no real motive to make such threats. Sure, Obermeyer ended their affair, but Wolf wasn't the vengeful scorned woman type, was she? She held an important position within the Socialist Democratic Party, and she was also a striking looking woman in her own right. She knew what a dog Obermeyer was when it came to women. She couldn't have been blind to the tabloids before dating him, so what was the connection? Political gain, perhaps? Sink Obermeyer before the election to help boost her own party? It wouldn't be unheard of, but it certainly jeopardized the investigation. How she knew what she knew was the key. For that alone, she would need to pay a call on Vera Wolf.

Mahler's phone rang. "Yes?"

"It's Levitz. We have Oppel."

"I'm coming in. Remember, Captain, no one can question him except Dieter. I'm calling him now." She hung up and dialed.

"Kelner," he answered.

"Dieter, it's Birgitta. We have Oppel at the station."

"I'm on my way. No one questions him but me."

"I know. I've already reminded Levitz."

"Good," he said. "I'll bring Lukas along."

He hung up. Birgitta looked at Salome. "I need to get back to the station house. I'll get you a cab." She hailed the first passing taxi.

As Salome stepped into the backseat, Mahler leaned down. "Thank you, Salome. I truly appreciate what you did to help me."

The woman smiled, placing her hand on Mahler's. "You're welcome. And thank you for keeping your word. I'll never forget it...or you." She leaned out, quickly placing a kiss on Mahler's lips. "Auf wiedersehen!"

She closed the door, and the taxi drove off. Mahler stood, stunned. Shaking her head, she made her way to her car and drove straight to headquarters. Vera Wolf would have to wait. They now had their bird in hand.

Chapter 28

The port in Stockholm was bustling with activity. Getting off the ship unnoticed was made easier because of it. Heinz, Faust, Elsa, and the child were just a group of many in the throng of dockhands milling back and forth to load and unload cargo. The first order of business was contacting HackTwice. She met them at a café located a mile from the dock. In short order, she arranged for two hotel rooms near the airport and began work on new passports for all of them for a bump in her usual pay, of course.

"The child's will take the most time. I have no information on her. You've provided me with your own faux identities beforehand. It's just a matter of printing them out. I need to know her name, age, place of birth, and birthdate, also mother and father."

Heinz sighed. "We don't know her birthdate. I know she's three years old. Her name is Nikola Schubert. Her mother was Marlessa Schubert. Her father is unknown. She was born in St. Petersburg, Russia. I suppose you could use her mother's birthdate. It's March 7th, and just subtract three years."

HackTwice noted the information. Then, she had Elsa hold the little girl in front of the white wall of the diner. She snapped a quick close up of her face for the passport. Afterwards, the gothic hacker dropped them at the hotel and arranged for room service. "I'll be back in the morning with your papers, and some travel cash. I'll expect payment to my account as soon as you get back to Berlin, Herr Direktor," she said, addressing Faust.

"Of course. Thank you for being so efficient." He watched her leave and turned to Heinz. "I had no idea she was so young, and so small!" His eyes reflected his surprise.

"Don't be so shocked, Herman. Women are strong no matter their age and size. Just look at how well this sweet angel is handling the change in her life." Elsa held Nikola who looked around the hotel lobby with big, blue eyes. "Come, Nikola. Let's go see our room!" Already, she was picking up on German words, absorbing everything around her like a sponge. Elsa led the child away, seeking out the room they were to share. Heinz and Faust would share their own.

All they had to do now was wait.

"I really need to call Birgitta, but I don't have a phone. Brezhnev's thugs took the one HackTwice gave me, and she's already mailed my phone back to your office along with my real passport."

Faust inserted the room key card into the slot. "Well, just call from the room in a bit. Put it on the bill. I guess it doesn't matter now, and you can begin building your barroom brawl lie. Best excuse to use the hotel phone I've ever heard."

Inside, the room was less than spectacular, but since they had no papers as of yet, it was the best that HackTwice could manage. Paid in cash and no questions asked. Either way, it was a world better than a cold cargo hold. Heinz chose the bed by the window, sinking down onto the brown duvet. "I'm exhausted." He laid back, stacking the pillows behind him to support his back.

Faust tossed the key card on the dresser, kicked off his shoes, and slowly lowered his out of shape body onto the bed by the door. "Almost like heaven," he mumbled, laying back and pulling the covers over him. Within minutes, both men were sound asleep.

⸻◄O►⸻

The interrogation of Rudolf 'Rudi' Oppel went on for hours. Korvettankapitan Dieter Kelner employed wartime tactics when Oppel refused to answer. Mahler watched from the other side of the two-way glass. Next to her, Lukas and Levitz stood, arms crossed over their chests. It was excruciating to behold. She'd never before witnessed what field-trained soldiers did to extract confessions, and what she'd read or seen in movies didn't come close to reality. Oppel made only the statement that he had no involvement in the attempted murder of Ritt Obermeyer, and that he absolutely did not murder Bierkit "Marilyn' Wiedner. He demanded his lawyer and then clammed up after that.

Kelner left him inside the interrogation room, handcuffed to the steel table for an hour. He then re-entered carrying water, which he did not offer Oppel, but rather, drank it in front of him. When Rudi continued to resist, Kelner left again, this time turning the thermostat up in the room, heating it. He also turned on loud rock music leaving Oppel to sweat it out. The music kept the man on edge, increasing his anxiety, and the heat wore him down. Still, he did not crack.

Lukas entered the fray after the third hour. He carried in a file, which he placed in front of Oppel. Opening it, he pulled out a series of pictures. All the prints were taken off Rudi's website showing him dressed up like Marilyn.

"Do you recognize these images?" Lukas stood, one leg on a chair opposite Oppel as he balanced on one foot. He pointed at the first picture.

Oppel refused to look. "I want my lawyer."

"It looks remarkably like you. Rachel, is it?" Lukas pressed on. "Just what is Benders and Enders? What do you do there? Who do you do there?" He paused. Oppel remained close-lipped. Lukas continued. "What a strange thing for you to do, the man who prostitutes women against their will, to quite literally prostitute yourself. I mean, you're the undersecretary to the Minister of the Interior. Are you so unsatisfied with your job? Lonely, perhaps? Twisted and perverted?"

Oppel's eyes narrowed.

Lukas pressed the next button. "Or jealous?"

Rudi's jaw tightened, but he remained quiet.

The chair scraped the concrete floor as Lukas pulled it out, and lowered himself into it, leaning onto the table. "Jealousy it is, then. Want to tell me why you murdered Marilyn? What or who did she have that you wanted?"

Oppel exploded. "I did not murder her!" Spittle flew from his lips.

"Then who did? Spit it out, Rudi! If you didn't kill her then you know who did or else you wouldn't have been on the run, hiding out!"

The petite man shook with rage, but he contained it.

"We know all about your side businesses, Rudi. As we speak, Madame Denouve is in custody, and my men are raiding all three of your brothels. You ran whores, prostitutes that were illegally kept. We know all about your strong-arm tactics, threatening these women and men, taking away their passports. Many of these so-called sex workers are victims of kidnappings, sons and daughters whose families have been searching for them for years. How do you even sleep at night, slime that you are? We already have you on sex trafficking, complicity in multiple abductions, so if you think a lawyer can help you escape the twenty to thirty year prison sentence you're already going to receive, then I suppose I can go ahead and give him a call. Still, I think many of these photos will find their way to the press...just for my amusement."

Oppel's face was red. A vein throbbed in his forehead, and he clenched and unclenched his fists. Sweat poured off him, drenching the collar of his button-down shirt. Being handcuffed to the table left him unable to remove his suit jacket. If left for too much longer, he'd dehydrate completely and need medical attention. But they weren't finished with him yet.

"Of course, you could cooperate with us now, and we could negotiate on your sentence. But make no mistake, you're going to do time. How much is up to you." Lukas stood, exiting the room. He turned the heat and the radio back up as he walked out and left the file of pictures laying spread out on the steel desk in front of Rudi Oppel. The enraged man sat alone in the room for another hour, left to consider what little was left of his future.

By the time Kelner decided to go back in, Rudi was crying like a baby. He was ready to talk.

"I didn't kill her. I loved her. Not a romantic love, but like a sister. It's obvious, you see! I admired her. She was so strong." He sniffed, wiping his nose on his sleeve. "She was Obermeyer's favorite toy. He's a complete whoremonger, but he always returned to her. He was not kind, though. He was abusive, not so much in a physical way, but verbally. He put her down, called her names, and played mind games on her. He would lead her on, and then he'd go off with Karl. She would always tell me these things. That's how we became friends. She cried on my shoulder, never knowing I was responsible for her predicament. She knew me only as Obermeyer's assistant. She did not know I owned her or the agency. Still, I never knew anyone could be so brave as she was, and I wanted to help her. She reminded me of my mother, how she used to be, before...I didn't want Marilyn to end up like her!" He looked at Kelner with sad eyes. "I was going to return her passport that night, set her free, so I arranged for the room. A girl's night out. I went back to the hotel to meet her, but she wasn't alone."

Dieter waited, and when Oppel continued to sit in silence, he prompted him by slapping the man across the face. "Who was she with?"

Oppel stared at the table. "They were arguing. I could hear them through the door. I thought it was going to be just the two of us. I was dressed up, happy. I had her passport with me. It was to be a surprise."

Mahler stepped closer to the glass. The man she'd met, who seemed so together and confident, now appeared beaten down and broken.

"I couldn't let him see me dressed like her. It would undermine my authority. No one knew my secret except for Marilyn. She was the one who first recognized my need, my desire to be a woman. It was with her when I first slipped on a pair of silken nylons. She helped dress me in her lingerie. I loved it. I'd never felt so beautiful before, but with her, it was just natural. So easy. She accepted me, saw me for who I really am."

His voice trailed off. Dieter sighed, trying to be patient. He tapped the table. "You said she was arguing..."

Oppel looked up, seeming surprised Dieter was there. His face tightened in anger as he continued. "Yes. They were arguing. He was calling her a second-rate whore, said she couldn't have *him*. That he was his, and now always would be. He told her that her time was over, and there was no one who could protect her now." He seemed lost in grief.

"Who was it? Who was she arguing with and about what?" Dieter pushed.

Oppel looked at him. "Karl! It was Karl in the room with her. Jealous, petty, angry Karl! They were arguing over Obermeyer. The shitty part is, Marilyn could have cared less. She'd fallen out of her infatuation with the minister. I knew this. She'd told me. Still, with everything I knew, I had to keep supplying her to him at his demand. I still can't believe she's gone. I shouldn't have left them there. If I'd knocked, maybe she'd still be alive. I left her...to save myself, my reputation." He dissolved into tears.

Behind the two-way glass, Mahler gasped. She'd interviewed Karl, but he hadn't triggered her alarms.

"The one that's still missing," Lukas shared.

"Then we need to put out a BOLO on him," Levitz said, and then turned to Birgitta. "You spoke with all of them, yes? You have his information?"

"I do."

"Good." Levitz pulled out his phone and called the desk. "I need all units to be on the lookout for Karl..." He looked at Mahler.

"Gephart. Age twenty-eight. Blond hair, blue eyes." She pulled her notebook out of her pocket, flipping through the pages, and read. "Approximately one-hundred and eighty-two centimeters in height. Weighs seventy-nine kilos."

"Did you get that?" Levitz asked the dispatcher on the line. "Good, good. I need this BOLO to go statewide. Karl Gephart should be considered armed and dangerous. He's wanted for the murder of Bierkit Wiedner and possibly the attempted assassination of the Minister of the Interior." He completed the details of the order and ended the call.

"It is certainly no great leap in logic that he tried to kill Obermeyer in a fit of jealous rage. It kind of makes sense. I did think the threats seemed more like they came from a woman. Except..." Mahler speculated out loud.

Lukas clapped her on the back, not paying attention to her trailing statement. "Almost there. Kelner still needs to connect the dots from Oppel to the authorized drugs and human cargo coming into and out of Hamburg."

Mahler remained at the glass, watching Rudi Oppel fall to pieces. Something still didn't add up. The argument he says he overheard happened in the evening. This was after the fact of the shooting of Obermeyer in the park. Why would Karl go to Marilyn after shooting the minister? Wouldn't he go into hiding instead? It would make sense if he was seeking help to hide him, but the argument Oppel described doesn't sound like a man asking for help. It sounded like someone rubbing it in, if what he stated is true. And something else emerged in the interrogation. Oppel mentioned something about his mother, that Wiedner reminded him of her, of "the way she used to be," and that the woman accepted him as he truly was. Did that mean his mother did not? That she knew her son was a transvestite? Why did this even matter? She pondered the last while focusing on the first. Karl Gephart might well be the man who murdered Bierkit Wiedner, but it was possible there was still another perpetrator in the wind.

Over the next two hours, Oppel spilled his guts. His lawyer arrived, and after complaining loudly about his client's rights, was allowed to come into the room. By then, it was too late. The BND knew everything, and Oppel cut a deal for a reduced sentence for helping with capturing a killer. His lawyer tried advising against it, but in the end, with the evidence before him, and his client singing like a bird, knew it was the best deal they'd get.

Kelner and his men now had control over the ships coming into port. They immediately issued arrest warrants for the dock master, and several officials involved, ranging from the ministry to the mayor of Hamburg. By the next morning, news stations were breaking across Deutschland with the salacious scandal of human trafficking, drugs, and murder, all tied to the offices of the minister. Ritt Obermeyer would awaken to find his career in the toilet, even though he was found to not be directly involved himself. His association with Bierkit Wiedner and the man accused of trying to kill him was enough to drop him ten points in the polls, pushing the Socialist Democratic Party ahead, and projecting a landslide victory in next week's federal elections for the Bundestag.

Mahler returned home that afternoon, weary to the bone, but glad that one case was now all but closed. While the BND took over, she could return to her normal duties and devote her time to her wedding. To her surprise, her answering machine was blinking, indicating she'd received a call on her home phone. The convoluted message left for her by Joseph had her chuckling in relief. She'd been angry for days, all the while, her love had been recuperating from a fight, which caused him to break his phone.

"I told him not to drink with Swedes!" Happy for the first time in a week, she allowed herself a moment to relax on the couch. Before long, exhaustion set in and she fell fast asleep.

Chapter 29

True to her word, HackTwice sent over a package containing four passports. They even appeared worn, all except for Nikola's which looked newer, but had two country stamps in it. One showing she arrived in Germany from Russia one month after her speculated birthday, and another showing her recent travel from Germany to Sweden. This would get the child through customs in Berlin where Heinz would then rent a car and take her to Potsdam to meet her grandparents.

The flight was arranged for later that morning. Little lead time was given, but they had no luggage, so not much was needed. At Arlanda airport, Elsa used some of the travel money to purchase Nikola a few outfits, new shoes, hair ribbons, and a bright purple backpack to put them in. She added in some other essentials, and at the last minute, bought a small snow globe showing the tall, golden minarets of St. Petersburg, Russia. It would be a reminder for her one day of where she came from. She allowed the toddler to carry on her own bag, worn proudly over her pink coat.

On board, Elsa made sure to have the little girl sit next to Heinz since she would be spending the remainder of her time with him. The look on her face showed how difficult it was for her to let go. She'd already begun to form an attachment to the sweet smiles Nikola showered on her.

"It's for the best," Faust said, patting Elsa's hand. "And you're sitting right behind her, just in case she needs you."

"I know." Elsa bit her lip. "Everything will work out, and Joseph is wonderful with children."

"Strangely enough, yes. Not bad for an old grouch, is he?" Faust chuckled. "He was rather good with Therese too. She loved him."

She was surprised by his easy sharing of what must be a painful memory. "Well, he had Ingrid. It wasn't like he was inexperienced."

"Therese was before Ingrid. Before he married Eva. They'd only just met then. I think, though, that Eva knew Joseph would be a good father when she saw him with our little one. Helga always said that's what convinced Eva to say yes. Apparently, those two hens had discussed Heinz's merits as a husband. I guess that was the tipping point."

Elsa laughed. "I can just imagine that. Well, part of it. I've never met Eva. Joseph has said very little about her. What I know has come more from Birgitta, and I don't think she knows the full score either."

"She knows the office gossip. Birgitta came after Joseph's breakdown. He'd been divorced for some time by then, and only just getting his life back together. At least he'd stopped drinking by then. He was still a cross bear to be around." He paused and smiled. "You know, she was a calming influence on him from day one. I remember he tried a few times to complain about her to me. He didn't want a partner, especially not a female. He said, 'Herman, she's too quiet! And you should see how small she is. I'll be spending all my time trying to save her from danger and will probably end up dead!' Now that I look back, I think it's safe to say she was the one who saved him...from himself."

A grin blossomed on Elsa's lips. She glanced between the two seats in front of her. Joseph was drawing pictures on a napkin and telling Nikola a story in his broken Russian. The little girl was leaning on him, laughing. Whether it was at his story, the pictures or his terrible accent, she wasn't sure, but the father she knew him to be was on full display.

As if sensing eyes on him, Heinz looked back, catching Elsa watching. "No peeksies!" He shoved a pillow over the opening. Elsa could hear him and the little girl giggling together.

Mahler awoke the next morning refreshed. Showered and dressed for business, she headed down to the station house and was immediately called into her captain's office. He was standing by the window, staring out at the cold, gray sky. He gestured for her to close the door.

"Good morning to you too." She sat, crossing her legs.

"I have news," he began. His face remained serious. "Three hours ago, two of our patrol officers received a tip on Karl Gephart's whereabouts."

"Have they found him?"

"They did. He was holed up in a cheap motel on the east end of town."

"That's great news. When do we get to question him?"

He turned to look at her. "We don't."

"What? Why not? Surely the BND doesn't need him. It was Oppel who was connected to their case." She sat forward, outraged.

"We don't get to question him because he is dead." Disappointment was clear in Levitz's eyes.

"Dead?" Mahler's eyebrow rose.

"He hung himself in the shower, or it appears that way."

"Suicide? Was there a note at least?" She blinked in disbelief.

"No note. But we found a laptop in the room. It was registered to Elite Worldwide, Oppel's business umbrella. Once we knew that, we had to turn it over to Kelner, dammit. I have no idea if it was in his possession by permission or stolen, but I'm guessing stolen, and probably the computer used to send the death threats to Obermeyer." Frustration marred his words.

"Damn Dieter! He could've at least let us run a forensic analysis on it first." Mahler blew out a breath. "What else?"

"The desk clerk said he'd checked in the night before last, around three in the morning. That puts him there at least five hours after the time Oppel says he heard the man arguing inside Wiedner's room." He walked to his desk and sat down. An open file lay in front of him. He turned it around to show Mahler. "And it means he checked into that room four hours after the coroner's official time of death for Wiedner. Want to know the interesting part?"

"Of course." She eyed the file, listening.

"Gephart made two calls from his room, both to the same number, around twenty minutes apart."

"And? Who did he call?" Mahler waited.

Levitz held her gaze. "Bierkit Wiedner's cell phone."

"What? Why would he call her if he killed her?"

"Exactly my thought," Levitz stated. "I reviewed the hotel's security tapes again. Gephart never stepped foot inside the Omni. If he did, he managed to escape every security camera from the front door to the room. He left only one message out of the two calls. He asked her to call him, and he sounded upset. Levitz chewed his lip, appearing disgruntled. "I'm not going to say you may have been right…"

Mahler narrowed her gaze, her expression revealing her frustration. It was one she was used to, not being taken seriously by male superiors, even when she was right. She said it for him. "But it appears I was right. Oppel lied." She let that sink in and moved on. "So, you got the autopsy results," she stated, sitting forward to read the paperwork. "When?"

Levitz was glad for the shift away from his own error in judgement. "About forty-five minutes ago. Preliminary results show a cardiac episode induced by an overdose of drugs. We still have to wait on toxicology. That'll be another week, but in the meantime, we know that an overdose killed her. What we don't know is if it was self-inflicted on purpose, by accident, or if someone else caused her to overdose."

She flipped a page. "Did the coroner offer any speculation into the type of drug or drugs?"

"He says opioids."

"As in heroin?" Mahler looked at her captain. "Inhaled or injected?"

Levitz pointed to a diagram on the page. "Doctor Menghala reports a fresh injection site located on her left arm just above the wrist. Whether or not it was murder is inconclusive at this time."

Mahler cringed. She was no fan of needles and could never understand how anyone could shoot up drugs. "But opioids," she muttered, thinking.

"I know. Oppel is still connected somehow, and now that he's made a deal with the BND, we won't be able to touch him. I don't give a shit that he denies killing her. I think you were right, he did it. He was involved in bringing drugs in as well as prostitutes to supply his businesses. We've shut them all down. More than half the employees were there against their will." He tapped the desk hard with his index finger. "But we have closed thirteen missing persons cases because of it."

"That many?" She looked up. "That's good. Still, something is off."

"He's a good liar."

"No, that's not it. It's something I can't put my finger on just yet." She considered why Oppel would create such an elaborate lie. The man was already caught on so many criminal violations, what's one more? He'd made a point of implicating Karl, but why?

"Now you sound like Heinz. It's never the obvious answer for him either." Levitz sighed, frustrated.

"And he's usually right, as you well know." She sat back, considering. "What about the money trail?"

"We're not privileged to what Kelner finds from here on out. They have the authorization to find and freeze all Oppel's bank accounts. They're not going to share that with the likes of me and you."

"No, I suppose not. But we have jurisdiction over Gephart's and Wiedner's. We can, at the very least, check to see if they even had bank accounts."

"Not likely since both were indentured by Oppel. You can't open a bank account without a passport or papers."

"Legally."

"What?" Levitz eyed Mahler.

"But what if they opened one illegally? It's not too difficult to get a fake I.D. card."

He stared at her for a moment. "See what you can find, but don't waste too much time on it. It's most likely a dead end. The real information is in what Kelner and Trommler uncover in Oppel's possessions."

"And Obermeyer's. Remember, he paid to play at the house in Reinickendorf. He may have also spent lavishly on his two favorite sex toys."

Levitz smiled. "And we have Obermeyer, by his own request. Look into it. Get back to me if you find anything."

Mahler stood. "Aye, Captain." She offered a mock salute and headed to her desk to do some digging.

An hour later, she had some answers, she just wasn't quite sure what to make of them. Karl Gephart had a savings account at a small bank not far from the ministry offices. This wasn't unusual in itself, but the amount revealed by the bank manager at Mahler's official request was fifty-two thousand euros. Prior to three days ago, there had only been two thousand accrued over a period of three years. The deposit of fifty thousand came in one lump sum by wire from a numbered Swiss bank account the morning after Obermeyer had been shot. There was no way to discover the owner of the Swiss account. Numbered accounts were protected to the highest level of privacy and usually belonged to criminals and corporations. One and the same in Mahler's opinion. If Oppel had such an account, she wouldn't be able to get the clearance required to look into it. Still, perhaps she could speak with Lukas, ask if an amount of fifty thousand had recently been paid out of any of Oppel's accounts.

Putting that aside for the moment, she pulled up the website for the Berliner Zeitung. Over the next half hour, she looked at articles and pictures of Obermeyer from the park opening to his paramours. There were quite a few of him with Marilyn, but none with Karl. He apparently never took the man out in public, probably to protect his own heterosexual image. Marilyn smiled in some but lacked expression in the most recent ones. In one, she was lifting a champagne flute, grinning. It was New Year's

Eve 2015. In another, she sipped a cocktail while Obermeyer rubbed elbows with elected officials. In others, she was eating dinner at lavish events, sitting next to the minister. Something sparked in Birgitta's memory. She scrolled back through them all, looking hard. Her brows furrowed as she concentrated.

"Oh, my God!" She stood, and quickly made her way to Levitz's office, throwing open his door without knocking. "It was definitely murder!"

He jerked, taken by surprise. Looking up, he stared. "What was murder?"

"Marilyn. She was murdered." She sat down across from him.

"How do you know?"

"Because, Captain, she was left-handed." Mahler reached across his desk, grabbing his keyboard, and accessing her files. She pointed at the screen. "Look." She scrolled through all the pictures.

Levitz watched them roll by. "There was no way she could have shot herself up in the wrist of the hand she would normally use."

"Exactly. It would've been too difficult. People always use the hand they favor." Mahler tapped the keyboard again, pulling up scanned documents. "See? This is her official employment application for Denouve's. Look at her signature."

"It slants to the right. Yes, left-handed."

"I also found that Gephart had a bank account. He received quite a large deposit the morning Marilyn was found dead." She went on to explain about the Swiss account.

"So, someone paid him off. But for what? To kill her or to kill Obermeyer?"

"That, Captain, is the question."

At Berlin Tegal Airport, Faust, Elsa, and Heinz went their separate ways. "This should get you through until Friday. Let me know how it goes. If they decide they don't want Nikola, I'll come get her." Faust handed over a wad of cash to Heinz.

"Thank you, Herman." He pocketed the money.

"Good luck, Joseph." Elsa hugged him, and then she squatted down to eye level with the little girl. "And good luck to you, too, sweetheart." She gathered Nikola close for a hug.

"Ich liebe dich," Nikola said as she threw her arms around Elsa's neck.

"I taught her that." Heinz grinned.

"She's a smart girl," Faust said, fondly ruffling the child's curls. "Despite everything she's been through, she's going to be all right."

"One way or the other." He waved at them. "See you at the end of the week." Heinz led the child away to the rent-a-car counter as Faust and Elsa walked outside to hail a taxi.

The drive to Potsdam was uneventful. Heinz secured an Audi sedan, navigating the autobahn with ease. When they reached the city, he located the nearest police station. With the help of local law enforcement, he found the current address of Anton and Marie Schubert.

As he drove there, he thought about what to say. He hadn't seen them in years. The last time they'd all been in the same room together, Marie blamed him for not bringing her daughter back home. Even though they both knew in their hearts that this was not his fault, and he'd certainly given it his all trying, it still hurt. The words, once spoken, could not be taken back, and the damage they caused could not be fixed. Years of friendship had shattered in that moment. Anton, once his dear friend, had to choose a side, and that side, rightfully, was with his wife. With regret, he gathered Marie and left the Heinz household. Afterwards, his own marriage fell to pieces as first his daughter, Ingrid, blamed him for not finding her friend, and his wife, Eva, grew tired of an angry, exhausted, and increasingly drunk husband crawling into their bed each night. The tension between the three of them continued to stretch thin until finally, it snapped.

The old feelings were still there, under the surface of scars. He knew he could never return Marlessa to them, but he hoped that bringing Nikola home would fill that hole in their hearts.

Heinz looked at her. She was strapped into a car seat, playing with her stuffed rabbit. "I'm not a praying man, Nikola, but I'm praying hard now that this all works out. You deserve it. So do your grandparents. They're very nice people, really. I promise."

She smiled, unaware.

"Can you say Oma?"

"Oma!" She mimicked.

"Very good! How about Opa?" He slowed, turning right off the round-about.

"Opa!"

Heinz chuckled. "That's very good, dearest. Remember that. It will help."

"Ich liebe dich!" She shouted, laughing, not understanding what she was saying.

"I love you, too, Nikola." Under his breath, he whispered, "And I sure hope you love her as well, Anton and Marie."

"You've arrived at your destination," The Audi's GPS stated.

Heinz parked in front of the house on Ahornstrasse. It was a typical German cottage style with a deep, steeled roof. The yard was fenced in by boxed hedges, which were bare of leaves and covered with snow. The tan siding was trimmed with a dark brown. The windows were slightly fogged over, and smoke escaped the chimney. He imagined that Marie was probably baking something inside. She loved to bake; cookies, cakes, pies, streusels, it didn't matter. It was the key reason Anton's waistline fought a battle every day, making him run a few miles each morning to keep the sweets from gaining ground.

He stepped out of the car and went around to help Nikola out of her seat. Together, they faced the sidewalk leading to the front door. "Be brave, little one," he said, but mostly for himself.

They walked forward, each step taking them both a bit further towards a new path in life.

Before Heinz reached the porch, the front door opened. Anton stood, staring at them.

Heinz stopped, taking in his old friend. It was clear that the cakes and pies had finally won the war. Anton's waist had grown, along with the hair on his chin which sprouted into a white beard. He looked older, and very much like a little girl's idea of a grandfather.

"Joseph, what are you doing here?" he asked quietly.

"Anton, I'm not even sure where to begin." He looked at the man, who was now looking down at Nikola. His eyes misted over, and his mouth hung open in disbelief as if he'd just seen a ghost.

"This is Nikola," Heinz began.

"Marie!" he shouted over his shoulder. "Marie! Come here, quickly!"

"What is it, Anton? I have cookies in the oven." Marie Schubert arrived behind her husband, and then glanced from him to Heinz. "Joseph!" Her voice revealed a familiar contempt.

She looked the same to Heinz, still trim, still attractive, but her faded blonde hair was liberally highlighted with silver, and her face contained more lines. His gut clenched in response to hearing her say his name with so much rancor. Fighting past it, he spoke. "Hello, Marie."

"Look!" Anton pointed as his voice shook.

Marie looked at the little girl. Slowly, the hard lines in her face softened. She sucked in a breath and grabbed Anton's arm. "She looks like..." Marie's eyes bounced to Heinz, questioning.

"Yes, she does look like Marlessa, quite a bit, actually." He looked at them both. "She's your granddaughter. This is Marlessa's daughter, Nikola."

Marie sobbed, holding onto her husband who now had tears running down his plump cheeks even as his lips split into a huge grin.

Anton was the first to step forward, shaking with emotions. He squatted down, bringing himself eye level with the girl. "Hello, Nikola. I'm your Opa Anton." He cautiously opened his arms.

Nikola looked from Heinz to Anton.

"It's okay," he said in broken Russian. "This is your Opa."

Nikola looked at Anton again. "Opa!" she said, and touched his nose with her tiny finger before raising her arms, and sliding them around his neck.

Holding his granddaughter tight, Anton cried. Standing slowly, he lifted her up and turned to Marie. He pointed at his wife. "This is your Oma, darling. Say hello."

"Oma," Nikola mimicked.

Marie's eyes flooded with tears. "Hello, darling dearest." She reached out, and Nikola went into her arms.

Anton turned to Heinz. "How?"

"It's a long story."

"Then you'd best come inside, my old friend. Come in! Come in." He hustled Joseph into the house followed by Marie who refused to let her granddaughter go.

By the end of the evening, and after a lengthy and difficult explanation fraught with tears, Heinz left the Schubert residence with an invitation to return. As he stood on the curb watching the scene through the window of the cozy cottage house, his heart healed. Joseph knew he'd finally been redeemed, and he could move forward, free of his haunted past, to a bright future with the love of his life.

Chapter 30

Lukas sat across from Birgitta at a small café in the Tiergarten. He'd returned to work that day for appearances sake. He still had quite a bit of work to do for the BND, but it could wait until the following day. Another Russian ship was scheduled to come in, and his unit would be there to intercept it.

"Thanks for meeting me, Lukas." Mahler sipped her coffee and waited as their server set two plates before them. She picked up her fork and knife, cutting into the steaming rouladen.

"Not a problem, but make it quick, Birgitta. I have a lot to prepare for." He took a bite of his buttered kartoffeln.

"We received the initial conclusions from Wiedner's autopsy, and it shows an overdose. Dr. Menghala speculates opioids, which I don't think is a coincidence. We're waiting on toxicology, but in the meantime, we know it was murder."

"So, there is no way her death was accidental." He didn't ask a question, but rather, made a statement."

"No. Marilyn was left-handed, and the injection site was right above her left wrist. People who shoot up do so using the hand they favor. Also, the site itself is an unusual spot to inject. I read through the file. There were no other track marks on her body. She wasn't a habitual user, if even a user at all."

"I see. So, what is it you're saying exactly?"

"I believe her death is somehow connected to your investigation."

"You think Oppel was lying about not killing her?"

"No, not that. I believe him, but he knows who killed her."

Lukas sipped the red wine in his glass. "Yes, you were there during his interrogation. Oppel indicated Karl Gephart as the killer. I understand he was found dead this morning, so there's no way to confirm that. All you have is the hotel security tapes and Oppel's confession placing him there. It's more than enough to convict a man. I'd say Karl's suicide is an admission of guilt."

"One would think so, but we discovered something of interest, something we missed initially. Hotel surveillance doesn't back up Oppel's story. Gephart was never at the Omni that night. Unless he's a master of disguise or can make himself invisible, he was nowhere on those tapes."

Lukas looked up but said nothing. Mahler could see the wheels in his mind spinning.

"I also discovered that Karl had a bank account. Want to guess at what I found in it?"

"I know you're going to tell me, so why guess?" He steepled his fingers, waiting.

"You're right. Gephart received a lump sum deposit of fifty-thousand euros the morning Marilyn was found dead. It came from a numbered Swiss bank account. As you're well aware, no one has access to discovering the owner without a warrant from the highest court, and even then, getting a name is hard."

He dropped his gaze, smiling to himself as he picked up his utensils and began eating once again. Between bites, he offered, "So you want our help in finding out who paid him. You've just cleared Gephart of Wiedner's murder yourself, according to what you just told me. Anything else puts Gephart out of your jurisdiction and firmly into ours. Any further investigation, as you say, would be related to the BND's case, not your own. And yet, you are still asking me to help you."

Mahler watched him. Lukas was a handsome young man, but annoyingly cocky. Elsa loved that about him. She called it 'confidence.' Birgitta called it being an ass. Still, she liked him even if sometimes she wanted to smack him across the back of his head.

"Yes. Will you?" She maintained eye contact, not backing down.

He stared back, thinking hard, and then looked at his plate. "I'll see what I can uncover, but I can't promise anything."

She smiled. "That's all I ask, Lukas."

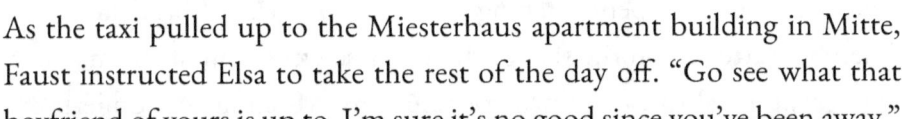

As the taxi pulled up to the Miesterhaus apartment building in Mitte, Faust instructed Elsa to take the rest of the day off. "Go see what that boyfriend of yours is up to. I'm sure it's no good since you've been away."

She sighed, smiling, and wondered exactly how much truth was in that statement. "I actually hope he is up to something, at work. I'm tired, Herman. All I want to do is sleep. I welcome a few quiet hours."

She stepped out of the cab. Faust rolled down the back window. "You did very well, Elsa. I'm proud of you." She grinned. "Don't get too cocky though. You have a great deal to learn. We'll begin tomorrow. I'm going to arrange for some classes for you beginning with linguistics and Global Politics. And I want to get you into martial arts training as well."

She leaned down, resting her elbows on the door. "You're going to kill me, aren't you?"

He patted her arm. "Nonsense. It's nothing you cannot handle. I have faith in you. Tschüs!" He tapped the roof, and the cab pulled away.

As they merged back into traffic, Faust gave new directions. "Head to the Landeskriminalamt, back entrance." The driver nodded and made a right at the next cross street.

It took twenty-five minutes to reach his office in the falling snow. The wind had picked up, blowing the flakes onto surfaces and frosting the windows of the building. Upstairs, in the corner office, Faust greeted his secretary.

"Any news?"

She turned and smiled. "Welcome back, Herr Direktor." She pointed at his office door. "Messages on your desk, and six new files with updates on operations in Saudi Arabia, Britain, Turkey, and America."

"Very good. Thank you, Lora. Efficient as always." He gave her a mock salute and entered the familiar space of his office.

He sat down and began going through messages first. One from Mahler caught his eye. He sighed. *Not going there just yet,* he thought. He put that one aside, intending to call her before leaving at the end of the day. The next hour was spent catching up on the progress of his field agents. Then he started in on the six new files. These were requests from above, new geopolitical threats in need of solutions. Much like an undertaker, there was always fresh business for the LKA, and much like that same undertaker, if left unattended, it began to stink. It was the last file that caught his attention. It was from the BND. As Herman read through, he sat up straight. The same ship, on which they'd escaped St. Petersburg, and the corrupt arm of the Russian Federation, was due to dock in Hamburg the next day. The Military Counterintelligence Service, under Captain D. Kelner, would be leading a raid to intercept the cargo, and arrest the crew.

Faust chewed his lip. He knew what this meant. Vladimir Brezhnev was going to be pissed. Somehow, he didn't think the Butcher would believe it was a coincidence or that he and Heinz had nothing to do with it. MAD was asking for the LKA's assistance with discretion, running interference with the media by deflecting any questions from their operation. The action was set to commence in the pre-dawn hours. The tip they received stated the Morskoy Drakon would arrive around 4:00 a.m. There wasn't much time to manufacture the cover up.

"Lora?" He called out. "Bring me the master list. Hurry, please."

Lora immediately went to her file cabinet and pulled out a large, blue book. The master list contained a compilation of past media stories used by the LKA in such events. Faust knew he'd have to dig back into the oldest section of the list to find a feasible, and unused tale to spin to keep the media, and the public, looking the other way. Deflection, or as he liked to call it, government slight of hand, was all part of the job. He made a mental note to include training of professional lying to Elsa. Knowing her past career, he figured she'd pass with flying colors.

Lora entered with the book which she handed over. Faust took it and glanced up. "Seems like the world started falling apart while I was gone."

She pursed her lips. "Yes. Minister Obermeyer was shot, not fatally, at a park opening, and the next day, one of his many paramours, a prostitute, was found dead in her suite at the Omni. The person police believe attempted to kill him, another prostitute from the same agency, was found dead in a motel the next day. As a result, the minister's campaign has dropped in the polls, and the Socialist Democratic Party has surged ahead, surprisingly with Vera Wolf being pushed to the top to lead." She turned and walked to the door. "And it always seems like the world is falling apart. It doesn't matter whether you're here or not, Herr Direktor. You're only one man. You cannot hold it all together by yourself, so don't fret. Just handle things one catastrophe at a time." Her voice trailed off as she returned to her own desk.

Faust sat stunned, staring after her. "Scheisse!" He quickly formulated a plausible news story for the media and sent it off to Lora to prepare the press releases. She would see that they went out exactly one hour after the raid, and that the LKA communications chief received his copy of the script. Arthur Muenster would brave the cameras, and field the questions for them. That was his job, and he was damn good at it. With that disaster averted, he picked up Mahler's message. He figured this mess with the minister had probably fallen to her while Heinz was out of the country. Between that and being out of touch with her fiancé, he imagined she was as mad as a wet hen. Now it fell to him to put out some of her fire before Joseph returned.

"I think I'd rather eat a shit sandwich," he muttered, picking up the phone.

---◆O◆---

Lukas stared at the telegram. It was from Piers Larsson, a former Marine and fellow soldier who'd served alongside him and Dieter in Afghanistan. Piers was German born, but his family came from Switzerland. After the brutality of war, he decided to give a neutral country a try. Piers was a numbers man, and accounting came naturally to him. What else was an accountant to do in Switzerland? He became a banker and quickly moved up the ladder. Still, ever the soldier, Piers Larsson became an invaluable asset to his old unit. Never was that more apparent than now.

"I'll be damned." Lukas stared at the name on the paper. It was the owner of the numbered account that sent a payment of fifty thousand euros to Karl Gephart. Now he understood. Gephart was someone who could easily get close to Obermeyer. Someone who made a good pawn. Disposable. Unfortunately, he was not a trained assassin and had flubbed the mission. Lukas wasn't sure if it was fear of retaliation for failing to kill the minister or perhaps some misplaced grief at choosing money over his lover that sent Karl over the edge and straight into suicide. Either way, it was not connected to the current BND operation. This was another intrigue altogether.

He sat in silence contemplating whether to share what he'd found with Birgitta. He promised only to try. He could say he'd come up short, finding nothing. However, this still didn't answer who killed Bierkit Wiedner. But there were no other suspects besides Oppel, and now that the man had cut a deal with them, murder was not on the list of charges. His collusion, kidnapping, and human trafficking violations along with breaking state commerce laws were enough to put him away for life. Thanks to his cooperating with authorities, his sentence would be no more than ten years.

He considered all sides. Who would benefit more from knowing? He weighed the good against the bad, and by his reckoning, the good outweighed all. In the end, he decided that it was best for all concerned, what with all that had already happened, and with what continued to unfold, that it remain a secret. He pulled a lighter from his pocket and flicked the flint. Holding the paper over the flame, he watched as it turned to ash and cinders. "I'm sorry, Birgitta, but this is definitely in your best interests, and the best interests for all."

Chapter 31

Elsa ran to the UBahn, hopping on the car right before the doors closed. Her workday had been spent meeting the new instructors who would be teaching her the fundamentals of being a good agent. All had been going well since she'd come back yesterday. When Lukas came home, he was pleasantly surprised to find her there. He cooked them a wonderful dinner and then made love to her with a tenderness that stole her heart until they fell asleep in each other's arms. She'd watched him quietly, and for the first time, didn't feel apprehensive about their relationship. He'd told her again that he loved her, in the middle of sex, of course, but she knew now that he meant it. As she reflected over their time together, she realized he showed her in a million ways, every day, how much he cared. Finally, she got it. Love wasn't just three little words uttered in a fairy tale. Love was a verb exercised every day, and she truly enjoyed watching him exercise it last night.

With her newfound perspective, she also decided to forgive him in regard to the email from Dieter, and even lying to her about having not heard from his old friend. He had no idea she knew otherwise when she'd brought it up. Her man had a secret, but she knew he was a good man. She had secrets of her own, and there would be more in the future. As long as he accepted hers, she would leave him to his.

Now she was ten minutes late for a dress fitting with Birgitta. After chewing her out for not returning her calls, Mahler informed her that Frau Kluge required them one last time, and she'd better be in attendance. It was like having her mother dress her down. How could she refuse such a lovely invitation? Elsa prepared herself to listen to a bit of fussing. Joseph was set to return in two days, and she already knew he hadn't been able to call his fiancé in some time, but Birgitta did mention hearing from him, so it wouldn't be too bad. She smiled to herself. Keeping secrets was not easy, but she had to admit, it was a little bit fun.

The swaying of the tube as it sped along soothed her. She was home, and for the moment, everything seemed right in the world. Joseph called her that morning, letting her know there'd been a happy ending after all in Potsdam. He sounded different on the phone, optimistic, for what she figured was the first time in a long time. He'd gone to a physician and x-rays were taken. No broken bones, only severely bruised ribs. He was thankful. The swelling in his eye had gone down, and the bruising was expected to fade away before the big day. Birgitta would be happy. Elsa knew no woman wanted a black and blue groom in her wedding photos.

More good news came her way from her brother, Anno. Her friend, Sarah, would arrive next week from Texas. She planned to stay for a month, which sent Anno into the clouds. She still couldn't ever tell her brother what happened between herself and Sarah back in the day. He really wouldn't understand, and the two of them were such great friends now that it didn't matter. What with all the love in the air, her inner matchmaker came to the surface. A spontaneous call to Amsterdam led to an invitation for Paul Christiansen to attend the wedding of Birgitta Mahler and Joseph Heinz. He was overjoyed to hear of it and promised to be among the well-wishers that day. Stories were shared, and she was glad to hear he'd begun to settle down, even as he continued to paint. Paul was in a good place in his life, and she thought now might be the chance for him to find love just as she and Birgitta had. Elsa didn't tell him about Sarah's upcoming visit. She left that out, figuring fate would take its own course.

The tube slowed, stopping. She got off, making her way up the snow-covered stairs and around the corner to Frau Kluge's shop. Birgitta was already inside, standing on the dais, wearing her gown. She looked beautiful. Tears blurred Elsa's eyes as she walked inside.

Mahler turned. "It's about time you got here. Some maid of honor you are..." Birgitta looked at the redhead reflected in the mirror and stopped. "What's wrong?" She jumped down from the dais, and ran to Elsa, earning a frown from Frau Kluge.

"Nothing," she smiled. "Oh, my gosh, Birgitta!" She grabbed Mahler's hands, holding them out as she stepped back, admiring her. "You look stunning. Joseph is going to melt into a puddle when he sees you!"

The alarmed look in Mahler's eyes faded away, replaced by sheer joy. She smiled, looking hopeful. "You think so?"

"I know it! You are the most beautiful bride ever," she gushed.

"Stop crying already. You're going to get me started." Birgitta hugged her. "Thank you, Elsa. I needed to hear that."

"Break it up. You'll ruin my work!" Frau Kluge stepped up, separating the two women. "You," she said, looking at Elsa, "go get undressed. Your gown is hanging in the first dressing room. Chop, chop! I don't have all day!"

"Yes, ma'am!" Elsa laughed, giving Birgitta one last kiss on the cheek before following Frau Kluge's orders.

Minutes later, Elsa joined the two women in front of the three-way mirror. Birgitta grinned when she saw her.

"Talk about stunning! If Lukas doesn't drop to one knee and propose when he sees you, then you should leave him."

Elsa stood before the three mirrors, admiring her dress. "I feel like royalty in this." She turned this way and that, one auburn eyebrow raised. The design of the gown was similar to Birgitta's. Off the shoulder, lined in delicate French lace over the décolletage, and cut to the curvature of her body. From her waist, it flowed in an A-line to the floor. Royal purple satin with a mock-wrap skirt held one fine line of silver piping running from the silver, tulle fabric rose at her left hip down and across the front to the far bottom right where it continued around the hem. Her shoes were strappy silver heels to complement the piping.

Birgitta came to stand next to her. Together, they admired each other, grinning like schoolgirls. Unlike Elsa's gown, Birgitta's didn't have the mock wrap style, but rather, it gathered at the back, and draped down into a full train. The delicate cream color brought out the roses in her cheeks, and set off her dark, sable curls. Silver threads were woven into the cream tulle fabric of the bow around her waist and also used in her veil.

Elsa reached out, taking Birgitta's hand. "I'm so happy right now."

Mahler laughed. "I guess absence made your heart a little fonder for your man?"

"Maybe. At least, I'm not going to worry about it anymore. I'm just going to enjoy everything."

"That's all you can do, Elsa. Life is too short to spend it waiting for the bottom to fall out. We see enough of that in our line of work. At least we can go home to someone we love, who loves us in return."

"You're right, of course. It just took," she stopped herself, rethinking what she was about to say, "it just took a little time away, I guess."

Birgitta looked at her. "I'm glad. You deserve to be happy. As long as Lukas makes you happy, I won't have to kill him, yes?"

Frau Kluge looked up from sticking pins in Elsa's hem. "Men, can't live with them, can't bury the bodies deep enough to stay out of jail."

"Frau Kluge!" Birgitta chortled.

The old woman looked at them. "What? I was married once. He drove me crazy." She stuck in a few more pins. "I miss Herr Kluge every day," she mumbled.

Elsa looked at Birgitta, whispering, "She didn't kill him, did she?"

Trying to smother a laugh, she responded, "I don't think so. They were married for fifty-two years."

"I am not hard of hearing, ladies. Stay still, Officer Kreiss," Kluge ordered. Elsa straightened, behaving for the rest of the fitting. When all was said and done, Frau Kluge informed them that the dresses would be completed and delivered to Mahler's home by Saturday.

As they left the shop, they passed a rally in the square. The Women's Socialist Alliance was campaigning outside of a school for gifted children. They were advocating for young girls to study science and medicine. There was quite a crowd.

"Elections are Sunday, and they're still campaigning," Elsa stated. "I'll be happy when it's all over."

Mahler nodded. "Their party is ahead. Obermeyer's shooting, and subsequent scandal, has sunk him and his party."

"Good riddance, I say. The bastard."

Mahler grew quiet, thinking about the recent events, and how she'd discovered Vera Wolf's involvement in leaking information to the press. With all the focus on Oppel, and the human trafficking case, they'd all lost sight of that small detail. Wolfgang Hachmeister all but stated out loud that Wolf was the one who gave him his scoop. Then Oppel had been picked up, and she never did follow up on that information. It seemed like a moot point after Rudi confessed to running illegal brothels and colluding to import drugs and prostitutes. Once he placed Karl in Marilyn's room that night, no one asked any more questions. Now she knew, Karl was never there, after all. Her intuition screamed at her, but Levitz had already closed the case, figuring Oppel had lied, and was, indeed, the killer. Her captain stated it was the BND's problem now. Rudi Oppel was their bird, and he was singing. Much was being laid at this bird's feet, but he would not be punished nearly long enough or tough enough for his crimes as long as he cooperated. The Obermeyer threats were a footnote in a case file marked closed. "He's awake. I visited him at the hospital this morning. He's fit to be tied, but too weak to do anything about it. His career is at an end, and he knows it."

"He's lucky he's not being thrown in jail," Elsa snorted.

"There were no grounds. Soliciting escorts is no crime, and he didn't know they were being held illegally."

"So he says," Elsa added.

"Yes, and that's all we have to go on. You should have seen his face when he read that his ex-lover, Vera Wolf, was being put forth as the SDP's candidate."

"I bet he loved that." Sarcasm dripped from her lips.

Mahler looked at her. "He called her a cunning cunt, and an ambitious bitch. I tell you, I was shocked. I asked him why he ever dated her if he felt that way."

"What did he say?" Elsa shoved her hands into her pockets. The temperature was dropping rapidly, and the snow fell in wet streams now.

"He said, and I quote, she really knew how to suck a cock." Mahler rolled her eyes.

"What a pig!" Elsa huffed. "Well, then I'm even more glad she's kicking his ass. She'll do far better for Germany than he has, and I know all law enforcement will benefit after that bastard's indecent budget cuts."

"True. I still can't understand what she ever saw in him."

"Opposites attract. I mean, what else could it have been? I don't think she necessarily needed him politically."

Birgitta shrugged. "I don't know. Being seen with him in public may have boosted her career, if in no other way than by providing a stark contrast between the two of them. The papers were cranking out articles left and right over their political differences."

"Maybe. Who knows? I fucking hate politics. It's a breeding ground for the worst scum of the earth."

They rounded the corner to the UBahn. "Yes, but in rare cases, it gives us some of the very best people who only want to help."

Elsa descended the stairs. "Did I tell you Sarah's coming next week? She'll be here for the wedding."

"What? No! That's good news."

She laughed. "And I may have added to your guest list."

"Who?"

"Paul Christiansen. I called him."

Birgitta looked at Elsa's face as a sly smile spread across the redhead's lips. "What are you up to? Are you matchmaking?"

The tube slowed to a stop in front of them. As they stepped off the platform onto the car, she chirped, "Possibly. Maybe." Seeing Birgitta's raised eyebrow, she sat down, laughing. "Okay, yes. Yes, I'm matchmaking, but don't scold me."

Mahler sat down next to her. "Okay, I won't. Actually, I kind of like the idea. I still remember the puppy dog looks he used to give her. Poor Paul, he didn't stand a chance with Anthony around then."

"Ja, but that was almost four years ago now. They're both a little older, a little wiser. Paul's in a good place now, and Sarah was attracted to him then. Maybe this time they'll make a go of it."

"Well, this ought to be fun, at least."

The doors to the car closed, and the tube slowly sped up, leaving the station.

Sunday's election was a landslide victory for the Socialist Democratic Party and its new Minister of the Interior, Vera Wolf.

Heinz sat on his couch, happy to be home, finally, and with the woman he loved. His barroom brawl ruse rolled off his tongue yet again as his fiancé asked him to explain how a man trained to take down criminals managed to get so beat up. He did his best to keep the lie to a minimum, claiming that after so many rounds of drinks, he didn't quite remember the 'fight' or even how it began. All he knew were the results which happened to be a black eye, split lip, and bruised ribs. His phone had been lost, and he was unable to call her while he recuperated. As a side note, he quietly reminded himself to purchase a new phone—even though Herman had his old one. The price of the new gadget, and the inconvenience of transferring data would be his punishment.

"How in the world did you manage to finish up the seminars?" she asked.

"Well, they were very accommodating at the hotel. One of the presenters lent me his computer to go through all the Power Point presentations. I was able to do most of the work in my room." He hated himself for the lies.

Birgitta kissed his cheek. "That was very nice of them. Still, I wasn't there to help take care of you."

He smiled, thinking maybe his lie might have an upside. "And how would you have taken care of me, my love?"

Sitting on her knees, curled up at his side, she ran her fingers through his hair. "With some tender loving care, of course," she said, then clenched a fistful of hair, pulling his head back, "after I kicked your arse for being so stupid. What did I tell you about Swedes?"

Heinz cringed, laughing. "Am I to be an abused husband?"

Her fingers relaxed. "Of course not. I'm sorry." She resumed caressing his scalp.

"That's better. There's my girl." He picked up her free hand, kissing her fingers gently. "You had your hands full here anyway."

"That's because you were gone. If you'd stayed, you could have dealt with Obermeyer. So, you see, it was all your fault."

Heinz watched her face, a happy smile on his lips. "One more week, and then you're all mine."

Birgitta sighed. "Yes, one more week."

He shifted, slipping his arm around her, and pulling her onto his lap. "I missed you," he whispered, and then kissed her.

She melted, allowing him to take the kiss deeper. Before they knew it, she was straddling his hips as his hands roamed freely over her backside. When his fingers slipped beneath her blouse, she shivered and pushed against his chest.

"Stop!" She pulled back, panting.

Heinz sighed. "Are we still waiting until our wedding night?"

She giggled. "Yes, Joseph, we are!"

He gripped her hips and pulled her against the evidence of his desire, rubbing. "Just so you know, you're killing me, woman!"

A soft moan escaped her. "It's killing me, too, but just think how wonderful it will be."

"I think it would be wonderful now, here, on this couch." He looked around the living room. "With the evening news serenading us."

"Joseph Heinz!"

He laughed low, kissing her nose. "Yes, Birgitta Mahler soon-to-be-Heinz?"

She touched his face, wondering how she could've been so mad at him. "Nothing. Just...I love you."

He kissed her lips, a soft, sweet kiss full of promise. "I love you too." They remained that way, staring at each other. "Will you marry me?" He broke the silence. When she laughed, he added, "I'm serious! I need to know. Last I heard, you were scolding me about drinking with Swedes and threatening me with bodily harm."

"You're a crazy man, you know that? Of course I'll marry you, but not until next week." She climbed off him, and grabbed the remote, turning off the television. "For now, let's just go to bed."

He stood, taking her hand. "I can't wait until that means more than just going to sleep."

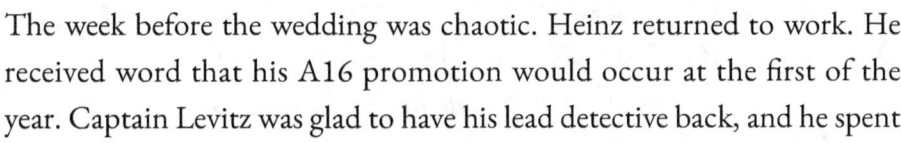

The week before the wedding was chaotic. Heinz returned to work. He received word that his A16 promotion would occur at the first of the year. Captain Levitz was glad to have his lead detective back, and he spent Monday getting Heinz caught up on recent events.

The news was full of stories about illegal smuggling of exotic pets following a raid at the port in Hamburg. With no one the wiser, the BND, with cooperation from the LKA, confiscated two tons of heroin and five abducted Swedish girls who were returned to their homes. With their cargo seized, the Bratva, and their business partner, the FSB, had a very public, and deadly falling out. Tensions grew between Russia and Turkey when millions in lost revenue could not be repaid. Incidents between the two countries escalated, resulting in the deaths of criminals, soldiers, and politicians. The underworld had erupted.

Mahler hadn't heard from Lukas. The mystery of the owner of the numbered Swiss bank account remained unsolved, but one new piece of information surfaced. After Dieter's men scoured the files taken from Madame Denouve's, they found, of all things, a stash of uncut heroin and a box of syringes in the Madame's possessions. Knowing the autopsy results showed Wiedner died from an opioid overdose, apparently her first usage, and finding heroin and needles in the Madam's possession revealed evidence he couldn't ignore. She was interrogated again, this time, by Dieter, using military tactics. When Denouve broke down, a startling confession followed. She murdered Marilyn. The BND and the local police hadn't caught it at first, but closer examination of the Omni Hotel security tapes confirmed not one, but two women in blonde wigs, dark glasses, one wearing a fur coat, and another in a more conservative Trench coat entered the lobby that night. The one in the Trench coat arrived first. Not thirty minutes later, the one wearing the fur coat showed, and proceeded up to the suite occupied by Wiedner.

The police and Dieter thought both were Oppel returning dressed as Rachel at the time, not noticing right away the differences in outerwear or the time stamps. He was surprised to learn the first one had been Madame Denouve. Lukas let Mahler listen to the taped confession.

"Is this you?" Dieter was clearly showing her printouts from the tape.

"It is."

"And why are you dressed this way?"

"Because I knew she'd open the door thinking I was Rachel," the woman answered. Her sultry voice was filled with contempt.

"How do you even know about Rachel? What's the connection? Why did you murder this woman, your employee?" Dieter hammered her with questions.

Denouve exploded. "Because he is my son! This slut thought she could take him away from me, turning him into some kind of pervert! I was not having it, I tell you! Rudi is mine, and I have sacrificed everything for that ungrateful brat! He is meant for more than one such as her. She only fed into his sickness!" She slammed her hand on the table.

Mahler sat shocked that day. She still couldn't believe it now. In a fit of maternal jealousy, Madame Denouve had killed another female considered, oddly enough, a rival for her son's affections. Now she knew why, for that one fleeting moment, the old woman had seemed familiar. She could see it now, the similarities between her and Oppel. Rudi was a bastard, his father unknown. Denouve used her real surname on the birth certificate and affected a French surname for business. She'd been a prostitute herself long before rising to the rank of Madame. Now she would descend to the rank of inmate alongside her son, but in separate facilities. He would get out in ten years for cooperating with authorities. Denouve would die in prison for murder, a murder her son knew she'd committed. It was clear now why he'd implicated someone else as being in the room that night with Marilyn. He knew his mother had been there. He may have even been there when she did the evil deed. Either way, he was complicit. His attempt to somehow protect his mother by pointing authorities in another direction failed.

That case was now solved, and she was glad for it.

Stepping outside, she headed to Frank's to grab lunch. Joseph was running an errand, so she was on her own. The sun decided to come out, melting some of the snow, but more was expected that night. September was winding down, and fall was upon them. The Schnitzel at Frank's was famous in this part of Berlin, and the counter was always busy. She went through her email while standing in line.

"Fancy seeing you here."

Mahler turned, hearing the familiar voice. Vera Wolf stood behind her, dressed in a red Prada business suit with black leather boots, and fine black wool coat.

"I see you enjoy Frank's too." She smiled.

"I do, Minister. Congratulations on your victory."

"Thank you, Detective. And you'll be happy to hear I'll be reversing Obermeyer's frugal policies, and reinstating funding back to all law enforcement and first responders with a ten percent raise."

"I am very happy to hear that. Thank you."

"No, thank you," she said. "Whatever would we do without our police, and firefighters, and EMS? What the old administration did was shameful."

"I agree." Birgitta stepped up and placed her order. Within minutes, her sandwich was packed in a to-go box. She pulled out her credit card.

"No, no. Let me get that for you. It's the least I can do." Vera Wolf stepped to the counter. "Please put Detective Mahler's order onto my ticket." She handed over payment.

Mahler pasted on a smile. "Thank you, again. You didn't have to, though."

The young man behind the counter handed the new minister her order, grinning as he recognized her, and whipped out his phone to take a picture. She smiled for him, posing with her Frank's bag. Looking at Birgitta, Vera Wolf winked. "It's only money. We ladies know how it should be used to everyone's best advantage. You know, Ritt never understood that. Always seeking money and power while taking both away from those around him, from the people who need it most. He was selfish. You know, yourself, the extent of his indulgences with whores. It was all about satisfying his immediate desires, and showing off, throwing his personal fortune around. He thought it would insulate him, save him from losing his lofty position." She turned, waving. "I guess his money didn't save him after all. Take care, Detective."

Mahler blinked, watching the woman walking away to the ministry car and driver waiting for her. *His money hadn't saved him after all.* Images of death threats carefully cut and pasted and mailed to Obermeyer flashed through her mind. In that moment, she knew. Vera Wolf was every bit as dangerous as her surname suggested. She'd fought her way to the top by intentionally sinking her opponent. When threats hadn't worked, she arranged to take him out of the picture permanently. It didn't even matter that Obermeyer survived the attempt; the result was the same. Dead man or dead political career. Either worked. Still, without proof of the payoff, Mahler had no case, only what her gut told her was the truth. That would never be enough in a court of law against a popular new Minister of the Interior. Sick to her stomach, she dumped the sandwich Wolf paid for into the garbage and headed back to work.

Chapter 32

The day dawned cold, yet sunny. A light snow fell the night before leaving a blanket of pristine white flakes glistening in the bright sunshine. Guests arrived at Berlin-Mitte's Soho House, gathering inside the Torstrasse event room overlooking Alexanderplatz. The AV area, usually used for business meetings, had been transformed into an intimate, romantic setting with seating for eighty-one attendees on crème-colored chairs tied with silver tulle bows. The altar was flanked by two large floral sprays standing well over five feet in height and filled with white peonies and white roses interspersed with purple freesia, lavender, and sprigs of dark green fern. The crème vases holding the giant bouquets were tied with purple satin bows. The wood paneled wall behind the altar was draped with a curtain of cream satin cloth tied with purple and silver ribbons, draping down in curling waves.

In the bridal suite, Birgitta stood before the full-length mirror, making last minute adjustments to her hair. Elsa helped while Sarah chatted in the background.

"I think you look perfect, Birgitta," she said.

Elsa smiled at her friend. Sarah Brown had grown into a lovely woman. No longer was she the naïve librarian she'd been when she first visited Berlin. After her experiences abroad, and her short-lived relationship with Anthony de Luca, Sarah had matured beyond her years. She'd returned to Texas and gone back to school, earning an associate's degree in liberal arts with a concentration in languages. She intended to continue to a bachelor's degree with a mind to becoming a teacher. And she had a surprise for Elsa.

"I'm moving to Berlin for a year as part of an exchange program. I'll finish out my degree here."

She dropped this bombshell on her first night at Elsa's. Her brother, Anno, had nearly done a backflip, but Lukas was quick to squelch his enthusiasm, taking him aside.

"You know it's never going to happen, right?" He chuckled as he put his arm around the young man.

"What do you mean? It could happen! I'm nineteen, not a child anymore." Anno stood nearly as tall as Lukas, almost as muscular now, but still appeared the boy next to a man like Trommler.

"Whatever you say, Anno. No, no," he held up his hands in mock surrender, "I applaud your ambition." He threw a glance at Sarah standing next to Elsa. Both women were beautiful, and quite striking in their differences. One petite and feisty, with flaming red waves, and one taller, blonde, and very much the girl next door type. He could see the appeal to a young man like his love's little brother, but he knew women, and Sarah Brown would never be interested in a boy. She was an intellectual. A woman like that needed a man, one who'd traveled, lived. "But surely you know she sees you like her own little brother?"

Anno huffed. "That could change..." His voice faltered, showing his uncertainty.

"I've not seen it change yet in all my years." He clapped Anno on the back. "But don't fret over it. You're not a bad looking sort," he grinned, ignoring the younger man's glare, "and you'll be at a wedding. There's sure to be a few possibilities closer to your own age. I'll even play wing man for you."

This caught Anno's attention. "Yeah? Well, I don't really need a wing man—"

"Everyone needs a wing man. Shut up and take my offer. It's a one-time deal."

"Okay."

Lukas shared this exchange with Elsa after everyone had gone to bed, much to her amusement. She still hadn't mentioned anything more about Paul Christiansen coming to the wedding. He wasn't Lukas's favorite person, but perhaps with Sarah to distract Paul away from flirting with her, something he used to do out of habit, Lukas would be more tolerant of the man.

Now, the three women made final preparations before the start of the ceremony, happy to all be together once more.

On the second floor, Heinz arrived with Lukas and Anno. Faust made it through the door in time with Helga in tow.

"You're almost late, Herman! I thought I was going to have to stand up there alone for a minute."

Faust flew him the bird. "As if I'd miss this, the day the great Kommissar Joseph A. Heinz gets his wings clipped."

"What wings? I'm happy to be a kept rooster," Heinz snorted.

"Cockadoodle doo, then, you crusty old bird."

Helga stepped forward. "Joseph, good luck, darling." She kissed his cheek.

Heinz hugged her close. "Thank you, Helga. Thanks for being here today."

"Like my husband, I wouldn't miss this for the world." She pulled back, touching his face. "You deserve to be happy, so be happy, eh?"

Heinz smiled at her, admiring the woman who'd stolen Herman's heart all those years ago, after clobbering Karl Keller, of course. That was the icing on Cupid's cake as far as Faust was concerned. The years had been kind to Helga. Her once long, red hair was now styled shorter, and liberally streaked with shiny white and silver 'highlights' as she called them. Her blue eyes sparkled with humor, creased at the sides from decades of laughter. Hers was a face that clearly communicated a lifetime of happiness despite losing her only child. She knew what he'd been through from the early days when he'd first met and married Eva to this, the day he would marry the love of his lifetime, the amazing woman with whom he intended to spend the rest of his days.

"I will, Helga, I promise."

She turned to Faust. "I'll see you inside. Don't be too rough on Joseph. Remember, he was there to hold you up on our wedding day." She reminded him of his own nerves at the altar almost thirty years ago.

"You take all the fun out of it, love." Faust kissed her cheek. "I'll behave."

"Good boy." She patted his behind on the way out.

Lukas burst out laughing. "I like her, Faust!"

Faust glared at the man. "She's taken."

"Down, you old dog. No one is going to steal your woman." Joseph laughed at them, feeling joyful.

A knock on the door interrupted their comradery. Anno answered while Heinz and Faust changed, putting on their tuxedos.

"A royal purple vest. Christ." Faust pointed at Joseph, snickering.

"I don't know what you're laughing at, Herman. Yours is purple too." Heinz unzipped the suit bag and handed out the vest to his best man.

"What? Oh, for fuck's sake. I'm going to look like a fat grape up there."

Lukas whipped out his cell phone and snapped a picture. "I overheard Birgitta gushing about how the color brings out your eyes, Heinz." He batted his lashes as he shared the picture on his social media, tagging Elsa.

"Did you just post that? Dammit, Lukas!" Heinz threw a thunderous glare at the younger man.

"What are you complaining about? There's a wedding photographer out there about to take hundreds of pictures. They're going to be all over your house, and on Birgitta's social media, not to mention her desk at work."

Heinz froze. "Not her desk..." He hadn't thought about that. "I'll never live this down."

"You and me, both," said Faust, shrugging into the vest. "Good lord." He stood before the mirror, tugging the vest down. "Even the sash is purple." He tossed a look at Joseph. "I don't think this falls into the parameters of our friendship agreement."

"Shut up, you fat grape!" Heinz stepped next to him. They stood together, sneering at their reflections. "At least the rest of the tux is black. I suppose I should be thankful she didn't turn us both into Liberace."

Anno approached Heinz. "Someone sent you a groom's gift." He handed over a small box about the size of his hand wrapped with gold paper and tied with gold ribbon.

"Who's it from?" Heinz looked for a card or a tag.

"I don't know. Some man dropped it off, said it was delivered earlier to the desk with instructions to make sure you received it before the wedding." Anno checked the clock on the wall. "I need to get out there and help usher people in. Jan is already dressed and waiting to walk his mom down the aisle."

"My soon to be stepson," Joseph grinned.

Anno left, and Lukas joined him. "Not much longer, gentlemen." He looked at Heinz. "I know I give you a hard time, but congratulations, Joseph. She's a wonderful woman." He extended his hand, and Heinz gripped it, giving it a shake.

"Thank you, Lukas. I'm a lucky man."

The groom and the best man were finally alone. "Well, what's in the box?" Faust asked, taking a seat.

"Don't know. Let's see." Heinz began unwrapping the box. Beneath the paper, the black box was embossed in gold with the brand name, Rolex. His eyebrows rose in surprise. "Did my love buy me a Rolex? Damn!" He looked at Faust, grinning. "What did I say about being a lucky man?" He pulled the lid off. "Still, a Rolex is very pricey."

Inside, a slim, gold Rolex watch sat upon a bed of black velvet. It was, indeed, quite expensive looking. A small envelope fell out from the lid, fluttering to the floor.

Heinz bent to pick it up. On the outside, it read *Kommissar Heinz*. His head cocked to the side as his brow furrowed.

"Well?" Faust noticed the look on his face. "What is it?"

Heinz read the note. A picture accompanied the missive. Red tinged his cheeks, and moisture gathered in his eyes. He couldn't speak. He handed the note and picture to Faust.

The Direktor read it and glanced at the picture. "Frau Karakova and her son," he said. He looked at his friend. "So, she's safe. But that's good news. Why are you upset? And what does this note mean? I don't understand."

Heinz paced and then turned to Faust. "Yes, she's safe. She and Alexei are in Sweden. I recognize Strandvagen in the background. But the note..."

Faust read it out loud. "A favor for a favor. The time will come." He looked at Joseph.

Facing his oldest friend, Heinz swallowed. "It's from the Butcher."

"What? Did you—"

"Yes," Heinz whispered harshly. "To save her and Alexei, I made a deal with the devil."

Faust was at a loss for words. He shut his mouth, and wadded up the note, throwing it in the trash. Pointing at the watch, he said, "You'd better put that away. Don't let Birgitta see it," he handed over the picture of Lana Karakova and her son, "or this. You'll never be able to explain your way out of it. You've come too far."

"What the hell can I do? I made a promise." Heinz chewed his lip.

"He hasn't asked for anything, and there's no need to ever follow through with—"

"There is every reason, Herman. He obviously knows where to find me at any given time." He threw his hands in the air, pacing again. "Worse, he knows where to find Lana and her son."

Faust knew this was true. "Well, there's no reason to worry over it now. It seems Brezhnev sought to remind you of your deal, and he did. I understand why you did it, Joseph. Honestly, I would have done the same. I'm glad you found a way to save her." He walked over and patted his friend on the back. "There's nothing for it but to put it aside and worry about it if and when the time comes. When it does, we'll make a plan. Right now, there's a roomful of family and friends waiting to see you get married, and a beautiful woman delusional enough to say I do is waiting to walk down the aisle."

Before he could stop himself, Heinz reached out and hugged his friend. "Thank you, Herman. Thank you for understanding, and for always being there for me."

"You're welcome. And I always will be." They remained that way, embracing, two friends who'd already shared a lifetime of adventures, both good and bad, and then broke apart. "But if you ever tell anyone about our moment, I'll deny you like Judas!"

Heinz chuckled. Faust handed him his jacket and put his own on. They stood staring at each other, purple vests, sashes, and all.

"Christ," said Faust.

"Suck it up, old man," said Heinz.

With one last look in the unforgiving mirror, Faust sighed. "Let's go."

Sneak Peek

The Making of Herman Faust
The Checkpoint, Berlin Detective Series, Book IV
A Prequel Novella

When the walls come tumbling down...

Herman Faust is the no-nonsense Direktor of the LKA (LandesKriminalamt, similar to the American CIA) and long-time friend of Kommissar Joseph Heinz. His career spans thirty years, and he is now on the cusp of retirement. Although usually cool and in control and a man of dry wit, it wasn't always so for Faust. With experience came wisdom, hard won wisdom for which he paid a high price.

***

In 1988...

Rookie officer Herman Faust apprehends a high priority defector during a routine traffic stop, but it quickly spirals out of control when the defector's brother vanishes, and the defector is found dead in her holding cell! Faust finds himself entangled in a web of CIA secrets, anonymous threats, and a Soviet plot to launch a biological weapon on the American Embassy. With the stability of West Berlin on the line, Faust must risk all to stop the deadly pathogen from being released on innocent civilians. It's a race against the clock, and the stakes couldn't be higher.

Fans of Tom Clancy's Red Storm Rising and Jack Ryan will enjoy this thrilling, Cold War era tale of espionage and high-stakes drama. Buy now before the price changes!

A Page Turner Awards 2021 & 2022 Shortlist Finalist for the Book Award and Screenplay (Book Adaptation Needed) categories.

Review: "Where the Checkpoint Series All Began...In this prequel to her Checkpoint, Berlin Detective Series, Michele E. Gwynn has spun a heart-pounding tale of Cold War intrigue...artfully recalling a darker age of Russian agents and secret plots that, until recently, we thought was gone forever with the fall of the Berlin Wall. I loved the suspense, the intrigue and the way Gwynn builds the relationships between Faust, his wife and the stalwart Joseph Heinz and I heartily recommend it to any fan of police stories and Cold War spy novels." ~ Aurora Dawn

***

Chapter One

"Please, get out of the car." The request was issued with authority.

Inside the sedan, a man with dark hair and a slight build began to exit the driver's side door. He pulled his coat tighter around him while shifting his eyes left and right.

"I really don't see why this is necessary..." he began. "I have my papers here." He reached inside his coat.

"Stop!" The blond officer pulled his service revolver out, aiming it dead center of the man's chest. "Raise your hands and turn around! Place them on the roof of your vehicle, and do not move!"

He approached the man, placing the gun at his back. With one hand, the officer reached around, patting him down first on one side, then the other. Finally, he retrieved the papers found inside the gentleman's coat. He stepped back, and attempted to read them, but it was dark on the side of the road, and rain fell in a soaking mist.

The man glanced over his shoulder. "I'm Gunter Meyer. A banker. I live at Number 52, Kreutznacherstrasse in Steglitz."

The officer nodded, muttering, "Figures. Jewish, and a banker." He handed the papers back. "You may turn around."

Gunter Meyer turned slowly as he put his papers back into his coat pocket.

"What are you doing out so late, and so close to the border of the DDR?"

Meyer shifted his weight. "I was merely out for a drive. Is that now against the law too?"

The blond officer remained quiet, staring at Meyer. He still held the gun in his hand, and it was still aimed in the man's direction.

Meyer cast his eyes down, and then back up. "Well? Can I go or am I being detained?"

"Is there a reason I should detain you?"

"What? No! Of course not. I was simply asking..." Meyer huffed. He clenched and unclenched his hands, a clear sign of his anxiety.

The officer shrugged. "You may go, but I would not make a habit of these moonlight drives. It's not safe out here." He began to holster his firearm.

Meyer's frame lost some of its rigidity. He turned, ducking into the driver's seat, relieved. A muffled sneeze broke the silence. Meyer froze, and then reached to slam the door shut while trying to start the car.

The officer cursed, pulled his gun once again, and aimed it precisely at Meyer's head. "Stop! I will shoot!"

Meyer was caught between his panic to flee, and the inner voice shouting at him to stay still, don't do anything to cause the officer to pull that trigger.

"Keep your hands where I can see them! Slowly exit the vehicle, and lay down on the ground, face first!"

The banker hesitated.

"Now!"

Defeat filled Meyer's large, dark eyes. He lifted both hands, moving at a pace he hoped would not antagonize the police officer. "Please, just please be calm."

"Shut up! Get down!" The officer came around to Meyer's side, and when he'd fully complied, quickly handcuffed the man. Meyer lay on the road unable to rise. "Stay there, or by God, I will shoot you like a dog!"

The officer searched the car. The sedan had a small backseat, barely any room for a person to sit comfortably, and no one was sitting there. The officer then pushed and prodded the cushions. At the last tug, the entire back seat popped up revealing a hidden nook.

Lying inside the hollowed-out space was a woman. She appeared to be in her early thirties with long, dark hair, and large brown eyes. She blinked at the German officer staring down at her.

"Please," came Meyer's plea. "She's my sister. Don't hurt her."

The officer huffed. He'd seen this a dozen times already. Since his first few days out of the academy, he'd witnessed people being smuggled out of East Germany. He didn't even know how they managed it since the guards inside the DDR were not only thorough, but brutal if they came across anyone trying to escape. Most of those who attempted it ended up shot right where they stood. Those that weren't killed on the spot wished they had been by the time the Stasi were finished with them. But the ones who made it never expected kindness from the police. It was foreign to them.

"I'm not going to hurt her, you fool. I'm not the Stasi. This isn't East Germany." He turned back to the woman and extended his hand. "You can come out."

She took his hand with some hesitation, carefully climbing out of the hidden well beneath the bench seat. When she stood on the pavement, he holstered his gun, and introduced himself.

"I'm Officer Herman Faust. Welcome to West Germany, Miss?"

"Edith Meyer Hoffmann." She gave her full name.

"And where is Herr Hoffmann?" Faust inquired after her husband. "Is he somewhere in the car too?" He lifted one thick eyebrow.

Her expression fell. "No. He's dead. Shot down not two hours ago." Tears welled in her eyes and began to fall down her gaunt cheeks.

"Edith..." Meyer's voice tried to offer comfort.

Faust sighed. "I'm sorry, Frau Hoffmann. You have my condolences." He turned to Meyer, bending down to release him from the cuffs. "No funny business from you, Meyer." Faust unlocked the wrist cuffs, and stood, reaching a hand out to help the man up. "You both will, of course, need to come down to the station to give a statement."

"Is that really necessary?" Meyer looked at his sister who was shaking visibly with grief.

"I'm afraid so. Come. You'll ride with me. I'll send someone to pick up your car and bring it to the station house."

Faust guided them to his own vehicle. Frau Hoffmann slid into the back seat of the police cruiser. Her brother reluctantly climbed in beside her.

"Will this take long?" Meyer asked. "My sister is not well."

Edith Hoffmann patted her brother's arm, a wan smile on her lips. "I'll be okay, Gunter." She coughed.

Faust looked in the rearview mirror. "It will take as long as it takes, I'm afraid, but we will be sure to bring in a physician if that is what she requires."

"That won't be necessary, officer," she said, looking out the window into the dark of night.

"Edith—"

"I'll be all right. Just let's get on with this. We're safe now, brother. We're safe." She spoke softly, seeming unconcerned.

Faust heard the resignation in her voice, and the relief. Even if her brother didn't realize it yet, Edith Meyer Hoffmann was correct. They were, indeed, safe now.

He cranked the ignition and pulled onto the road. The ride back to the station was slow-going as the rain began to fall in sheets. With the December temperatures dropping below freezing overnight, there would be nothing but ice covering the roads by morning. Herman was glad he'd remembered to put the chains on the tires. His wife, Helga, would need the traction to make it into work. He would be getting off shift only an hour before, just in time to make it home to take care of Therese, their daughter. At three, she was the apple of his eye, and had her papa wrapped around her dainty finger. Still, she was a handful, especially when he had to work overnight. At least his mother-in-law, Margaret, would arrive in the morning to watch the tike while he got some sleep.

Margaret stayed until Helga came home, and by then, Herman was getting up for his next shift. It wasn't an easy schedule, but it worked for them, for now.

Before he knew it, they'd arrived at the station. Faust pulled into the parking lot and found a spot. He had no umbrella on hand, but he did carry an extra jacket. He handed it to Frau Hoffmann after opening the back door to let her and her brother out.

"Here," he said, throwing the coat over her shoulders, and flipping the hood up, "this should help keep you dry."

Meyer exited the vehicle, and they ran for the front door. Inside, the station house was quiet. Faust took Meyer and his sister to in-processing. He left them both in the desk Sergeant's hands while he reported in to his Captain.

"Another made it across. She's in with Herring right now."

Captain Rolf Rheinhardt looked up, his keen green eyes locking with Faust's as his dark eyebrows lowered. "She?"

"Yes, a widow. Recent widow. Her husband did not make it."

"I see. She had help?"

Faust nodded. "Yes, her brother. He's one of ours, a Jewish banker."

Rheinhardt grunted. "Have you run his background check yet?"

"Nein. I'm on my way to my desk now. I'll run it and fill out my report."

The captain nodded, dismissing Faust who turned to leave.

"Faust?"

Herman paused, looking back.

"What's her name?"

"Hoffmann. Edith Meyer Hoffmann. The brother is Gunter Meyer."

Rheinhardt froze. "And her husband?"

Faust returned to the doorway. "Herr Hoffmann?" he offered.

The captain rummaged through his desk, locating a file folder. He pulled it out, flipping through the pages. Finally, he stopped, and pointed at the two pictures on the page. "Is this her?" He turned the folder toward Faust.

Hermann approached, looking down. On the page were two faded photographs. One was of a tall, good-looking man with prominent cheekbones and a thin mustache. He wore wire-rimmed glasses over his blue eyes and was dressed in a dark suit. The other picture showed a young woman with long, dark hair and creamy cheeks, smiling, wearing a wedding gown. She was the picture of health and happiness holding a modest bouquet of white roses. Despite the difference in age and obvious declining health now, there was no doubt this was a picture of Edith Meyer on her wedding day.

"Yes, that's her. Why? Who is she?"

Rheinhardt ran a hand over his mouth. "She is the wife of one of the top microbiologists in the world. Solomon Hoffmann. Back in the early '70s, Hoffmann was caught on the wrong side of the wall while on a special dispensation to visit his dying grandmother. He was recruited by Vector to help develop biological weapons for the Soviets. Since then, we've lost track, but he more than likely moved on from Vector to Obolensk, the newest branch of their germ warfare division. You said he didn't make it?" He looked at Faust.

"Frau Hoffmann said he died not more than two hours before I came upon them. What does this mean?"

"I don't exactly know yet, but now we have her. She was his wife. She'll have information." He picked up the phone.

"Who are you calling?" Faust asked. His captain seemed agitated, a clear shift from his usually calm demeanor.

Rheinhardt chewed his lip. "The Landeskriminalamt will want her." Dialing, he glanced over his shoulder. "Good work, Faust. Now, go write that report."

***

An hour later, Faust finished his report and dropped it into the inbox on his Captain's desk to be signed off. Rheinhardt was away from the office.

Faust sighed, knowing he would need to return to patrol now that his paperwork was completed. He thought about what his Captain said. Frau Hoffmann's husband was apparently a high priority acquisition for the west. In Hoffmann's absence, his wife became second prize. After all, as his spouse, she would most likely have knowledge of his work, might even be in possession of his research—whatever it happened to be—although Faust had not searched her person himself. She wasn't a criminal. Her lack of criminal status, and her non-threatening appearance had made him complacent, allowing her to escape a pat down. Still, he was curious if Sergeant Herring had discovered anything. He decided to stop by the holding cells on his way out. It wasn't often something this intriguing occurred.

It was quiet save for the sound of rain slapping the tin roof of the small station house. Herring was nowhere to be found. Faust sniffed, raising an eyebrow as he bypassed the Sergeant's desk and headed back toward the holding cells. He felt all alone in the world in this moment, what with no one about. It appeared the night shift had it easier than the daytime crew, at least, the ones who weren't assigned to patrol. Faust entered the back rooms and came to the secured door that led to the cells. He punched in the authorization code and waited as the light on the lock turned green, buzzing. The loud sound pierced the silence. He turned the knob and entered.

Inside, there were six independent cells, all 4 x 8 feet in size. Just enough room for a cot, a toilet, and a sink. Each also contained a small window approximately 12 inches wide and 18 inches long. The glass was unbreakable, but at least it allowed for the smallest of views outside. The grayish-green paint on the concrete walls showed its age as it cracked and peeled, revealing an old building and its lack of funding.

He didn't know which cell she was in, so began peering through the small windows of each door. The first three cells were empty. The next contained a gray-haired man loudly snoring off a beer-bender. The fifth cell was also empty leaving the last cell on the left the only likely spot where Frau Hoffmann would be held. Faust peeked into the window, speaking before laying eyes upon her.

"Are you okay in there, Frau...?" The words died on his lips.

Edith Meyer Hoffmann's body was sprawled across the cold concrete floor. Blood oozed from her nose, lips, and one exposed ear.

"Guard!" Faust shouted, running back to the security box by the main entry to punch in the code that would open that door. "Guard!" He yelled again, throwing the steel door wide.

Herring came running from the bathroom, tucking his shirt in. "What is it, Faust?"

"Frau Hoffmann, she's unconscious on the floor! Call an ambulance!" He ran back in, punching another code. The door to cell six slid open. Herman Faust ran inside, dropping to his knees beside the woman.

"Frau Hoffman," he pushed two fingers against her carotid artery, feeling for a pulse. "Edith! Can you hear me?" With no pulse found, he straightened her neck and leaned down, turning his ear toward her nose and mouth. There was no breath. Not waiting one minute more, Faust began chest compressions.

"Well?" Sergeant Herring stood in the doorway, another officer behind him peeking, wide-eyed, over his shoulder.

"No pulse, not breathing. Did you call for help?" Faust continued depressions.

Herring turned to the lackey behind him. "Call the ambulance! Schnell!"

"Get over here, Herring, and do the breaths. Hurry!" Faust directed the Sergeant in CPR, telling him to check for any obstruction in her airway. "Pinch her nose and blow in two breaths."

Herring wiped the excess blood from her mouth and did as bid. Faust began counting out compressions once again. "Where the hell is the Captain? We need to inform her brother. She may have a medical condition we don't know about. He's here still, yes?"

Herring blinked, clearly rattled by the situation. "No. Rheinhardt took him out of here about an hour ago."

"What, why?" Faust pointed, and Herring blew in two more breaths.

The sergeant sat back up. "I don't know. He didn't say. I figured he was taking him home. We didn't have any reason to hold him."

"Shit! A fine time to take off." Faust and Herring kept up the life-saving measures until the emergency medical responders arrived. One short man in his late thirties, and a tall, young woman who looked fresh out of school took over, checking again for a pulse.

The young woman opened Frau Hoffmann's shirt, pushed her bra straps out of the way, and grabbed a defibrillator. Lifting the paddles, she said, "Clear!" before shocking Hoffmann's heart. The machine continued its monotone. She increased the amplitude and repeated the task. Still nothing. The man filled a syringe and injected the intravenous line he'd only just inserted. Once complete, the woman, again, tried to shock Frau Hoffmann's heart back to life. The monotone stretched out like a siren in the silence, never once breaking off into a steady beat.

"I'll need to inform her brother. Which hospital will you be taking her to?" Faust stood back, looking at the techs.

The short EMS technician sat back on his heels. "Whichever one has an open morgue." His partner, the tall, young woman, set the paddles back on the defibrillator, and pulled out a sheet from her bag. She shook it out and laid it over the body of Edith Meyer Hoffmann.

"What? Why did you stop?" Faust looked down at them, eyes wide and filled with shock.

"She's gone, officer. I'm sorry, but it took us more than thirty minutes to get here, and despite all your efforts, and ours, we've been unable to revive her. She's been down too long. She's gone."

Herman Faust stood, unsure what to do next. This was his first death on the job. He ran his hand over his face, chewing the inside of his cheek—a nervous habit that helped him think. His wife, Helga, often joked he would one day chew a hole right through his face.

"I need to contact the captain. If he's still with Herr Meyer..." Faust walked out of the cell and left the block. Herring followed.

"I can't believe it. She was fine when I put her in there. Maybe a little cough, and she looked rather thin, but otherwise, she seemed okay. Normal for those from the other side of the wall. And what do you think was with all that blood coming out of her nose and ears?"

"Maybe a brain hemorrhage? I don't know, Herring. That's for the coroner to figure out now."

Herring went behind his desk, wiping blood off his hands and chin with a towel. "Well, at least you didn't get blood all over you." He picked up the phone. "I'll call the captain. As soon as I get him on the line, I'll transfer him to your desk."

Faust stood, unsure of his next step. "Okay. I guess I'll be at my desk." He wandered off to his area in the back corner of the quadrant.

He sat down, stunned. Only once before had he been involved in a life-or-death situation, a choking. A perp he'd picked up for drug possession had tried to swallow the bag of drugs he carried. The bag got stuck, and the fool began to choke. Faust had immediately grabbed him around the waist, applying pressure just below the breastbone. The Heimlich maneuver was successful. The baggie of drugs was expelled, and the dealer went to jail. Alive. But this was his first death. The silence in the station house was briefly interrupted by the paramedics wheeling the body out to the ambulance. He couldn't see her face, but Edith Meyer Hoffmann was there, under the white sheet, dead.

The junior officer followed, a Polaroid camera in hand. He'd been taking pictures before the body was removed. Standard procedure. There was also closed-circuit footage inside the holding area. All of it would be collected as part of the evidence to close her case. A woman who'd escaped communist rule only to be jailed in the west, dies alone inside a cell. It was a fucking tragedy. Such shouldn't happen to anyone in Faust's opinion.

He realized he'd been sitting there for quite some time, and still, the phone hadn't rung. He looked up, seeking out Herring. The man was leaning over the front desk, rubbing his temples.

"Hey, Herring. Any luck yet?"

Herring straightened. "No, not yet."

"Keep trying." Faust sat forward. The clock on the wall showed it was 0437. His shift would end in less than three hours. There was still much to do, beginning with informing her family, which they were trying to do with zero success.

"Where are you, captain?" he muttered under his breath. No longer capable of sitting still, Herman Faust pulled out the requisite forms for an inmate death and began filling them out.

Read *The Making of Herman Faust* today!

Also By Michele E. Gwynn

Visit my website for these books plus updates on upcoming releases!
micheleegwynnauthor.com

Checkpoint Novels

Exposed: The Education of Sarah Brown (novel)
The Evolution of Elsa Kreiss (novel)
The Redemption of Joseph Heinz (novel)
The Making of Herman Faust (prequel novella)

Green Beret Series *(18+)*

Rescuing Emma
Loving Leisl
Freeing Fatima
Saving Christmas
Loving Freddie
Saving Major Morgan (A Green Beret Series prequel novella)

The Soldiers of PATCH-COM

Secondhand Soldier (18+)
Second Chance Soldier
Second Breath Soldier
Silent Night Soldier

C'est la Vie Soldier

The Harvest Trilogy

Harvest
Hybrids
Census

Section 5 (A Harvest Trilogy Spinoff)

Stand Alones

Darkest Communion (Paranormal Romance, 18+)
Waiting a Lifetime (Contemporary Romance, Mystical)
Hiring John (Romantic Comedy 18+)

Foreign Language Translations
Il faut retrouver Emma (La serie des Bérets verts: Tome 1)

www.ingramcontent.com/pod-product-compliance
Lightning Source LLC
Chambersburg PA
CBHW071204100726
47908CB00002B/505